Summer of Love

Summer

 of Love

Lisa Mason

Drawings by Tom Robinson

BANTAM BOOKS
NEW YORK · TORONTO · LONDON · SYDNEY · AUCKLAND

SUMMER OF LOVE

A Bantam Book / July 1994

Copyright © 1994 by Lisa Mason.

Book design by Richard Oriolo.

Library of Congress Cataloging-in-Publication Data

Mason, Lisa.
Summer of love / Lisa Mason ; drawings by Tom Robinson.
p.   cm.
ISBN 0-553-37330-7
I. Title.
PS3563.A7924S86   1994
813'.54—dc20   94-7592
                                                          CIP

Published simultaneously in the United States and Canada

Bantam Books are published by Bantam Books, a division of Bantam
Doubleday Dell Publishing Group, Inc. Its trademark, consisting of
the words "Bantam Books" and the portrayal of a rooster, is
Registered in U.S. Patent and Trademark Office and in other
countries. Marca Registrada. Bantam Books, 1540 Broadway, New
York, New York 10036.

PRINTED IN THE UNITED STATES OF AMERICA

BVG   0 9 8 7 6 5 4 3 2 1

Gratefully dedicated to flower children,
past, present, and future;

and for Tom, Ara, Alana, Luna,
and all the beautiful cats.

Acknowledgments

For their assistance and enthusiasm in locating rare resources and sharing memories, I want to thank the following:

Helen Strodl, owner of Cheshire Cat Books in Sausalito; Jack Rems and Jay Sheckley, owners of Dark Carnival Books in Berkeley; Adam Phillips, independent book dealer formerly with The Holmes Book Company in Oakland; Marshall and the folks at Walden Pond Books in Oakland; and Bibliomania in Oakland, whose fine collection of first editions is invaluable. Special thanks to David Scherr for lending me his collection of the *Berkeley Barb*, published by his father, the late Max Scherr; to Faren Miller, Associate Editor of *Locus*, for sharing her diaries and memorabilia; and to Louis Collins, of Collins Rare Books in Seattle, for sending me Jerry Mander's *In the Absence of the Sacred*, locating the 1964 edition of *Notes from Underground*, and sharing his recollections of 1967 as a North Beach bookseller. Thanks to Mark Weiman of the Regent Press in Oakland for including extra footage on my *Oracle Rising* videotape produced by Claire Burch, and publishing the *Oracle Facsimile Edition* edited by Allen Cohen, a beautiful and invaluable resource; to Lenore Kandel for her effervescent wit and indomitable spirit; and to Yoshio Kobayashi, the translator of my novel, *Arachne*, for Hayakawa Publishing, for sharing his interest in American music and culture of the sixties. Thanks to Dale Harrison Miller, formerly of *Image Magazine*, for locating back issues. And special thanks to Tom Robinson for his tireless research and editorial assistance, his visionary ideas, his superb drawings, and his detailed recollections of the tall, slim, red-haired artist who journeyed through the Haight-Ashbury long ago.

Contents

Tenets of the Grandfather Principle

[Developed for tachyportation projects by
the Luxon Institute for Superluminal Applications]

Tenet One: You cannot kill any of your lineal ancestors (prior to his or her historical death), including yourself.

Tenet Two: You cannot prevent the death of any of your ancestors (at the point of his or her historical death or thereafter, if applicable).

Tenet Three: You cannot affect any person in the past, including aiding, coercing, deceiving, deterring, killing, or saving him or her (except as defined and authorized by the project directors).

Tenet Four: You cannot affect the natural world in the past.

Tenet Five: You cannot reveal your identity as a modern person to any person in the past, including yourself.

Tenet Six: You cannot reveal the personal future of any person in the past, or of his or her immediate family and descendants, to that person, including yourself.

Tenet Seven: You cannot apply modern technologies, including tachyportation, to past events or people, except when the result conforms to the Archives, and, in that case, you cannot leave evidence of a modern technology in the past.

The CTL Peril: You are capable of dying in the past, including your personal past (but see Tenet One). If this occurs, the tachyportation is transformed from an Open Time Loop (OTL) to a Closed Time Loop (CTL). You are trapped in a CTL.

June 21, 1967

Celebration of the Summer Solstice

She's Leaving
Home

Susan Stein clings for dear life to a Ford flatbed truck five years older than she is. *Jig-jig-jig* up Twin Peaks. Four-thirty A.M. High in the hills. San Francisco slumbering at her toes. Pitch-black beyond feeble street lights. West wind from the ocean, salt scent of sea dragons. Never smelled anything like it in Cleveland. Wild and free, oh the sea, the sea.

Bone-chill, teeth chattering. Butt really sore, three hours or more on Pan Am flight 153. Now bouncing on the flatbed, she feels frostbit all over. Fog tousles her hair, stirring rowdy frizz. Eyelids sag with fatigue. A frantic all-nighter, her daring escape from the oppression of Shaker Heights, Ohio.

"Beam me up!" cries the skinny girl in the cowboy hat. "Om mani padme hum," chants the shaved-bald boy in the long orange robe. "Purple haze," sings the guy with the big blond 'fro.

Transistor radio blares, "If you're going to San Francisco . . ."

Flag flapping above, a swatch of tie-dye stapled to a stick. Must be twenty kids jammed onto the flatbed. Body stink, patchouli oil, musty secondhand velvet, sexy leather.

Grass? Sharp smoke pinches her nose. Last spring she and Nance caught Nance's big brother with some. Paul wouldn't give them a hit, but Nance's cousin Don turned them on to a joint, which they smoked to *Rubber Soul*. It was okay, not great. Same for the music. That stuff about a guy threatening to kill a girl if she sees another guy. Gross. Barely got a buzz, but Mom and Daddy would turn forty shades of pale if they found out. Susan looks around. Who's got a joint?

Brass bells, finger cymbals, warbling flutes, awkward guitar. Someone sick off the starboard bow, Captain Kirk.

Susan clutches her purse and overnight bag. Teddy bear comforts, paunchy and safe. The purse holds a hundred fifty bucks, the overnight bag a hundred twenty and change. Under-the-table wages earned after school at Mr. Rosenstein's art supply store. Plus the hundred for when Mr. Rosenstein pressed his hand on her stomach, down low, asking if she'd got her first period yet. Worst of it was, she just had. Wouldn't Dr. Stein, with his groovy new dental office, flip his lid if he knew his daughter got felt up by a dirty old shopkeeper. Well. That was just another thing Daddy would never find out. He'd make things worse for her than for Mr. Rosenstein. Took the job, didn't she? And all her needs provided for. She'd be equally to blame, if not more so. She always was.

They seized her. "Hey, you! Chick with the bag!"

Susan shivered, terrified and thrilled.

"What's your name?" they called.

She had just stepped off the 6 Parnassus bus running a red-eye from Market Street. Dragging the overnight bag, which had become awfully heavy.

She was ready with the alias Nance had scrawled on the postcard. "Starbright." Clever Nance. When they were little, they always wished on the first star of the evening. Like Jiminy Cricket in *Pinocchio*. "I'm Starbright," she called back.

"Beautiful! Come on, Starbright," they said. "You're either on the bus or off the bus."

On the bus, off the bus? She didn't understand, since they were riding in a truck, but she let them seize her, anyway. At the corner of Haight Street and Ashbury, an unruly chortling horde barreling through the dawn like there's no tomorrow.

"We're gonna see the sun rise!"

"Celebrate the Solstice!"

"The start of summer!"

They crest Twin Peaks, top of the town. Night is lifting. The truck's motor sputters off. The kids pile out. Bongo drums quicken everyone's pulse. Plum incense spices the scent of sea dragons. People everywhere; so many! A couple hundred or more, milling in the mist.

Never saw anything like it!

Oh, she and Nance used to sneak away to Coventry Street where the boys slicked down their Beatle bangs and the girls in miniskirts showed off their shocking pink tights. Cool for Cleveland.

But these people!

People stranger than aliens on *Star Trek,* the new TV program she loves. A woolly man stalks by in pointy-toed boots, a Davy Crockett jacket, swooping hat like a Mexican bandit. Another man preens at his embroidered gauze shirt and jewelry. Not the cuff links, tie tack, and plain gold wedding band Dr. Stein wears. The man—a man!—wears a necklace of shells, an earring, bracelets stacked on his slim wrists. A wild woman brushes past her. No coif or white lipstick for her. God—and no undergarments either beneath her silky dress. Susan lowers her eyes; nipples, a crotch. Other women climb the hill in buckskin shifts or Hindu saris, velvet gowns, feathered headdresses, gypsy bandannas of red and purple.

There are cameras, too, slung about necks, and long-snouted movie cameras balanced on shoulders. Guys in jeans or mod suits stride through the crowd, jotting notes on clipboards, whispering into microphones. The fringed and feathered people ignore them with regal disdain or pose with extravagant gestures. An electronic eye whirls into her face. "Hollywood, babe," says a guy with fluffy sideburns from ears to chin. "I'm the producer. We're making a flick. You want to take off your top?"

Susan is stunned. Looking at *her*! Like *she's* an alien, too, and she'll be watching herself on *Star Trek* tonight. The first season is in reruns now. Still! She hides her face. The enormity of her escape strikes her for the first time—*what if Mom and Daddy see me?*

She's known fear. The prickle waiting for penicillin shots to treat her earaches. The dread when the Steins moved from the small familiar streets of South Euclid to the mansions of Shaker Heights. Her anxiety muffled in a pillow before eighth grade at her new school. But this fear is so intense and strange—*what if they see me?*—her breath catches in her chest. She darts from the crowd, seeking refuge in the shadows west of Twin Peaks.

She glances down the steep hillside. A girl in a long black cape stands below her, a peaked hood drawn over her head, hiding her hair and face.

At the moment Susan sees her, the girl stirs, turns, and looks up the hill. Another jolt of fear. Like looking in a mirror! The girl stands twenty feet down slope in dawn light and swirling fog. Suddenly Susan is *awake,* and there's no mistake. It's *her.* Her own face looking back! From beneath the hood, hair frizzing out of control, the eyes she likes, the cheeks she hates, her pouting mouth. Her vision becomes preternaturally clear. She can see each trampled blade of grass at the girl's feet.

The girl smiles. Her smile glints for an instant, and it's all wrong. Little upside-down triangles glitter beneath her lip. Her eyes glow and flicker coal red. A freezing breeze blows up slope. Her cape billows, wide curves and sharp points like the wings of a bat. A blackness deeper than the receding night forms an aureole around her, as though she stands within the mouth of a cave in the hillside. But no, not a cave, not a bat. Gleaming panels surround her like the hull of a machine, pulse into view for a moment, fade out. Weird electricity crackles, black sparks sputter.

The girl with her face holds a staff or rod in her left hand. She slowly raises it, points the top knob at Susan. Cold surrounds Susan's hand. An odd tugging wraps round her, pulling her.

Drawing her forward. Susan steps.

The hillside falls away.

She scrambles for a foothold, clawing at the dirt. Her purse bangs against her thigh, she slides against the overnight bag. The bag snags on a sapling tough enough to hold her. She digs her heels in, halting her fall before the cliff angles to nothing. Scratches, scrabbles up the slope, pure fear propelling her. She hoists herself back onto the ledge.

The girl watches. Then disappears.

Susan gathers her bags and runs.

Up slope, to the dawn side, where people are gathering and chanting and laughing. Sunlight peeks. Pink beams filter through the fog. The fireball rises from the east hills. People shriek and sigh as though they've never seen the sun before. Cameras click and whir. A woman unbelts her purple shawl, gifting everyone with the vision of her nipples and navel. A firework rocket arcs up. Overhead, flares form red and white blossoms of light.

"Hare Krishna, Hare Krishna, Krishna Krishna, Hare Hare."

"Om."

"Whee!"

"Charlie Artman," someone says. "Do it, Charlie."

A man wearing a necklace of chicken leg bones and a huge wood ankh stands before the crowd. He beckons to the sun, calls out in a voice thick with wonder and joy, "Let the Summer of Love begin!"

WEATHER REPORT

Between 1821 and 1824, thirty-three million pioneers came to America, felling ninety percent of the trees in New York, Massachusetts, Ohio, Michigan, Wisconsin, and Minnesota. By 1850, the pioneer explosion was sending half a billion tons of carbon into the atmosphere each year. George Callender, Steam Technologist to the British Electrical and Allied Industries Research Association, reported that from 1888 to 1938, temperatures worldwide rose precipitously. This global warming could be traced to the volume of carbon dioxide that the industrial nations injected into the atmosphere since the introduction of Mr. James Watt's steam engine. Mr. Callender concluded that the world's climate would surely be improved, since carbon enrichment of the atmosphere would fertilize every farmer's crops and stave off the killing glaciers of previous Ice Ages for a long time to come.

o

This Summer, the youth of the world are making a holy pilgrimage to our city to affirm and celebrate a new spiritual dawn. The Summer of Love is a family and a seed-bearer.

We carry to you this message:

The activity of the youth of the nation which has given birth to the Haight-Ashbury is a small part of a worldwide spiritual awakening. Our city has become the momentary focus of this awakening. The reasons for this do not matter. It is a gift from God which we may take, nourish, and treasure.

The facts are these: many thousands of young people, our children, our brothers, and our sisters, will soon arrive in this city. *They seek meaning.*

There will be great celebrations all Summer long, celebrations which affirm the universal values of Love, Peace, and Self-Knowledge.

We call upon the world to help us celebrate the infinite holiness of Life.

—From "Proclamation of the Council
for a Summer of Love," *The San
Francisco Oracle*, Vol. 1, No. 8 (June, 1967)

"Say hey. Professor Zoom. Check it out. Flower children," the man says. Brash baritone, a smoker's throat. His growl slides into Susan's uneasy dreams. Falling, grasping, trying to hold on . . .

Her eyes pop open. Flutter shut against the sun. She peeks through purple lashes.

"Seek and ye shall find, Stan the Man," Professor Zoom says. Somnolent chuckle, flat effect like Jack Webb on *Dragnet*. Just the facts, ma'am. "You always do. The roving eye, et cetera. Bears a resemblance to the Moving Finger. A jug of juice, a wad of bread, and sweet pretty pussy."

Laughter. Not boys. Men.

"Turn on the world!" voices shout nearby. She peeks again. A huge canvas balloon painted like the Earth bounces high into the thin blue sky, rebounds onto outstretched hands.

"Rise and shine, wild things." Mock daddy. Noticing her. "Say hey. Foxy lady awakes."

"Sweet pretty pussy in droves and droves." Professor Zoom drifts away, chuckling like the pull of a saw through wood. Muttering, "Verily, in droves and droves."

Noon. Solstice sun on high. Susan nestles in the back of the flatbed truck against the girl in the cowboy hat, the shaved-bald boy, another girl she's never seen before curled up in a poncho, face buried beneath yellow wool. Strangers several baths short of clean. She checks her purse and overnight bag, the inside pockets where her cash hides. The others snore, heedless of the flatbed's rock-hard floor. Susan sits, shivering violently. Her back and ribs ache worse than three summers ago when she and Nance slept on the lawn and saw a great, glossy raccoon prying the lid off their can of Cheerios.

A great, glossy man bends over the flatbed, stealing out of the sun's glare, stunning her. A mountain man, chiseled and fierce. His proud chin declines a beard. His suede shirt is open to his chest, jeans slung low.

"Wake up, flower child. The Celebration of the Summer Solstice"— his hand sweeps over the meadow as though granting it to her—"awaits you." Gray eyes flicker all over her. His smile dazzles.

Before she can catch her breath, he turns and strides away.

Foxy lady? Flower child?

She does what she always does: tries to understand what the world sees in her at going on fifteen years old. She climbs off the truck, crouches, wipes the mud from a chrome bumper. Peers at the silly reflection as though she can't place who she is till she can see her own face, however distorted. God! Unkempt hair, unwashed face. She slaps some color into her cheeks. Awful!

She can just see her mother's look. Even in the best of circumstances, nothing is ever right. Nothing ever good enough. That long, disapproving scrutiny mixed with . . . what? Some terrible, nameless thing her mother holds against her, no matter how hard she tries.

Where is Nance? The postcard was signed "Penny Lane." Where is her best friend, the only person she knows in San Francisco? She figured she would step off the 6 Parnassus bus, and there Nance would be, one of her dreadful Kool Menthols dangling from her lip.

Now she doesn't know where to start.

Susan stands. Despair, near tears.

The mountain man is looking at her from across the field. He grins when he catches her glance. Waves grandly, come on! He is a magnet, a pot of honey, a good-luck charm. No boy she's ever known comes close. Is he really waving to her? She looks over her shoulder, to the right, to the left. Yes, to her!

The truck is parked on one side of Speedway Meadow, a long, tree-lined field in Golden Gate Park. Small wooden stages, frail against the backdrop of huge trees, are set up along the three other sides. Bands gather or are already playing. The reedy voices and guitar twangs are lost in the air, even the drums are diminished, but Susan knows their sounds, their songs, and all of their names: the Grateful Dead, Big Brother and the Holding Company, Quicksilver Messenger Service.

A man in a Mickey Mouse cap perched over his wrinkled forehead leaps about, blowing soap bubbles from an oversized hoop. A woman skips by in a thigh-high smock slit to her waist. The smock unfurls in a passing gust, showing her dimpled bare butt. A boy of perhaps ten, his face painted with stars, lies atop a small girl, her face painted with flowers, and pumps his hips against hers. A five-year-old, headband tied over her curls, squats on the sandy soil and negotiates with another five-year-old in a baseball cap. Her pear for his half-eaten hamburger.

What's young? What's old?

The scent of beef grilling makes Susan's stomach turn somersaults. She has not eaten since the TV dinner the maid left before her parents went out last night.

Something snags at the corner of her eye. A ripple of deep black, the swirl of a hooded cape, sparks of strange electricity. In the dappled shade behind the trees. A freezing breeze nips her face.

She whirls.

People are laughing by the barbecue pits. The cook drops a patty of raw meat in the mud, picks it up, throws it back on the grill. A reveler offers his plate to receive it.

There is nothing. Nothing at all.

* * *

Susan catches up with the mountain man halfway across the meadow. She stands several paces away, struck with shyness.

He speaks with a regal woman. The woman stands nearly six feet tall. Her turquoise dress is sewn with little mirrors set in chrysanthemum designs. Curly black hair forms a cloud around her face. Ebony eyes, full lips, high cheekbones in skin like coffee with extra cream. She wears a ton of Navajo turquoise and silver, a squash blossom necklace. Expensive. If Susan's mother has taught her anything, it's how to spot Nice.

"Won't stand for it," the woman says. She does not speak. She proclaims. Voice of a jazz singer, like a storm about to break. "I want my calculating machine. I want it back to*day*."

"Can't do it." He beams at her. "Got one more shipment coming next week. Got to figure the numbers."

"No! No more shipments, no *more*! Won't cover for you, Stan the Man, not ever again. Those days are long gone."

"The people will think . . ."

"I don't give a *shit* what the people will think. I don't give a *shit* about figuring your numbers."

"Say hey, Ruby A. Maverick." Stan the Man drops his smile. "We made a deal. Take the calculating machine, you said, as long as I need it. I need it. And I'm keeping it. You'll get it back when you get it back."

He is so beautiful to Susan, calm and strong. That woman; what does she mean? Why is Ruby angry?

"No deal," Ruby says. "The deal is off."

"One more shipment, Ruby. You have my word."

"Your *word*."

People are staring or laughing. It's embarrassing. Susan shifts the overnight bag to her other hand.

"Don't be uncool, Ruby. Look how you fuck with the energy of this beautiful day."

"Uh-huh, uncool. Look how you fuck with the energy any time you got a notion."

Repulsive; Susan is fascinated. Mom and Daddy fight. Always voices behind closed doors. What do they fight about? Susan can't sleep sometimes after hearing them, their muffled rage. Or over their cocktails or dinner, innuendos she doesn't understand. Sometimes she has to excuse herself, go to the bathroom, press fingers to her throat.

Stan turns to two other men. The first is another god-man, towering, razor-thin. Tough as leather, his boyish features are dusted with a patina of poverty. A fisherman's cap tilts over his brown curls. A threadbare suit coat is paired with patched jeans, cracked cowboy boots. His gold earring gleams.

"Say hey, Gorgon," Stan says. "You're a man of many heads. Talk some sense into her."

Gorgon shrugs. "Your calculating machine is just an object, Ruby. Private property. A bit of your capital. Ownership is the phony bullshit upon which this society of greed is based. What's the big deal?"

"That's just it, Leo," Ruby says. "He's using my calculating machine to *deal*."

The second man is frail in a loose purple shirt, grass-stained jeans two sizes too big. Feet bare, although the afternoon is quite chilly, his toes are caked with mud. Aquiline nose, sunken cheeks, Dracula's complexion. A door knocker strung on a leather thong hangs over his delicate breastbone.

"That's your reality, Ruby," the stickman says. Flat effect, refined accent. Professor Zoom's eyes are all pupil. His face, even his lips, barely move. "*Dealing* is in your mind. Dealing *is* your mind. Deal your *mind*, Ruby."

"Go back to Yale, Arnold," Ruby says. "You're full of shit."

"Don't call me names," Professor Zoom says. "Besides, I'm not full of shit. I'm full of Owsley white lightning."

A sight to see. Amid the laughing, leaping people, Ruby's anger burns. It feels wrong to Susan. Yet the men are intent on diffusing Ruby. That feels wrong, too. It's confusing.

They notice her suddenly, hovering at the edge of their circle.

"Foxy lady." Stan greets her like a long-lost friend. He embraces her, stoops, plants a long, hard kiss. Not the sloppy stuff Bernie MacKenna or Allen Weisberg tried. She is petrified and elated.

She wants . . . Not sure what she wants. She forgets herself for the ten seconds he takes to kiss her. Forget it, her messy hair, messy clothes, unwashed face. She is foxy lady. Mindless, such a smart girl. Numb, except for a spot somewhere north of her thighs, deep inside. If she had to give it a name just now, she would call it her heart.

He scoops her under his arm, sweeps her back to the circle. "Our newest flower child."

Ruby glares. "Uh-huh." She looks her up and down. "What's your name, flower child?"

"St-Starbright."

"Starbright. Let's see, Starbright. Just blew into town from some burb outside Chicago. Right? Am I right?"

"Cl-Cleveland."

"Speak up, Starbright."

"Cleveland."

"Uh-huh. And daddy's an executive. A vice president, they're the straitjacket type. Or, say, a doctor."

"Dentist," Susan whispers.

"Ruby's psychic," Professor Zoom says. Just the facts, ma'am.

"A *dent*ist. A real sadist, right? Wears a plain gold wedding band. Beats up everybody's mind at home. Everybody uptight *all* the time."

Susan studies the squash blossom necklace. They *are* uptight all the time. She can't stand it.

"Eat good." Ruby circles her. "Maybe a little too good. Have your own li'l bedroom painted purple. Got all the Beatles posters tacked on the walls."

Susan stares. Her room is lavender, actually.

"And you've come all the way to the Haight-Ashbury. Come to find your soul 'cause sweet Isis knows ain't no soul in Cleveland."

"I've come to find Penny Lane," she says.

"Penny . . . Uh-huh. Another darling daughter from the soulless burbs. Name's really Debby or Nancy. And *she's* run away to the Haight-Ashbury to find her soul. Am I right?"

Tears pool. Susan blinks them back.

"Go home, Starbright," Ruby says. "Sally or Suzy, whoever you are. Go home to your purple bedroom and three meals a day. I'd love to take your daddy's money. Damn right, I would, Leo." She glares at Gorgon, rubs her thumb across her fingers. "But you and your kind were old news *last* summer. You hear me, kid? It's 1967. You are *old news*."

"But it's all new to me!" Glances up to see the black eyes are furious.

"You're too late. There's no place for you in the Haight-Ashbury, Starbright. Cleveland needs you more. *Go home*."

"No!" How dare she! The tears melt away, the stutter steadies. "You can't tell me what to do!"

"Beautiful." Ruby throws up her hands. "Another teenybopper for Stan the Man. That's beautiful." She turns, strides away. "Have a ball," she calls over her shoulder.

"Bummer, Ruby," Professor Zoom yells after her.

"Cleveland needs them more," Gorgon says to Stan. "She has a point, even for a capitalist pig." He takes off after Ruby.

"Methinks Sir Leo the Gorgon intends to pick up the piece, as it were," Professor Zoom says to Stan the Man.

Stan hugs Susan closer. "Pick up the piece." His growl has a knife edge. "Yeah. Gorgon wants to try some dark meat. Well, that's her karma. Bitch."

"Not *bitch*, my good Stan. *Witch*," Professor Zoom says. "Every scene needs a witch, with psychic powers, et cetera. And a troll and an ogre and a fairy. Say, Stan, which are you?"

He shrugs, still staring after Ruby.

"Don't be attached, my son," Professor Zoom says. He takes out a corncob pipe from some hidden pocket, lights it. "Nothing is real. Reality is nothing."

Stan laughs. "Professor Zoom is a very wise man," he says to Susan. To Professor Zoom, "I'm not attached. I just never saw a Digger anarchist make it with a HIP merchant. Leo Gorgon and Ruby A. Maverick? Maybe they'll off each other."

"Life is an attachment," Professor Zoom says with a deadpan chuckle. The smoke smells like bitter chocolate. "But a sleep and an awakening. I am content if Ruby offs Leo Gorgon. I am content if Leo offs Ruby A. Maverick. I am content if they off you. Try some white Lebanese pollen?"

"Or you, my man." Stan takes the pipe.

"So be it. However, if it's you, bequeath to me the calculating machine," Professor Zoom says. "A useful tool, if a military-industrial deviltry. I'm still searching for the Final Expression to my equation proving God equals a hit of blotter."

Susan doesn't understand them. She shivers, leans against Stan's sturdy warmth. He hugs her back, quick and natural. When did someone last hug her? Maybe Nance before Susan moved away, and that was nearly a year ago. Body heat, oh the comfort of arms. She snuggles closer, dares to glance up at his face.

He winks at Professor Zoom as he hands back the pipe.

"Methinks the sweet pretty pussy is very hungry and very very thirsty," Professor Zoom says. He gazes at Susan. His eyes are like tunnels boring into his skull. What goes on in there? "Let's go trip with the Double Barrel Boogie Band."

* * *

The Double Barrel Boogie Band sets up.

Susan can hardly believe her eyes. It's them! On the bass drum, two circles conjoin like a shotgun snout or the symbol of infinity. She and Nance *love* the Double Barrel. They brought the *Let's Boogie Boogie* album to Cheryl Rubinstein's birthday party, took off the Beach Boys, and danced all night. Nance wore a black T-shirt, black jeans, and a strand of black plastic beads she got at Sears. Susan was so proud of her. The crowd from Greenview Junior High had been shocked.

That's Paul on keyboards, Mickey on drums, Stevie on bass, Rodg the Dodg on lead guitar. The Double Barrel Boogie Band! God!

Then something even more amazing happens. Stan the Man hops onto the stage, just like that. He slaps hands all around. He confers with Rodg the Dodg, barks orders at two scruffy boys connecting wires and setting up equipment. He hops down, goes behind the stage. Three beautiful girls pose in velvet and lace, stare at Susan with caterpillar eyes, whisper and laugh.

She is shaking so hard the overnight bag wobbles in her clenched fist. Nance, oh Nance, where are you?

The band's set begins. Stan comes back, wraps his arm around her. A blond woman in a sheer black blouse calls to him from the crowd. Her nipples bounce as she waves. Stan smiles at Susan, eyes lingering on her breasts nestled inside her jacket, sweater, blouse, bra.

Deafening chords of "Drop a Double Barrel."

He shouts in her ear, "How old are you, Starbright?"

She is ready with that one, too. "I'm eighteen."

He laughs. "So am I," he shouts back.

He gets her a paper cup. Professor Zoom squats at the foot of the stage, ladling juice from a wide-mouthed jug, handing cups to passersby. "Orange juice? Free orange juice?"

She takes the cup, annoyed. How stupid does he think she is? He's not eighteen. Maybe twenty-eight? She never can guess people's ages between young and ancient. Wrinkles crease his brow, fan from his eyes, his mouth. In fact, with his weathered, leathered look close up, he doesn't seem much younger than her father.

He is nothing like her father. A thrill ripples through her.

She drinks. Yum. Loves orange juice. Gulps it down. So hungry her stomach is yelping. "Can I have some more, please?"

"You can have anything you want, Starbright."

Professor Zoom ladles bright juice, soupspoon spilling. Bees buzz, free sweets. Yum. A cup to the dew-stained boy in blue, to the denimed college couple, to the fat girl in the gown. A cup to the barbarian with a fur hat and a vest that says Hells Angels on the back, to the fellow in a scarlet wig and ballerina's tutu, to the black guy in a beret and leather jacket. Buzz, buzz.

Another cup to Starbright with a smile.

Cup with a smile.

A cup does smile, if you hold it just so. Has a mouth. Why not smile?

The band is wailing, the day is sailing, her throat is getting gulpy. She catching something?

Sick. Stomach pitching, rolling around. Stan the Man bends over her. Strong hand on her neck, thumb pressed in the soft spot between her collarbones.

Sitting. Suddenly. Rank dandelion smell, mud like dog shit. Hands, monkey hands rest on her thighs. Thighs like sausages, stuffed skin over thick bones, moving, breathing like alien things. Monkey hands, *her* hands. A million wrinkles crisscross crude knobby knuckles. Fingers just like the monkey she saw in her biology textbook with electrodes stuck in its shaved-bald skull. Body like some heavy beast, a thing, not *her*. Ugly, so ugly ugly ugly.

She feels every function, heart pounding, squeezing blood into her head, breath wheezing like a wind through her mouth. The girl with her face, only it's all wrong. What if she comes, on wings of a bat, sparks crackling from her fingers? A rushing noise deafens her ears. Falling off a cliff, what if she falls?

There are no bats here, the man's voice says. There is no cliff here, Starbright.

His voice reassures her, the terror flows away. A sour, metallic taste rises in her throat. Hard to swallow, numb all over.

Another wave hits her.

Sobs tear from her chest. Grandpa! Grandpa who loved her, the only one who ever has. His vegetable garden, and grown-up tea with milk and sugar. His eyes that really twinkled, beaming just at her. Grandpa with tubes up his nose, in his arms, impossibly thin. His frightened eyes, his fear terrifying. The awful smell, the light too bright. And there was nothing she could do. Grandpa, this cannot be happening to you. Grandpa, don't leave me, please, please.

Other ghosts menace at the edge of her mind. Thoughts loom. Realizations thunder like a freight train, she is tied to the tracks. No, I don't want to!

Is she screaming?

She hears singing. People are singing. All around her. Voices creep into her ears, insistent and subtle as cats. The weird skinny elf in the purple shirt is singing. The barbarian with Hells Angels on his vest is singing. Scared again. Then the man, the mountain man. So beautiful! He smiles, bright as an angel. He beams at her, beaming right into her soul. He smiles and sings and sings and sings, like he knows she cannot hear him till she *hears* him:

> First there is Starbright,
> Then there is no Starbright,
> Then there is.

It's so . . . *silly*! It's so . . . *funny*! The elf is singing, the barbarian is singing, the mountain man is singing, the beautiful girls are singing. The Double Barrel Boogie Band—it's really *them—they're* singing, "First there is Starbright, then there is no Starbright." Everyone is smiling and singing.

To her!

She laughs and laughs. The trees sway, going *ssh-ssh* to the beat. The clouds rearrange themselves into lizards, butterflies, sea dragons, scorpions, schools of fish. A multicolored checkerboard erupts across the stage, gorgeous arabesques sprout in the dandelions.

Ecstasy! Everything is connected to her, she to everything, and it is so beautiful, the trees, the clouds, the singing people. She feels so much love for the world and all these people, for the Summer of Love, that she starts to cry again.

The mountain man says, "Stop it, Starbright."

Stop it, yes! Stop it, stop it. No more pain, no more sadness, no more anger, no more fear. No more fear! She will celebrate, celebrate the Solstice! She is bold, filled with wild abandon. She has crossed over. She *knows*! She has the power! She waves her arms, shakes her hips, she swoops and dives. No one tells her what to do!

She is leaping, laughing, free.
Dance, Starbright.

The first star of the evening winks on in the west. Night stains the sky, the wind blows from the ocean. Susan's chilled again, just as her bones were warming. A lifetime has passed in this day. She realized something amazing. Trying to remember. Cannot, her thoughts are tumbling.

The awesome explosion is gone. But everything is still luminous, numinous, streaked with mystery. Afterimages dance with the movements of objects. Professor Zoom hands her his corncob pipe. She takes it, holds it, examines the stem curiously. He guides the stem to her mouth. She opens her mouth. What else is there to do?

The night ripples with shapes, feelings. Nothing is real? Reality is nothing?

Everyone drifts from the meadow. Some jam onto flatbed trucks or crowd into vans and buses bound for the beach. They want to see the sunset. "Come on, Starbright!" someone calls. "You're either on the bus or off the bus!"

Yes. You're on the bus. You've been initiated into the mystery. Seen trees sway to the music, arabesques sprout in dandelions. You have stripped the plastic face off civilization and glimpsed Truth.

But she is off their bus this time. Night lights flash. The scene is humming in a different way. Excitement of nocturnal things, the darkness, the hunt.

Where will she go?

The bands break down, pack up.

People gather blankets and picnic baskets, collect the trash, wander into the dusk. Children grumble sleepily. They all have some place to go.

Where will she sleep?

Voices pass and fade. "Jimi Hendrix, man. He makes love to his guitar."

"See him at Monterey Pop?"

"Yeah, and he's playing the Fillmore tonight with the Airplane!"

So many things that were a unity now are separating. Susan can see this, this constant process, unity and separation. She and Grandpa, she and the Greenview Junior High crowd, she and Nance, she and Mom and Daddy. So many painful separations. But where are the unities? How she hungers for a new unity.

Hungry. Where will she eat?

The city has become a citadel, gleaming with electric jewels. In the dawn before, she saw empty streets, tired shop fronts, sidewalks strewn with trash. Now: the scene! On a Wednesday night in June. People milling about; so many! Bongo drums quicken everyone's pulse. Plum incense stirs in the stench of gasoline.

Lonely. Nance, where are you?

The postcard was addressed to "Starbright," and signed "Haight Is Love, Penny Lane." A Technicolor Golden Gate Bridge, emerald hills, turquoise sea and sky. "Monterey popped! Meet me here! Be sure to wear some flowers!"

Susan knew Nance's looping scrawl. She knew about the Monterey Pop Festival, which was advertised in the *Berkeley Barb,* an underground newspaper that Nance's cousin Don got from some guy who knew some guy in faraway San Francisco. She also knew the number five tune on the hit parade for May. Who didn't? "If You're Going to San Francisco." The tune says there is a new explanation, whatever that meant. Everyone was humming it, such a pretty tune.

Nance Jones ran away from her parents' home in South Euclid. She didn't have the decency to wait to graduate from the eighth grade. It was a scandal. Since Susan and Nance were best friends for years before Dr. Stein moved the family to the mock Tudor in Shaker Heights, Nance's stepfather and her mother came looking for Susan to see what she knew about it. Susan knew Nance ached to go to California for the festival. "*Every*one will be there!" she told Susan on the phone in a trembling voice.

Susan's father turned the parents away at the front door. "A bad influence," she heard him telling them as she crouched at the top of the second-floor stairs. He was using That Tone. Susan knew he had been listening in on her conversations. He was no good at picking up the phone in the den without making a click. There were words. Nance's parents said something about Susan being the bad influence. Then her father, "Since we've moved, I have kept my daughter away from her. Susan doesn't know a thing about it." Loud words. God, Daddy! Susan ran into her bedroom and shut the door. Glad he hadn't forced her to tell. Appalled he hadn't allowed her to tell.

Then a week ago she got the mail from the chute inside the front coat closet. Her mother was walking in the door with shopping bags. She managed to slip the postcard down the front of her jeans. Later, she studied it. She even called the airlines. She counted out her secret bank account stashed in the bottom of her toy chest. A hundred twenty dollars for a one-way red-eye on Pan Am, nearly three hundred dollars left over, plus the hundred for Mr. Rosenstein's roving hand. She was rich.

But it was a fantasy, however thrilling. She didn't decide to go for real till her mother found the postcard in her underwear drawer beneath the Tampax.

They called her to the kitchen. Anxiety swelled her throat. Chills ran down her spine. It was like going to be executed. She began twirling a lock of hair round her finger, bit the split ends, and spit them out.

"Stop it," her mother said. "I can't stand it."

But Susan's finger found another lock. Twirl, bite, spit.

"Get me some scissors," her mother said. "I'm cutting off her hair right now."

Daddy had That Look. His face was flushed, his eyes shone, his cheeks quivered. His mouth turned down, making his chin unsightly. "What the hell is this?" He shook the Golden Gate Bridge in front of her nose.

Bad news. She was grounded for the summer, her telephone privileges were taken away, she was forbidden to *ever* speak to Nance again. There was a question about new clothes for the ninth grade. Her mother sat beside her father on the other side of the table, a strange look of grim satisfaction and something else Susan never could place on her face. Two against one.

She said, "Nance is cool, she never puts me down. She's like my sister. She's my best friend!"

"You have new friends," her father said.

"No, I don't. They're gross."

Her mother was saying, "You haven't even tried . . ." when her father said, "You are *stupid*, Susan. You are wasting your time with that no-good girl, that little tramp."

There was more, but she didn't hear it. All she heard was the word her father had never applied to her before. A violation of the one thing she thought he respected her for, the fragile trust she possessed with him.

Stupid.

He tore the postcard into tiny scraps, put the scraps in an ashtray, lit them. He made Susan sit and stir the scraps till nothing but ashes was left.

She left that night. When Mom and Daddy went out to their dinner engagement, Susan booked Pan Am flight 153 and called a cab. They would get home from dinner an hour after she lifted off. She didn't leave a note.

It was like the time she and Nance climbed the old ironwood tree in Cheryl Rubinstein's front yard. On a dare from Cheryl, who they thought was conceited, they jumped from the big branch fifteen feet up. It wasn't hard till she hit the ground.

"Starbright," Stan the Man says. "Got a place to stay?"

If she's stupid, she might as well be really stupid. Does he guess she's going on fifteen? Who gives a shit? "No," she says. "I've got nowhere to go."

He takes her hand.

The Double Barrel Boogie Band's house is a slim, three-story Victorian with intricate gingerbread and peeling paint. A steep stairway leads to the porch and front door. The living room boasts a crumbling fireplace, a scuffed wood floor, battered chairs and swayback couches strewn about. The air smells of wood rot, dog shit, burnt chocolate, incense. A mutt slinks by, growling when someone stoops to pet him. Professor Zoom cuts chunks from a brick of vegetable matter on the coffee table. The table is decorated with grease-lipped glasses, brown apple cores, tweezers, a kazoo, a brass pipe, a can of half-eaten SpaghettiOs with the lid bent back. The floor is thick with more of the same. The profusion of junk forms a tapestry of chaos with its own weird beauty. Susan thinks of her mother's precise living room, the curving peach couch with its custom slipcover that she only takes off for company. The stereo blasts. People everywhere; so many!

One of the caterpillar-eyed girls who stood at the back of the Double Barrel stage comes to her. Sarah turns out to be sweet and shy, a fine-boned blond with freckles and bloodshot eyes beneath her false lashes. Not nearly as intimidating close up as she was at a distance. Susan thinks about that revelation. Sarah takes Susan's hand, leads her to the room she shares with Mickey. She shows Susan her chalk drawings. Asymmetrical flowers, clouds over a beach. It's sad. Sarah is not very good.

Susan knows how to draw. She doodled hours away at Mr. Rosenstein's art supply store. She takes a scarlet chalk, draws a bold, lidded eye, a star for the pupil, a teardrop hanging at its tip. Her mother says her drawings are not proportional.

Sarah says, "That's beautiful, Starbright. But what do you think of this? I want to do my thing, too." She shows Susan a man who might be Mickey, long hair drawn in psychedelic swirls. "Mickey wants me to make posters for the band, but Stan says no," she complains. Susan can see why.

Looking at Sarah and her drawings, Susan thinks of "The Menagerie" from *Star Trek*. The bleak landscape of Talos IV. And Vina, the human girl made ugly and deformed in a starship crash that stranded her there. The Talosians make her whole and beautiful, but her beauty is an illusion. Yet Vina chooses to remain on Talos IV. She gets to stay with Captain Pike, who was crippled, too, and now is strong and handsome—but only on Talos IV. Given a choice, Vina prefers her illusions.

To Susan's luminous, numinous mind, this is another revelation: the saving grace of illusion.

"That's beautiful, Sarah," Susan says. She means it, too.

Stan the Man carries her overnight bag and purse in one hand. With the other, he takes her hand, leads her up two stairways to his room.

The penthouse cubbyhole is layered with paisley blankets and old smoke. Her perceptions swell and ripple. She breathes hard from the climb. She is aware of being dirty for over twenty-four hours, of a tart sweat gathering under her arms, filming her skin.

They sit on a mattress on the floor. She has never seen someone living with a mattress on the floor, but it looks like a fun idea. Like a pajama party. He takes her jacket, easing stiff wool from the May Company off her shoulders. Unshells her feet from the mod ankle boots, kicks off his own boots.

Her sweater goes next, the lavender mohair Grandpa gave her for her twelfth birthday. He throws the sweater on the floor. She follows the trajectory unhappily. He seizes her chin, chews her eyebrows like a cat. Nips her nose, ravages her mouth. His hard kiss, so exciting in the open meadow, is frightening in the small room.

He tears at her blouse, at buttons she denied Bernie MacKenna and Allen Weisberg. She fights back, clawing, clutching herself.

No!

He turns away.

Is he angry? He leans back on the mattress, props pillows against the wall. No, not angry. Sad; melancholy falls over him. "I won't hurt you," he says. His face is extraordinary. He shrugs off his shirt, beckons to her. She gladly scoots next to him and snuggles, her back to him, wrapping her arms over her chest. She feels all right like this, but so cold. Shadows curl and pulse across the room.

Feelings shift, thoughts drift.

She is suddenly aware of his living force beside her. She turns to watch him talk. His eyes are alive. He murmurs strange things. "You're with me, but you're not with me. You're not with me." He turns away, he will not look at her. His voice rumbles, a thrilling sound she almost can touch.

She is part of a huge and complex pattern, like a curtain woven of space and time. With him, not with him? How did he know she was thinking about separations and unities?

The realization he knows what she's thinking loosens a tide of warmth inside her. Stan the Man; he *knows*.

There's something she must do. Get up and leave? This occurs to her, but she dismisses the thought. Anyway, she isn't sure how to do it. Cannot get her legs to obey just now. She feels paralyzed. Is destiny a paralysis? She almost laughs out loud. God, Susan, she tells herself. You are becoming wise.

Mostly it's the cold that gets to her. Bone-chill, teeth chattering. He turns to her at last, cuddles her. Gently, they lie together. He finds a blanket, throws it over them. Dust tickles her nose. Stiff, she hugs herself.

He surrounds her like a cocoon. He strokes her hair. Her arms loosen, unwind. It's unnatural to fold your arms over your chest. It's natural to unfold them, let them fall away. Her shivering stops. It's natural to hold someone holding you. She unbuds like a flower, be sure to wear flowers. She drowses. He kisses her forehead. Lightly, lightly. He kisses her eyes. His lips slide over the bridge of her nose.

His lips on her mouth. Sleepy, her lips yield. She tastes his tongue, tastes tobacco, white Lebanese pollen. Relaxing her hand, she touches his waist. Somehow his jeans have vanished. She feels his flesh, his stirring cock.

Awake.

He's got her blouse halfway to her elbows by the time she can rouse herself. He undresses her with ease, overcoming the logistics of buttons, zippers, hooks and eyes, elastic bands. Her clothing slides off before she can struggle. Red lights literally flash in her face. Every nasty conversation whispered in the girls' lavatory jabbers in her ears. Her parents' faces, stern and pasty, rise up like ruined moons.

He licks her nipples. His mouth slides down her stomach to the place where Mr. Rosenstein put his hand.

He kisses her knee, pries her thighs apart. She splits open like a shell. His tongue parts her labia. She falls back, fluttering. The ceiling plaster forms red and white blossoms of light as she shivers with pleasure so intense it's almost painful.

He lunges up, defeats her tightness, buries his cock in her. He pounds against her till it's too much, she can sustain him no longer. Is she screaming? He slaps her face, covers her mouth with his mouth.

He shudders. The heat of his climax shocks her. Is she crying?

He rolls off, rolls away. Then rolls back, tickling her ribs, biting her ear, kissing her tears. "That was groovy, Starbright," he says and slaps her butt.

Astonishment and aching. She stares at him. He grins, he *laughs*. He doesn't ache?

He zips his jeans, pulls on boots, grabs a shirt, and stalks out. She hears him clatter downstairs to the party. People shout and laugh, a glass smashes, a woman shrieks. Motorcycles gun, someone turns up the stereo.

Wild and free, oh take me.

Night shines through the rain-dappled window. Stars wheel, forming patterns: Orion the hunter, a bridge made of clouds, a girl dancing, leaping.

"Star light," she sings softly. "Star bright. First star I see tonight. Wish I may, wish I might. Have the wish I wish. Tonight."

Then she goes down to the party, and they boogie till four that morning.

2

Do You Believe
in Magic?

They never prepare you for the shock of the Event.

Chiron Cat's Eye in Draco steps through the Portals of the Past. After the subjective second it takes to cross over, he proceeds, as required, to check points of reference:

The dome;

the carving;

his time of arrival.

But wait, wait. He tries to stand very still as perceptions rush into his eyes and ears. Not dizzy like some, nor nauseated, nor faint. Just . . . emptiness. They say you don't feel the ME3 Event, but they're wrong. He feels it, all right. The pulse of his essence, a sensation of *being* pure energy. Ah!

He is shaken to his core. For a moment, reality seems dead. A weight round his neck, a disappointment so vast he quells the urge to weep. They don't tell you reality is the same everywhen, but the ME3 Event is a quantum leap, translation-transmission an epiphany. The only true ecstasy one can know.

The project; move, Chiron! He starts again, more slowly: points of reference.

First, the dome. The cosmicist dome that's spanned New Golden Gate Preserve for nearly two centuries. Right, it's gone. Only sky above, nude as a rad-vacc lass defying the sex police. Gorgeous. Criminal. And dangerous as a maser on blue. The sight of the summer's eve unshielded by PermaPlast sends a jolt of terror up his spine. He throws his hands over his face, *now* he's dizzy. Nearly crashing like a telelink going down.

Damn it, Chi! The sky is prime, thick and whole, wet with clouds, ozone perched atop the stratosphere where it should be. Like it did once.

Like it does Now.

Never crashed his telelink in his life. He is fitted for professional link, rigged with a neckjack that interfaced his mind with telespace. Telespace: computer-constructed reality, the latest technology of the New Renaissance. Jack up, link in, space out. Cool, tool.

Fuck it. If he can handle telespace, he can handle a tachyportation.

But when you jacked out of telespace, you unlinked from the workstation and went home. A t-port isn't that easy.

He touches cool marble, steadying himself.

And with his touch on the mysterious ancient stone comes the second shock:

The carving at the bottom of the Portal's left column. *It's gone.*

The dome shouldn't be there, but the carving *should.*

Mere graffito. A forgotten, indecipherable set of glyphs carved on the column, discovered only after the massive research effort led by his skipfather. The carving proved to be a final piece of the puzzle. Once evidence supported Open Time Loop probabilities, the directors of the Luxon Institute for Superluminal Applications threw fifty million International Bank Units at the project. Never mind that Chi's skipfather held an executive post with the Archives, or that his skipmother owned LISA stock and one-sixth of the patent on the ME3 Event. If anything, their position made t-porting their own skipson to a hot dim spot in the middle of the Crisis all the more compelling.

As he stood in the Portals of the Past, waiting for the ME3 Event to translate-transmit him, he had stooped and pressed his fingers, learning the shape by touch, as well as by sight.

What did it mean?

Who could say? The Eye of Horus was a prehistoric charm signifying wisdom, prescience. The heart symbol was even older, depicting not the organ of circulation at all, but the buttocks of a beloved as a lover would see them from behind. And the old-fashioned key? A concept and device from the first millennium. A key unlocked secrets, secured possession and ownership. There were associations with music, translations, maps, ciphers and codes.

As it turned out, the key could also—at a probability just over fifty percent—refer to *him:* Chiron Cat's Eye in Draco. The fanciful, mythological name he'd been born with twenty-one years ago. Calliope had chosen it. She of the slanting blue eyes, golden skin, strawberry hair. How Calliope had loved fanciful, mythological things. In myth, Chiron was the centaur, his symbol the key.

He wishes he could doubt his eyes. The link to the loop, the piece of the puzzle, the final bit of evidence sealing his ticket to a dangerous tachyportation.

The damn carving is gone.

An awful thought strikes him: *What if they made a mistake?*

And with that bitter thought, seventy-six days in this forsaken past, days he loses forever in his personal Now, he checks his time of arrival. Looks at his wristwatch and sees:

He is twelve hours and ten minutes late.

Late?

His microfusion wristwatch loses a second every two millennia, and he's only t-ported five hundred years. The watch has got a counterclockwise chronometer that the LISA techs set most meticulously, checked and rechecked, up to the moment when he translated-transmitted through the Portals of the Past.

June 21 to June 21, San Francisco 2467 to San Francisco 1967, portals to portals.

It should be ten-fifteen in the morning. Precisely five centuries, one hundred twenty-five days, fifty-three minutes, thirty-nine seconds, three hundred nineteen milliseconds, minus one picosecond. The ME3 Event is instantaneous, merely a shifting of energy in the One Day. A when to another when. The minus-picosecond accounts for superluminal drift, but registers on the human mind as a second in duration. A subjective second.

Instead, it's nearly half-past ten at night.

He's fucking *late*.

Chiron sits on the steps, stunned. Rank green water shimmers before him, the surface splintering from the dance of night insects. Lloyd Lake. He wishes he could laugh at the pretentious name for this swampy little pond that will dry into a dust bowl in a hundred years. Taste ocean salt in two hundred years, be restored beneath the first cosmicist dome after three hundred. Serve as sanctuary for rare fish and birds after four hundred years, provide the site, plus the desired atmospheric humidity, for consummating a t-port in five hundred. Five hundred years.

The awful chasm of centuries yawns before him.

Huge eucalyptus trees rustle in a cold breeze. Bamboo on the littoral shore stirs and murmurs. An insomniac duck quacks. He is alone in the Portals of the Past.

He stands.

Says softly to himself, "Let the Summer of Love Project begin."

A woman's laughter floats across the water from John F. Kennedy Drive, a bright chuckle recalling his lass, Venus Rising. People stroll arm in arm beneath electric street lights in the summer night. Ah; a woman's laughter. Still the same.

What did he expect? Humanity hasn't changed. His neurobics, his neckjack, the aftereffect of the radiation vaccine, even his DNA editing and gene tweaking. These improved upon the original design, certainly, but didn't make him a new breed of human. These are modern people, he reminds himself, neither Neanderthals nor devolts. Differing from the impact of circumstances, but not in fundamentals.

Two women walk around the lake. A Cherokee maiden and an Elizabethan lady, from their costumes. "Got any spare change?" they call to him. He jogs past without a word. "Asshole," they call again.

He can barely swallow his outrage. He didn't ask for this project. He was summarily drafted. It was a grievous interruption, an imposition on his rights. On his *life.* His thesis on the effect of macros in the growth trends of liver clones—an extremely important topic!—was placed on hold. Worse, he had just started the affair with Venus Rising. A rad-vacc lass from a prominent Eurasian cosmicist family, rigged for telelink and specializing in the new thing, cosmospherology. Their dynasties were much excited by their meeting, which could have been arranged, but was random. The randomness added a keen edge to their lovemaking. Not to mention their free-linking.

Give it up? Give *her* up? For *how* long? Hadn't his family done enough for the Great Good?

Apparently not. He was a cosmicist, the heir to a distinguished cosmicist dynasty. To give is best; live responsibly or die. He was expected to sacrifice for the Great Good. You *lived* what you advocated, with joy. Those born with privilege gave up privilege. Now the data was disappearing, the Archives were riddled with holes. He had witnessed the dreadful Vision of the Other Now with his own eyes. The world faced a Crisis unlike any other before. It was his duty.

He glances over his shoulder, but the women are gone. He unsnaps a neurobic bead from his pharmaceutical necklace, pops it open, inhales the metallic-tinged vapor.

His head clears instantly, his sight soars. Better, better.

Half a day late, but he made it. He wriggles his toes in the Beatle boots, examines his fingers. All in one piece. Early t-porters lost fingers or ears or got buried in sidewalks, thrust through trees. When-to-when wasn't the only calculation, and he'd arrived on target. Right where he started from: on the threshold of the Portals of the Past. Free and clear of the marble columns, brick supports, concrete steps. The portals have stood exactly in the same place for nearly six hundred years. A majestic doorway in the Ionic style, it was all that remained of the Towne mansion after the Great Fire of 1906. Set upon Lloyd Lake thereafter, the graffiti-blighted portals proved an ideal shuttle site. Permanence, in the face of flux.

The huge installation of the tachyonic shuttle had surrounded the portals. Beams and wires and steelyn lattices. Arrays of calcite crystals, an artillery of photon guns. Banks of microframes networked to offsite mainframes. A thousand imploders arranged in a half-moon that instituted-consummated the ME3 Event. The awesome dish of the macrofusion chronometer that coordinated when-to-whens within the shuttle site. The SOL Project staff scurried about, his skipfather stood near, whispering final instructions. The Chief Archivist and her three top ferrets checked and rechecked their sources on supersmart knuckletops.

His skipmother hovered, too. Fidgeting, more nervous than usual for her, even under stress. Parental anxiety, he thought. But to his amazement, just before he stepped, she slipped something into his back jeans pocket! Whispered, "Consider impact before you consider benefit, my son."

Now all of it, all of them, gone.

Chiron strides through the park. Apprehension knocks in his chest, giving way to slow anger. Mistake. He can't afford a mistake! He feels like the first passenger on the EM-Trans, wondering if the maglev train will hold to its tracks or fly off at a thousand miles an hour.

Fifty million IBUs, and the Archivists didn't find the right dim spot? The SOL Project directors didn't choose the right loop? It could happen. The Save Betty Project directors were confident in '66. The object of that project seemed simple. Yet the Save Betty Project got complicated in no time. Dangerously complicated.

Chiron's project is anything but simple.

But the fact that you arrive means you *will* succeed, the Chief Archivist insisted. It's an Open Time Loop; evidence supports your presence. Any fool could see this logic itself was a loop. Yet he'd swallowed her claims like a good cosmicist, done his duty, and crossed over the Portals of the Past.

He quickens his pace, apprehension deepening to dread. The Chief Archivist neglected a key point, of course. He clenches his fist, punches it into his palm. A *key* point, ha! *Punch.* He has *not* succeeded till he *returns.* What if he goes to the portals in seventy-six days, the tachyonic shuttle fails to engage this spacetime, and he can't translate-transmit? What if he can't get to the portals at all? *Punch.*

Then he's trapped in a Closed Time Loop, that's what. A CTL, from which there's no escape, never has been an escape, never will be an escape. When does a CTL commence? No one knows. It just *is*.

Oh, the Archivists plot their probabilities, but they never arrive at absolute certainty any sooner than reality itself. A ninety-nine percent probability of success permits a one percent probability of failure.

In the beginning and the end, it's all a crapshoot. The Cosmic Mind *does* play dice. Loves to gamble, in fact.

You cannot change the past. Under the Grandfather Principle, the first commandment of tachyportation, changing the past is logically, theoretically, practically, historically, physically, over-under-and-sideways *impossible*. Everyone has known that for as long as people have asked the question.

But Ariel Herbert finally proved in her famous experiment that particles traveling faster than the speed of light—tachyons, these particles are called—correlated information superluminally, regardless of conventional distance or Newtonian causality. Physicists will be physicists. And the theoreticians, not to mention applications specialists working with luxons—particles traveling *at* the speed of light—began to reconsider the impossible.

Physics got sexier and sexier. While Dr. Herbert proved tachyonic correlation of information, a team of techs learned how to translate matter to its energy equivalent and back again with less than a picogram-picosecond of loss. And once you can translate matter to energy, you can transmit it superluminally. Piece of cake.

How did translation work? Krafkat and O'Lawless, who always had been daring, mastered the Dead Stop—a matter-antimatter annihilation exchange halted like a hiccup before the moment of completion. Due to its danger, the process of translation-transmission—driven by the Matter-Energy Equivalence Equation, or the ME3 Event—was first permitted only to correlate pure information. But, once done, tachyportation of matter proved a mere increment of application. Everyone started to relax about that antimatter stuff. Krafkat made a world tour during which she swallowed coordinate particles onstage and disappeared and reappeared all over the auditoriums. She made a fortune before the gig in Bombay during which she mysteriously disappeared and never came back.

So it went like this: Superluminal correlation permitted the ME3 Event, the ME3 Event permitted superluminal correlation. Was this the grandmother of all loops? Chiron wonders. Or could there be another loop? A secret loop, snaking deviously, insidiously, way beyond human sight? Is it a CTL, an OTL, is it closed, is it open? Who could know?

Tachyportation was quickly applied to development of the solar system. The Luxon Institute for Superluminal Applications was owned and largely staffed by cosmicists. They prided themselves on a philosophy of radical extrapolation of theory coupled with conservationist, impact-correct action/nonaction. T-port destinations beyond conventional observation technology were approached with caution. None of the superluminal probes sent beyond the Milky Way returned but one, which came back crushed flatter than a pancake. The probe cost thirty million International Bank Units. No more intergalactic probes for the next three fiscal years till you raise another thirty million IBUs, sorry.

The arduous and delicate terraforming of Mars owed much to t-ported shipments of personnel and materiel, however. Mars was so close you could see planetside activity with a child's telescope. T-portation gained daily in efficiency and ease. It wasn't long before the LISA techs began to observe paradox.

Terraformers on Mars discovered ashen-faced arrivals wandering about the base before they'd stepped through the tachyonic shuttle on Earth. Three laborers went insane. The paradox was hushed up till a telelink pirate broke into the encrypted file, deciphered it, and uploaded the news over public telespace. It was a scandal; not the last scandal. The institute was embarrassed, but pleaded the privacy rights of the victims, none of whom were cosmicists, just ordinary citizens thankful for a high-paid job.

Paradox became the hot topic. Probability physicists gleefully abandoned linearity, embracing super-determinism and multiple realities with a passion repulsive to free-will proponents, but oddly congenial to cosmicist philosophers. After all, every one of the t-porters who paradoxed on Mars ended up stepping through the shuttle. No one didn't. A statistic of one hundred percent. A Prime Probability.

The next step down the road to hell was even easier. If humanity has succeeded in t-porting to the past, said the theoreticians, we have already done so. And if t-porting to the past creates probabilities, we're already mixed up in any number of realities that are consistent with our spacetime and therefore resilient. By and by, we'll invent a past-travel application to the tachyonic shuttle. In fact, no one will invent the application. All we need do is wait till someone remembers the specifications.

Chiron slows, breathing hard against the steady upward slope. Chaotic noise beats in the distance. The rumble of a crowd, he can practically smell them, like passing near a zoo.

A team of techs at the Luxon Institute for Superluminal Applications *did* remember the specifications. In no time at all.

Someone shrieks in the night.

Ahead, around the bend. To his right, the flat, undistinguished roof of the De Young Museum rises above the trees. A stone sphinx crouches in the dark.

Adrenaline shoots through his blood. Demons? For that is another theory the Chief Archivist holds: that demons are targeting the hot dim spot.

A knot of people gathers in the shadowed street.

Wary, he joins them.

A girl, perhaps no more than fourteen years old. Cropped black hair plastered over her tearstained face, she lies writhing on the ground. A teenage boy tries to hold her, but her frantic, flailing strength nearly overpowers him.

"My heart!" she screams. "Jesus Christ, my heart!"

"What is it?" Chiron quietly asks, jumping at the sound of his own voice. Half a day late! Blown it, could he have blown it? But no, she cannot be the Axis. Her hair is way too short to be the Axis.

"Her heart, dincha hear?" says the struggling boy. "Some dude in the band wouldn't look at her, an' her heart is broke. Shit!"

"Serenity, Tranquility, and Peace," says his companion, a boy in a bush hat, glancing anxiously over his shoulder. He digs out a capsule from his shirt pocket. "Hey, Bobby, get this red down her fuckin' throat, and let's split, man."

"Don't do it," Chiron starts to say. "You need to—"

The boy in the bush hat whips around, thrusts his face into Chiron's. He must be sixteen, but his cheeks are as gaunt as an old man's, skin sunbaked tough. "Need to *what,* man?" Hard eyes flick over Chiron's hair, clothing. He has foul body odor. He is shaking.

Chiron backs away. Is his costume wrong? "You need to be cool," he says softly. "You need to . . . ah, leave her alone. Just . . . leave her alone."

"Yeah?"

"I'm having a heart attack! Jesus Christ, I'm dying! Bobby? Bobby?"

"That's all," Chi says.

That's the best he can do. The Axis has much longer hair. This girl cannot be the one he's looking for.

"Just be cool," he says.

GOSSIP, INNUENDO & ALL THE NEWS THAT FITS

Psychotomimetic amphetamines (DOM or, more popularly, STP) are seen in the Haight-Ashbury in June, 1967 and represent a shift in drug consumption from the LSD preference of the hip community existing prior to the Summer of Love. Stanley Owsley III, the LSD chemist, allegedly named STP after Scientifically Treated Petroleum, the popular oil additive, "because it makes your motor run smoother and lubricates your head." Dealers claim STP produces three days of Serenity, Tranquility, and Peace.

Five thousand hits of STP were passed out free near the barbecue pits during the Celebration of the Summer Solstice in Golden Gate Park. Users experienced, over a period of twenty-four hours or more, heart palpitations, muscle tremors, hallucinations eighty times more potent than mescaline, acute anxiety, and, in certain users, paranoid psychosis. Barbiturates typically used to calm a bad LSD trip, such as Thorazine and Seconal, intensify STP's adverse symptoms and should be strictly avoided.

> —Adapted from David E. Smith, M.D.,
> and John Luce, *Love Needs Care*
> (Little, Brown and Company, 1968)

The boy in the bush hat hands the red to Bobby, who tries to push it in the girl's mouth. She clamps her lips, moans. Bobby pinches her nostrils. When she gulps for air, he tosses in the red, makes her swallow.

"Jesus, I'm . . . You're trying to *kill* me!"

"Shut up, Penny Lane," Bobby says.

"Help! Help me, please!"

He slaps the girl. "I said shut up!"

"He . . . he's trying to *kill* me!"

Chiron jogs away.

The girl will probably go to the Haight-Ashbury Free Medical Clinic on Clayton Street. She may be one of the patients who will be treated there in the days following the Celebration of the Summer Solstice. She may even turn out to be the young woman who will be admitted under one of her numerous street names to the Immediate Psychiatric Aid and Referral Service, be diagnosed as psychotic, and escape back to the street. Not long after, she will die from a rape-beating in Golden Gate Park. Her street names are lost to the Archives, her legal name will never be known. She is an a.k.a., then a Jane Doe.

The Archives documenting this summer are hot with holes burning out the data, erasing the past so completely that the most obsessive ferret on the Chief Archivist's staff couldn't find certain information. There is no cross-reference. Jane Freaking Doe. Chiron doesn't know. Hair plastered over her face, screaming, "Help me!"

So young.

Ah, forget it. He must find the Axis, that's all. That's the object of the SOL Project: find *her*. Only *her*. What other responsibility does he have to these people?

These are people who out of their greed and selfishness, their lack of responsibility to themselves, their children, and the future, will perpetrate so many crimes against the Earth, against the creatures and the life of the planet, against even themselves, that their heirs for the next five hundred years will suffer and sacrifice and hide from the sky itself.

He finds himself shaking with rage.

Why should he help that girl? He may not make it back home himself.

Ah, but he's a t-porter. And it's worse than that.

He pops off another neurobic bead, snorts it.

Under Tenet Three of the Grandfather Principle, he cannot affect any person in the past, including deterring, aiding, killing, or saving her. He's not *allowed* to help her. Not even if he wanted to.

You cannot change the past. Everyone knows that.

But what *is* the past? How is it defined? How does anyone know what the past really is?

They knew from the Archives: the records, books, photographs, artifacts, magnetic tapes, microfiche, films, CD-ROMs, hypertexts, holoids, and, for Chiron, telespace backups. In bacterial microproteins, every single piece of retrievable information from the last ten thousand years could be stored in a room the size of a small closet. Applying telespace technology, data could be accessed in seconds. Whole industries sprang up around search and access, not to mention the Archives themselves. The Chief Archivist rivaled the Chief Executive Officer of the International Bank in power and importance.

But even the Archives failed to preserve *everything*. Things crumble, become dust, become lost. An empire, a city, or a clay pot. So much is lost.

And who could say, the techs asked, what happened in the past *every second*? There were gaps in the Archives that, when examined closely, appeared enormous. What became of the small moments, details so vast as to be nearly infinite? Did it matter if we knew? And what about people's minds? Their thoughts, their feelings, their intuitions? Didn't reality consist of these, too? Another virtual infinity, another set of probabilities.

What happened when you kicked the sand? Everything? Or nothing? A rearrangement of the entire beach? Or a spray of grit, settling down again? The beach was always shifting, gliding with the tides.

You would think people trembled at the frailty of existence, but no. Everyone congratulated each other. We *created* paradox! Do you realize what that means?

What a temptation! A tantalizing notion: If you could find soft data in the Archives, places where the evidence supported a set of probabilities, you could get away with flinging in a bit of new probability. Go ahead. Spacetime was resilient, the timeline was conservable. Want proof? If you do so, you have *already* done so. Indeed, you *must* do so. And vice versa, said Ariel Herbert, Chiron's skipmother. The very same Herbert who cracked tachyonic correlation.

Giddy with optimism, the Luxon Institute for Superluminal Applications took that as permission, a reasonable warranty they could not do very much wrong. Cosmicism, as an ontological philosophy, couldn't find much fault with this. We are cocreators of reality with the Cosmic Mind, aren't we? We claim responsibility; we make destiny.

Easy. As it turned out, soft data in the Archives was not very hard to find. The Archivists called these places dim spots.

And through the study of dim spots, they found the holes. Data that was thinning, then vanishing, sometimes wildly, beyond the best backup and retrieval techniques known. With typical aplomb—another cover-up; they were desperate—the LISA techs called *those* moments hot dim spots.

A hot dim spot. Like the Summer of Love.

Chiron steps to the corner of John F. Kennedy Drive and Stanyan Street, looks south to the mouth of the Haight-Ashbury. Bongo drums thump, laughter soars. Bells clang, tambourines jingle, automobiles and motorcycles roar, horns honk. A crowd swarms over the sidewalks, in the park, down the Panhandle, on the street. It's appalling. The stench of gasoline and body odor, mixed with sickly sweet incense, nauseates him.

A vision of hell? To the technopolistic plutocracy, this would be paradise, ripe and ready for exploitation.

All right. Evidence supports Chiron's probable presence at this hot dim spot. His skipfather traced the OTL himself. An act of love, good old Brax kept insisting.

What is the evidence?

The carving, of course, with the key. But the carving is gone. There goes the only fifty-one percent probability he's got on his side.

Second, the advertisement. A local newspaper called the *Berkeley Barb* ran certain classified ads. Personal ads, they were called. Hardcopy of the paper was long gone, the microfiche was mostly gone, too. But there, among guys looking for swinging chicks and chicks looking for swinging times, was an ad placed during the summer by someone looking for a guy with red hair. And, yes, Chiron is a guy with red hair. At least, he *would* have been a guy with red hair if he hadn't taken the radiation vaccine and turned out to be a rad-vacc lad. He has red hair now thanks to implant technology, an unpleasantry required for the project to which he submitted reluctantly. Venus Rising was understanding, if distant. On reflection, he realizes the red hair is a loop, too. A small loop, but a loop nonetheless.

And third, the news clip. The news clip that caused such excitement among the Archivists. The clip shows a tall, red-haired person who appears to be speaking with a girl. They stand in the background of a scene shot on Haight Street. The original film had deteriorated in every known Archive but for the clip, which, when discovered, was reconstructed in holoid, supercopied, and backed up in four mainframes. And *still* was fading.

That's the evidence.

His skipfather said, "You're the one, Chiron." He had tears in his eyes, but he was sure. His skipmother said, "Consider impact before you consider benefit, my son," and slipped him contraband at the very last moment. Ariel Herbert must have been sure, too. Or was she?

The noise, the stench, the high nervous energy, the sheer weirdness overwhelms him. Chi decides to avoid the main drag. He's in no shape to deal with bright lights, not tonight. Hungry, but he decides against a nutribead from his nutritional necklace. Drowsy, but he decides against another neurobic bead from his pharmaceutical necklace. To give is best, live responsibly or die. Right; he's got limited supplies. Find a place to rest, that's what he'll do. He can sleep anywhere. His t-port training included camping on the ground.

A thousand thoughts scatter through his mind. He struggles to hold on to one. Don't underestimate the ME3 Event. Analyze the probabilities. Get his bearings. The enormity of the t-port strikes him again: *What if they made a mistake?* He forces the thought away.

He sets out down Oak Street, but people crowd the back alleys, too. Try the cosmicist tack: if you take no position, you encounter no opposition. He keeps to the shadows, avoids people. A bad taste sours his mouth.

Is he a coward for not helping the girl in the park?

He forces that thought away, too. No. He is a professional telelinker at twenty-one years old, on the verge of his doctorate degree in medical modeling, an heir to a domed estate in Sausalito. He never feared telespace; he does not fear reality, present *or* past. He is a conservator, charged with conforming to the Tenets of the Grandfather Principle. A t-port is tough. The Tenets are there to guide you, not make you feel guilty. He's got a touch of past-shock, that's all.

What else is a mistake? The shrewd inspection of the boy in the bush hat gave him small comfort.

His costume was designed by Archival specialists. With scrupulous attention to authenticity, so they claimed. Beatle boots, with absurd toes and heels. Generic denim jeans. They assured him straight-leg Levi's have been cut much the same since 1849. The pharmaceutical necklace and a nutritional necklace, which look like love beads. A French flight jacket in a tough brown synthy that looks, feels, and smells like goatskin.

Everything is bacteria-resistant, waterproofed and dustproofed. He's got no bags, no change of clothes. Five centuries for fifty million IBUs got you tools bundled close to the body, and that's about it. The payload is tight. He can't risk infection from clothing of this time, so he'll have to wear the costume for seventy-six days. The Archivists assured him that wasn't unusual. Runaways to the Haight-Ashbury often brought nothing but their ideals and the shirts on their backs.

His pockets are stashed with supplies. Plenty of Block, a stack of patches tucked in one pocket. The maser fits into the other. The scanner, slim and compact, fits next to the maser. Mega! That's one pocket full of power. Three antique Kleenex packets are each stuffed with ten thousand filters, ten thousand wipes, ten thousand prophylaks. It's imperative that he avoid the pollutants, bacteria, and viruses of this time. All the antiseptics, antibiotics, and antifungals in his pharmaceutical necklace may not help if he gets contaminated. Got a pocket scope with 2000× magnification, too.

The knuckletop is the largest payload, the costliest tool, and the last item of fiercest negotiation, though in size and weight it's indistinguishable from a large man's ring of carved silver and onyx, the bezel raised slightly higher than most. The SOL Project directors violently protested his t-portation of the knuckletop. No t-porter had ever been equipped with such a modern tool. The possibility—and the temptation—of violating any of several Tenets of the Grandfather Principle was too great.

His skipfather took no position, but his skipmother excluded the knuckletop from her list of sealed objections. About that, she was explicit, precise, and vehement. My skipson must have it. Everyone was surprised, even Chiron. Ariel Herbert was known for her radical conservationism. Yet she insisted. He gets the knuckletop, or he doesn't go.

In the end he got the knuckletop, plus a solar palmtop calculator, but only after she pointed out he could analyze probabilities, plus view Archival files the directors had authorized. This was the most radical t-port the institute had ever attempted. They were asking him to spend an extraordinary length of time in the past. Perhaps, she argued, he could avoid too many mistakes. Perhaps he could avoid a disaster like the Save Betty Project.

Chiron pats his back jeans pocket, knows exactly what his skipmother slipped him the moment he touches it. Carefully, he works it out of the pocket. A stash cube! What's inside? Holoid disks, a slew of them! Slivers of crystal he can insert in the knuckletop's H drive and view in holoid projection.

Her last words, "Consider impact before you consider benefit." The classic cosmicist injunction. And the mandate of nonintervention for tachyportation projects, as articulated in the Tenets of the Grandfather Principle.

Prime. But what's on the holoids? If possession of the knuckletop was deemed dangerous for a t-porter, what about holoid disks unauthorized by the directors? He shakes his head. His skipmother did not prevent his t-port. Yet she allowed him to smuggle contraband. *Allowed* him; she *gave* him the cube! Why? Did she pity him?

His elation deflates into resentment. Her pity does him no good now.

Or did his skipmother slip him something subversive?

He breaks into a jog. Where to? Just keep moving. He dodges the crowd, seeking someplace quiet, someplace hidden.

Sprints down Page, crosses Clayton. Then suddenly he sees something that stops him in his tracks, stops him right in the middle of the street. A flatbed truck jammed with kids screeches to a halt. The driver yells and flips him a gesture he knows right away. The finger.

Chiron doesn't care. He jogs down the block. There, at the corner of a three-story Victorian commercial building. The address is 555 Clayton.

Above an arched door on the ground floor is the sight that draws him. A shop sign.

Like the carving on the column of the Portals of the Past!

But not like the carving. Lacking the other two symbols.

Still, the correspondence is striking. He smiles. Correspondences are signs of the Cosmic Mind, manifest behind the face of spacetime, showing meaning in things great and small.

He raises the knuckletop to his lips. "K-T," he says, and cups his hand behind the ring. The holoid field pops up halfway between his palm and his face. Strings of alphanumerics and command sequences flash through the slice of blue light.

The knuckletop has voice recognition and visual display, but in the compromise over his possession of the tool and the real limits of t-port payload, the LISA techs took out its voice chips. Which strikes him as sad. He can talk to K-T, but the knuckletop can't talk back. The tool can only respond mechanically in its holoid field. Well, he should be speaking to people, not chatting with his artificial intelligence. He knew telelinkers who preferred the company of AI to human beings. That won't help him here. Still, he could use a friendly voice just now.

He whispers a description of the shop sign into the knuckletop.

The knuckletop analyzes the information against the Archival files in its memory and calculates how meaningful the information may be. Glowing red numerics flash. Not great probabilities, but good enough. Suddenly he's so tired, he's falling asleep standing up.

The sidewalk outside 555 Clayton Street ducks down beneath the arch, turns left, and leads to a heavy oak door bristling with lock devices.

Chiron slides a prophylak out of the Kleenex packet, shakes it free of its folds. With a gesture he's practiced hundreds of times, he sweeps the fine PermaPlast over his hand. The prophylak instantly adheres to his palm and fingers, forming an unobtrusive but impermeable shield.

He grasps the brass door handle and enters the Mystic Eye.

3

Somebody

to Love

Dig it:

The Establishment media loves to moan and whine that they don't understand these crazed folks, with their strange costumes, their eccentric frolics, their illicit TITillations. And since the media doesn't understand—and why should they try? diatribe and invective make such good copy—it follows that the hip stand for nothing. Who knows what their principles are, let alone their MORALS? Yet when Mayor Shelley and Chief of Police Cahill officially decline to do a THING about the stampede of kids—who were *never* invited by the hip community, the hip community had *nothing* to do with the number five song on the hit parade—why, the HIP community sets up crash pads in garages and in the backs of stores. The hip community cooks food and gives it away. The hip community sets up a free medical clinic and free switchboards and free stores and free boxes on the street and free entertainment in the park. The hip community gets a tent to shelter a thousand people, only Parks and Recreation won't approve a site. The hip community sets up a job co-op and a merchants' association so the poor li'l refugees from AnyTown, U.S.A., from Mr. and Mrs. Jones's sad and sorry households all over this great nation, can earn a bit of bread, won't starve, or freeze their buns off. The hip community does all these things at its own private and lean expense. But GEE it's strange, the Establishment media moans and whines. HEAVENS, it's awful puzzling, isn't it? What *do* these crazed folks *do*? Why, they chant, they dance. They talk about Peace and Love and Nature. They meditate, they study strange philosophies. They protest war. HOW SHOCKING, they try to organize a *New Community*. And after the Man spies on them and pries into their lives and J-Edgar-Hoovers them till it's not funny, ALL OF A SUDDEN, the hip don't want to hang out with the Establishment media anymore. To *Post* and *Time* and the *Press Democrat*, the hip say fuck OFF. And THAT'S not nice, is it? So the Establishment media can't understand— since the hip stand for nothing—why are so many kids flocking to these lawless, immoral, fornicating, stoned, dirty, lazy freaks?

Uh-huh.

And you don't know *half* the story.

"I don't sell Zig-Zag rolling papers," Ruby A. Maverick tells the scruffy teenybopper. She struggles with a fiver minus two dollars and ninety-four cents, scrawls out the receipt, makes change. Damn Stan the Man. Holding onto her calculating machine like he once held onto her common sense. Her hostage days. Not anymore. He's on a power trip. Won't shuck her, running that game. Won't get her back in his bed, either. "You want Zig-Zag," she says, "you go round the corner to the Psychedelic Shop. The Thelin boys, they sell Zig-Zag."

She keeps one eye on the red-haired cat who charges in the door, the other on the teenybopper whose hands are a little too busy. Twenty minutes till closing on a Wednesday night, another twelve-hour day for her, and the cash drawer's jammed with loot. The Solstice Celebration brought a crowd, plus Hendrix and the Airplane at the Fillmore. Mercury is transiting Cancer, and the street is *jumping*.

"Then like how 'bout some oth' kinda rollin' papers?" the teenybopper says. "What kinda fuckin' shithole is dis, anyway?"

Checks out his hoodlum friends, see if they see how he walks the walk and talks the talk. His Beatle bangs finally hide his eyes, he hasn't washed in a week, and his voice is gravelly from pothead's throat. Thinks he's cool, rapping trash like a wino who never got over Korea.

At thirty-five, Ruby is old enough to be his mother and big enough to tan his hide. Bend the little asshole over her knee and whack his butt till he cries.

Leo Gorgon, lounging behind the counter, takes in the scene. "Say, Ruby," he calls in a fake-nice voice. "How come you don't sell Zig-Zag rollin' papers?"

She bestows a withering glance. "This *shop, my* shop, is the Mystic Eye." She leans across the counter, lowering herself nose-level to the teenybopper. "We're into magic, sonny. *Real* magic." She expertly palms his quarter, pulls it from his ear, takes a ballpoint pen from his other ear.

His hoodlum friends stare. Their bloodshot eyes bug out.

"Like wow!"

"You see *that*?"

"Shit," the teenybopper says. Mr. Know-It-All. "So she's got th' power. Lotsa people got th' power. I saw this holy dude on the Haight th' oth' day, an' he had th' power, too. Pulled flowers right outta thin air. I fuckin' saw it."

Gorgon rolls his eyes and snorts. Like, what a shuck, Ruby, moonstoning flower children with parlor tricks. Right. He's a mime and she's a psychic. Why should they talk?

What *does* this Digger cat want with her? The Diggers do some fine works, sure. Free food, free stores, street theater. But Gorgon has his very own agenda. She has her spies. They say this rooster's boosting goods all over town. Donations to the Free Store, uh-huh. No one outside the tribes is supposed to know what Gorgon looks like, who or what he is. Part and parcel of the Digger legend playing in his mind. Leo the Gorgon, the man of many heads. Not a real person, stupid. Like Buddha or Robin Hood or Batman. A myth.

She trusts the mythical man about as far as she could pick him up and throw him, and you know how far *that* is 'cause the cat's got five inches on her and is built lean and mean. And now you know what *she* wants with *him*. Why she lets him situate his fine ass behind her counter and shoot the breeze as if they're old pals. 'Cause booster or not, he is one righteous cat, and she hasn't made it with a man worth a second how-do-you-do since she and Stan called it quits.

Adios, common sense.

The red-haired cat gives her a sharp, questioning glance. They all look too young to Ruby, but at least this one's not still sucking on his ma's teat. Does she know him? Uh-uh, got to be brand-new. Tall and slim, he's got rich-kid written all over him. Tourist? With a touching sense of wonder, he looks around like he's never seen a shop like this.

Across one whole wall are rows of mason jars filled with leaves and powders and bits of bark. Acacia, angelica, black cohosh, cascara sagrada, damiana, dragon's blood, ginseng, kava kava root, mandrake, periwinkle, quince, rattlesnake grass, Saint-John's-wort, tree of heaven, witch hazel. Special orders that never got claimed are stashed below, including a half-jar of sun-dried banana peel. The heads clean her out of catnip and parsley every time rumors of a legal high hit the street. She had the presence of mind two years ago to get a Health Department certificate, which she hangs next to her diploma from the Platonic Academy of Herbal Renaissance and her Bachelor of Arts from Mills College. But Sergeant Billie Dillon and the beat cops still rattle her cage now and then. She's got a running tab at HALO, the Haight-Ashbury Legal Organization.

That's one wall. Another wall holds crystal bottles filled with essence oils, scents for astrological signs, planets, and twenty saints, both European and Haitian. There are scented wax candles, magic bath salts, spice soap, loofahs, herbal brews, plus seven varieties of incense that she gets from the importer for a nickel a package and sells for a buck. Seems the people can't get enough sweet smoke.

And the Mystic Eye stocks books. Books you can't find anywhere else. African spells, alchemy, American Indian lore, the dark arts, dreams, hypnosis, the *I Ching* or Book of Changes, out-of-the-body experiences, past lives, voodoo. Ever since Ken Kesey and the Pranksters spread the word that you can find psychedelic secrets in certain novels, she can barely keep in stock Heinlein's *Stranger in a Strange Land,* the three-book sets of Tolkien's *Lord of the Rings,* and Arthur C. Clarke's *Childhood's End.* She herself tells friends that psychedelic secrets are hidden in the stories of Cordwainer Smith, but that's her opinion.

These are strange and wondrous days.

In glass-faced cases are talismans and jewelry. Mojo coins, Chinese coins for casting the I Ching, ankhs, pentagrams, Sicilian figs, magic elephant beans. Beads of wood or lapis lazuli, fetish necklaces, peace signs strung on chains. Bronze sphinxes, faience Bastets, copper ceremonial goblets. Devotees of the neighborhood band, the Grateful Dead, keep buying out her collection of skull and skeleton charms.

The red-haired cat takes it all in, starts to touch a porcelain statuette of Kuan Yin, pulls his hand away as though he's not allowed. He plants himself by the incense burners, a vantage point from which he can see the whole shop. Alarm nicks Ruby's peace of mind. He stands there, alert, like he's waiting for something, and surveys the shop with lucid blue eyes.

She can't figure him. A big-time booster or a knickknacker looking for kicks? The teenybopper is trouble, but this one? She doesn't pick up the vibe. He's a strange one, though. Foreign-looking. Pa is a bigwig at some slick European conglomerate, Ma is a class act dripping with whatever she wants to drip with, and sonny's got a mind of his own. Accounts for his too-cool *haute couture.*

She sighs. Zig-Zag rolling papers; right.

It never used to be this way. Every punk demanding rolling papers? High school kiddies flaunting roaches, puffing pipes on the street like it's nothing?

Sweet Isis, how the Man shook folks down in North Beach seven, eight years ago. You hear the knock on the door, squint at the flashlight in your face, get slapped around just *once,* one time is all it takes, and you never *ever* want to mess with the fuzz again. It is not a moment in the brevity of life to treasure.

Some folks dig danger; not Ruby. That's the way she felt about dope. Never again. She would dump her whole herb collection—which took her five years to acquire—if she had to. Like when the Drugstore Café changed its name to Drogstore 'cause the heat wasn't worth it. Never mind a mom-and-pop drugstore with calamine lotion and Band-Aids had stood in the same location on Haight Street for fifteen years. Just not worth it. She thanked her lucky stars a crazy colored chick like herself could make out so good in a white man's world circa 1967 San Francisco, U.S.A. Wasn't *anything* worth more than her liberty and the pursuit of free enterprise.

And some thirteen-year-old hoodie is cussing her out for not selling Zig-Zag rolling papers?

Ruby smacks the quarter in the teenybopper's grimy palm. "No hash pipes, no water pipes, no opium pipes. No chillums, no bongs, no roach clips, no plastic baggies. No spoons, no rollers, no tweezers, no screens. No Zig-Zag rolling papers. Get the picture, sonny? So I lose a couple hundred a month 'cause I don't stock paraphernalia. Money isn't everything."

Gorgon says, "Holy shit!"

She flips him the bird. To the teenybopper, "Can I interest you in jasmine soap?"

"Excuse me," the red-haired cat says. "But he just took something."

Ruby seizes the teenybopper's wrist, lunges around the counter. The teenybopper twists away, sprints. He and his hoodlum friends clatter out the door.

"Get him!" Ruby cries.

But the red-haired cat shakes his head no, doesn't budge.

She dashes after them onto the street. They career into a troop of Krishna devotees, orange robes, shaved heads, finger cymbals, "Hare hare." Ruby donates two hundred bucks a year to the local ashram. The devotees dance in place for a moment, a jangling wall of feet and arms. Ruby catches up, seizes the teenybopper, grabs his wrist but good, twists his hand back.

"Give it up, you little shit."

Like a bitty boy, which is what he really is, tears pool in his eyes. Contrition puckers his face. He drops a packet of pine incense.

"So, sonny. You wanted to buy this?"

He shakes his head, eyes cast to the pavement. "I just got a quarter."

"Uh-huh. I should turn you in to the fuzz. You want to go to the slam?"

His hoodlum friends are jumping up and down across the street, whooping and catcalling. The teenybopper looks up at her, and she sees how his pals harass him, maybe he's not very bright, maybe a big brother bullied him back home or Pa laid a strap on his back, and the Cuban missile crisis gave him bad dreams.

"Like, I'm sorry," he whispers.

"You bet your ass you're sorry, flower child."

"Don't get me busted, lady." A beat. "Please."

He's such a sorry kid that a hangnail of mercy scrapes across her conscience. They're pests, kids like him. They're ruining her beloved neighborhood. But they *are* children, barely out of grade school, ears glued to transistor radios playing the number five song on the hit parade. The song is sung by the best friend of the rock entrepreneur who wrote the lyrics and sold thirty thousand tickets to the Monterey Pop Festival, the profits from which he took back to Los Angeles. The song tells them there's a New Explanation, and if you're searching for something, you can find it in San Francisco. They all know the address. Talk about pressure.

"All right, scram. But don't you and your hoodlum friends ever come in my shop again unless you're there to buy something. You dig?" She lets him go.

He darts away like a wild rabbit.

She is hopping mad when she gets back to the shop, madder now at the red-haired cat than at the teenybopper. But when she storms back inside, she sees him standing quietly by the counter. He leans against the wall, his stance anything but casual. He stares at Gorgon, and Gorgon pretends to read, uh-huh, with his racehorse legs stretched out, his eye on the drawer that is packed with maybe five hundred dollars cash. She left the drawer wide open, dashing after a packet of dollar incense that cost her a nickel wholesale.

Her eyes lock with the young cat's. He did the righteous thing. But how does this stranger know to distrust Leo Gorgon? Nobody knows who and what Gorgon is. And what about the cat himself? *He* could have ripped off the drawer and split. Why is he so good?

"Closing in five," she calls to the stragglers. Exhaustion drags her down. Too many weird trips today, and it's only the first day of the damn Summer of Love. She taps Gorgon on the shoulder. "You, too, Leo. Scram."

He jumps up, towering over her. Sweet Isis, she's a soft touch for a tall man. "Ruby." He slides a finger down her shoulder, toys with her neckline, touching her skin. "Don't call it a night. Maybe we could go upstairs. I hear you like wine. I like wine, too."

"Oh, and I got me a fine bottle of chablis." A soft touch for a tall man, but her well-developed sense of outrage kicks up. "So what is this? Hey, Ruby, I'd like to go upstairs with you. I'd like to drink your wine. What else is there you'd like to do, Leo?"

He looks puzzled. She might be telling him true, and she might be shucking him, but he's not sure 'cause she says all this in a sweet, low voice. Sugar or poison? Possibly both.

"A lot, Ruby. There's a lot I'd like to do." Husky voice, a little rough. Just the way she likes it.

Right.

"And there's a lot we could do," she says. "Some fine day."

His genuine disappointment almost makes her change her mind.

But no. It doesn't feel right. What does he think? What does he see? That she's got a cash drawer with five hundred bucks? That she's still on the rebound from Stan the Man? An easy mark? An easy lay? It's too mixed up, and it's too fast. Happens a lot these crazy days. Flash, people meet on the street, fall into bed. Flash, longtime lovers fall apart. Did people used to be *this* fast? Even Roi, who turned out no good, courted her. Or is she feeling her thirty-five years?

"Leo, scram."

He goes, along with everyone. She locks the door, dims the lights. Sweet Isis, she has stashed some cash to*day*.

Turns.

The red-haired cat stands silently at the back of the shop, with such a strange look in his eye that the needle of alarm angles up her spine again. She walks back to the counter, calm as the moon. Should have got a gun, after all. Been thinking about a sweet little number called a Beretta.

"So, sonny." She tidies up. "Why didn't you chase after that knickknacker?"

"Well. For one thing, he was dirty."

"Dirty. *That's* a new one."

"Yes." Aloof, disdainful. "I didn't want to touch him. Besides, you left your money drawer unattended. I watched it for you."

"My friend was behind the counter."

"He's not your friend."

"Oh? How do you know?"

"I calculated a positive ID from the files."

"The files, uh-huh." She gets the broom from the closet. "So, what. You a narc, or something? 'Cause if you're a narc, I can tell you right now, I don't deal. I don't even sell paraphernalia. I want nothing to do with that shit, understand? I study the ancient ways, that's all. My herbs are legal substances used for medicinal purposes. I mean headache remedies and menstrual tonics and such. You cannot get high on catnip unless you're a cat."

"A narc? You mean a police informant?"

"Oh, shit!"

"No, no! Please! I'm not!" He gets a little too close. "You're not doing anything illegal."

"You bet your ass."

"But there is something I'd like to know. Are you sheltering any runaways?"

"Sheltering runaways! Sonny, I live *alone*."

"Hmm," he muses. "But there's a probability you will."

"A probability." She brandishes the broom handle. A nasty rod, quite sturdy. "There's a probability that with proper aim, I could poke your eye out with this thing." His eyes widen. "Out you go."

"But—"

She jabs the broom handle at him. "But, nothing. You think I'm gonna let a little shit like you sting me? Get out. Get out of my shop *now*."

Through the peephole, she watches him go. He hesitates, then sits on her stoop. Groovy; better him than the winos. She hits the three deadbolts home, hooks the chain lock. Runs the broom over the floor, but her heart's not in it. Sweet Isis, what a day. Should she dump the herbs now or tomorrow morning? Either he's stupid or he likes her, and *that's* stupid, and neither explanation gives her much comfort. A sting? She'll have to call Brian at HALO first thing, find out if stocking an herb collection is probable cause for a search warrant and what to do if they plant something. Damn it, anyway.

She tallies and bundles the cash. Takes down the two-by-four, spray-painted-gold Eye-of-Horus-in-a-triangle, pulls aside the red velvet curtain, opens the safe, and deposits the bundle. The Mystic Eye has grossed a grand since Sunday, and it's only Wednesday night.

She landed the lease on 555 Clayton in the spring of '62. Three thousand square feet altogether, two-fifty a month for five years. A nice commercial space, plus a residence above. The landlady didn't much care what Ruby did, as long as it wasn't a whorehouse. As it turned out, Mrs. Andretti was a good Catholic lady who liked to read tea leaves and the tarot. From spring of '62 to fall of '65, the Mystic Eye broke even, with a little fun money left over. In fall of '65, the Mystic Eye started grossing five hundred a month, then a grand, then two. Three grand a month, come fall of '66.

In spring of '67, in anticipation of the mass pilgrimage of world youth this summer, people in the Haight-Ashbury community were asked to join the Council for a Summer of Love. The council consists of HIP merchants, local publishers of underground newspapers, political leaders, spokesmen for the mystic, and tribal chiefs, several of whom are known drug dealers such as Stan the Man. The council looked for camp-grounds, planned festivals, sought donations for the various free services offered to newcomers. Leo Gorgon was invited to sit on the council. Gorgon arrived in San Francisco from New York City in December '66 for the New Year's Eve bash and has done his Digger thing ever since.

But not Ruby. Ruby was not invited to sit on the Council for a Summer of Love, even though she has owned a business and lived in the Haight-Ashbury since '62 and has been a HIP merchant since the day the Thelin brothers organized the Haight Independent Proprietors.

Dig it:

The Council for a Summer of Love invited men. The council is all men. Like Leo Gorgon, they are tall, good-looking, and white. They like to party. They've been partying with each other forever. Well, six months *feels* like forever when you are wasted from morn till eve.

The boys are pleased with themselves. They issue proclamations, which get published. They hold press conferences, which get televised and covered by the papers. The council predicts that two hundred thou-sand people will pass through the Haight-Ashbury for the Summer of Love.

At first, Ruby was stung by the council's invitations, which she had trouble understanding till she finally got it. Two hundred thousand peo-ple? Far out. She wants five dollars from every one of them.

No wonder Diggers like Leo Gorgon are jealous of HIP merchants. Who believes his shuck that money is dead?

Ruby climbs the stairs to her living quarters above the shop. Two floors of Victorian manse, all for her. Pa would have been so proud to see her success as a grown woman. Ma would have been proud, too. How her hard work at Marinship and the modest settlement paid out.

She goes to her kitchen on the second floor, gets that fine bottle of chablis, takes glass and bottle to the living room, lights the fireplace.

Her cats rouse themselves and come around. "Girls and boys," Ruby coos. There slinks Sita, a tiny seal point queen, and Luna, a petite blue point princess. Rama, a regal seal point king, perches on the arm of the couch next to Ara, a flame point prince, all amber and ivory. Alana, the Turkish Angora, winds round Ruby's ankles, white fluff, plumy tail, gold eyes. They crowd onto her lap, nuzzle her fingers, trilling and purring.

Sweet Isis, the old times.

The Beats ranted and raved, they were a crazy cabal, but they inflicted their neuroses mostly on each other and they read books. They took pride in the intellect, schooled or self-taught. They actually wrote and read poetry: Kerouac, Snyder, Ferlinghetti, Lamantia, Kaufman, Ginsberg. Words, jazz, ideas turned them on. Oh, the Beats smoked grass and ate peyote. Those traveling through the *haute intelligentsia* in L.A. got their hands on a shaman secret called LSD. A crazy scene down there in the fifties. Aldous Huxley turned on Cary Grant. During her twenties, Ruby tried just about everything once. She didn't regret it. It was part of the exotic philosophies, otherworldly cultures, and mind experiments on life's odyssey. Beat for Ruby meant the quest for freedom.

The junk scene happened, too, as Ruby well knew. Junk had blown through the underground for a long, long time. A few got into it, a few lost their way to it. But the hip in late fifties California generally looked down on habits. Drugs weren't an obsession for the folks Ruby knew. Habits hung up your freedom. A square gig on Monkey Street or a spike in your valley, they both boiled down to the same thing. Trips that stole your mind and your time and, finally, your soul.

That's why she and a lot of folks got out of North Beach in early '62. Everything was getting too wild and too mean. Cops hassling parties for grass, tourists gawking like they were a freak show, sailors sniffing for free love, even suits from Monkey Street slumming after Beat chicks or queens or both. It got so you couldn't stage a decent blabbermouth night without some drunk taking a swing at a Poet and bringing down the house.

So they split to the Haight-Ashbury, where the rents were ridiculous, the air fresh and chilly, the park gorgeous. No heat, no tourists, no salts, no suits. The neighborhood was strictly lowbrow, on the wide, full lip of the Fillmore, a scary black ghetto. They set up shops, studios, cafés. They smoked some more grass and ate some more peyote and drank a whole lot more Papa Cribari, despite the hangover. The colony was cool in '62, private and civilized. In the face of crew cuts and white gloves, mean police and the atomic bomb, church on Sunday and kill the Commies, folks in the Haight-Ashbury just wanted to do their thing. No one chased after Establishment media. No one binged on the messianic urge. No one wanted to be pigeonholed, let alone holed up in a cell at the Big Q. The colony got behind poetry and art and novels, philosophy and jazz and folk music. Unmarried couples lived together, or two cats. Or two ladies, or married couples with other married couples, or grown-up people by themselves. Ma and Pa and Buddy and Sis was not the only family you had to have. The scene was rather Zen.

They called it the personal revolution.

And dope was not some monstrous, all-consuming, demon force. A cultural demigod. A cruel, obsessive commerce. A means and an end in itself.

When did it change?

Grandmother Says: Meng (Youthful Folly)

The Image: A spring wells at the foot of the mountain. The spring
 escapes stagnation by filling the hollow places in its path.
The Oracle: Youthful folly has success, provided truth is sought and
 character is fostered.

In the time of youth, folly is not an evil. This is the initial stage of all things. One may succeed in spite of youthful folly. But one must seek experienced teachers and maintain proper attitudes toward them. Such attitudes include modesty, receptivity, perseverance, and thoroughness.

—Hexagram 4, *The I Ching* or Book of Changes

Stop to think of the wonders that have enveloped our young people. They were children during the golden age of written and cinematic science fiction—a window to other worlds, other forms of life, other ways of consciousness. Then Sputnik went up, and fiction became fact. They are the children, too, of advertising, that enormous and still underrated channel of communication that so dazzlingly displays the diverse wares of our civilization and that, as much as any other force, is making the new age arrive. The young will not believe you when you tell them there is only *one* way of doing or feeling anything. They have lost that old, secure faith in the impossible.

—From George B. Leonard,
"Where the California Game is Taking Us,"
in *Look, America's Family Magazine*
(June 28, 1966)

It was the next wave of kids seeking something they weren't getting from AnyTown, U.S.A. Mostly college students admiring the Beats, who were slouching toward thirty in the early sixties. This was the chicken-in-every-pot crowd, while most Beats came from blue-collar. The new-wavers were raised with just enough privilege and freedom from the gap-toothed specter of poverty that they could afford to reject ambition without a heart-stab of terror. Their parents had spare change for the first time since the war. A ten-thousand-a-year income qualified you as middle class. Affluent, even. A three-bedroom house in the burbs with wall-to-wall carpets and electric appliances might cost you fifteen thousand dollars. Everyone was rich.

The corporations—Ike's military-industrial complex—schemed to get at all that extra cash. Hard booze and sexy cigarettes, disposable consumables of every description. Glossy advertisements urged the squares to loosen up. Urged them, begged them, baited them shamelessly. Live it up, Mr. and Mrs. Jones. Old Crow Traveler, Dial with AT-7, Total Electric Living. Ruby never saw such a concerted media effort to get people to consume.

So it was college kids schooled on Beat poets who shook a tail feather to rock 'n' roll on transistor radios plentiful as gumballs. Kids raised on television. People born in '45 and after were the first generation baby-sat by television. Shortened attention spans, quick cuts of stimulation, self-absorption. Turn it on, lie back, enjoy.

These kids disdained Pa's Johnnie Walker Red and Ma's Camels. The avant-garde developed an overweening taste for marijuana. Pot, grass, weed, hemp, doo, maryjane, good shit. Heightened colors, quick cuts of consciousness, self-absorption. Turn on, lie back, enjoy. In fact, a lot like television.

Junior hipsters, the Beats mocked them. Hippies.

But another new group, hot and restless at twenty years old, infiltrated the scene. A new breed of drifter, kids on the road. Teens who shot junk, did time in juvie, ran with biker gangs in New York City, New Orleans, Los Angeles. They slid in and out of jail or the nuthouse. A whole underclass who aspired to much and got little, even in chicken-in-every-pot America. But kids everywhere were discovering drifting could be all right. A groove, in fact. This is America. Rebels built the place.

Hip to the dope scene, doing the bicoastal circuit, cooler than cool. Finding willing lovers and generous friends on all those lovely campuses brimming with easy rich kids and earnest intellectuals. Though the Beats knew hoods and rustlers, they never made bedfellows of them the way the middle-class, television-suckled, thrill-seeking students were willing to do. For an important reason: The young hoods had an entrepreneurial streak that the students appreciated in a way the Beats had always disdained. The hoodies didn't just deal to survive, they dealt to thrive. They had ambition. They hustled. If you did it with style and wit, hustling could be fun and exciting, not to mention lucrative. A beautiful market was opening up. A ripe market, a huge market, bigger than big. The college scene, the youth scene, the swinging scene. Where hip local citizens connected with hip young hoods willing and able to smuggle drugs from Mexico or deal with old-timey gangster pushers.

That's when it changed.

Everyone began to talk about dope. Write about it, joke about it, sing songs about it, recommend it, revel in it, glorify it, find salvation in it. Ruby counted at least a dozen drug jokes in *A Hard Day's Night*. No, the squeaky-clean Beatles? Yeah, yeah, yeah.

Turn on, tune in, drop out. Leary is lecturing about it, Kesey is partying on it, everyone who's anyone is turning on. They say lawyers and doctors and politicians, even judges and cops, will be turning on in another twenty, thirty years. And all the laws, propaganda films, and paranoia couldn't put that shattered value system together again.

But dope was never the New Explanation. Not to Ruby.

A breeze kicks up. The wind chimes on the deck off her kitchen clang loud as doom. She sets down her wine, goes outside. The willow and the lemon tree toss about, casting restless shadows across the small weedy yard behind her garage. She breathes the damp night, catches a few sprinkles of rain in her palm, smiles at a whiff of plum incense lingering in the air.

She drags the bench over, steps up on it, balances, reaches for the wind chimes. The breeze kicks up again, and, for a moment, she's dizzy.

The long day, the wine, the lateness of the hour. She wavers, loses her balance.

Starts to fall!

The stairway going down from the deck looms below her, like a cliff in the dark. She seizes the wind chimes, which are strung on tiger-tail fishing line. Her foot slips off the bench, scraping skin. Jammed together, the chimes make an awful clamor. She dangles from the tiger-tail, testing claims the line supports up to two hundred pounds. Catches herself on the banister, swings back. She loses her grip, falling back against the bench. "Shit!" she mutters. Heart pounding like mad. She wipes sweat from her upper lip.

As she sprawls, breathing heavily, her eye catches on something. A tall, dark figure standing inside her fence! Standing stock-still in a pose of arrested motion, forearms raised. Silhouette of hands extended, fingers outspread. Eerie light glows round the fingertips. A low ominous hiss. She sees something like sparks, glowing purple-black.

Burglar, murderer, dealer, drifter, narc, cop, FBI, CIA? Leo Gorgon? The red-haired cat downstairs?

How many people does she have to be afraid of?

What *is* it?

The wind moans. Black shadows swirl like living things. A cloud of black hair, but gleaming somehow with that eerie light. Where eyes would be are two black holes, and within, evil flickers of red like the eyes of a nocturnal predator. She can make out high cheeks, a full snarling mouth.

A deep awful cold rushes up from the yard.

Crazy thoughts tumble. Has her double come to take her soul?

The figure takes a step toward her.

No! She didn't fall. She's not dead, not yet! She runs inside, slams the kitchen door and locks it, slaps the light off, grabs the phone.

Call who? The heat? Sergeant Dillon and his goons?

She turns, and, in a flash, she sees a face, sweet Isis, *her* face smashed against the glass of the kitchen door, lips writhing off shattered teeth, an eye dripping down the cheek.

She screams.

The face disappears.

Ruby peers through the peephole in the door of the Mystic Eye. The red-haired cat still sits on her stoop, his back propped against the wall, long legs stretched before him. Arms akimbo, he nods gently, eyes closed, chin drooping on his chest.

She cracks open the door, the chain lock still locked.

"Hey," she says. "Wake up. You hear me? Huh? Now you tell me. You tell me why you stayed and watched Leo Gorgon. What do you know about him? What do you think you know about me? Huh? Wake up, you."

He wakes, yawns. Eyes shiny from the street light, but no evil red glow burns within them. "Told you," he says, sitting, stretching painfully. "I calculated the probabilities. I . . . ." Big yawn, another stretch. "Extrapolated."

"Shit," she says and slaps the door. "Don't give me that probabilities shit. No one outside the Haight-Ashbury knows about Gorgon. I've never seen you before, sonny. So come on. Tell me something good. Something that'll convince me."

"Convince you?"

"That you're not the Man. That you're not setting me up for a bust." She grinds her teeth. "Damn it, I need somebody. . . . To help me now."

He stands up at once and huddles by the door. Earnestly, he says, "I'm not a narc, I swear. Your sign"—he points up at her blue neon sign, which she leaves on all night for good luck—"is a sign. If my calculation is correct, you're another point of reference. I searched my files after you kicked me out. I have a record of a woman, probably a shop owner. She's described as a quadroon, dark curly hair, light skin."

"There's a *record*?" Her adrenaline goes through the roof.

He presses his thumb to his lips. "Don't worry about it."

"Sonny, I'm not worrying. I'm panicking."

"Forget I said it. Please tell me how I can help you. Is something wrong?"

A point of reference. *A record of you, a record* keeps echoing in her ear.

"Someone's messing around in my backyard," she says. "There's something . . . *weird* about it. I . . . I don't want to call the cops."

He turns, bends, deftly picks up a square of something that looks like plastic sandwich wrap. He's sitting on a square of sandwich wrap? She only notices it as he plucks the corner and shakes it like a stage magician. The transparent square flutters thinner than a butterfly's wing and vanishes in his hand.

"I'll go look." Young cat's got to prove himself, they all do.

"Don't get your head blown off, you hear?"

"How do I get back there?"

"To the right of the garage, there's an alley with the trash cans. But it's all fenced in, the gate's locked."

He disappears before she can tell him to stop. She slams the door, hits the three deadbolts home, races up the stairs to the kitchen, and out to her deck.

Down below, he pushes the gate open. Must have picked the lock. Beautiful, she thinks. Not sure which makes her happier: that he's a narc or a lockpick. He takes something from his jacket pocket and proceeds to creep along her fence line, north to south and back again.

Nothing. The intruder is gone.

"You see anything from up there?" he calls to her.

"No. He—she—it; it's gone."

He stands at the foot of the stairway to the deck. If she'd fallen down it, she could have broken her neck or her back. His face is as pale as peeled potato. That awful, sputtering shadow could not have been him.

"Lock the gate," she says, "and come on up."

She goes inside and sits at her kitchen table.

He clatters up the stairs, comes cautiously inside, locks the door behind him. Polite. A respectful young man, now how often do you see that? He takes out an astringent-smelling square of tissue and carefully swabs his fingers, his palms, his knuckles, between and around his fingers, underneath his fingernails, digging at the quick.

"You jimmied the gate."

"It was open."

"Uh-uh."

He shrugs. "My name is Chiron Cat's Eye in Draco. I need a place to stay."

She sniffs. Isopropyl alcohol. A needle freak? But folks like that are notoriously nonchalant about their cleanliness. "Can't help you, sonny. Like I said, I live alone."

"But you shelter people. Runaways, and people."

"You must be mistaken. I don't, I never have. Except for a friend now and then. Or a lover. I don't rent rooms. This isn't a crash pad. I don't take in runaways. I could probably get busted, corruption of minors or some trumped-up thing."

"But you will. You will shelter people."

"*No,* I never *will.* I'm not into communes. I like my privacy. I *need* my privacy. I've worked long and hard to get a place of my own, sonny. I don't *want* to shelter people."

"I won't disturb you."

"You need a place to stay, try the Print Mint. People crash on the floor sometimes. Try the Trip Without a Ticket on Cole Street, that's the only Digger pad left since the Man busted their other pads. Try Huckleberry House or Glide Church or All Saints'. Or walk down the street. There's always a party; someone will take you in. But you can't stay here."

"I'll pay rent. I'll sleep on a couch. I'll sleep on the floor. I'm used to floors." He finds a few new-looking dollars in his pocket, handles them clumsily.

"What are these? Marked bills?"

"Then I'll work for you. You need someone to watch the shop for knickknackers on the busy nights. Isn't that true?"

Yes, she does. Knickknackers could account for a couple hundred a month flying out the door. But what would *he* take? She studies him. "Why? Why here? Why me?"

He smiles at last, and it's a lovely smile. A rich kid smile with perfect, sparkling white teeth. He shrugs. "Let's just say I like your sign. And I like you. You're different."

"Uh-huh." But different is good. Different is what she's tried to achieve. "My pa was half Cherokee and half Irish, and my ma was Haitian black with a splash of Southern cream. I am Ruby A. Maverick, and you may call me Ruby."

"You're beautiful, Ruby. And you're going to let me stay."

"Beautiful." She likes flattery as much as anyone, but he's much too young for her. She's old enough to be his mother, she thinks for the hundredth time. Hell, she's old enough to be *everyone's* mother. What will people say on the street?

What will people say. The mere thought of gossip makes her smile. Let them flap their jaws.

"I must be crazy."

"You won't regret it."

"We shall see." She shakes her finger at him. "Listen up, you little shit. No dope and no funny stuff in my house. You rip me off, I'll get you busted, I swear."

"I won't rip you off."

"We'll see." If only she could believe him.

She takes him in to her hardwood floors, laid with Persian and Navajo rugs. Shows off her herb and cactus gardens, teak and rosewood furniture. Her Chinese antiques, porcelain vases handpainted with dragons and phoenixes. Her superb stereo record player and reel-to-reel tape deck are connected to speakers on the second and third floors. On the whitewashed walls hang Op Art and Mondrian prints, a few abstract expressionist paintings that she bought because they were interesting and are now worth triple the price. Tibetan tankas, Japanese screens, surrealist prints. The best dance posters of '66 from the Fillmore and the Avalon Ballroom drawn by Rick Griffin, Wes Wilson, Stanley Mouse, Victor Moscoso are carefully framed in oak and ebony.

"No thumbtacks or tape on *my* collection," she tells him. "Oh, they're just posters, I know. But I dig the psychedelic look."

"I like it, too," he says, with the sense of wonder she saw earlier.

"Bill Graham fired Wes in May," she rattles on. "Rumor is they had a hassle over money. The Family Dog's complaining they can't afford full-color art anymore. Won't be posters like this before too long, Chiron. They'll all disappear."

He stares. "Yes, they will. They'll disappear. And people will only guess what the real thing once looked like."

Uh-huh. Appreciates art. That's a good sign. She finds her glass of wine, offers him some. He declines, also a good sign. Sometimes young cats can't handle the booze.

"It's sad," she says, taking the rocking chair while he gingerly sits on the couch. "Just a hustle, these days. There's no quest for freedom anymore. Today was the Solstice; first day of the Summer of Love. And you know what I say, Chiron? I say, it's all a shuck. The Haight-Ashbury has up and died. The love is dead and gone. There's nothing left for anyone here."

"No!" he says. "It's not dead."

"You don't know how it used to be. You could walk down the street, and some cat would come right up to you and put his arms around you, and he wouldn't be putting the make on you or trying to hustle you. He'd be there *loving* you. He really would. People believed in freedom. Believed in love. They really did. There was joy." She wants to cry or scream, it's so damn sad.

"Then it's up to you and me to keep the Summer of Love alive," he says.

"You can sleep on the couch," she says and goes to find blankets, a pillow.

She takes her bottle, goes upstairs, and collapses on her big double featherbed. Her cats nestle with her. Could it be true? That folks his age still believe in the New Explanation? The vision and the New Community she and her people once believed in, built their lives upon, before things got so crazy in 1967?

Is Chiron for real?

Ruby wakes, smiling. There were times, since Stan left, she didn't want to face the day. Cold dawns when she lingered under the covers, curled up like a baby. But not this morning. Up 'n' at 'em, despite the fog. And she realizes: It's good to have someone here in the house. For the first time in a long time, she isn't all alone.

She wraps herself in an embroidered silk robe, drifts downstairs.

His boots are neatly stashed beneath a chair hung with his posh leather jacket. Chiron lies on the couch beneath the blankets, very still. He squints through half-open lids. He smiles. The cats have taken him over.

Sita crouches on his chest, staring at his face with her sapphire eyes. Luna curls in a ball behind her, gray-blue face nestled against fawn fur. Rama perches in his usual spot, while Ara watches the new human curiously. Alana props herself between his ankles, grooming her tummy with a rhythmic bobbing of her head.

"Morning, Chiron. Hope you like cats." Ruby laughs. "They seem to like you."

"Oh, we like cats," he says. "Schrödinger's cat is the fundamental of probable reality theory."

We. His distinction of himself and his people from her is unmistakable. And this probable stuff again.

"Look, sonny," she says, perching on the edge of the rocking chair. "Let's get this straight. Files and records. Of me, or someone who might be me. I once got hassled by the heat. But I've never been arrested. I've never caused any trouble. I'm not a singer or an actress or someone famous. I'm just folks. So tell me true. What do you mean you have a record of me?"

"Well," he says slowly. "There are journalists and reporters observing the scene, right?"

"I'll say."

"Well, someone's seen your shop, and you, and mentioned you in an article that's preserved in the Archives."

"Really!" She doesn't want to be flattered, but she can feel the rush of pleasure on her face.

"That's all," he says, smiling.

"What article? Where, show it to me."

"I don't have hardcopy with me. It's stored electronically."

"You mean like microfiche, in the library?"

"Exactly! I saw the article in the Archives—that's like an electronic library. And that's how I know about the files. And you."

He is too triumphant, like his lie worked out better than he hoped. He makes it sound so innocent and plausible Ruby is instantly suspicious. But his explanation will have to do. For now.

"Chiron," she muses. "That's the dude with the body of a horse and the torso of a man."

"The centaur, very good. You know mythology?"

"In my business, I know all sorts of things. And you?"

"In my business, I know all sorts of things, too." But his smile suddenly disappears. He frowns. He sits bolt upright. The cats scatter.

He throws back the blankets, pulls up the leg of his jeans. There, in the skin above the edge of his expensive-looking socks, are three or four nasty red splotches.

"Damn, those fleas." Ruby is embarrassed. "I'll get you some calamine lotion."

"Fleas!"

"I'm sorry." She hurries back with the lotion, sits at the end of the couch. "I comb these cats every day and bathe them, too. But that's California for you. It never freezes, so the fleas never go away. With five cats . . ."

"Fleas. Did you know that neuvo-typhosa is transmitted by fleas interchangeably parasitical on dogs and human beings? Five million people died in Asia last year!"

"Five million people?" And she prides herself on keeping up with the news. "No, I didn't know. Imagine how the cats feel about it."

He fusses and fumes, scrambles for his jacket, takes out another of his astringent tissues and scrubs at the flea bites till his skin bleeds. With a motion so quick she has trouble following his hands, he whips off one of his necklaces, somehow detaches a turquoise bead and reattaches the remaining beads, crushes the detached bead between his thumb and forefinger, and sprinkles bright turquoise powder on the bites.

She watches, amazed. "Take it easy. A couple cat flea bites won't kill you."

"I don't know that," he says, with a look approaching panic.

She tries to help, hovering with calamine lotion dripping from her fingertips. His skin is dead white, almost luminous, like he's lived under a rock his whole life. The calf of his leg swells with nice muscles, but the skin is as smooth and hairless as the cheek of a baby girl, though clearly he's a grown man. She can see his veins, pulsing blue.

He waves away the calamine lotion, extracts from another pocket a little clear square, like a plastic membrane. He lays the square over the bites. It adheres, vanishing on his skin. He attends to himself with an air of expertise.

"Sweet Isis," Ruby mutters. She's never seen this kind of thing before, but his quick motions and the streetwise medical self-administration are unpleasantly suggestive. "Listen, Chiron. Tell me true. You're not a junkie, are you?"

"No!" Offended, he pushes up the sleeve of his shirt, shows her his milk-white arm. No tracks. Nothing but smooth white skin, hairless. Not even the fine down a baby girl has.

"A hemophiliac?"

"Do I seem unhealthy?"

"I don't know!" She caps the calamine, suddenly struck with concern. "You're so . . . *pale.*"

"I sunburn. I stay away from the beach."

"And . . . well, excuse me, but you don't have any hair."

"Sure I do." He tosses his beautiful long red hair back from his milk-white face. Clean-shaven? Not even a hint of stubble on his jaw in the morning light. Stays away from the beach, uh-huh. His face is a mask of alabaster.

"Well, I mean on your . . . body."

He shrugs, like he won't answer even if he could. He rolls down his sleeve, his jeans leg. "I like your cats, Ruby. But I can't risk flea bites. There must be something you can do."

She thinks about it. "I don't believe in commercial flea collars. They've got poisons that could harm a creature as small as a cat. The poisons wouldn't do you much harm, though. I've seen kids on the street, the ones who sleep with their dogs? They strap flea collars around their ankles."

He makes a face. "I'll pass on flea collars."

"Myself, I rub my ankles with eucalyptus oil. Keeps the fleas away pretty well."

"Eucalyptus oil. That sounds all right. May I try some, please?"

Please. She ties her robe tight against the chill, runs downstairs to the shop, finds the oil.

Never saw a man that pale and smooth. Ruby's seen a lot of things in her thirty-five years, but she *never* saw anyone like Chiron.

He's like some kind of . . . stranger. A stranger in the very strange land of the Haight-Ashbury. Sweet Isis! The unexpected glimpse of his smooth manly leg is as startling as if he'd extruded antennae from his ears. What is he, who is he?

These are strange and wondrous days.

She runs back upstairs, bearing the eucalyptus oil, wondering what she should cook him for breakfast.

July 1, 1967

Festival of Growing Things

Foxy Lady

Days vanish, and nights last forever. Reality unfolds, an origami of dreams. The tribe takes Susan in, with love. Magic manifests. The party never ends.

She crouches behind the driver's seat in the Double Barrel Boogie Band's van, clutching a map of Marin County in her right hand, the side door handle with her left. The band is playing at the Festival of Growing Things at the Mount Tamalpais Outdoor Theater. High atop the Tam, with Quicksilver Messenger Service, the Charlatans, Big Brother, the Fish, everyone who's anyone but the Dead and the Airplane, who've got gigs out of town. Over the meadow and through the woods, beam me up, up, up. Terrified and thrilled. Been tripping with the Double Barrel for what seems like eternity but, in fact, is only ten days.

Yet things are not entirely a groove this Saturday morning. It's freezing outside. How did everyone get the idea California is some tropical paradise? She shivers, wipes her nose on the back of her sleeve. Little needles stab her sinuses in the middle of her forehead, behind both her eyes. She has lost a couple pounds on a diet of dexies, hash, and occasional bowls of spiked rice. That's cool. But her throat is sore and her cheek is dappled with an itchy rash. She has to pee for the tenth time this morning.

Professor Zoom sits in the driver's seat, hunched over the steering wheel. He is constantly in motion, finger-combing his hair, fiddling with the radio, kicking at the gas, clutch, brakes, slapping the stick, thrusting through gears that the van may or may not possess. The engine goes *hunnh-hunnh-huh*! He cackles in his deadpan way and mutters things like, "Seek new life, new civilizations," and "Grok it, chief," and "Thou who did with pitfall and with gin, beset the road I wander in; thou will not with evil round enmesh, and then impute my fall to sin."

When they approach a freeway on-ramp, or pass an intersection, or sometimes merely lumber up a stretch of road with no turnoffs on either side, he calls out, "Hey, naviga*trix*. Which way, naviga*trix*?" Pretty soon he's calling her Trixie, and that makes her mad.

"Hey Trixie, hey Trixie."

"I'm Starbright, Professor Zoom."

"Which way, Trixie? Wake up, Trixie."

"Why don't you slow down, Arnold."

"Don't call me names."

"Don't call me Trixie."

"So which fucking way, Starbright?"

She wins. Five points for Susan.

Professor Zoom is banged on acid, which is no big deal since he drops some kind of cap, barrel, or blotter every other day. Banged. Like gang bang, when guys rape a chick. She heard about the awful thing that went down at an Ashbury pad last week. They beat her up, too. Anyhow, that's how Professor Zoom talks about tripping. Starbright, I'm banged.

But he's driving, and that, to Susan, *is* a big deal, though no one else in the van seems to think so. The van climbs Route 1, a winding seacliff road, one shoulder of which is no more than a foot of gravel in some places, beyond which the mountain drops, sheer and clean, to nothing. Nothing but a hint of wooded valley far below through the thick, gray fog. The morning is nearly as murky as night, worse really, since they cannot see more than six feet ahead with the headlights on, when there *is* six feet of straight road. Yet the sun somewhere above infuses the fog with a hellish glare that is dim and bright at the same time, revealing nothing and giving Susan a blinding headache.

Thank God they can't muster more than thirty miles an hour uphill, Susan thinks, strained from her vigilance. She is custodian of the map and navigatrix since no one else is fit or willing for the task, and she's too young to drive the damn van herself. Too young, hell. She never learned to drive a stick. Daddy's Cadillac is automatic. Ditto Mom's Mustang. It was easy as pie the time Daddy took her driving on Christmas Day and let her spin the Cad around the May Company parking lot. She wasn't the least bit afraid the time she and Nance took out the Mustang when he and Mom were in France.

But this funky Volkswagen van covered with blue clouds? Forget it. The stick is as intimidating as an algebra equation. She forms a plan. If Professor Zoom blows a mean curve and deep-sixes off the cliff, she can pop the side door open. Jump out before they tumble into oblivion.

"Fare thee well, oh world of illusion," Professor Zoom mutters, as though he's read her thoughts. It's not the first time he seems to read her mind, especially when he's banged. Does he really possess the power of telepathy when he's tripping, or does he only seem to because he claims to? It's confusing.

Professor Zoom drops acid or STP or DMT every other day in his quest for the Final Expression to his equation proving God equals a hit of blotter. On days when he isn't banged, he speaks somberly with Susan of his quest. He saw the whole equation written in the sky. But when he came down, he could not remember the Final Expression. Tears pool in his eyes. That's why he must trip. Must trip till he finds the Final Expression.

He is On To Something, he tells her. Buddha was psychedelic. Jesus was psychedelic. Every great Teacher and Seer through history was psychedelic. Illumination is the door, LSD is the key. To pass through the door, the self must die, the ego must die, and you will be reborn into a New Consciousness. All who trip are on the verge of the New Consciousness. The New Consciousness will save the world from greed, military ambition, exploitation of nature, all the evil propelling Mother Earth to the brink of destruction.

Get banged, Starbright. Change your life.

They climb the last switchback to Tam Theater. Susan sighs with relief. Made it. How banged will Professor Zoom be when they go back down the mountain? She shudders. Maybe she can get someone to show her how to use the stick. The road is jammed with vans painted with hearts, eyes, flowers, and slogans. Plus bugs, flatbeds, buses, a glossy black Mercedes-Benz, a green Jaguar. They swing around the traffic, smug as royalty. Their van is waved through the barricades, to the stages. The usual circus.

Susan's life *is* changed. In the days after the Solstice, a transcendent awareness lingered.

Her life in Cleveland. What a dreadful treadmill, a psychic death. So much frustration, guilt, insecurity, fear. Why? Her father is a lapsed Jew, her mother a lapsed Catholic. Her father is fond of saying religion is the opiate of the masses. He dispenses opiates in his dental practice when he extracts wisdom teeth. What wisdom is being extracted from the masses? Why are he and her mother always so troubled?

What is the purpose of her parents' lives? What do they *believe* in? They believe in:

Getting as much money as possible, no matter what gross thing you have to do to get it.

Paying taxes, but complaining loudly.

Paying bills, but complaining louder.

Dial with AT-7.

Mr. Clean.

Getting drunk on Friday and Saturday nights.

Arguing about everything.

Hassling Susan about everything.

The Vietnam War, because LBJ says we have to stop the spread of Communism in Southeast Asia.

What *don't* they believe in? They don't believe in:

Gods and goddesses.

Love.

Magic.

Happiness.

Truth.

Beauty.

Freedom.

Peace.

Star Trek, which they threaten to turn off when they're deciding how to punish Susan.

Then there is school. She's appalled when she thinks about school. She recalls the time when she was eight years old, and she came inside from recess. The sun was shining, the sky blue, the air fresh and sweet, and she was skipping down the hall. Her third grade teacher caught up with her and seized her forearm in a grip like the band they wrap when they're taking your blood pressure. The teacher forced her not to skip.

What was that teacher trying to do?

That teacher was trying to break her spirit.

But why would school do that? So you could become someone like her parents and believe in the things they believe in. So you won't believe in the things they don't believe in. And believe you're a happy person whose life has meaning. So you will go to your job and do whatever gross thing someone tells you to do and get drunk on Friday and Saturday nights and pay taxes and bills. *That's* why.

An image she flashed on tripping keeps haunting her. The photograph of the monkey in her biology textbook with electrodes stuck in its shaved-bald skull. Wires were attached to the electrodes. The wires led to a machine with a dial, which was watched by a man with a crew cut, steel-rim glasses, a white lab coat. The caption said the man in the white coat could measure the waves occurring in the monkey's brain, and, by measuring these waves, they could figure out why people sleep. The monkey's eyes squinted with terror and pain. Bernie MacKenna and Allen Weisberg laughed when they turned to the photograph in class. Bernie scratched his armpits and went, "Ooh-ooh," while Allen jumped up from his desk, took his ballpoint pen, and pretended to drill the pen into Bernie's head, making a shrill buzzing noise through his teeth. Everyone had laughed.

But Susan hadn't laughed. It was disgusting, grotesque, cruel beyond belief. Any idiot knows why people sleep. You sleep when you get tired. Why torture an innocent creature? Who could do it? Did the man in the white coat drill holes into the monkey's skull so he could pay taxes and bills? Did he get drunk on Friday and Saturday nights to try to forget he stuck electrodes into a living creature's brain?

You are either the man in the white coat or you are the monkey. Susan sees herself as the monkey.

The other image she flashed on haunts her, too. Her grandfather's death two years ago. Grandpa had been sick for a while. When he finally went to the hospital, her parents took her to see him. The visit was horrible, the worst thing that ever happened to her. Afterward, her parents didn't speak to her about him.

One afternoon she came home from the park with her new butterfly collecting set. The saddlebags on her Schwinn bike were filled with frantic butterflies she'd caught with her net. She was going to chloroform them and pin them on a corkboard and spread out their wings beneath strips of paper. She was in the garage, taking out the killing jar, when her mother came to the door. "Grandpa died," her mother said. Then her mother's face collapsed. And she slammed the door.

Susan sat down on the garage floor. She must have sat there for an hour. Finally, she opened the saddlebags. The butterflies were crushed. She took the net and the stickpins, the corkboard and the jar, even the saddlebags, and threw everything in the trash. Later, her father yelled at her. The butterfly collecting set had cost him twelve bucks.

That night, her parents had one of their big fights behind closed doors. Her father went away for days, while her mother stayed upstairs in the bedroom with the TV on all night. Susan wandered about the house, weeping and eating cheesecake and corn chips. She ached all over. She missed Grandpa. Worse, she couldn't forget the terror in his eyes. The funeral was open-casket. She had to go up to the front of the funeral parlor and look at his corpse. Her mother shrieked like a crazy person and wept more fiercely than Susan had ever seen. It was frightening, her mother's wild grief.

There was a big party after. Lots of booze. Her parents and relatives she didn't know at all or hadn't seen in years got falling-down drunk. Later, Mom and Daddy went into their bedroom and turned the TV on full blast. She heard their drunken moaning. The stink of whiskey lingered in the living room for days.

She is going to die.

Sometimes she cries, lying on the edge of Stan the Man's mattress. That she'll die; it's terrifying and strange. One morning she was up with the birds. Everything quiet. She sat on the stoop, tears drenching her face. Professor Zoom materialized. He sat beside her without a word, puffing his corncob pipe. He passed the pipe to her. She passed it back.

"Professor Zoom," she said at last. "I'm sad we have to die."

"The spirit is eternal," he said.

"But our bodies—this body," she pinched the skin on her arm. "It *dies*. There's pain and suffering. What do our minds *feel*? And then the body goes cold. I mean, it *rots*."

"That's why I want to be cremated," he said. Just the facts, ma'am. "Fire is pure, not to mention hot."

"But I'm . . . *afraid*. It's so *awful!*"

"Oh, it's not so awful," Professor Zoom said. "Think of it this way. We live on the Earth, and we kill things. You see, everything is alive. You kill a cow, or you dig up a carrot, it's all the same. It's all killing. So when you die, you give your body back to the Earth. It's like payback. You give a little of what you took. I think that's fair."

She thought about that, and, after a while, the pain in her heart began to fade. "Yeah," she said and dried her tears on her sleeve. They had smiled at each other. "I think that's fair, too."

Rodg the Dodg, Paul, and Mickey huddle in the back of the van, working on some righteous dope—splash, horse hearts, serenity. Up to the last minute, they are working out three songs they intend to play but haven't been able to practice. The energy at the house has been strange. Sarah split, after knickknacking some expensive things. Stella and Fawn freaked. Mickey got wasted. The next day Mickey brought home someone new. She wears a glittery pink boa clipped in her hair, a leather vest over nothing but her olive skin, and jeans slung below her navel. Her stringy biceps are tattooed with a lightning bolt. Lady May, she calls herself. The guys get mileage out of that. "Lady May?" they call in cajoling voices. Stella and Fawn are still freaked.

"Oooh-wah-oooh." They sound okay, not great.

Stan the Man sits in the front seat, ignoring everyone. Especially Susan, which fills her with sadness and a deep, nameless fear. He's working, she reminds herself, bagging ten thousand caps of LSD. He decided to call this batch dragon's blood after an herb in an occult shop he says he used to own. The caps are bright red. Dragon's blood. It's got a ring.

Suddenly, things are happening, everyone is jumping. They pile out of the van.

"Starbright, you can carry the mikes and tambourines," Mickey says.

She hops out. She is always carrying the mikes and tambourines, or fetching a bottle of wine or a hash pipe, or passing out postcards of the album covers. Clapping her hands, cheering when they finish, admiring the men up on the stage from down below. She's grateful for such a groovy place to stay, of course. They don't charge her rent. But she keeps thinking of Sarah's bloodshot eyes beneath her false lashes. "I want to do my thing, too," Sarah had said.

Susan wants to do her thing. Her mother says her drawings are not proportional, but Professor Zoom and Stan and everyone thinks her drawings are beautiful. She goes to Mendel's Art and Stationery Supplies —a store on Haight Street like Mr. Rosenstein's but bigger—and buys a box of pastel chalks. She draws two posters for the Double Barrel Boogie Band. She can imitate the psychedelic style pretty well. Eyes, women's faces and bodies, swooping letters.

Do her thing. There's this tricky thing about her mind. She seems to think faster than other people. It's odd. While Stan the Man labors over the calculating machine, a big metal monster that goes *ka-chunka ka-chunka-chunka-chunka* when he hits the Equals button, she works out the numbers in her head. She says, "Um, Stan, at seventy cents profit a hit, you'll make seven hundred dollars per thousand. Um, that makes seven thousand dollars per ten thousand. That's a lot of bread, huh?" And he gives her a look. What you'd call a dirty look.

She's seen the look before. Bernie MacKenna and Allen Weisberg stand at the blackboard, working out equations or diagramming sentences and clowning around, and they are popular, they are in with the cool kids at school. But when she works out an equation or reads her poem—she doesn't dare clown around—the girls whisper to each other behind their hands. The boys snicker or stare coldly. Even teachers give her the look. She feels like a freak. Like something's wrong with her. Her school counselor told her she's in the ninety-eighth percentile. What does that mean? That means, the counselor said, her I.Q. is in the top two percent. What good does that do her? The girls, the boys, the teachers, they still give her the look. So she stops speaking up, stops offering the right answer, stops challenging the discussion. It's sad and confusing.

Now she wonders if the spooky girl with her face has something to do with it. The encounter on Twin Peaks seems so unreal, after all she's seen and done. Was the girl an awful omen, a dreadful prophecy that she would have to face herself and see the truth? She shivers at the memory and looks over her shoulder for that weird spark of black.

Professor Zoom is the intellectual of the Double Barrel house. The resident shaman. And Susan is the one he seeks when he wants to discuss his quest for the Final Expression. She's the one he takes aside when he wants to debate something. One night he found a Sacramento station that was rerunning "This Side of Paradise" at three in the morning. Susan had talked a lot about this episode of *Star Trek*. This is where the *Enterprise* comes to Omicron Ceti III and finds that all the colonists are really groovy. Mr. Spock reunites with Leila, a woman who once loved him. Leila turns Mr. Spock on to spores that pop out of pretty pink flowers and hit you in the face. Mr. Spock gets spores in his face and becomes really groovy, too.

Professor Zoom is impressed. Psychedelic secrets on national TV?

The whole house dropped black beauties and stayed up to watch. But Susan was appalled seeing the episode again. The spores turn the colonists on Omicron Ceti III into silly, passive know-nothings, who must be led back to a useful life by the Federation.

But Professor Zoom was not deterred. "Wake up, Starbright," he said. "The spores set Mr. Spock free. The spores make him give up his intellectual games. There he is, this uptight supercilious robot—"

"Mr. Spock is not a robot," Susan said. "Mr. Spock is half Vulcan."

"There he is," Professor Zoom said. "This uptight half-Vulcan schmuck . . ."

They went at it like that till everyone got tired and went to bed. Are the pink flowers opium poppies? Are the spores pot or LSD? Do the spores enlighten the colonists or oppress them? In the climax, Captain Kirk incites Mr. Spock. He insults him and challenges him to a fistfight. The release of adrenaline breaks Mr. Spock from the spell of the spores. Violence restores Mr. Spock to his old, uptight self.

"That's pretty fucked," Professor Zoom pointed out. "What kind of message is that? That's like Army propaganda."

"It's confusing," she admitted.

"Forget it, Starbright. I really dug the beginning. The spores healed wounds and conferred physical perfection! Who knows? Maybe acid will end up curing cancer. Maybe acid will alter our chromosomes so our DNA isn't linear anymore and we can all achieve cosmic consciousness."

But Susan could not sleep. Propaganda? Maybe, but there's no mistake. *Star Trek* says the love spores from the pretty pink flowers are bad.

Tam Theater looks like a Greek amphitheater, with stone seats sloping to the modest stage. Professor Zoom takes out his corncob pipe. "Got some gold," he calls to the tribe. That routs stragglers out of the van. Stella and Fawn crowd around. Lady May struts up. They pass the pipe, lips to lips. Sniffling, Susan pretends to toke. The pain in her throat is excruciating. "Hold it in, Starbright," Professor Zoom coaches her irritably. He crooks his arm round her neck, thrusts the pipe into her mouth, and holds it for her.

"God," Lady May says, toking deeply. She dropped acid with Professor Zoom an hour ago. "I am so fucked up!" She laughs. A nipple slips out of her vest.

"The ego must die," Professor Zoom whispers ecstatically. "The self must die."

Susan slips away, looking for Stan the Man.

She is going on fifteen. She doesn't want to die.

Her body, this awkward, sausage-limbed body, has turned into a woman. A sexual being. Her new awareness of sex goes hand in hand with other hard questions.

On the first magic morning when she woke in Stan's bed, she realized—revelation!—that she was young and healthy and perfect. She could accept herself; why shouldn't she? Then she did what she always did: tried to understand what the world saw in her. She looked in the filmy mirror in the john, and it's all wrong.

How can she deny it? She thinks of the photographs in *Seventeen* and *Life* and Mom's *Vogue*. The ideal of beauty everyone adores. Bony face, thin lips. Bone-straight platinum hair. Bone-thin hips and stomach, bones sticking out everywhere. Limbs like twigs. She is nothing like that. And all the revulsion she feels about herself floods back, worse than ever. Her mother is right. She's just not good enough. She's ugly. She cannot reconcile the new realization that she is young and healthy with the desire to claw off her flesh.

But Stan the Man accepts her as she is, doesn't he? They have sex nearly every night.

As she walks up to the van, he jumps down, lithe as a panther.

"Hi," she says and lifts her face.

He seizes her, wrapping her in one of his hugs, hands hard on her body. He kisses her forehead, nuzzles her ear. She's delighted. The motion of his tongue in her mouth suggests what he does between her legs.

Dizzy from his kiss.

"Listen, Starbright," he says. He slips the package filled with dragon's blood beneath her arm. "I want you to do something for me."

"What?" An ominous feeling chokes her throat.

She woke the other morning to find him rooting in her overnight bag. He found the hundred-dollar bill from Mr. Rosenstein. When she asked what he was doing, he demanded the money. When she said no, he got weird. Said she'd be sleeping in the park if it wasn't for him. She got frightened and silent. He came over to the mattress and pressed her down. She let him keep the hundred-dollar bill. A loan, he said. Front money for the dragon's blood deal. He'd pay her back. Afterward, she tucked the rest of her cash, along with her library card, into the secret place in her purse where the lining is torn. Now she keeps the purse with her always, sleeps with it tucked beneath her pillow.

"I want you to give the dragon's blood to my connection." His eyes are cold.

"What connection?"

"They'll be looking for you. Hand it over, that's all. You can do *that*, can't you?"

She is struck with guilt. She *does* feel bad about giving him a hard time over the hundred-dollar bill.

Sizzling with his kiss and paranoia, she goes over to the face-painting tent like he tells her and waits. Watches and listens for anyone looking for dragon's blood. An electric guitar starts to wail. That's Rodg the Dodg's lick. Damn, the band is starting, and she can't be there!

Half an hour crawls by. Children and their mothers come and go from the face-painting tent. No one pays her any mind. The Double Barrel finishes their first set. One of the songs they were rehearsing in the back of the van turns out better than she feared. She hops from foot to foot, trying to keep warm, furious at Stan. She is only getting her hundred dollars back. He is clearing close to a year's income, tax-free. Maybe she should get a piece of that seven thousand dollars for fronting some of the money, plus making the delivery for him. She wonders if she has the nerve to ask when two men wander by.

A child with a painted clown face cries, holding up her crushed packet of green bean seeds.

"Didn't I tell you?" the child's mother says. Deep lines in her forehead push against her beaded headband. "Not everyone with long hair is cool."

Susan looks to see who crushed and dropped the child's seeds. A squat guy in a stovepipe hat that says "L-O-V-E" on the crown set firmly over kinky black hair brushes past the child. Steely black eyes set in an unsmiling Buddha face. A scar angles across his sallow cheek into a Fu Manchu mustache. His partner is short and wiry, nut-brown skin etched by hard times and harder living. A yellow Happy Face button is pinned to his lapel. His psychedelic regalia cannot conceal his reptilian aura. She can just see a lizard's tongue flick out of his mouth, snag a fly, and chew.

Even on Haight Street, Susan has never seen men like this. They operate on some level she doesn't know. Violent and dangerous and mean. They drift about the face-painting tent.

She is about to turn and flee when she hears them murmuring.

"Dragon's blood? Got dragon's blood?"

"Here," she whispers. "Got d-dragon's blood."

Stovepipe is in her face in two seconds. "Dragon's blood?"

"Y-yeah." His eyes are so cold!

"Where's the guy?"

"Around, I g-guess."

"Who is he?" the Lizard says. "What's his name?"

"Just a guy," she says, confused. They don't know who Stan is?

"Give it here," Stovepipe says.

She hands over the package.

Stovepipe and the Lizard fade into the trees. Will they dash off with the dragon's blood? But in a moment they come back, hand her a smaller package, and disappear as quickly as they came.

The package could be filled with newspaper for all she knows. It's not her fault! Shit! Why did Stan make her do this!

She runs to the Double Barrel stage. The band is well into their second set. It's the usual scene, fans gathered around, dancing, bobbing their heads. Beautiful girls in exotic costumes. Stan stands at the edge of the crowd, pointing at something on the stage. A platinum-blond girl, bone-thin in her jeans, stands beside him, laughing.

Susan taps him on the shoulder. He turns. She gives him Stovepipe's package. "Groovy, Starbright," he says. Eyes bloodshot. He's had a few hits of the gold by now, holds a smoking roach beneath his palm. "Everything was cool?"

"Sure," she says. Her demand for a share vanishes into thin air.

The girl turns. Bony face, thin lips, limbs like twigs. She smiles at Susan, sunny and open. She must be seventeen. The ideal of beauty everyone adores.

"Starbright," Stan says. "This is Maryann. Her daddy owns half of Mill Valley."

"Marilyn." The girl laughs and slaps his shoulder. "Isn't he a pig, Starbright?" Her eyes assess and dismiss. "Give me." She pries the roach from his fingers.

"I'll give you," Stan growls in her ear.

Susan wonders if she can stop the trembling in her lip.

Give me. Back at the Double Barrel house, this is Marilyn's big line. She says it over and over. She makes the guys scream with laughter. She is so enticing, she even upstages Lady May.

Susan huddles on the swayback sofa. She is shivering cold. A fever? The never-ending party is in full swing. People pour in the front door, laughing, smoking.

Give me.

Stella, who has gotten wasted, leaps on the coffee table and begins to dance. She stretches out her arms in a beckoning gesture.

Susan suddenly recognizes that gesture. For a moment, Stella looks just like Juno, the transparent woman.

Only girls and their mothers were allowed in the auditorium at the Cleveland Health Education Museum. Juno, the transparent woman, stood eight feet tall upon her dais, her arms outstretched and beckoning. The room dimmed. A don't-be-afraid voice came over the PA system. The transparent woman lit up her internal organs. Her heart was bright purple. Her blood pulsed neon red through arteries, cool blue through veins. Her yellow lungs billowed. Her green stomach showed where food went, her pink bowels where waste products left.

Then the transparent woman lit her reproductive system. The girls stared in silence. The mothers coughed. The ovaries sent tiny turquoise eggs down graceful fallopian tubes, to the uterus, which got redder and redder. Gathering monthly blood, the voice said. The red spilled through the cervix and down the vagina. The voice said the vagina was the birth canal. Like the Panama Canal or the Suez Canal. The birth canal was where the baby came out.

But how did a baby get *in*? The transparent woman went dark. The man, said the voice, deposited his sperm—like seeds—into the woman. The transparent woman lit her canal again. But *how*? How did the man deposit his seeds? The seeds got deposited in the birth canal. The transparent woman stood stiffly on her dais, smiling her transparent smile, giving no hint of the task at hand.

Susan went to the ladies' room after that. Three girls consoled a friend who was sobbing. "You mean he *sticks* it in you? No, never, never, never!"

It was shocking, all right. Sticks his seeds in the birth canal.

"Someday you'll want it," said a friend of the sobbing girl with trembling authority. "You'll love each other, and you won't mind."

"Never, never, never!" the girl cried.

"Well, that's that," Susan's mother said as they drove home through the dark.

They never spoke about the transparent woman again.

Susan knows how the seeds get in now. Losing her virginity and sleeping with Stan every night is as powerful a revelation as her trip. Sex is a lot like tripping. There are people who know and people who don't.

She craves Stan. In her eighth-grade science class, the teacher showed how goslings raised with a bowling ball become imprinted on it and follow it everywhere. Stan is her sexual bowling ball.

Susan's first period came not long after the transparent woman lit up her reproductive organs. After the Cleveland Health Education Museum presentation, she imagines her uterus glowing redder and redder, streams of red light flowing out of her birth canal. For a year, the streams of red light have been as regular as clockwork. Twenty-two days exactly. The red light traces its path between noon and one o'clock on the twenty-second day.

Susan swallows tears. Her throat is killing her. Her nipples tingle, she can barely keep food down, she has to pee every half hour. The transparent woman dances on the coffee table before her.

She is five days late.

WEATHER REPORT

In 1967, at the Geophysical Fluid Dynamics Laboratory in Princeton, New Jersey, two climate experts, Syukuro Manabe and Richard Wetherald, are using the latest computer technology to create what they call global circulation models (GCMs). GCMs will improve the capability to predict the weather over the entire planet, a capability that has long eluded the best scientific analyses. A reliable predictive technique could bring dramatic advances in our agricultural production, as well as advantages to our industrial production and other untold benefits. Manabe and Wetherald will find that when they inject an extra three hundred parts per million of carbon dioxide into the atmosphere of a GCM —as could reasonably occur within a few decades of the go-go economy of the sixties—the surface temperature of the Earth begins to climb. Slowly at first, then faster and faster.

          o

    I know that a lot of girls are doing it, and a lot of boys are doing it. People who don't know that don't know anything. Times have changed, that's all. Mother always talked about how things were when she was young, the whole time I was growing up, but I always knew that things were different today. I guess I was pretty innocent and everything, though. Five years ago, I never thought I'd be here. Maybe I've always been out of step in other people's eyes. . . .

I've never stopped to question my morality, just my
luck.

> —From "Conversations Parents Never
> Hear, No. 4, The Unwed Mother," in
> *Look, America's Family Magazine,*
> Vol. 30, No. 19 (Sept. 20, 1966)

Fawn leaps up and dances with Stella on the coffee table. They
proceed to kick everything off, grease-lipped glasses, brown apple cores,
the half-eaten can of SpaghettiOs, their clothes. People drift in and out,
sit down in circles, pass joints, dance, wander through the halls.

Stan the Man has disappeared.

Susan is burning up. She's beat. She just wants to go to sleep. She
crawls up the two stairways to her room.

Stan's room.

The door is closed. Voices; not just his. Laughter, the chuckle of
seduction. She pushes the door. It swings open.

Marilyn's Mill Valley thighs. And between them, Stan the Man.

As she flees down the stairs, Susan wonders if she can stop the
trembling in her heart.

5

White Rabbit

Chiron sits in the catbird seat for his noon-to-three shift, daydreaming of imploders, calcite crystals, the awesome dish of the macrofusion chronometer. The catbird seat, which Ruby rigged, is a ragged chair cushion tied round an amputated chair seat. The seat is nailed to the top of a rickety stepladder set in the back of the Mystic Eye. Ruby is boundlessly resourceful, but the tachyonic shuttle it's not. He folds his arms in the djellaba she gave him, a scarlet-striped robe that goes over his clothes, head to toe. He pulls the hood about his face, letting a lock of his hair fall across his brow and sunglasses. Ruby gave him the sunglasses, too. She calls them candy-apple red.

Thus anonymous, swathed in red, hunching over gargoyle-style, he watches people mill about the Mystic Eye. Down below, shoppers hesitate. Some touch the merchandise, glance up at him, and replace a mojo bag or conjure wand just so. Two women in the uniform of Beat intellectuals—turtlenecks, jeans, sandals, woven shoulder bags stuffed with Alan Watts, Marshall McLuhan, the *Bhagavad-Gita*—smile at him and whisper to each other. Others can't conceal the larcenous intent crossing their faces. A boy no more than twelve, in dirty denim and floppy hair like a thousand other boys passing through the Haight-Ashbury, fingers a brass butterfly strung on a leather thong.

Chiron lets loose a booming, "The Mystic Eye Sees All!"

The would-be knickknacker jumps, so badly startled he dumps the butterfly and dashes out the door. The young women giggle.

College girls, maybe twenty. Mega. The tall, slim one is so prime she could compete with Venus Rising, but for her gooey black hair. He pictures her nude. Without her clothes, of course. But better, without the wild extrusions from her scalp, her furry eyebrows, the fuzz on her forearms beneath pushed-back sleeves. And without the trauma to her skin: her suntan. He still can't get over seeing people so young look as weather-damaged as centenarian day-laborers without domes or proper Block. The sight is as disturbing to him as a peg-legged beggar would be to this vivacious student.

He longs to tell her: Stay out of the sun, even this sun. Would his warning violate Tenet Three of the Grandfather Principle? He sighs. Can't affect a person in the past, except as authorized by the project directors. After the Save Betty Project, the LISA techs were adamant about the Tenets and the mandate of nonintervention. Still, dermatologists of this Now know about skin cancer and malignant melanoma. They're just not telling.

But it's tricky. If he *could* tell her, would she believe him? In pop wisdom, a suntan is healthy. Forget healthy. A suntan is cool.

"The lady looks lovely in the tie-dye scarf," he calls out like the voice of doom. The shopper blushes, pretends to preen, and reluctantly unties the scarf.

Sometimes he enjoys the abnegations of the catbird seat, like a cosmicist on a giftday. The day each month when you rose with the sun and fasted, consuming no resources but a water ration. You did not jack into telespace. You went nowhere except by your own exertion and even wear-and-tear on shoe soles was frowned upon. You read or wrote on rationed hardcopy, meditated on True Value, or worked, if you could work without consuming anything. Neither candles nor fires in the fireplace were allowed. Even reserves in your solar cells were conserved, along with utility credits that you bicycled on a Path. You talked with friends, sang, or made love. You slept when the sun set or sat in darkness till you tired. Cosmicists were invited to gift twelve days a year, one a month. Some cosmicists gifted more. Chiron and Venus Rising gifted forty-eight days between them last year.

Giftdays. To give is best. Be still, and let the world rest. Two billion people participated in giftdays, and more were gifting all the time.

Ruby gives him the thumbs-up. She loves being in the vanguard. He's started an antiknickknacking trend among the HIP merchants. All the shops that can afford them are installing watchmen on stepladders.

"*Achtung*, Beelzebub," Leo Gorgon says. He clicks his heels and holds out his arm in a ramrod salute as he lounges behind the counter with Ruby.

Chiron makes no reply. From this vantage point, he can see Gorgon's hands, too. The Archives contain the autobiographical novel he will publish in 1973. By his own admission, Gorgon is a thief, stealing goods and food for the Diggers' Free Store and dispensation of stew. The free-thieves, a radical cosmicist faction during the height of the brown ages, supported thieves' rights. Free-thieves theorists claimed that taking private property when needed was supported by the U.S. Constitution and, in any case, by the law of necessity. After a long and ugly debate, the cosmicist majority declared the free-thieves were not working toward the Great Good and quickly suppressed them.

Gorgon never loses a chance to express his contempt for Chiron. A contempt earned, it seems, because Ruby befriended him and gave him shelter. And because he's helping Ruby turn a profit at the Mystic Eye. Chi believes in free enterprise, especially grassroots entrepreneurs like Ruby. He never thought much of the free-thieves. The contempt is mutual.

"Forget him," Ruby says and winks. "You're cool, Bub." She glares at Gorgon, who never sees the sharp looks she aims at the back of his neck. Still, she's sleeping with Gorgon, which Chi cannot understand. But Ruby's affairs are not his business. What women have to go through in these primitive times is not his concern. He can't get involved.

"You're the boss, Ruby," he says for Gorgon's benefit.

The red watchman has become a minor celebrity on the scene.

Gorgon dubbed him Beelzebub as an insult, but the kids take to the name and call him that or the Bub when he's perched in the catbird seat. It's a kick, being a minor celebrity.

One day, a longhaired girl sat below his feet, glancing up at him from time to time. He paid her no more attention than anyone else. Still she lingered, attracted to his minor celebrity. He was half-awake, thick-headed with tachyonic lag, when suddenly it occurred to him: *Is it her?* Excitement seized his chest. "Need a break," he called to Ruby and leapt down from the ladder. But the girl lost her nerve before he could untangle his legs from the hem of the djellaba. She fled, darting out the door and onto the street, disappearing into the crowd, pale hair flying. He cursed his hesitation. He never got a good look at her.

Was she the Axis? Who knows, he thought with a leaden heart. When the tourists, day-trippers, military personnel on leave from nearby bases, transient criminals, local teenagers, and college students were added to the runaways, pilgrims, emigrants, parents looking for run-aways, law enforcement personnel, and local settlers, a million people could pass through the Haight-Ashbury this summer. Perhaps ten thousand newcomers on any given day, some who stay, some who leave as quickly as they came. How is he ever going to find her?

Now high in his perch, he raises the knuckletop to his lips. "K-T," he whispers and cups the holoid field in the shelter of his palm. The djellaba's generous cuff hides the slice of blue light. Tucked in the H drive beneath the bezel of the knuckletop is a sliver of crystal. The first of the contraband holoid disks he's been able to access without being bounced out of drive.

A tiny red message appears in the holoid field:
"Date: 07-01-1967. You may insert Disk 1 now."
"Go, H drive," he whispers.
The holoid field disappears. A scene pops up in his palm.

GOSSIP, INNUENDO & ALL
THE NEWS THAT FITS

The sandy-haired man in a suit and tie steps off the curb at
the corner of Haight Street and Ashbury, surrounded by a
group of young people. Over his shoulder, in the upper left
corner of the frame beneath the street signs, stands a
longhaired girl in a high-collared shirt speaking with a tall,
slim, red-haired person. The red-haired person's face is
androgynous, blurred, little more than white skin and a long,
smooth jaw. The sandy-haired man and his escort walk
across the intersection toward the camera. The scuffing
sound of their footsteps, the jingle of necklaces and bells,
fill the audio. The man says, "CBS News, without any
flowers in its hair, is in San Francisco because this city has
gained the reputation of being the hippie capital of the
world." The man glances down at a scruffy young boy
walking next to him. From the left background, the girl
darts behind the group, reappearing in the near right side of
the frame. She catches up to the man, darts behind his
shoulder, and falls into the rhythm of his step. The man and
the group step onto the curb on the opposite side of the
street and stop. The girl looks straight at the camera. She
nods slightly. The wind whips her hair. She shakes the hair
from her face and smiles. A radiant smile, an enigmatic
smile, as though she knows the secret to everything. In the
background, someone says, "Beautiful!" The man says, "I'm
Harry Reasoner."

> —"The Hippie Temptation," CBS News
> (televised Aug. 22, 1967)

The holoid disappears. The blue holoid field returns.
"K-T, off." He lowers his hand. Back to work. Ruby looks up at him
curiously.
He can't get over the way the girl smiles.
"Axis," he whispers. "Where are you?"
Could the red-haired person be him? He never thought so. He never
felt the shock of recognition other t-porters claimed after seeing evi-

dence supporting their presence in the past. The Chief Archivist assured him that was only because human consciousness knows time as a forward-moving experience and he had not experienced this moment yet. He never was convinced. Only annoyed that the Archivists, especially his skipfather, could believe the red-haired person was him.

No, he concludes, the girl who sat at his feet had been too small and too blond. She couldn't have been the girl in the CBS News holoid. She wasn't the Axis.

But it's hard to tell the hair color of the girl in the holoid. Not light, not dark. Long, but not extremely long. She's taller than most girls, but not towering. Slim, but not emaciated. Lovely, but not exotic. In hip clothing, but not outrageously costumed. Her eyes are two dark ovals in the sun's glare. Even at the highest magnification, the Archivists never could determine the color of her eyes.

It frustrates Chi beyond bearing. The SOL Project is insane! And it gets worse.

He knows what they believed her legal name was, but the Axis will use an alias. A street name. Some people used more than one street name. Who knew the thousands of street names this pack of transients used? Who correlated all the street names to legal names? CBS News never identified the girl or the scruffy boy or, for that matter, the red-haired person in the background. Of all the names, street or legal, of people who came to the Summer of Love, the Archives contained but a handful.

And she will change her looks, the Archivists said. Seems everyone who came to the Haight-Ashbury transformed themselves, however briefly. Transformation was one of the traditions arising from the Summer of Love, emulated and echoed down the centuries by truth-seekers and romantic artists in gathering places all along spacetime. The Vivas, the free-thieves, the Sino-hipsters, the handcrafters, even certain cosmicists in the early days of the movement. Plus, the Axis is fourteen years old. A time when a young woman's looks often change under any circumstances.

The first object of the SOL project, then, is to find her. Find the girl in the CBS News holoid as soon as possible. Then verify her identity, determine at one hundred percent probability that the girl in the holoid is who they think she is.

For even if he can find her, the girl in the holoid may *not* be the Axis, after all.

The probability that the girl in the holoid is *not* the Axis was so high that certain staff at the Luxon Institute for Superluminal Applications dissented. They disagreed with the Chief Archivist and the SOL Project directors that the t-port should target the Summer of Love. "You must remember, it's a *dim* spot," his skipfather argued. "Yes. A *hot* dim spot," his skipmother countered. She was one of the dissenters. "The remaining data is unreliable." His skipfather had to agree, distress tugging at the corners of his mouth.

A million people. And one may be a fourteen-year-old girl. A girl who holds the conservation of all spacetime in her hands.

Chiron's relief comes for the three-to-six shift. Howie loves the djellaba. He pulls the hood about his face, smooths back his hair but for one lock falling over his brow. Chiron lets Howie take the candy-apple red sunglasses, too. Chi doesn't need sunglasses, since his corneal shields protect his eyes from ultraviolet radiation a hundred times more brutal than what beams down from this gentle sky. Howie is sixteen, from Kansas City. His parents never fixed his buck teeth. He could have only gotten a groovy gig like this—he doesn't have to cut his hair or anything—through the HIP Job Co-op, the employment referral service set up by HIP merchants. Howie is grateful for Ruby's dollar an hour. He pays the crash pad where he's staying fifteen bucks a month for a spot to lay out his sleeping bag, toilet privileges, and all the brown rice he can eat. Working maybe ten afternoons a month, Howie's rich on three dollars a day.

Chi goes to the cash drawer to collect his three dollars. Ruby insists he take it, though he said he'd work for free.

"Wages of sin," Gorgon says, tipping his chair against the wall.

"Because he stops knickknackers in my shop?" Ruby says.

"Because you're payin' him less than minimum."

"It's tax-free."

"For you or for him?"

Can they last much longer? Chiron sighs.

"For us both," Ruby says. "I deduct his wages, he pays no income tax. That's the best kind of game, right? We both benefit."

"Typical capitalist pig," Gorgon says. "Profitin' from the love-shuck boom."

"Been running my shop since this street was a sleepy little ghetto," Ruby says. "When did you get here, Leo?"

"Seniority doesn't make priority."

"I'm not Bank of America or Standard Oil."

"Typical capitalist pig, begrudgin' knickknackers," Gorgon says. "They need a buck more than you."

"I give to charity," Ruby says. "I give to the Free Clinic. Not to knickknackers."

"Typical capitalist pig, hirin' desperate runaway flower children."

"Who couldn't find work otherwise. Who would starve or hook themselves. Listen. I didn't ask these kids to come here."

That stops Gorgon for maybe half a minute.

"But you're scorin' all this bread!"

Ruby smiles. "You bet your ass. I'm half Cherokee, half Haitian black, and half Southern cream. My ma taught me. She said, 'Daughter, don't you ever depend on some man.' "

Chiron takes his three dollars. "Thanks, Ruby."

"I bet these watchmen are savin' you twenty bucks a day," Gorgon says. He gets up, goes over, wraps his hands round Ruby's shoulders. He always changes his tactics when he can't push her around with his politics. "Since you're passin' out all this bread, lay a fiver on me."

"Why should I?" She shoots him one of her looks. "You're a young, able-bodied, white man. Why don't you work for it?"

"I'd be glad to work for it." He kneads Ruby's skin, nuzzles her ear.

Ruby flutters her eyes, flexing her neck against his touch. "Uh-huh."

"First, I'll go get some of that grape juice you dig," he says. "And then? This is how I work." He whispers.

She chuckles and smiles her bedroom smile. She hands him a five-dollar bill. Gorgon grins and winks at Chiron.

Chi shakes his head. In his novel, Gorgon will flay the exotic HIP merchant. Impugn her character, cast her as an evil, manipulating, stupid, greedy whore. A blush creeps into Chi's face. Gorgon laughs, taking his reaction the wrong way.

And what about the glass from all the wine bottles Ruby tosses in the trash? Tons and tons, a mountain of glass, it will wind up as acid-safe retorts, flexiglass, neckjack housings, building insulation. But only after billions of IBUs in reclamation costs, another century and a half of waste, and conservationist laws that will skid perilously close to an unconstitutional invasion of privacy, not to mention fines so high they'll bankrupt companies.

Damn it, Ruby, Chiron wants to say. So many things he wishes he could tell her. Ah, but Tenet Three forbids him. And what about Tenet Six? He cannot reveal Ruby's future to her. How the exotic HIP merchant will sue Leo Gorgon for implying she prostituted herself, and she'll win. But by then Gorgon will have years of a junk habit in him, and he'll be judgment-proof.

It's too depressing. He tucks his three dollars in his pocket and strides out of the Mystic Eye.

All he can say is, "See you later."

"Whatever you do, son," his skipfather had said, "don't get busted by the Man."

"The Man?" Chiron said.

That was Brax, showing off. During Chi's training for the tachyportation, his skipparents learned the argot with childlike glee and practiced on him every chance they got.

"They'll search you. They'll take your good shit," his skipfather said. Tears had misted his eyes. His skipfather had become emotional since he tapped Chiron for the SOL Project. Chi wondered if Brax was having a midlife crisis. He was pushing ninety-six. "They'll freak out over your neckjack. If they throw you in the laughing academy or X-ray the hardware in your head, there's nothing we can do."

Laughing academy?

"Yes, and don't let the Man rip you off," his skipmother added, and Brax had looked at her like *Not quite, Ariel.*

Chiron smiles, thinking of their gentle, scholarly disputes. But he hadn't smiled ten days ago, standing in the Portals of the Past, dread beating in his chest.

The Archives were unclear about so much. "The Man" was the military arm of the civil service—the police, the heat, the fuzz, the pigs. "The Man" also meant a dealer, especially a pusher, a major criminal trafficker in drugs. Which was an extremely odd contradiction, if the Archivists were right. How did people know which usage someone meant? Even the context might not clarify.

Contradictions appealed to the ferrets. They loved finding twenty contemporaneously applied usages for a single word of slang. The more conflicting, the better. That was why the seventh decade of the twentieth century had attracted their scrutiny. It was a rich, confusing time, exploding with new expressions, and loaded with contradictions, contexts and subcontexts. A classic dim spot.

Sometimes the Archivists guessed. There was a popular song that went, "Over, under, sideways. . . ." *Down* was the obvious choice, of course, fitting rhyme and context. But there were advocates of *found, sound,* even *astound* and *confound.*

No authority could settle the matter. The ferrets were delighted. The missing lyrics became the subject of contests and rivalries. A game, a challenge.

Then telespace crashed, the Vision of the Other Now appeared, and the Chief Archivist ordered a complete review of the Archives.

The ferrets went back to "Over, under, sideways. . . ." In every Archive *in the world,* the end of the lyrics was gone. A smudge, a blank space, a burn hole or a worm hole. In every recording of the song *in the world,* the singer sang, "Over, under, sideways, nnn-nnn." The recording skipped or feedback crackled. You could not hear the words, could make no sense of them.

And that's when the ferrets realized they'd found a hole.

A team of sixteen Archivists working in twenty-four-hour shifts for thirty days, with the latest searchware on a network of mainframes, could find no trace of the end of the line.

A complete hole in the data.

And a hole with no disaster to justify it. Missing data could be explained after the burning of the Library at Alexandria, the eruption at Pompeii, the Holocaust, Hiroshima, or the Hundred Nights of Blackness in Beijing. The blank sixty seconds after the Crash of telespace before the Vision of the Other Now could be amply justified.

No, this was a loss of data *that had once been there.*

It was uncanny, shocking, devastating. No one had ever cross-checked and verified a complete hole in the data. The dim spot wasn't just dim, it was *hot.* Conservationists panicked. Past data was a nonrenewable resource.

But why? Why was the data disappearing?

Chiron grits his teeth. He has no intention of getting busted by the Man. *Or* ripped off by the Man.

He takes off down Clayton, walking the loop. He has walked this loop every day for the past ten days in the peak of the afternoon. Across Clayton, up to Haight, east to Broderick, cross over, west to Golden Gate Park, across Stanyan, and back.

For ten long days, he has searched for the girl in the CBS News holoid.

And watched for demons.

He visits the Haight-Ashbury Free Medical Clinic first. The clinic is housed at 558 Clayton, another faded Victorian house typical of the neighborhood before this architecture vanished from the urban landscape. The ample stoop is packed with people. A queue straggles down the sidewalk.

Beaded hipsters, bikers in leather. Vacant-eyed teenyboppers, bums on the nod. And children. So many young women with their dirty babies. Chiron stares at the mothers with stern disapproval. They're not even licensed. President Mitsui, who first required prequalification of parents and the licensing of children, would not be happy to see this disgrace.

He climbs the stairs, taking care not to bump against anyone. He slides a prophylak from the packet in his pocket, folds it over the door handle, opens the door, and drops the prophylak in a wastebasket. As soon as a prophylak becomes contaminated, he's got to dispose of it. But the disposal always makes him queasy. What about Tenet Seven, which forbids leaving evidence of a modern technology in the past? This grade of PermaPlast will decompose into vegetable components in twenty years. For now, it looks like nothing more than a wad of petroleum-based plastic wrap. The SOL Project directors authorized the necessary disposal of prophylaks. Still, Chi can't get used to casual trashing.

More stairs inside, and a sign.

NO DEALING. NO HOLDING NO USING DOPE. NO PETS ANY OF THESE CAN CLOSE THE CLINIC

WE LOVE YOU

He's made friends with Dr. Smith and Nurse Peggy, Dr. Dernberg and Miss Laurel, Dr. Reddick and Hallie. Necessary acquaintances, whom he keeps as distant as possible. For one thing, he has no authorization to affect these people. He has little business with them. For another, he's always embarrassed at the inferior position of the women, how they're demeaned in such pervasive ways. President Mitsui, who advanced the rights and protections of women more than any previous American president, would not be happy to see this disgrace, either. Chiron is as embarrassed as these people would have been appalled to witness a whipping of slaves a century ago.

Here, it's Dr. Dernberg and Nurse Peggy, Dr. Reddick and Miss Laurel.

"Find your cousin yet?" Miss Laurel says. He shakes his head. "Let's see her picture again."

He pulls out the blurry print downloaded from the CBS News holoid.

The clinic staff looks him up and down. He's still something of a curiosity to them. When he first came in, Dr. Reddick exclaimed over his pallor and slim build. The doctor tried—forcefully—to persuade Chiron to submit to a blood test. Chi had refused, resorting to Ruby's speculation about him. "I'm a hemophiliac," he said. The explanation seemed to work, even with these sharp-eyed doctors. But they still stare curiously every time he visits.

"Isn't she cute!" Miss Laurel exclaims.

Papa Al and Teddybear come over at once. Two burly, bearded hipsters in their thirties, they are volunteer staff. They don't try to slap hands with Chi anymore. He always refuses.

The clinic crawls with contagion. Ailments that don't exist in Chi's time, like mumps and yellow fever and hepatitis B, could kill him. Not to mention any of a thousand ancient bacteria that might be harmless to these people, but could kill him, too.

He can touch nothing, according to the SOL Project directors. He can touch no one.

Miss Laurel holds out the print.

"Nope, I'm afraid we haven't seen her," she says. "How about you guys?"

"Not yet, man," Papa Al laughs.

"We'll let you know, man," Teddybear grunts.

When Chi doesn't take the print from her, Miss Laurel lays it on her desk. He fumbles for another prophylak. He picks up the print, wraps the prophylak around it, and tucks the whole package in his pocket. Miss Laurel watches his performance with bemused interest. New patients clatter up the stairs. A biker with a bleeding knee poking through his torn jeans, a woman with a baby who can't keep milk down, a bearded man with a second-degree burn on his lip. Miss Laurel gets busy.

Dr. Smith waves from across the room. He's sniffling and blotchy-faced today. Founder of the clinic, David Smith is a curly-haired twenty-eight-year-old professional with a sensitive mouth and eyes glistening with sympathy. "Measles," he calls to Chiron. "Seen twenty cases today, not counting me. I think we're working on an epidemic, don't you, Peg?"

Nurse Peggy looks up from her desk, red-eyed, puffy-faced. "Whew," she sniffles. "All this bad boy takes is a sneeze. We'll keep an eye out for your cousin, Chi."

He clatters down the stairs again, recoiling from people's faces, their breaths. Such a ripe and ready contagion—measles! All it takes is a sneeze. His skin crawls.

Two girls sitting on the sidewalk caress the dog crouched between them, pass a joint back and forth, pick at calluses on their bare feet, and eat potato chips, licking the salt from their fingers.

For a moment, his stomach turns over.

He reminds himself: We had to shield ourselves from the sky itself before the radiation vaccine. Shield ourselves because of *them.*

He turns and studies the people in front of the Free Clinic. No one here looks like the girl in the CBS News holoid.

Onward.

To Haight Street.

The Archivists classified the Haight-Ashbury during the Summer of Love as an authentic spontaneous, integrative, interactive social setting based on random activity outside the private residence and focused on scheduled or impromptu celebratory activities.

A street scene.

There are other authentic street scenes. Paris during the Surreal-ists' Ball, Rio during Carnival, New Orleans during Mardi Gras, New York and San Francisco during the week-long celebration of New Re-naissance Day, Beijing on People's Independence Day, the Vivas' Spring of Life Festival. Street scenes are romantic to view in holoid, exhilarating to jack into as a telespace simulation.

What Chiron actually confronts is a bustling, hustling, babbling, twittering, tinkling, pounding, stinking, unsanitary insanity. Nothing but trouble walking down this street. He avoids getting jostled or sneezed on as best he can. He avoids interactions and confrontations. He cannot get involved, can leave no imprint of his own. But it's hard. The small street, which was never meant to contain such a crowd, is packed this afternoon.

Why the crowd?

He sees a sign painted on a wall.

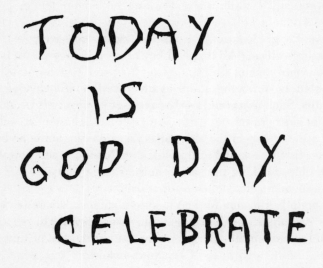

A cacophony: flutes, whistles, tambourines, bongo drums, voices singing and laughing, bells and finger cymbals, cars honking. A chopper gunning, spewing petroleum fumes. In an upstairs flat, a party rages. Two young men prop big boxes—stereo speakers—in the open, windows and blast music onto the street. "Sergeant Pepper's Lonely Hearts Club. . . ." Two women clad in bikini tops and denim cutoffs step out the window onto a narrow fire escape and gyrate to the beat. "Turn on!" they shout. "Turn on, tune in, drop out!"

"I'd walk a mile for a camel!" someone yells.

A woman in a lacquered hairdo stands with a clean-cut man in a mod suit. He lugs a huge reel-to-reel tape recorder, while she wields a gigantic camera. They detain an old man shuffling down the sidewalk. The young man thrusts a microphone into the old man's face.

"Sir, I'm the Question Man from the *Chronicle*. Would you mind answering a few questions?"

"Eh?" says the old man. The woman aims her camera. The old man has got thick spectacles over a deep frown between his eyes, a straw fedora perched on his balding pate, lips collapsed against his gums.

"What's your name, sir?"

In a quavering, but dignified, voice, he says, "I am Alfred Baumann."

"And what do you do, Mr. Baumann?"

"I'm retired."

"Mr. Baumann, what would you do if your child became a hippie?"

"I would beat him up," says the old man and totters on.

A procession marches past Chiron. Four pallbearers carry a coffin draped in black. They wear black gowns and four-foot-high papier-mâché masks depicting a dog, a ram, a bear, and a rat. "Hear ye, hear ye, money is dead!" they intone. "Money is dead!" Three kids in fake beards and Nazi helmets follow the coffin, banging garbage can lids with drumsticks. A man trails behind them in a black cap with mouse ears, a black clown's nose, round sunglasses with black lenses, a black leotard and tights, and a long black cape. In his right hand, he carries a wand topped with a skull. In his left, a brass bell, which he rings to a somber rhythm.

A flatbed truck jammed with devotees rolls slowly down the street. The devotees chant, beat drums, clang finger cymbals. Two barefoot women in flowing smocks dance before the truck as it advances. They fling daisies from the baskets they carry, kick their legs, whirl and bob, twirling their skirts. Chiron sees a bright spot of blood on a dancer's toe.

A girl glides by in a cotton dress so sheer Chi can see her nipples *and* her pubic hair. A towering man in leather pants does a double take, promptly turns and follows her. The mouse magician promenades in the opposite direction.

Chi cranes his neck. Any television cameras? No, only journalists and photographers today.

He smiles at the astonishing variety of hats and headgear. Bowlers, high-peaked Stetsons, Edwardian top hats, military caps and helmets, Greek fishermen's caps, a Victorian lady's hat that resembles a drooping bowl of velvet blooms, Moroccan fezzes, an extravagant spray of plumes held in a band of rhinestones, a full Sioux headdress worthy of a museum, gypsy headscarves, headbands of leather or suede, fresh flowers or silk woven into garlands and entwined in all that hair.

Where else has Chi seen such delight in headgear? Among his peers, of course. The bold and golden rad-vacc lads and lasses, jacked into telelink, heirs to telespace. Venus Rising would adore this. If only she could see for herself!

And a sadness strikes him as he stands in the crowd, searching the faces. A strange sense of longing. A sense of the innocence of this celebration, which he knows will pass as swiftly as the summer itself. Of course, these times aren't innocent at all. A wasteful military adventure rages in Southeast Asia, a prelude to other military adventures to come in the next centuries. Ignorance, fear, prejudice, and bigotry abound. Women are abused worldwide. The sex and drug practices in which these people revel will cause problems for centuries, challenging even the most compassionate humanists.

Still, he finds himself watching this authentic, spontaneous, integrative, interactive social setting outside the private residence with a feeling he can only call sentimental.

And frustration. Can he admit it? The mood is contagious. He taps his toe, in spite of the gravity of his purpose here. He longs to take a pull from a joint, swig from a bottle of wine, and yell the telelinkers' slogan, "Jack up, link in, space out!" Seize a pretty woman and dance in the street.

No. No. No. He can't do it.

A girl drawing on the sidewalk with chalk abandons her art and moves from her spot in front of the Psychedelic Shop. Chiron claims the spot. He deftly pulls out and positions a prophylak. His clothes are bacteria-resistant, but he still feels squeamish about sitting on the sidewalk without a prophylak. He blows on the PermaPlast, trying to hasten the descent of the damn thing, which takes its time floating down. But there are so many strange people doing so many strange things, he finds no one pays much attention. He gingerly sits and leans against the shop front.

A guy in fringed jeans strolls by, murmuring, "Grass, hash, acid, speed?"

To Chi's right sits an intense young man with chin-length hair nearly as red as his own. The young man wears a burgundy corduroy coat and jeans, brown suede Beatle boots as pointy-toed as Chi's. He draws on a clipboard with a thick black-and-tan Rapidograph pen. Next to the red-haired man sits another artist sketching in colored pencils on a drawing pad. A burly black fellow, he wears a red and yellow knit cap pulled over his dreadlocks. The intense young artists confer, trade talk. They are amazingly good and extremely serious, comparing techniques and tools.

The girl's abandoned chalk drawing depicts a bouquet of flowers. Within each flower petal is an eye. The red-haired artist draws an intricate jungle around an eye. His black friend sketches the eye of a spouting whale. A boy to Chi's left sells buttons laid out on a piece of junk velvet, and on each button is an eye, rows and rows of eyes. Eyes in suns, eyes in clouds, eyes on trees, eyes with legs, eyes with wings. Wings!

There! A film crew wends its way through the crowd, cameras whirring. Is it CBS?

Chiron jumps up and crosses the street to a shop called Mnasidika. The film crew climbs into a double-parked van and pulls away. He pauses before Mnasidika's window display, green and hot pink dresses printed with peace signs. They're gone.

He bumps into tourists. A fortyish guy in a plaid suit coat drags his scandalized wife along. The wife stares, her hand poised at the base of her throat as though she's about to vomit, while the guy clicks his Kodak camera as fast as he can. Four young men stride by, military crew cuts and potato-fed faces. They gawk at the women, hoot when they glimpse the girl in the see-through dress. Chi sees a lot of clean-cut men stalking the street.

A black man saunters by in a ragged suit coat and mismatched slacks. "Mystery! Hey, Mystery!" another black man calls to him. They slap hands, glance warily about. "What's happenin', Superspade?" The second man wears a stylish leather jumpsuit, mirrored sunglasses, and gold chains. The men make a quick exchange, a package for a package.

A barefoot girl in filthy jeans and a moth-eaten sweater creeps up to them. "Spare change?" she asks. Her name is Cyn. Cyn's always working the street. A platinum-haired runaway from Texas, she must weigh ninety-five pounds. She is nothing like the girl in the CBS News holoid, but sometimes Chi gives her his three dollars for the day anyway. "Later, Mystery," Superspade says. He takes Cyn's hand. "Spare change nothin', sugar, you're comin' with me. You want somethin' to eat?" Cyn nods. "I'll get you somethin' to eat," he says.

Chi pushes through the crowd, searching, searching. Where are you, Axis? Past Wild Colors and the Phoenix, the Blushing Peony and the I/Thou Coffee House. Socialist Worker's Party representatives sit at a card table with a petition they want him to sign. The Sexual Freedom League leaflets the crowd, along with the Recall Reagan Committee, the Berkeley Anti-Draft Union, and the Metaphysical UFO Convention. Down the block, a party spills onto the sidewalk from the Double Barrel Boogie Band's house.

By the time he returns to the Psychedelic Shop, his spot is taken by a boy in an orange dashiki who juggles four silver-colored balls. Suddenly, a man appears above the Pall Mall Cocktail Lounge. He wavers on the rooftop. "Hey, you!" yells a beat cop. "Get down from there!" The man pushes down his jeans, takes out his penis, and pisses over the rooftop. People cheer and clap. Horns and kazoos toot.

Chi dashes as piss sprays the sidewalk. A bearded man strolls east in a white robe belted at the waist. A bearded man strolls west, a white robe belted at the waist, plus a wreath of withered roses set firmly on his skull, little trickles of blood dried on his forehead. Or maybe it's makeup. He's got on red lipstick, too.

Another street vendor crouches with his display of knickknacked roach clips, Day-Glo paperclips, and other worthless odds and ends. A hoodie pulls his chopper to the curb. The hoodie wears black leather and a perpetual sneer, military boots, chains wrapped round his wrists and ankles. The hoodie's hands are heavily tattooed, "L-O-V-E" in blue on his left knuckles, "H-A-T-E" in red on the right. "Hey, Billy." The hoodie kicks the street vendor's display. "You owe me for that nickel bag, Billy." The vendor squawks, crawling across the pavement, chasing after his wares. The hoodie steps on the vendor's hand, seizes his scalp hair, jerks his head back. "Gimme some bread." The vendor extracts a handful of change from his jeans and hands it over. "Huh." The hoodie picks through the quarters and dimes. "You still owe me for that nickel bag, Billy." He takes a roach clip, too.

"Leave him alone," Chi says.

The hoodie whips out a switchblade.

Chi sprints across Haight, dodging cars.

On the other side, he nearly collides with two Hells Angels in full colors, shoving people out of their way. Chi steps off the sidewalk, back onto the street. A gangling man in shorts trots after them, playing a flute. He pauses to catch his breath. "Keep playin', you li'l fuck," says one Angel. "I dig it." He smacks the flutist on the back of his head. The other

Angel guffaws and flings a Ballantine Ale bottle into the gutter. The bottle smashes, spraying glass at Chi's feet. "Come on, you li'l fuck." They both punch the flutist in his bare ribs. A third Angel catches up with the pair. A barbarian in a fur hat and a denim vest. "Beat it, kid," he tells the flutist, who stumbles gratefully away. "Aw, Chocolate George," the two Angels complain. But Chocolate George shrugs. He's a head taller.

Chiron steps back on the sidewalk, anger pounding in his throat. His hand rests on his maser. The blue beam could slice open the Angel's head like a machete through a coconut. But Hells Angels aren't the sort of demons he's searching for. Don't get involved, Chi. Yeah; he's getting tired of that.

The guy in fringed jeans murmurs, "Grass, hash, acid, speed?"

An old man staggers and falls against The House of Richard. He reels over kids on the sidewalk. Chiron can smell him, the stench of fortified wine and body odor. The kids laugh and push him away. The old man pulls himself to his feet, goes to the curb, and vomits. He brushes off his frayed jacket, rolls over, and begins to snore.

Winos sprawl everywhere on the curbs of Haight Street, congregating in front of Pacific Liquors and Drugs. Alcohol addiction; Chi shakes his head. The trait dates from bappir fanciers in prehistoric Persia to gin-soused telelinkers careening through telespace, causing crashes with their static. Standard gene scans identified strands associated with the addiction, and DNA-editing was widely available. But most alcoholics Chiron knew tweaked only half their suspect strands. Seems a good drunk was such a pleasure, even modern people didn't want to give it up.

A shiny red Jaguar cruises. A bushy fellow in a cowboy hat drives with a beautiful woman in cascades of beads. "Stevie! It's Stevie!" A young girl sitting on the curb yells and points. She and her friend leap to their feet, dash after the Jag. The car speeds away.

Chiron recognizes the hip elite as he makes his loop: Jerry Garcia, Grace Slick, Allen Ginsberg, Timothy Leary. Images of people who attained international stature are strewn all over the Archives. But most of the hip elite will leave the Haight-Ashbury before the Summer of Love is over.

A short woman sashays arm in arm with another woman, toting a jug of wine, encouraging a lively dog who leaps about. "George," they call to the dog. "Here, George. Get it, George." The short woman has a worn-out young face bare of makeup, a wide toothy grin, a strong peasant's nose, frizzy brown hair beneath her crushed velvet top hat. Her plump little body is curvy under her paisley brocade smock and jeans. Her hands are stacked with silver rings. She takes the jug from her girlfriend and swigs it. She sees Chiron, stares, and saunters up to him.

"There you go, honey," she says in a voice like molasses and grit. She finds a pencil in her purse, digs out a hundred-dollar bill. She scribbles something on the bill, rips the money in half, tucks the half in his hip pocket. "That's for being so beautiful."

"Aw, Janis," her friend says.

"Don't you worry, Sunshine," the short woman says. "I got more where that came from."

The short woman cackles, and they saunter on. Chi finds the torn bill, looks at it. In pencil is her address.

The afternoon slips away. Sun slants through the trees. The scent of onions grilling in butter makes his mouth water. But he can't eat. The microorganisms in this food of the past could kill him. Salmonellae, shigellae, cholera, e. coli, staphylococci, viral hepatitis, microbial toxins, not to mention botulism, which is fatal anywhen. Instead, he pops off nutribeads from his nutritional necklace. Two thousand calories. Still, his mouth waters.

Another film crew barrels down Cole Street on the back of a flatbed truck. The men whoop and holler, young women cling to them, hair flying. But the truck speeds around the corner before he can get a good look. Damn it!

Thrills. It's a thrill a minute in the Haight-Ashbury during the Summer of Love.

And dangerous. So many dangers. The Man or the Man. Rustlers, bikers, hoodies, military crew cuts. The Axis is a fourteen-year-old girl, all alone.

There! A slim girl in jeans and a high-collared shirt, light brown hair flying. She sprints across Haight, disappears down Belvedere.

And there! As though a shadow has lifted from the concrete and become a solid thing, a dark figure darts after her.

Chiron pushes through the crowd, touching strangers without a prophylak over his fingers. "Hey!" people say. He finds a clear path along the curb and darts around couples arm in arm.

Where is she? Where did she go?

"Hey, you! Snot-nose." A beat cop with his billy club, grizzled jowls and quivering indignation, seizes him by the elbow. "Outta the street, snot-nose, or I'll bust ya for jaywalkin'."

Chi points up Belvedere Street, starts to protest.

"Swear to Jesus, snot-nose." The cop slaps the tip of his billy club into his beefy palm. "I'd dig bustin' ya."

Whatever you do, son, don't get busted by the Man.

"Okay, okay!" Chi hops back on the sidewalk. But the cop still comes after him. He ducks into the stream of people walking in the opposite direction, hunkers down with bended knees. He's six foot four with bright red hair, but he manages to slip through and fade into the crowd.

Will he ever find her? And find her in time? His easy defeat by a petty beat cop makes him sick.

For aside from all the dangers lurking in the Haight-Ashbury, demons could come to the Summer of Love, too. That's what the Chief Archivist believes. Demons: Devolved Entities Manifested from the Other Now.

Demons that seek her. Demons that want the Axis dead.

Purple Haze

The never-ending party rocks on as Susan sits on the stoop of the Double Barrel house, staring at a trail of ants. She studies them, precise little beings fulfilling their function in life. They're all over the kitchen. No one puts out ant traps or worries much about them. Why kill an ant? Around the corner, the Haight-Ashbury hums and jangles.

"They're just like those ants, all these damn people, aren't they?" the woman says. The tall, exotic woman, the one who cut her down in Speedway Meadow. Only this time the woman is dressed in scarlet, and Susan knows a thing or two. To Susan's surprise, Ruby A. Maverick sits next to her on the stoop.

"The ants have more nobility and purpose," Susan mumbles. How much more misery can she take today? This woman humiliated her once. What's she here for? To do it again? She can feel the woman's fiery eyes burning holes through her shame.

"The ants have more nobility and purpose," Ruby says. "Sweet Isis. That's good for a teenybopper." Her voice still rings with that haughty tone. "Find your girlfriend?"

"No." Susan shakes her head. "I haven't found Penny Lane."

"What did you say your name was?"

"Starbright. And you're Ruby Maverick. How come I can remember your name, but you can't remember mine?"

Ruby snorts. "Get off your high horse, kid. I meet a lot of people in my shop. Got a real name?"

High horse, oh really. "That *is* my real name. *No* one's turning me in to the Man, so you can forget it. I'm not telling anyone *anything*, including you."

"Uh-huh." Ruby shakes her head. "Listen, Starbright. I acted like a pig last time we spoke. I admit it, right, all right? So . . . I'm sorry."

Susan shrugs.

"You gonna accept my apology?"

"Why should I?" Susan looks up at her. Ruby isn't smiling. She looks as intimidating as ever, a bold, proud woman with a cloud of black hair out to there. But those fiery eyes, staring out at the street, then back at Susan, then out again, are unmistakably friendly. The eyes twinkle, beaming just at her.

Suddenly, Susan isn't afraid.

"You have to understand," Ruby says. "This is my turf. I've lived here for years. This hippie thing, all you kids. The journalists and film crews. The cops and the crazies. All the dope, all the dealing. The cars and the hogs. It's turned into one big drag. Oh hell," she throws up her hands. "I can't explain it."

"No, you explained it just fine," Susan says. "I understand. At least, I'm trying to. I love the Haight-Ashbury. The Summer of Love is the most amazing thing that ever happened to me."

"Uh-huh," Ruby says, but her tone is not sarcastic.

They sit together a while, watching the boisterous crowd and the busy ants.

"How's Stan?" Ruby says.

"He just did this big acid deal at the Festival of Growing Things."

Everything sort of tumbles out of her mouth, but she's too embarrassed to tell Ruby about the hundred-dollar bill Stan took from her. "Ten thousand hits. His profit is practically a year's worth of income. He used your calculating machine to figure his profit, but I could do it in my head. Stan can't figure anything out after he smokes white Lebanese pollen."

"Sweet Isis." Ruby gives her an inscrutable look. "He inside?"

"He . . . he's upstairs with some chick he met at the festival." Susan stares at the ants till her eyes tear.

Ruby sighs. "Stan's not like he used to be either, kid. We've all changed."

"The chick is really beautiful," Susan says.

"Chick?" Professor Zoom strolls out and sits on the stoop. He dropped a hit of dragon's blood on top of the hit of white lightning he dropped this morning. He practically glows in the dark. "This isn't a farm; where's a chick?"

"Shut up, Arnold," Ruby says. "Starbright and me, we're talking."

"Chiiiick, chick-chick-chick," Professor Zoom says in a falsetto. He chuckles in his deadpan way. "He-ere chickie-chickie-chickie." He presses his thumbs together and flaps his fingers like wings in Susan's face.

She recoils. "Chick. Like a . . . stupid little bird."

"Like prey," Ruby says. "Wolves go after them. And dogs."

Professor Zoom starts to chant. "Chick, bird, broad, bimbo, pussy, cunt, gash." He laughs. "Bird, broad, bimbo. Witch bitch! Chick-chick-chick!"

"God!" Susan looks at Ruby, openmouthed.

Ruby stares back. Their eyes connect.

"Dig it, kid," she says. "Once chick was Beat. But I guess chick isn't very hip. Not anymore. Not for us, anyway."

Professor Zoom gets into it. "Bird, broad, bimbo! Chick-chick-chick!"

"Let's you and me not use that word anymore," Ruby says.

"Okay," Susan says. "What shall I call you?"

"You may call me Ruby," she says and takes her hand. "Come on, Starbright. We've got work to do."

They go into the house. Someone's plugged in an amp. Fawn is stripping on the coffee table. She's down to her panties and boots.

"Know where Stan keeps my calculating machine?" Ruby shouts in Susan's ear.

"In his room. On the desk by the door."

"Think you can help me go get it?"

"They're up there now. My overnight bag is up there, too. I think I want to get it."

"Right," Ruby says. "I think you should. You help me, I'll help you."

They steal up to the third floor. Susan cannot believe her nerve, but Ruby closes her hand round the doorknob, turns it, and silently opens the door. Marilyn from Mill Valley moans in loud, long sobs. Ruby puts her fingers to her lips, *Sh!* Hands her shoulder bag to Susan, creeps inside. Susan holds the door ajar, turning her eyes away. Ruby creeps out, cradling the calculating machine in her arms. She sets it down on the floor with a thump, creeps in again.

"Aaah! Aaah! Aaah!" Marilyn cries.

Ruby scurries out with Susan's overnight bag.

"Hey! Who's there?" Stan calls.

They steal back down and out of the house. Made it! Aaah! Aaah! Aaah! They slap hands, flushed and laughing.

"Sweet Isis, this thing must weigh thirty pounds." Ruby grunts, resting the calculating machine on the front steps of the Double Barrel house.

"What monster dost thou cradle in thy arms, o witch?" Professor Zoom says, still sitting on the stoop, eyes popping.

"Go back to Yale, Arnold," Ruby says.

"Don't call me names," he says.

Susan can't help it. The laughter vanishes. She starts to cry.

"Hey, flower child," Ruby says. "He's not worth it."

"That's easy for you to say."

"Is it? Kid, you don't know. Stan and me, we once had a life, too. At least, I thought we did."

"Oh, Ruby, I don't know what I'm going to do!"

"Find somebody better. We all do."

"I'm pregnant."

Susan's cheeks burn. She clutches her purse and overnight bag. Teddy bear pouches. But there is no more comfort in childish things.

Stan dashes out the door in barely zipped-up jeans, towing Marilyn, dazed and naked, on his arm. "Say hey! I'm not through. . . ."

"Let's go, kid," Ruby says. "You better come along with me."

* * *

Ruby hoists the calculating machine under her arm and hikes as fast as she can down the quiet way on Page Street. Damn, the thing is heavy, but not as heavy as the sharp repentance in her heart. Regret is the worst because there's nothing you can do. You can't change the past.

The kid trails three steps behind, dragging her overnight bag and her feet. Ruby looks back to see if she's still following. She is, eyes glued to the ground. Ruby can't flash the smile waiting on her lips or catch the kid's glance with a look of apology.

Chick-chick-chick. She should have hauled off and belted Arnold in the chops. Dropout Yalies, they are the worst.

Up the block, Haight is packed with the Saturday night crowd. Stragglers coming back from the Festival of Growing Things. Folks heading to the Fillmore where Eric Burdon and the Animals, Chuck Berry, and the Steve Miller Blues Band are playing. Hustlers and hunters, bikers and dealers, tourists and college kids, heads and hangers-on too poor for more than the street scene, which can be as entertaining as a paid-for engagement.

Regret. Ruby recalls Speedway Meadow only too well, how she lashed out at the kid. A lamb thrown to the wolf with the most bodacious appetite in the Haight-Ashbury for Little Red Riding Hoods.

She could have been cool, if her head had been on straight. She could have guided the kid to Huckleberry House or All Saints' Church, the back room at the Print Mint. Hell. Ruby could have put her up on the couch. She took in Chiron readily enough, and he's worked out fine. Favoring a young man, is she? The couch is taken now. She could put the kid in the sitting room off her bedroom. She's got space. Lots of space in her house. What about in her heart?

Sometimes flower children fresh off the bus have a friend. Sometimes they don't. Now look at the trouble she's in. Sweet Isis knows what dope Professor Zoom turned her on to. She's lucky to be as coherent as she seems. She might have VD and not know it. These kids from the burbs are unbelievably naive. Crabs and the clap are rampant in a pad like the Double Barrel house, even syphilis, who knows. And Stan? The man has gone too far this time. Getting a kid pregnant. Does he know?

Pregnant. She doesn't doubt it. Ruby got pregnant once. Not much older than the kid, no less miserable, and under circumstances equally unsavory. "Never again," she mutters to the evening sky. "Never ever again."

She sighs and grips the calculating machine tighter. Just goes to show you. She wouldn't act so stupid if she didn't still feel lousy about Stan. The sight of him in bed. She feels ill. Damn it!

Because there *was* a time when he wasn't like this. And that time, their time together, is all mixed up with her longing for the way things were before the crazy Summer of Love. For the time when Ruby was happy.

She'd been juicing it up at Vesuvio's in North Beach. Jazz was blowing, and the '60 edition of *Beatitude* had just hit the newsstand. She and Bob Kaufman and Lawrence Ferlinghetti were whooping it up in the John Wilkes Booth. Her poem, "Hot Bitch," got published in the collection, and there were rumors the heat was going to bust City Lights Bookstore for peddling pornography. After studying Emily Dickinson and Edna St. Vincent Millay at Mills College, she felt positively wicked. She was still dumb enough to be proud of a line like "Her nipples burn, hot bitch." And so on. Bob and Lawrence had been kind.

In strolled this fine young cat, tall and rangy as a racehorse, in boots and a leather jacket. His hair was cropped. He was clean-shaven like he is now. Vain about the chin and the cheekbones, well, why not? He went by the name of Harry Oar, which made a sophomoric joke or a lousy come-on. Harry or . . . ? He toasted her literary success and—disappeared.

He was doing the bicoastal thing, which should have been a tip-off he'd turn out no good. The underground, dope and stolen cars, broken paroles and broken hearts. Still, when he showed up on the Beach again, he hadn't lost his illusion of purity. Ruby was turning thirty, an intense age, full of fate and magic. She could have anyone she wanted. When the Beats lusted after spades for their dose of cool, they dug the spade in her. When the hipsters turned to Native Americans for their dose of natural primitivism, they dug the Cherokee in her. She considered them all racists, which gave her an implicit sense of superiority. Her skin was the palest toffee, her nose a narrow Irish snoot. She was one fine babe, and she knew it. She thought Norman Mailer's *White Negro* was hilarious. That was no metaphor when it came to Ruby A. Maverick.

He was now Stan the Man, possibly on the lam. Their paths crossed again at Vesuvio's. This time he came home with her to the view-apartment on Vallejo Street.

When she split to the Haight-Ashbury in '62, Stan came, too. Ma had died in '61 from lung cancer, though she never smoked, and Ruby made a stink about working conditions at Marinship to its successor, a rich steel company. The steel company settled out of court for fifteen grand. Ruby sprang the rest of Ma's inheritance out of probate and, with a third of her holdings—ten thousand dollars cash—opened the Mystic Eye. Get your own, Ma always said. Ruby did. The shop was her dream, after a lifetime of fascination with the ancient ways. Stuff Pa knew from his mother in Oklahoma, stuff Ma knew from her mother in New Orleans and *her* mother in Haiti. Stan grew his hair—sweet Isis, he was beautiful —and helped set up 555 Clayton. He built the shelves and cases by hand. She hoped he'd pursue his talent for carpentry and woodworking. He moved in with her upstairs and stayed true for nearly two years.

It was no secret how women panted after him. Even the squares in their spit curls and girdles. They joked about it at first: Harry or Stan?

The Pill and rock 'n' roll and bikinis and James Bond movies. Cigarette ads urged women to let loose, booze ads showcased gorgeous dames lapping bright drinks from tall glasses, tampon ads insisted nothing should hold a woman back from doing what she wanted to do. Even the ads for Dial with AT-7 showed a girl in the shower, her pursed lips ready for fellatio, soapsuds ejaculated all over her face.

There was no containing the sexual tension those days.

Grandmother Says: Kaou (Temptation)

The Image: A hot wind arises under heaven, disrupting the world
    and its rulers.
The Oracle: The maiden is bold. The man delights in her and does
    not recognize her power. He is seduced, then finds he cannot
    control her.

It is necessary for elements predestined to be joined and mutually dependent to come to meet one another halfway. However, the female principle unexpectedly obtrudes from below the male principle. The dark goes all the way to meet the light and overpowers it.

—Hexagram 44, *The I Ching* or Book of Changes

to fuck with love
to fuck with all the heat and wild of fuck
the fever of your mouth devouring all my secrets and my alibis
leaving me pure   burned into oblivion
the sweetness UNENDURABLE
  mouth   barely touching   mouth

  nipple to nipple we touched
  and were transfixed
  by a flow of energy
  beyond anything I have ever known

  we TOUCHED!

  and days later
  my hand embracing your semen-dripping cock
  AGAIN!

  the energy
  indescribable
  almost   unendurable
  the barrier of noumenon-phenomenon
        transcended
  the circle   momentarily complete
                          the balance of forces
                              perfect
  lying together, our bodies slipped into love
  that never have slipped out
  I kiss your shoulder and it reeks of lust
  the lust of erotic angels fucking the stars
  and shouting their insatiable joy over heaven
  the lust of comets colliding in celestial hysteria
  the lust of hermaphroditic deities doing
  inconceivable things to each other and

SCREAMING DELIGHT over the entire universe and beyond
and we lie together, our bodies wet and burning, and
we WEEP we WEEP we WEEP the incredible tears
that saints and holy men shed in the presence
of their own incandescent gods

I have whispered love into every orifice of your body
        as you have done
           to me

my whole body is turning into a cuntmouth
my toes   my hands   my belly   my breasts   my shoulders
my eyes
you fuck me continually   with your tongue   with your look
                      with your words   with your presence

        we are transmuting
        we are as soft and warm and trembling
        as a new gold butterfly

        the energy
        indescribable
        almost   unendurable
at night   sometimes   I see our bodies glow

    —Lenore Kandel, "To Fuck With Love," in
    Notes from Underground (Underground Press,
    1964)

Who married? Why marry? No one married. Who was faithful? Why stay faithful? What did faithful mean, anyway? Nothing. Or at least, not very much.

Ruby recalled the first time she saw the personal ads in the *Berkeley Barb* and the *Village Voice*. Even she was amazed. They gave out phone numbers. "Man seeking boys for Greek encounters, expert at B&D" and "Man seeking girls for French dates, expert at oral stimulation."

That was Stan. An expert. And expertise required practice.

Where did all those women come from? They would open their thighs at a wink of his eye. So many hip chicks, eager to fuck with or without love.

She should have known he could not possibly stay faithful to her. Instead of an occasional score, Stan turned into a cottage industry. Late-night calls came weekly, daily. He spent more and more time on the street. One evening Ruby was confronted outside the shop by a stringy woman with bad teeth who demanded to see Stan. He went to Mexico three times. Her paranoia went through the roof. She had a legitimate *business*. She was working on a pretty cool *life*.

He moved out when he got the gig as manager of the Double Barrel Boogie Band. Never was the settle-down type, Ruby consoled herself.

Now he's got everything he wants: a bountiful supply of connections and easy girls. In the time since they broke up, Stan got a gorgeous suntan and a singular reputation, and has become a caricature of himself. Ruby got a silver '66 four-passenger BMW Sports Coupe and a fifty-grand-a-year business, and has become a respected HIP merchant.

There's some justice.

Still, taking things out on the kid at the Solstice. Crazy; the man still makes her crazy. She doesn't dig it. Not cool at all.

So what does she turn around and do? Takes it up with Leo Gorgon, of all crazy things. Thighs still sweet from their tryst. Better to do it in the afternoon than at night with young Chiron sacked out on the living room couch. Gorgon. Another bad cat, more into strange power trips and funny politics than sex and dope, though he takes his fair share of the latter and indulges her lusts with finesse. You're so sensitive, Ruby, he would sneer, if he knew she'd rather not hump him with Chiron downstairs.

Why does she keep falling for bad cats like Stan and Leo? Sometimes she thinks that Roi, her beautiful lost Roi, for all his failures, had more nobility and purpose. Right, Starbright.

She grits her teeth, turns the corner at Clayton. The kid turns the corner too, looks down the block, looks up at Ruby. And Ruby sees in the kid's eyes self-loathing and insecurity and pain and fear, and it's like falling down a well. Dizzy, falling into the past, her past. Was she really that vulnerable once? How can young women bear it?

Shifting the calculating machine to her other arm, she comes to a decision. She will not turn Starbright over to Huckleberry House or All

Saints'. She's heard of rip-offs at the crash pads, folks turning in run-aways to the fuzz for sixteen bucks a head. Bounty hunters are every-where during the Summer of Love.

The kid can stay. In the sitting room, on the third floor. Chiron can continue on the living room couch. She has given up trying to understand Chi, but one thing she can say is he's an aloof and sober young man who observes her house rules, as far as she can tell, and who doesn't look twice at girls. He won't bother Starbright.

What vice cop could pin her on that?

She'll tell the kid to contact her parents, of course, and go back home. That's the right thing to do, presumably, but only if the kid wants to go. If she hasn't burned her bridges. If she's not getting beat up. If she's not getting diddled by her pa or a big brother. So many ifs. It's frightening. Ruby can imagine them all.

But to shelter another kid, a real live runaway this time, and preg-nant? Sweet Isis, don't make this a trend. She feels good about it, but not that good. She is not the custodian of the disaffected youth of America for the Summer of Love.

And with a small shock Ruby remembers: *I don't take in runaways.*

But you will, Chi said. *You will shelter people. Runaways, and people.*

Where did he see her description before, what article, where? He didn't—after all—show it to her, did he? Electronically stored, right. If the article is on microfiche in the library, she should be able to go look it up, shouldn't she? What journalist could have written about her shelter-ing runaways if she hasn't done it yet?

Who is Chiron Cat's Eye in Draco? And who is watching Ruby A. Maverick?

It's a scene.

Half a dozen young cats are sitting on the sidewalk with a girl. The girl's face is shaped somewhat like a frog's: a narrow, wrinkled forehead, round eyes, a thick, wide jaw around a thin-lipped mouth. Flower petals are painted on her eyelids. It doesn't help, poor thing, Ruby thinks. But the frog-girl is thrilled to be sitting with so many young cats. The cats ignore her. It's not clear whom she's with, if anyone. But the frog-girl is cool. She doesn't have to be with anyone.

The mob slouches about the stoop in front of the Mystic Eye or sits

cross-legged down on the curb. On the door of the shop is the sign Ruby
left.

One cat balances a skull on his knee. Not a pendant or a button, but
the real thing, bony eye sockets and grinning molars, minus the lower
jawbone. Another cat's got large black eyes with long curly lashes
painted in kohl on his prominent cheekbones. His real eyes are rimmed
in kohl, too. Then there's the usual cat in a headband, a cat in a military
cap, and an older cat with a graying beard and hair halfway down his
back.

A jug of dago red makes the rounds, plus a huge bong billowing like
a smokestack.

Ruby swoops down on them, breathing fire. She deposits the calculating machine on the stoop.

"Okay, boppers. Break it up and move it on, 'cause you're not gonna
trip at *my* door."

She might as well be speaking in tongues, because no one bats an
eye. They are so far into their game they neither see nor hear her, but
continue to laugh and jive and pass around jug and bong.

Ruby stands at the edge of their circle, tapping her toe. "Listen! I
want to open my shop."

What they do notice, instantly, is Starbright sidling up behind
Ruby. Starbright. She's got to lose a week's worth of grime, the mod look,
which doesn't suit her at all, the white lipstick, and her attitude of abject
depression. Still, she's got a lovely face and a pretty young body and
wavy light brown hair, however unkempt. Her overnight bag is a red flag:
Runaway. Meaning she won't sass, won't ask much, won't put up a fight.

In other words—to these hard young cats skulking about Haight Street—an easy lay. Beautiful.

They do what young cats do. Their shoulders square up. Their voices get louder by two decibels. Their gestures broaden and swoop. They start to hassle each other. The headband sitting next to the cat with the skull gets an ash flicked in his face. "Hey, man!" "Heads up, sumbitch." Sweat pops out of unwashed armpits, the stink of competition.

Flash of red hair. Suddenly Chiron is there, taking everything in. To Ruby's surprise, he notices Starbright, too. He practically cranes his neck. Ruby knows Chiron well enough to know he'd walk away from a scene like this, a look of disgust on his smooth, pale face. But, no. He sits. He doesn't even take out a square of his weird plastic wrap to sit on. Talk about distracted.

Ruby glances back at Starbright. She doesn't notice the stir she's caused.

"Where there's dope," says the cat with the skull, passing the bong to the headband, "there's hope."

"Dope gets you through times of no money," says the headband, passing to the guy with the eyes, "better than money gets you through times of no dope."

"Reality is a crutch for people who haven't got the courage for acid," says the guy with the eyes, passing to Chiron.

"LSD is a psychotomimetic," says Chi.

"A what?" says the guy with the eyes.

"A mimicker of madness." Chi doesn't take a hit, but passes the bong to the military cap.

"Oh. Yeah," says the guy with the eyes. "I knew that."

Starbright's eyes widen. Uh-huh, Ruby thinks.

"I usually trip once a week," says the military cap. "If I went for two weeks without acid, I'd grow so much ego that I'd blow to pieces."

The military cap passes the bong to the frog-girl. She tokes and says nothing. The girls in these circles seldom do. The frog-girl passes the bong to the elderbeard.

"I trip," says the elderbeard. "Every two or three days. Then I wait a day to do body work."

"What sort of body work?" asks Chiron.

"Y'know, sleep. Eat." The elderbeard passes to the cat with the skull.

"I was walkin' down the Haight," says the cat with the skull. "An' I looked up an' saw this sign that said NO STOPPING. It like jumped out an' like *dragged* me 'cross the street. An' as I'm steppin' up on the curb, this Angel comes by on his hog doin' eighty miles an hour, I swear, an' he juuuust missed me, like by *that much*." He holds up his thumb and forefinger.

"That's omens for you," says the elderbeard, nodding.

"Acid," says the guy with the eyes, "raises your powers of integration so that everything is important."

"Acid," says Chiron, "lowers your powers of discrimination so that everything seems important."

"Huh?" says the guy with the eyes.

"Why aren't you smokin'?" says the military cap.

Everyone turns. Suddenly tension is thicker than smoke.

"Ah," says Chi. "Measles. I went to the Free Clinic today. There's an epidemic of measles, that's what Dr. Smith says."

Measles. The circle coughs. Ruby is struck with concern. Chiron is some kind of clean freak. He is obsessed with germs like no one she's ever known. He's got measles?

"The health of the body is a matter of the mind," says the elderbeard, handing a tiny foil packet to Chiron. "Here. Owsley white lightning. Do wonders for your measles, brother."

"That's all right," says Chi.

"Take it," says the elderbeard.

"Take it," says the military cap.

"We want to see you take it," says the headband.

The frog-girl turns and stares. Her greasepaint flower petals shine.

Chiron unfolds the foil packet. He sticks out his tongue for all to see and places the tab on the tip of it.

The cats relax, the circle is restored.

Chiron coughs gently. Ruby sees him palm the tab. He does a pretty good job of it. He slips the tab into his pocket.

"Tripping yesterday," says the headband, taking the bong again, "I saw the mandala of a thousand eyes."

"Oh, I've seen that," says the elderbeard. "I've seen the mandala of a thousand eyes a thousand times."

"You have not," says the headband.

"Sure I have," says the elderbeard. "I saw a formation of flying saucers cruising over the park on the Solstice, *whoosh*! I shot a rainbow out of the top of my head. *Shoosh!* Shot it all the way across the Panhandle. Everyone on Hippie Hill saw it."

"I can see through solid rock," says the headband. "I can read minds."

"Myself, I do magic," says the elderbeard. "It's easy 'cause I was a magician apprenticed to Merlin in 1467. I made it with Morgan le Fay."

"Oh, you're an incarnation?" says the guy with eyes.

"No, man, I'm five hundred years old," says the elderbeard. "I'm living backward in time."

"I'm reincarnated," says the headband. "I was a Navajo chief."

"Shit, *every*body's been a Navajo chief," says the elderbeard.

"I'm from Egypt," says the military cap. "I built the pyramids. In my past life, I was, like, Ramses the King. And *she*," he stares at Starbright, "was my queen."

Starbright turns scarlet.

"Weren't you my queen? Come here, Nefer-tit. Sit down next to me."

She hovers behind Ruby. The pressure of their bloodshot eyes is too much. She goes and sits down behind the military cap, next to Chiron.

Chiron smiles at her. She ignores him.

"Fuck Egypt," says the guy with the eyes. "I'm from Mars." He produces a sheaf of spidery ink drawings and proudly shows them to Starbright.

"Wow," Starbright says.

The guy with the eyes flips through the drawings. "These are our machines. I design these machines, you see? I've come to Earth to give Martian technology to you Earthlings. How do you like our machines, brother?" he says to Chiron.

Chiron tries to catch Starbright's eye. She gives him a withering look. He jerks back, rebuffed.

Oh, these young cats, Ruby thinks.

Chiron's shoulders square up. His voice loudens two decibels. His gestures broaden and swoop.

"There's no advanced life native to Mars," Chiron says. "No life at all, except for some insignificant bacteria we discovered centuries ago."

"You callin' me a liar?" says the guy with the eyes.

"There wasn't any life on Mars," Chiron says with haughty authority. "Till we terraformed the planet, restored the atmosphere, and made it habitable for humanity."

"Terrify the planet?" says the elderbeard, chiming in. "That's what we're trying to do in the Haight-Ashbury, man. Terrify the planet."

The circle laughs, warily. Not everyone gets the joke.

"And we couldn't terraform Mars," Chi continues. His tone is harsh, condescending. "Till we could finance such a massive project out of positive cash flow. A positive cash flow in International Bank Units, based on True Value. After spending for conservationist control and crime control and birth control, it took us a hundred years of savings and investment just to fund the first year of the project. And *that* was after a delay of two hundred years from the turn of the millennium. Financing terraformation was a long-term commitment, requiring long-term discipline. The government lacked the ability. The rich lacked the compassion, the middle class lacked the willpower, the poor lacked the means. It was cosmicists who got the job done. My family donated fifteen percent of our income for a hundred years to Mars terraformation. *We* brought life to Mars."

"Dig this shit," says the guy with the eyes. "He sounds like an accountant. *I'm* a Martian."

"I'm not an accountant. I'm a tachyporter."

"A tacky-poor-*who*?"

"My personal Now is in your future."

"I think you're a narc, man."

"And I think you're dirty." Chiron slips something out of his pocket, flips it in his palm, flicks it. An orange beam shoots from the tip of a metal tube the size of a Bic pen. He aims the beam at the sidewalk in the middle of the circle and twirls his hand, tracing a shape. A puff of pulverized concrete spews from the beam's path. He flicks the pen again and tucks it in his pocket. Dust lingers like smoke. And carved in the concrete, perhaps half an inch deep, is a figure.

Ruby can't believe her eyes. She knows a thing or two about stage magic. She barges through the circle and crouches, touching the sidewalk. She doesn't even think twice about the wisdom of this till her forefinger tells her the concrete is still hot.

"What the hell?" she says to Chiron.

He shrugs, triumphant and apprehensive at the same time.

The frog-girl and the circle stare at the heart, openmouthed.

The elderbeard starts to cackle, "Man oh man oh man."

Then Ruby sees something else she cannot believe. Chiron—the aloof Beelzebub in his high tower—whips out one of his squares of plastic and punches his hand through it with a practiced gesture. He reaches over and, while everyone's eyes are still riveted on his trick in the concrete, he presses his fingertips into Starbright's jacket between her breasts.

"Hey!" She recoils, startled. Her eyes widen. "Ouch!"

He tries to take her hand, her fingers. She seizes her hand back, slaps at him, pushes him away. He holds a small, dark, oblong stone. The circle looks up from the heart carved in concrete, slowly taking interest in their struggle. Chiron pockets the stone. His face is solemn, intense, faintly ashamed.

"What *is* your name, man?" says the guy with the eyes.

"Where *are* you from?" says the headband.

Chi's got them all rattled when a cop car turns the corner at Haight and Clayton and commences prowling down the block. Two cops hop out, hips thick with holstered revolvers. Their hands dangle, expectantly.

"Party's over," Ruby says. "All of you, *scram!*"

At Ruby's nod, Chiron hustles Starbright around the back way.

Ruby hoists the calculating machine and heaves it with a *thump* inside the front door of the Mystic Eye, tosses her CLOSED sign in, too. She slams the door, stands in semidarkness with her eye to the peephole, heart pounding. The cops disperse the circle and clear the sidewalk. She waits, one beat, two. Are they coming after her? Charge her with instigating a public nuisance? Or is this the night to raid her herb collection and plant a joint on her premises? Stranger things have happened.

But the cops hang around for a minute or two, exchange a few laughs, get back in their car, and take off.

Damn! It's a Saturday night. The street is still packed with paying customers. But paranoia drains her dry. She doesn't know how much more she can take. She shuts the shop, triple-locks the front door, and dashes up the stairs.

Chiron and the kid stand on the deck by the kitchen door. Starbright is almost as pale as he is. She furtively checks him out. He stares at her from just about every angle.

"But what's your *real* name?" he says in a wheedling tone.

"That *is* my real name," the kid says, eyes flashing.

Uh-huh. Now Ruby *has* seen Chiron glance at the ladies *some*times. And she has no idea what the young cat does with his days and nights outside the Mystic Eye. But this is the first time she has seen him stir his royal self over a female person. A pretty child, yes, but what is happening? There is something odd about the gleam in his eye.

She steps out on the deck. "Hey," she says to Chi. "What the hell do you mean by pulling a stunt like that in front of my shop?"

"I'm sorry," he says and looks it.

"You bet your ass you're sorry, sonny. What if the city tries to make me replace the sidewalk you ruined?"

"I didn't ruin the damn sidewalk, Ruby."

"None of your smart-mouth," Ruby says, shaking her finger at him. She tosses Starbright's overnight bag into the kitchen and slams the door. "You're gonna help me," she says to him and heads down the stairs. "Come on, kid."

Ruby takes them back to the garage, heaves open the doors, pulls the chain to the lightbulb hanging from the ceiling. Her BMW Sports Coupe is parked there, plus assorted boxes of inventory and a huge, eight-armed brass statue of Kali she's not sure what to do with. She unlocks the storeroom, picks her way through the rubble. A lawnmower with rusty blades, a ten-inch black-and-white TV the previous tenant left behind, a couple of Hula Hoops. She keeps forgetting to dump the box of desiccated peyote buttons from Morris Orchids in Laredo, Texas, that Stan got through mail order in '63. Ah, there's that old box mattress.

Ruby slides her hand through the loops on the left side of the mattress. Chiron takes the right side. Starbright navigates from the rear. Ruby has never seen such a skeptical look on a flower child's face, but then a week or so is a long stretch for anyone to do time at the Double Barrel house. They struggle with the unwieldy mattress through the narrow storeroom door.

"You can help us upstairs," Ruby tells Chiron. "Then you can take your things and get out."

They stand in the musty garage beneath the bare bulb swinging on its chain.

He looks up, startled. "Ah, come on, Ruby."

"Come on, nothing."

"What did I do? I thought you liked me."

"*Liked.* Past tense. You got it, sonny." Her hand slips, tearing three nails below the quick.

"But why? What's wrong?" Chiron steadies his side. "I'm here to help you, Ruby. Haven't I helped you?"

His face is so pained, she almost changes her mind. Almost. She is Ruby A. Maverick, and she will tolerate no nonsense.

"Measles. You got measles? You know how bad measles can be? I've got a young woman here who . . ." *Who is pregnant,* she starts to say. She shuts up the second she sees Starbright's horrified face. "Who doesn't need that, and neither do I. You know how contagious measles is?"

"I don't have measles, Ruby," Chiron says slowly and patiently like she's being dense, which makes her even madder. "I would probably die from measles."

"You would probably die. Then you lied?"

"I didn't lie. I implied." He tugs at the mattress. "They were trying to force me to communally ingest drugs."

"Trying to force . . ." Ruby softens. "Yeah. Well. You had better go to the Free Clinic and get treated. Don't be spreading measles around here."

"Ruby," he says again, less patiently. "I never *said* I had measles."

"He *touched* me," Starbright speaks up. Her voice is shrill. "He *attacked* me. With that black stone-thing of his. He *stabbed* me." She rubs her breastbone.

He starts to laugh, then stops himself. "I didn't stab you, Starbright. The scanner's got a small probe, that's all. The probe is a hundred times finer than a sewing needle. You felt a little prick, that's all. Isn't that true?"

"He *stabbed* me." Starbright glares at him with such venom, Ruby revises her opinion of the kid. Not such a little lamb, after all.

He turns to Ruby. "Look, pot's all right, but I can't smoke from a bong passed mouth to mouth." He makes a face. "Besides, I'm complying with your house rules, Ruby."

Of course he is. But her stubbornness and her paranoia won't let it go. "But you sat down with those cats. Maybe you didn't partake, but you passed the bong. Tell me true, once and for all, Chiron. Are you a narc? Have you come to the Haight-Ashbury to get evidence?"

"Well, in a way, I *am* here to get evidence."

"A nonparticipant witness, isn't that what they call it?" she says in her sweet-as-poison voice.

"Actually, that's a fair description."

"Damn it, Chi!"

Starbright drops the back of the mattress, poised to run.

Ruby gestures to her, *cool it*. Damn her foolishness, but she is suddenly worried about the kid. Out on the street, in the Haight-Ashbury, at night. "You're not going anywhere, Starbright," she says firmly.

"I'm *not* a narc!" he says. "I have no wish to harm you! I swear it! I swear it on anything you want me to swear on."

"Swear it on your mother's grave, and we'll never mention it again."

An unexpected look of sharp sadness crosses his face that arrows right into Ruby's heart and hits bull's-eye.

"Oh, I can do that," he says. "I swear it on my mother's grave."

They set up a makeshift bedroom for Starbright in the sitting room off Ruby's room. At first the kid is unsure, but then she joins in Ruby's enthusiastic rearrangement of the bits of furniture, Chiron's placement of the carpets and potted plants. Soon they've got a cozy little nest all for Starbright, with a door that closes and locks, a sloping skylight, a private bath two steps away, and sheets. Clean sheets. The kid's face begins to shine. She takes off her jacket and carefully hangs it on the hook on the back of the door.

Chiron beams as though he's the one responsible. "I'll go downstairs now," he says, slipping quickly out the door and clattering down the stairs, "and let you lasses rest."

"Not so fast, sonny," Ruby calls to him. "You're packing some kind of weapon. Aren't you. Well, aren't you?"

He stops, slowly climbs back up.

"I, for one, will rest a whole lot easier when you tell us what your magic show was all about. Carving up my sidewalk with that . . . thingie."

"This?" He pulls out the Bic pen.

Both Ruby and Starbright duck.

"It's just a maser," he says mildly. He turns it, showing tiny graphics along one side. "Microwave Amplification by Stimulated Emission of Radiation. This tool is cool. Got quite a range." The maser is striped in bands of purple, blue, green, yellow, orange, and red, with gradations of those colors in between. Each colored section is subdivided in tiny, millimetric measurements like the divisions on a ruler.

"Pretty," Ruby says. "That Japanese?"

"Yes," he says. "You set it like this." He slides the tiny black pointer up and down the length of the tube along the colored bands, clicks it in at the divisions. He points to the red band. "Red is good for microlevel jobs. Microorganisms, bacteria, small insects, and such. The beam destroys the target, but doesn't affect anything else." He points to the orange and yellow bands. "These are higher intensities. I can cut various materials, cauterize a wound, perform surgery, if I need to. Concrete is pretty soft. You can carve concrete with orange. The serious fire-power is here." He points to the green and blue bands, taking care not to touch the black pointer. "Plus, I've got a frequency that doesn't apply normal physics. The purple beam is an antimatter emission similar to the Dead Stop near-annihilation exchange used in the ME3 Event."

"I don't get it," Ruby says.

"Neither do we, not completely," he says darkly. "I've got an active purple beam only if I need to affect antimatter. Hope I never need to use purple." He tucks the maser away. "Under Tenet Seven, I'm only to use the maser under strict necessity, anyway. Can't be masering up your world with a modern tool."

"Antimatter, uh-huh," Ruby says, nonplussed. He's so earnest, so convincing. An awful thought strikes her. Is Chiron insane? Still, she saw him carve concrete with her own eyes. Suddenly, her head is spinning. She's exhausted. "The royal *we* again. *You* and *us*. Who's *we*?"

"He said he's from the future," Starbright says, looking him up and down skeptically.

"Guess I told everyone." He brushes back his red hair and blushes. Charming, to see this young cat blush, his pale face as chiseled and fine as a movie actor's under the soft light in the sitting room. "They were too intoxicated to take me seriously, though, weren't they?" His look of contrition competes with a smirk of triumph. Won *that* competition, brother.

"But I'm not intoxicated," Ruby says. "Not yet, anyway. And I remember you used a weird word."

"Tachyporter. I'm on a t-port, and I've blown the shit out of Tenet Five now." He paces about the tiny room. Got himself a bit of a temper. "Ah, the Summer of Love. It's getting to me, you know? I'm not supposed to get involved. But I am involved. Only ten days, and I *am* involved. Sometimes I give my three dollars to little Cyn." He faces them. "I'm not supposed to reveal my identity. But now you know, and it's true. My personal Now is in your future. So you must know for sure I'm not a narc, Ruby."

These are strange and wondrous days. These are also paranoid days, when your old man turns out to be a dealer, and his best friend turns out to be a narc, and the best friend's old lady turns state's evidence, and you wind up in the slam.

"You've got a more interesting rap than the average head," she says. "But you can't fool me. I got weaned on Superhero comics. In between Hemingway and Flannery O'Connor at college, I read Heinlein and Arthur C. Clarke. I've done all of Tolkien. Lately, I've been getting into this strange new guy, Phil Dick. You say you're from our future. What you mean is, you're just a time traveler. Right, am I right?"

"I'm not *just* a time traveler," he says, annoyed. "I'm a tachyporter. Developing tachyportation technology cost us a fortune. And it isn't exactly *traveling,* either, like going from one place to another. All space-time is One Day, you see. With a superluminal application called the ME3 Event, I *translate-transmit.* From my Now to your Now. A when to when."

He looks around the room with such tangible anxiety that alarm needles up Ruby's spine. She looks around, too.

"The good news is, everything hasn't disappeared just because I've told you," he says, voice thick with relief. "Just because you know."

Starbright's jaw just about reaches her collarbone.

"Let's see what we know," Ruby says. Teach these kids a thing or two. "Whereabouts in the future are you from, sonny?"

"From here. I'm from San Francisco." He still looks worried, like she might find out something she isn't supposed to know. "Sausalito, actually."

"Then we're next-door neighbors," Ruby says. "I grew up in Marin City."

"Sausalito, 2467. The when-to-when is five centuries, one hundred twenty-five days, fifty-three minutes, thirty-nine seconds, three hundred nineteen milliseconds, minus one picosecond."

"Minus one picosecond," Ruby says. "Is that B.C. or A.D. or A.C. or D.C.?"

"You don't believe me?" he says, widening his eyes.

"Sonny, there is this guy in South Bay. He wrote himself a pretty good novel, and he got himself a fine party pad, and he has been taking himself on some mighty strange trips. He's got himself an entourage, plus a harem, and they all think he is Valentine Michael Smith. Excuse me; not that *he* is Valentine Michael Smith. That Valentine Michael Smith is *him*."

"Excuse me," Starbright says. "But who is Valentine Michael Smith?"

"The cat from Mars. I mean, the man who was abandoned by his human parents on Mars, and was raised by Martians, and has come back to Earth with exotic Martian wisdom and powers."

"Excuse *me*," Chiron says. "Are you saying there *are* Martians? Here? Now?"

Ruby guffaws. "I'm talking about Heinlein's novel!" But she sees she had *him* moonstoned for a moment. Ha! Gotcha! "We may be psychedelicized in the Haight-Ashbury, but we are also science-fiction-alized. Ken Kesey is equating his group mind experience with *Childhood's End*. Timothy Leary writes about mutating our genes into starseeds, evolving consciously through the use of mind-expanding drugs. Some local folks have started an alternative elementary school called the Shire. This has all happened since 1962. Our lives have become a metaphor, and metaphors are becoming life." She laughs. "These are strange and wondrous days."

"Yeah," Starbright says. "Look at the guy with the eyes. He said he was from Mars, too."

"I never *said* I was from Mars," Chiron says.

"Where's your time machine?" Starbright demands in a militant tone.

"My time machine?"

"Yeah! Like George's sleigh."

"George's sleigh?" he says.

"Like in *The Time Machine*," she says impatiently.

"Oh, that's my favorite H. G. Wells novel," Ruby says, pleased.

"There's a novel?" Starbright says doubtfully.

"Since the turn of the century," Ruby says.

"Oh. I saw the movie when I was seven," Starbright says. "Oh, but I loved George's time machine. It's the prettiest thing, like a gold and leather sleigh, with a crystal-knobbed stickshift, and everything." She blushes. "I haven't learned how to drive a stickshift yet."

"Ah," Chiron says. "I don't have a time machine."

Ruby says, "Why am I not surprised?"

"The tachyonic shuttle doesn't work that way," he says quickly. "The shuttle exists only in my Now, not in yours. We install the shuttle at a site that's been stable a long time."

"And then what happens?" Ruby says.

"I step through the site to get to your Now. On a certain day at a certain time, I step through the site to get to my Now. The shuttle engages this spacetime, and the ME3 Event translates-transmits me."

"Uh-huh," Ruby says. An eerie feeling creeps over her as she sits in the half-lit room, shucking with this strange young man. But she doesn't want to surrender to the feeling, doesn't want to let her mind spin off in some half-comprehended revelation. She's got work to do, damn it. She's got a pregnant runaway under her roof, plus this tourist. She doesn't want her whole life changed just this moment. "Why aren't you supposed to reveal your identity? I mean, aside from getting thrown in the laughing academy."

"Laughing academy?"

"That's Beat for the nuthouse."

"Ah." He nods. "I'm not supposed to reveal my identity as a modern person under Tenet Five of the Grandfather Principle. All the Tenets turn around the mandate of nonintervention to preserve the timeline and conserve spacetime."

"What's the Grandfather Principle?" Starbright says.

"That's the fundamental controlling contact with the past," Chiron says. "Under Tenet One, for example, you can't murder your own grandfather. If you could, you wouldn't exist in the first place to go to the past and do the deed."

"Dig it," Ruby says. "If you allowed for that sort of anarchy, reality would be mighty strange. The world as we know it could disappear. Right, am I right?"

He looks around again with sharp apprehension. Ruby's skin crawls.

"Why would anyone go and murder her grandpa?" Starbright says.

Ruby turns to find the kid is crying.

"Well, you wouldn't," Chiron says to her gently. "It's a Tenet developed for t-port projects. A thought experiment, you see? It's just a way of thinking."

"Just a way of thinking," Starbright says, sniffling. "I think it's *terrible*. It's a terrible way of thinking. My grandpa was the only one who ever loved me. I could *never* go and kill my grandpa. *Never*. Not for *anything*."

"The kid's got a point," Ruby says. "The way you think about things shapes the way your reality is. All this talk about killing someone's grandfather. It's not very cool, man from Mars."

He stares at her, aghast. "I don't want to kill anyone, either! I don't want to kill a flea," he says, scratching his ankle.

Uh-huh. And they say goodnight.

The Haight-Ashbury is mobbed with Navajo chiefs, Merlin's magicians, Egyptian pharaohs, guys with four eyes, men from Mars.

And time travelers. The Summer of Love has plenty of time travelers.

July 9, 1967

A Dog Day

There Is a

Mountain

 Life is sacred; her life is sacred. Children are the godhead manifest; she is the godhead manifest. Freedom means nothing left to lose; she has got to get free.

"I'm eighteen," Susan lies to the law clerk in the waiting room outside the hip lawyer's office next door to the Haight-Ashbury Legal Organization. Hip lawyers are in such demand, HALO can't keep up with the caseload. An annex has sprouted in the adjoining suite on Ashbury Street.

The lie comes no easier. The lie has not helped Susan one bit. She's not even sure why she keeps telling it, except now she's got a fake ID proving she's eighteen, though the photo doesn't look much like her. She is so paranoid about coming to the hip lawyer's office, despite the fact he is, by definition, cool, that she doesn't want to show the fake ID to the law clerk. He doesn't ask.

The law clerk, a rabbinical guy with a beard and doglike eyes, peers at her through steel-rim spectacles. He aims a long-suffering, skeptical look at Ruby. Ruby shrugs and stares out the window at the foggy dawn. Her face is set in stone. She taps her toe. Next to "NAME: 'Starbrit,' " the law clerk scribbles. "AGE: Teen." "Even if that's so," he says, shifting the clipboard to his other knee, "and frankly I find it hard to believe, miss, but even if that's so, at eighteen you're still um a minor. So even if you could meet the other requirements of Section 25951, I think it's likely you'll need parental consent to get a legal abortion."

At going on fifteen, Susan has read Rilke *auf deutsch* and mastered intermediate algebra. She can identify the bones in the human ear and would have won her debate against the Vietnam War if the Poli Sci teacher hadn't been a hawk. So this thing with the law clerk in the hip lawyer's office is weird. This monkey-knuckled, sausage-limbed beast Susan finds herself inside? This is *her* body. Doesn't her body belong to her? If *she* doesn't have a right to say what happens to her body, who does? *They're* not inside her skin. *She* is. She thought she had say-so in the United States of America. She thought she was supposed to be free.

Now suddenly she finds she doesn't control her own body. She doesn't have say-so about her own life. She isn't free.

God. Her head is fuzzy. Her stomach rolls around. She thinks of the demonstration of the milk churn in third grade, how they sloshed the milk till gobs of butter floated up. She takes out a Tums. Each morning she goes through a whole roll, sometimes two. Ruby agreed to sneak out of the house and come early to the hip lawyer's office so as not to disturb Chiron. Ruby is cool. She knows Susan doesn't want Chiron to know. It's embarrassing.

A trio of Gypsy Jokers whoops it up with the hip lawyer in his office. "So I sez to him I'll get mine up, off'cer, if you get yers up. Haw-haw-haw." A traffic violation or a midnight bust. Another groovy Saturday night, apparently. No one's gone to bed yet. The Gypsy Jokers are accompanied by Dirty David, a member of the Double Barrel Boogie Band's entourage. Dirty David is a small, gaunt man with a nimbus of brown curls that he tosses about and preens incessantly. At first, Dirty David ignored Susan like he'd never seen her before. Then she catches him giving her the up-and-down, what're-*you*-doing-here? written all over his face.

"Have you been to Planned Parenthood?" the law clerk asks, suppressing a yawn.

"They gave me the test." As if there were any doubt in her mind.

"Um. The test," the law clerk says. Too bad. He can't get rid of her that easily.

"What if she claims rape?" Ruby says sharply.

Susan shakes her head, but Ruby ignores her. Susan doesn't want to claim rape. She doesn't want to face Stan the Man—whom she hasn't seen since the Festival of Growing Things—and accuse him of rape. She just wants this nightmare to be over.

"If she claims um rape," the law clerk says, blushing, "the committee must notify the district attorney. She'll need to make out an affidavit attesting to the facts of the alleged rape, and the D.A. um would need to find probable cause that a rape occurred. If the D.A. doesn't find probable cause, the committee can't approve the abortion."

"Wait, wait," Ruby says. "You mean she hasn't pressed criminal charges, but she has to prove this probable cause business according to a criminal standard in order to get medical treatment?"

Susan smiles. She loves to see Ruby go at it.

The law clerk is unimpressed. "An unapproved abortion is not medical treatment, ma'am. An unapproved abortion is a crime in California."

"This is a crime," Ruby says.

"This is the law. Now, even if the D.A. finds probable cause, it's been our experience—and I admit it's scanty experience—that the committee may still require parental consent before an abortion is approved for a minor."

"The committee," Susan says. "What is the committee?"

The law clerk takes off his spectacles and rubs his eyes. "The committee consists of three licensed physicians on the medical staff of an accredited hospital. They must agree unanimously. The committee must find either a substantial risk that continuance of pregnancy would gravely impair the physical or um mental health of the mother or that the pregnancy resulted from rape or incest. We've um been through the rape angle. I don't suppose," the law clerk says gloomily, "there's an incest angle?"

"No incest angle," Susan whispers.

Ruby pulls herself up all her nearly six feet. "What does that mean: 'grave impairment of mental health'?"

The law clerk fumbles with the clipboard. He doesn't like Susan or Ruby. Susan isn't intimidating like Ruby, just pathetic. He doesn't want to think about any of this. He would much rather try to beat a drug bust. "Under Section 25952, the impairment of mental health means the infliction of mental illness to the extent that the woman is dangerous to herself or to the person or property of others or is in need of supervision or restraint. As a result of the pregnancy. The um would-be pregnancy. You know what I mean."

"Dangerous to property," Ruby muses.

"We'll shove this rap up their ass, no sweat," the hip lawyer says. The Gypsy Jokers clatter out of his office into the waiting room.

"How come you don't know more about this law and how we can get her a legal abortion?" Ruby says.

"The statute just passed," the law clerk says. "California now has one of the most progressive therapeutic abortion laws in the United States, ma'am."

"No, I'll tell you why," Ruby says. "You don't really want to go up against the committee, either."

"You want my advice, I think you should get parental consent," the law clerk says to Susan. "Can't you get parental consent?"

"I couldn't get parental consent to talk to my best friend on the phone," Susan says.

"We'll plead illegal search and seizure," the hip lawyer tells the Gypsy Jokers.

"We *was* holdin' five thous'n fuckin' hits," one of them says.

"Piece of cake," the hip lawyer says.

The Gypsy Jokers slap hands with the lawyer. Two of them stick out and lick each other's tongues. "Seizure!" says the third, rolling his pupils back in his eye sockets, making claws of his hands and shaking them violently. He seizes Susan, plunging his mouth onto her mouth.

Susan goes limp. Don't struggle with the kiss of a biker, flower child. That's what she's learned on the street. You struggle, he may haul off and whack you one. He tastes of beer and bile and pot smoke.

Ruby waits till he's through. Then she seizes Susan's elbow. "Let's get out of here, kid."

WEATHER REPORT

Beginning in the sixties, a team of geochemists headed by Professor Hans Oeschger of the University of Bern has commenced a project in which the team is perforating the ice sheets of Greenland, Antarctica, and the Alps. They extract and collect cores of ice, some up to six miles long. The team intends to locate within these ice-cores bubbles of ancient air. Eventually they will crack the ice surrounding the bubbles and, using the latest computer technology, analyze the air as it rushes out of the ancient bubble. In this way, they can examine the content of the Earth's air hundreds—even thousands or tens of thousands—of years ago. They will find that just before James Watt invented the steam engine, the amount of carbon dioxide in the Earth's air was two hundred eighty parts per million. In 1958, the amount had risen to three hundred fifteen parts per million. Between 1858 and 1958, eighty billion tons of carbon have been injected into the atmosphere. Since 1958, the amount has risen sharply, with another eighty billion tons of carbon expected in the atmosphere within the next thirty years.

o

"The new abortion law is one big hoax. It's a fraud on women," says Rowena Gurner of the Society for Humane Abortion in an interview with the *Barb*. The society plans to teach women dupes to get around the law. "We're going to instruct women in the arts of phony psychosis and false hemorrhage," said the indomitable Pat McGinnis, head of

the Abortion Society. She plans to help women prove to law
enforcement officers and physicians that they have been
raped or are psychologically in danger of their lives so that
they can get legal abortions.

—From "Abortionists Will Pile Hoax
on Hoax," *Berkeley Barb*, Vol. 4, No.
24, Issue 96 (June 16–22, 1967)

"Are you sure?" Ruby asks her for the hundredth time.

"I'm sure," she says for the hundredth time.

"You don't want to tell Stan?"

"No way!"

"Tell me true, Starbright," Ruby says, furrowing her brow. "You
can't be more than sixteen. Right, am I right?"

She nods. How did Chiron say it? She doesn't lie; she implies.

Sometimes Susan imagines having the baby. A little girl with big
brown eyes like hers. She will name her Jessica. Jessica will be beautiful
and brilliant, of course. Susan understands—she will never forget—what
it's like to be a child. She knows so many things she could teach Jessica.
Important things. Love and sex and death, sadness and happiness, finding yourself in life, finding meaning. She could be a good mom. She'll be
fifteen in September.

Mostly, though, she has the nightmare, and all her fantasies about
Jessica fade away. In the nightmare, the baby grows and grows, pushing
past her bowels, sliding around her stomach. The baby reaches up
through her throat. Its tiny wrist wriggles out of her mouth like a snake.
Its palm slaps against her tongue, making her gag. The baby's hand
seizes her teeth. Its fingers are surprisingly strong. Then she wakes,
heaving for breath. Her teeth are always sore, and she is always sick to
her stomach.

She cannot have a baby. She doesn't have a husband or even a man
who loves her. She has to finish high school. She was hoping to finish
college before she had a baby. She needs to figure out what she wants to
do with her life. She was hoping to have time to enjoy the world, too. She
has only begun to taste the sweetness of freedom.

Of course she wishes it hadn't happened like this. She wishes Stan
the Man loved her, that he were someone else, that she were someone
else, in another space and time. In another lifetime, that's an obsession

in the Haight-Ashbury. Other lifetimes, other worlds. Susan thinks it's possible. That we have lived before and will live again. In some other world, she is ten years older, in love with the father of her child, and pregnant on purpose.

But she is not in that world now.

She's sorry she fucked him. Ah, forget it. She's *not* sorry she fucked him. She's sorry she's pregnant.

"You really *really* sure?" Ruby asks her for the thousandth time.

"I'm really *really* sure," she tells Ruby for the thousandth time.

"Absolutely positively?"

"Absolutely positively."

"Don't you come crying to me later."

"I won't come crying."

"Don't you tell me you regret it, and why didn't I warn you. You remember I'm telling you this."

"I'll remember."

Ruby quietly backs the BMW from the garage. Chiron is still sleeping on the couch. He often sleeps till noon. Says he's got tachyonic lag; something like jet lag. They whisk across the Golden Gate Bridge. Fog cascades, thick and eerie. Ruby flicks on the dims. She is a superb driver, but Susan is edgy. Ruby's face is still as grim as granite.

Ruby is not an easy person to live with. Not that she's mean. Susan just hasn't figured out exactly what Ruby believes in, the full extent of her point of view, the parameters of her philosophy. She is different from anyone Susan has ever known. She flies into a rage if you question whether tincture of hemlock could really cure cancer, but with a laugh she forgives spaghetti sauce spilled on a good rug, an offense that would propel Susan's mother into shitting bricks. Ruby hates television. She never watches it. She calls television the devil box. But when Susan wanted to draw a life-size mural of the goddess Isis in chalk on one wall of the Mystic Eye, Ruby just said, "Put an ankh in her *left* hand and a sistrum in her *right* hand, you hear me?" With a squirmy vague memory of her hands—baby hands—slapped beet-red before she finally dropped an offending crayon, Susan drew a six-foot-tall goddess right on the whitewashed plaster.

What's really weird is that Ruby permits no grass or acid or speed in her house. No dope, period. As far as Susan can tell, Chi abides by the house rules. But then, for all his hip appearance, Chi is straight in the most peculiar ways. Susan tries to abide, too, but it's hard after the never-ending party at the Double Barrel house. She doesn't miss grass or acid so much, but dexies are tough to give up. That surge of clarity and power, plus she lost weight without even trying. Sometimes she's tempted to score some speed, but she doesn't want Ruby to kick her out, and she has to be careful with her dwindling cash. How is she ever going to get that hundred dollars back from Stan?

Ruby drinks a lot of wine. Susan sees this as an unseemly hypocrisy. Wine makes Ruby poetic, maudlin, or hostile, or a volatile combination of the three.

"Isn't grass a superior high?" Susan challenged her one night.

"Is it?" Those glinting black eyes.

"That's what everyone says."

"To hell with what everyone says. What do *you* think, Starbright?"

"Well. I don't like grass that much. It mixes up my thoughts. Plus, it makes me hungry and paranoid."

"Hungry and paranoid, uh-huh," Ruby said. She had half a bottle of chenin blanc in her at the time. "Otherwise, you'd be toking up in my bathroom, wouldn't you?"

"But I don't think grass is any worse than your wine. I don't think grass should be illegal."

"Neither do I. But it is. So don't you get *my* house busted."

"But," Susan tried again, "isn't LSD a superior high? Professor Zoom says alcohol produces an anesthetic state, whereas acid is an enlightenment."

"You took LSD?"

"They gave me some orange juice. I don't know what was in it."

"And was whatever it was an enlightenment for you?"

"I thought so. Yes!"

"Had a wonderful trip?"

"I had an amazing trip."

"Lucky you. Never wanted to come down?"

"I was very glad to come down. Besides," Susan admitted, "I've seen people freak out since then."

"Tell you what, kid," Ruby said. "Drugs is drugs, and that's that. I know drugs. I had a cousin. He was a beautiful cat, and I loved him. But Roi was a junkie, Starbright. I'm talking shoot-'em-up stuff. He was a handsome young cat in the prime of life, and it *killed* him."

"Everyone in the Haight-Ashbury is against junk, Ruby."

"Are they? I'm not so sure. I see a lot of folks taking that speed crap, and speed is just as bad as junk. Maybe worse."

Susan had cringed. But Ruby meant crystal, meth, stuff that freaks shot up. Not her little green-and-white dexies.

"I know drugs, kid," Ruby mused. "I've known drugs since you were knee-high to a grasshopper. I ate peyote when you were still wetting your pants. Made me sick as a dog."

"I *never* wet my pants."

"So don't you be giving me this shit about the superiority of this drug or that drug. Dig it, all drugs are fucked." With a flourish, Ruby had downed her glass. "Sweet Isis, and don't we love to get fucked."

God! Ruby loves to mess with Susan's head like this. Susan is often left with more questions than answers.

When things get bad, though—like at the hip lawyer's office— Ruby is a rock. She is . . . Susan struggles for what to call it. Well, she's like Nance, only she's practically as old as Susan's mother. Ruby is . . . a *friend*. She stands up for Susan against the whole world. Susan cannot remember the last time her father and mother stood up for her against the whole world. No, her father and mother always seem to stand *against* her. Two against one. Her parents, she realizes, do not act like friends.

"This is it, kid." Ruby pulls into the parking lot in San Rafael.

"Okay. I'm ready."

But as Susan sits in the general practitioner's sunny office, a shiver of fear cuts through her, though she's boiling hot in her mohair sweater, which she needed against San Francisco's chill. Church bells toll. Mid-morning worship services are commencing in the suburban hills of Marin County. Neighborhoods a lot like the ones she knows in Shaker Heights, only with palm trees mixed among the oaks.

The general practitioner gazes at a framed photograph on his desk. The photograph shows three children, seated in an opulent rose garden. The children hold pets in their laps, kittens and puppies. The youngest, a brown-haired toddler, cuddles a white rabbit nearly as big as she is.

"Yes, I'm still a rose gardener," he says. "I've been pruning roses since '52. Isn't that so, miss?"

Susan senses the tension. She's got antennae for covert emotions, like a termite seeking wood rot. She looks to Ruby for help, but Ruby is more remote than she was before.

"A public service, as I recall, Doc Clyde," Ruby says. "That's how you like to think of your work. For which you get paid very well."

"My technique has improved. But you must know that, miss, or you wouldn't be here."

"Uh-huh. Haven't killed anyone lately?"

"I've never killed anyone, miss. Well! Not counting the rosebuds."

"Cool. We're depending on you this morning, Doc Clyde."

"You've had the HCG test?" he says, glancing at Susan. He manages to check her out in about two seconds, then looks away. She has the clear impression she's keeping him from something. He is a lot like Daddy that way—keeping him from something, always keeping him from something more important. The general practitioner looks older than her father, a squashy bland man with salt-and-pepper hair combed straight back, probably a bald spot beneath the Brylcreem, a potbelly swelling out of his modest, soft frame.

She looks at Ruby. HCG? Ruby says, "The standard Planned Parenthood test. Of course."

"You still keeping cats?" he says to Ruby.

"Five now," she says.

"Ah, five cats." He says to Susan. "How about you? You like little animals?"

"Oh, I love animals!" Susan says. "Animals are high spiritual beings. I love life! I celebrate the infinite holiness of life!"

"Is that so, is that so?" he murmurs. "Then what do you suppose is growing inside you, miss? A crystal? A flower? A vegetable?"

She blushes fiercely. His condescending smile and his fancy office and his pretty family picture make her instantly furious. "I know what it is, doctor. It's a fertilized egg. Like what you get at the grocery store and fry for breakfast."

"Yeah, get off the pulpit, Doc Clyde," Ruby says. For the first time this morning, her eyes connect with Susan's, and Susan sees a coiled-up spring of darkness inside her. "You're a fine one to interrogate her."

"I'm merely asking a question," he says mildly.

"Uh-huh. Dig it: the circumstances aren't right for her to have this child. That's all you need to know. Right?"

"That's all I need to know." He stares at the photograph, wipes a speck of dust from the face of the brown-haired toddler. "HCG means human chorionic gonadotropin, miss. It's a hormone that's essential for enriching the endometrium so that the fetus is nourished from the mother. Production of HCG begins right after implantation of the egg. When they do the HCG test, they take your urine sample and inject it into the abdomens of lab animals. Female rabbits, to be exact. They kill the rabbits after two days and examine their ovaries. If HCG is present, the ovaries of the rabbits will have swelled and hemorrhaged. They take each rabbit by her ears and twist her little head back. Snap! Breaks her neck. Rabbits don't have very strong necks, you know. They sacrificed three rabbits just for you. Got to be sure. Got to be accurate. Do you have any idea, miss, how many female rabbits are killed for pregnancy tests each year?"

Susan swallows a Tums. Two tears fall out of the corner of each eye exactly at the same time.

"What's your price, Doc Clyde?" Ruby says in her sweet-as-poison voice.

"Five hundred bucks for a D and C."

"After that bedside story, make it two hundred."

"Three."

"Forget it."

"Two hundred fifty."

Ruby explodes. "Go to hell, you son of a bitch! I hope you crawl with guilt. I hope you can't sleep at night and lose all your hair and get raging ulcers. You owe me."

Susan stares, horrified.

"What do you want, miss?" the general practitioner says.

"I don't need you, but this young woman does, and her fate is in your hands. So this one is gonna be on you, Doc Clyde. And you better do the job right."

Ruby storms out of the general practitioner's office. Susan can see her stalking about the parking lot, pulling leaves off trees, kicking at the gravel.

The church bells toll.

"She gets crazy sometimes," Susan mumbles.

The general practitioner pulls out a fresh file folder. "You're not pregnant, are you, miss? No, *don't* answer. We both know you're not pregnant. Just a menstrual problem. Because if you *were* pregnant, what we're going to do here would be illegal. You're married, of course, or over twenty-one? No, *don't* answer. Don't tell me your name. Don't tell me anything. I don't want to know anything about you."

"My daddy is a dentist," she whispers. She isn't sure why she says it, but, when she dares to glance again at his face, she knows exactly why she said it.

"Are you allergic to penicillin?" he says gruffly. His face is purple, stricken with compunction. "Good. Go in there, take off your clothes. Put on the hospital gown. I'm just a rose gardener, miss. I've been pruning roses since '52."

Because she's so early, Susan only has to have a menstrual extraction. A sipping of her uterus without cervical dilation or anesthesia. A slipping-out of the lining and the troublesome egg. It hurts when the general practitioner withdraws the suction from the syringe. A short, sharp pain, not a whole lot worse than a bad cramp. Afterward, she doesn't bleed much. She gets up on her feet. The general practitioner tells her to come back in three weeks for a checkup.

She will never see him again.

Ruby drives her back over the bridge. A tear slides down her face.

"You okay, kid?" Ruby is brusque. It's amazing what she's just done for Susan. They have known each other, Susan realizes, for a week or so. "He did the job, and no funny stuff?"

"I'm sorry." Another tear.

Ruby guns the BMW between two Volkswagen vans painted with swirls and flowers. "Damn it, you said you were sure."

"I'm sorry," Susan says, "about the female rabbits."

It's past noon by the time they get back to the Mystic Eye. Haight Street is just beginning to stir. The Sunday crowd wakes late.

Ruby's cats saunter down from the bedroom to greet them, tiny lionesses and tigers looking for their lunch. Ruby spoils them shamelessly. She feeds them roast turkey and leg of lamb, cottage cheese and chips of cheddar, brown rice with corn seasoned with catnip and alfalfa, pumpkin-oatmeal cookies for dessert.

The Summer of Love is like that. A fellow who calls himself Red walks an Irish setter named Man. A Beat friend of Ruby's named Feather carries Penelope P. Parrot on her shoulder. A tattooed girl known only as Tangerine wraps a python she calls Sir Galahad around her neck. And a boy who seems too young for the street even to Susan sits shivering without a shirt, clad only in filthy oversized jeans, next to a fat, piebald guinea pig known to everyone as God. God reclines in a laundry basket lined with threadbare towels. The boy nibbles on the tips of carrots God leaves behind.

Ruby fusses over her cats so much sometimes Susan gets jealous. When did Mom and Daddy fuss over her like that? And when did her parents realize she had gone for good? Did they reconstruct their memory of Nance's postcard from the ashes and conclude she had fled to San Francisco? Will they hire someone? That would be like Daddy. He'd pay for a detective to look for her, but he wouldn't come looking himself. She's always looking for the Man, for anyone following her. It's weird *and* gross. Her very own personal spy show, added to the paranoia all over the Haight-Ashbury, shrouding the Summer of Love like the fog.

Or do her parents give a damn?

Ruby goes to the kitchen. Susan drifts after her. Ruby seems more wound up after the ordeal with Doc Clyde than she is. Ruby takes a sweet Sonoma sherry from her good liquor shelf. Susan aches, but she feels dreamy. No more Section 25951. No more law clerks. No more nightmares. She's free!

Susan goes to the window.

Chiron bends over the garden he's digging in Ruby's backyard. He says dirt is clean, unlike doorknobs and bongs passed around. He says a lot of strange things, the five-hundred-year wonder. Oh, excuse me. He's really only twenty-one. She likes to shuck him. "Are you *really* five hundred years old?" she asks. "Are you living forward or backward in time?" He hates that. He sulks. Susan has seen and heard so many things in the Haight-Ashbury, she doesn't believe Chiron's tachyporter rap for one second. So he's got a maser. Ruby says they'll probably see masers at Macy's next year. It's just some foreign high-tech junk that hasn't hit American stores yet. And so he's got a stone-thing that pricked when he pressed it to her chest. The so-called scanner is like one of those jokes you get in a magic shop, a whoopee cushion or a joy buzzer that goes *bzt* when you shake someone's hand. She won't let him near her with that thing again. He doesn't have a time machine, not even a tricorder like the crew on *Star Trek*.

In the yard below, he's taken his shirt off, which is weird since he usually acts like a prude, cuffs and shirt collar buttoned up tight. The oddity makes her pause and watch. The skin on his lean, muscular back shines like wet ivory. Rainbows ripple off him like the wing of a mayfly.

For a moment, he is a tall, slim, pearlescent being under the sun. Strange; almost alien. As though he senses her presence, he suddenly looks up. His face breaks out in a big smile, and he waves.

Chiron Cat's Eye in Draco. He isn't mean or crude or pushy. Maybe she's being unfair. She was so sick with the pregnancy, she has barely said two words to him since she came to Ruby's. After her crazy time at the Double Barrel house, she has slept whole days away in her little room.

He *is* beautiful, in his way. From some rich European family, that's Ruby's theory. People who own property in the Sausalito hills. Susan blinks, trying to dispel the hallucination of rainbows rippling around him. She waves back.

He's always watching her.

When she lived with Stan the Man—nine days or ten?—she was always trying to catch his eye. On the first miraculous day, she'd look at him and there he'd be, the mountain man, smiling at her. But his smile got harder and harder to find.

Now Chiron watches her. Every time she turns around, she finds his eyes. But there is nothing flattering or appealing or comforting about his surveillance. He watches her like you would watch a fly crawling up the wall. It's annoying, distressing. He sneaks past her room. He watches her doing dishes in the kitchen. He tries to follow her when she goes out. He's always asking dumb questions like he thinks she wants to tell him the story of her life. Maybe other people want to tell him the story of their lives. Not Susan. If she could, she would *forget* the story of her life.

Could Chiron be a detective sent by her father?

Ruby chats on the phone, checking up on business downstairs. "How's the drawer doing, Morgana?" she says. Susan thinks it's amazing how Ruby runs her own shop. Susan's mother doesn't do anything. Mom is like a servant to her father.

Susan climbs the stairs to the sitting room on the third floor. She loves her room. The skylight lets in the sunset and the first star of the evening, to which she sings the Starbright song every night. She talked Ruby into letting her take the funky old black-and-white TV from the storeroom in the garage. They have a deal. Ruby must never hear the voices on the devil box when she is trying to sleep, and Susan may only watch *Star Trek, Time Tunnel, The Twilight Zone,* or *Voyage to the Bottom of the Sea.*

A knock on the door. Ruby pokes in her head. She's got the bottle of sherry, two cordial glasses. "I got this out for you. Want a nip?"

"Okay." Susan does not believe in drinking alcohol, but she takes the glass and sips.

"Any pain?"

"A little here." She rubs her abdomen below her belly button. The sherry rockets straight to her head. "A lot here." She rubs her chest over her heart.

"Forget Doc Clyde's nasty story," Ruby says. "I hear they're working on a new pregnancy test that's faster and more accurate and doesn't rely on killing female rabbits." She slugs back her glass, refills it to the brim, and gulps half.

"Yeah." Another sip for courage. "What did you mean, Ruby? About Doc Clyde owing you?"

Ruby tops off her glass and sighs. "Oh hell, kid. I knew Doc Clyde when he didn't have that potbelly. We're talking fifteen years ago. Mediocre GP, fresh out of med school, greedy and stupid. He had this cousin, a nice Beat lady. Black sheep of the family, right? She hung around North Beach. She put out the word he did D and Cs, clean and with decent dope. I had friends who went. Mostly he did okay. A couple of times, though, in his early days, he screwed up. I mean, he never did give a shit, he was just doing it for easy money. He got scared, and he got a couple of his patients scared. So scared they didn't go to the hospital like they should have. Things got ugly." She downs her glass, pours a third. "I don't forgive him for that."

"I'm sorry."

"Oh, he's okay now. He's the only local I know who's a real doctor and will do minors. Otherwise, you'd have to go to Switzerland or Brazil." Ruby reaches over, tucks a stray lock of hair behind Susan's ear. "I wouldn't have taken you to him if he wasn't cool. You know that, don't you, kid?"

"I know, Ruby." Not used to sherry at all. Head spinning. Susan turns on the TV. At Ruby's skeptical look, she says, "I can get a San Jose station that reruns *Star Trek* in the afternoon. Will you watch it with me? Just one time?"

The episode is "Mudd's Women," in which a con man, Harry Mudd, wants to trade three stunning women, Ruth Bonaventure, Magda Kovas, and Eve McHuron, to Rigel XII miners in exchange for dilithium crystals. The miners are crude and rough-looking. They are not exactly prizes. Why would the women settle for these men? It turns out the women have a secret. They keep popping a pill called the Venus drug, which is highly illegal and which instantly turns them from hideous crones into beautiful women.

"I'll be damned," Ruby muses. "Pimps on *Star Trek*. I had no idea."

But Susan is appalled. She cannot believe she ever watched the episode in her parents' den and went to bed without a second thought. "Oh, Ruby," she cries. "I want a Venus drug."

"What?"

"I could never look like Eve or Ruth or Magda. Or Twiggy. I could never look like Twiggy. I couldn't get my thighs that thin if I took dexies for a whole year."

"Why would you want to look like Twiggy?"

"Doesn't everyone? Isn't she the ideal of beauty everyone adores?"

Ruby guffaws. "You girls from the burbs are nuts! You are from another planet! You know what Twiggy looks like to me? To me, Twiggy looks like a junkie. Or a speed freak. Or both. You want to look like a junkie speed freak, kid?"

"I'd do anything." Sadness spills from a well of pain. *You're not good enough, you're ugly, no matter what you do.* Where does it come from? "I'd take anything if it made me beautiful. I'd take the Venus drug in a second. I don't care if it's illegal. Maybe Stan would have loved me."

Ruby slaps the TV off as the trailer music is playing. She slides next to Susan, reaches over, and rubs her shoulders. "Listen, Starbright. Stan loves no one. And you're all wrong about the Venus drug. At the end, Eve realizes she's beautiful *without* it. The Venus drug itself is an illusion. Eve really *is* beautiful. Think about it. Right, am I right?"

Susan thinks about it. "But Captain Kirk still doesn't love her. He goes off without her."

"Captain Kirk is a swinger. He will never *ever* settle down."

"Captain Kirk is not a swinger. He's dedicated to the *Enterprise*!"

"That's what all the space-age swingers say. I've heard *that* before. Warping around galaxies, bumping into girlfriends on exotic planets. Lovin' 'em and leavin' 'em. Uh-huh."

"God." Susan thinks about *that*. Captain Kirk—like Stan the Man? No, no, no. Captain Kirk is a hero. He's the *captain*.

"And so are you, Starbright. You really are beautiful."

"I'm ugly, that's what my mother thinks. She made me eat hard-boiled eggs for ten days. She said my breasts are getting too fat."

Ruby shifts again, sitting on the mattress in front of her. She gives Susan the up-and-down. "Do *you* think your breasts are too fat?"

Susan notices Ruby's eyes are almond-shaped and slanted above her cheekbones. "Don't you? I ate nothing but dexies for ten days, and they still won't go away."

"You have very nice breasts," Ruby says and cups her hand around Susan's left breast. "Talk to any woman who hasn't got any, and I bet she would love to have these breasts. I bet Twiggy would kill to have breasts this nice."

"My mother *looks* at them."

"You want to see fat breasts, look at this." Ruby takes Susan's hand and cups it over her breast. And she's right. Ruby is stacked.

"But you're *beautiful*, Ruby."

"Beautiful, huh! I'm half Cherokee, half Haitian black, and half Southern cream. You want to know how hard it is for a girl to feel she's beautiful in America when her skin isn't white and her hair is kinky?"

"Daddy's a Lithuanian Jew, and Mom's a Yugoslav Catholic. And I'm American. I'm nothing."

"You are angel food cake, kid. If *I* can be beautiful, so can you. What else about you is ugly?"

"My hair. My mother hates my hair. It's not blond and it's not straight like in *Life* magazine."

Ruby strokes Susan's hair. "Starbright's hair is golden brown like wheat, wet sand, or new-baked bread. And wavy, with little curls. Like a mountain stream washing down or those high fine clouds they call mare's tails or the curlicue leaves on Queen Anne's lace. Why would you think your hair is ugly, little one?"

"Oh, Ruby," Susan whispers. She notices how lush Ruby's lips are.

Ruby slides Susan's overnight bag over, digs in. "Let's have a look. Uh-huh. White lipstick. White eyeshadow. You want to look like a vampire *and* a junkie speed freak?"

"It's mod," Susan says, depressed. The tubes and cakes look like ground-up termites, chalk sludge.

"You have rose-colored lips and big dark eyes. Throw it out! Out, out, out!"

They take turns tossing white lipstick, hair straightener, and blue eyeliner across the room and into the wastebasket.

"Out, out, out! Throw it out!"

They shriek with laughter. They tumble together on the mattress.

Ruby brushes back Susan's hair. "You're beautiful, Starbright. Don't let *anybody* ever tell you different."

Overcome, Susan kisses her, quick and hard. "Oh, Ruby," she says, "I love you."

Ruby seizes her ear, pulls her down. She kisses her back. A little slower. Much deeper. Susan tingles all over. She tips her face for more.

But Ruby pulls up. She smiles, a strange light in her eyes. "Ah, kid," she whispers, shaking her head. She sits and pulls Susan, so she's sitting up, too. Then she pushes Susan away.

Susan is still laughing. This is fun! Ruby is wonderful. Ruby's so beautiful. She never wants to stop laughing and hugging her on the mattress. Body heat, oh the comfort of arms. "You're my best friend in the whole world," Susan cries. "Nobody's ever been as good to me, except maybe Penny Lane. But that was when we were little."

Ruby stands on the mattress, walks unsteadily to the door, and sits, propping her back against the wall.

Susan stops laughing. Not sure what's happened. Not sure how to read Ruby's face. "Ruby? Is something wrong? Did I do something wrong?"

She pours herself more sherry and shakes her head. "Nothing's wrong, kid. Everything's fine. You're just fine."

"I *do* love you, Ruby. You're the best!"

"I'm the best, and don't I know it." But her smile is wistful.

They sit in the sun for a while, sipping sherry.

"Listen, Starbright, you want to know a secret? Beauty is a fine thing. A beautiful woman is a joy. Not just to men, but to women, too. But don't go looking for your beauty in magazines or on that damn devil box."

Susan looks at the wastebasket brimming with mod cosmetics.

Ruby nods. "You don't have to reject the beauty thing. But beauty isn't everything. Sweet Isis, you got to go beyond all that, stop worrying about it, and get on to the important business of running your *life*. Before anything else, you got to use that brain of yours, kid. Doesn't your school in the burbs ever tell you that?"

Susan shakes her head. She thinks of Bernie MacKenna and Allen Weisberg and the way she has come to view school after she came to the Haight-Ashbury. Has Bernie MacKenna or Allen Weisberg ever cried over a mirror? Does everyone try to make them feel worthless? They would probably think she's stupid, feeling worthless because she doesn't look like Mudd's women or Twiggy.

The Summer of Love is like that. Things that seemed stupid become important, and important things become stupid.

"You know something?" Susan says. "My school doesn't tell me anything except that I'm in the ninety-eighth percentile. I just feel weird there. So I shut up. Or I don't make the numbers line up. It's not important. I'm just a girl."

Ruby sucks in her breath. That dangerous, coiled-up look pops into her black eyes. "Stop it, Starbright!" she practically yells. "You are important!"

Shock ripples down Susan's back. Who ever told her she was important before?

No one.

Ruby springs to her feet and paces. "Doesn't your pa tell you about these things?"

"Oh, he's always yelling at me. Nothing I ever do is right. He criticizes everything. It's always my fault."

"What about your ma?"

"I told you. She *looks* at me. Like I'm all wrong."

And Ruby looks at her. Not with long, disapproving scrutiny. Not like her mother at all. Ruby looks her up and down and all around, and Ruby sighs.

"Kid, I'll tell you another secret. Something no one will ever tell you. Not your pa, not your school, not your friends. You know what I think about your ma? It's the green-eyed monster. The Evil Eye. Your mother is jealous of you."

Susan stares, a familiar anxiety chilling her heart. "Jealous! But why?"

"Well." Ruby thinks. "When a woman has a child, she gets attention. A lot of attention. She's the star of the show. And the child is her possession. Look what *I* made, look what *I've* done. But you're not a little girl anymore, Starbright. You're not your ma's little dress-up doll. You're your own person. You're a young woman. Now *you're* the star of the show. *You* got things to do. Maybe your ma's having trouble accepting that. She's got to bow out."

"But why does she put me down?"

"Because you're young. Just because you're young." Ruby winks. *"And* smart. *And* beautiful."

That terrible, nameless thing her mother holds against her, no matter how hard she tries? The cold look she never could place?

The sherry wears off. A dull ache throbs in her belly.

"Ruby," Susan says. "It hurts."

8

Ball and Chain

 Like a ghost tapping on his shoulder, an impulse strikes him.
Chiron turns in time to see her at the kitchen window. At last!
They're back at last! He waves, overcome with relief. She
hesitates, then waves, too. He flings the shovel down, shakes sweat from
his face, brushes dirt from his hands on his jeans. He dashes up the
stairs to the kitchen.

But they're gone again. He hears Ruby's voice upstairs, Starbright
murmuring. A laugh. Is that the television? Impossible, Ruby can't stand
TV, never watches it. Then soaring music, a reedy soprano. The opening
tune to the program Starbright loves. Ruby's watching *Star Trek*?

He calms the pounding in his chest. Damn them, stealing out before he woke! But she's safe. The girl is safely tucked upstairs.

Is Starbright the girl in the CBS News holoid? There's some resemblance. But the match isn't perfect. Her hair doesn't look right. Her face doesn't look right. She is heavier than the girl in the holoid, her breasts are bigger. Her style of clothing, her purse, even her posture; not even close. Since the CBS News Special was filmed sometime before the program aired on August 22, any discrepancy in such a small time frame can't be easily overlooked. It's like an optical illusion. Or peering in an atomic microscope. The more closely he studies her, the less sure he becomes.

Yet if she's the Axis, he must verify and document her authenticity as soon as possible. Verification ought to be easy. One day, he crept behind her while she was dreamily washing dishes in the kitchen, clapped his hands as loud as he could, and shouted, "Hey! Susan!"

She had dropped a plate and shouted back, "Shit!" She threw a cupful of soapsuds in his face. "God, Chiron! Don't scare me like that!"

"You're Susan, right?"

"I'm Starbright!"

Who could have known she would flat-out refuse to tell him her real name? Starbright. A typical juvenile street name. Completely untraceable, as the Archivists suspected.

Ruby is no help, either. "Who *is* Starbright?" He could get away with asking the question twice before she gave him an evil look. "Who wants to know?" was Ruby's first answer. "Get that jar of kava kava down for me," was her second. "How about that accent," he tried again. "She says her vowels like she's got a tongue depressor in her mouth." That made Ruby laugh, at least. "She from the Midwest? Like Cleveland, some place like that?" "From the moon, sonny." He doesn't press her. Ruby distrusts him enough. He doesn't want to give her a reason to kick him out of 555 Clayton.

The girl is positively compulsive. With single-minded vigilance, she keeps her purse by her side, sleeps with it, takes it into the bathroom with her and locks the door. "Why is Starbright so paranoid about her purse?" he asked Ruby. "Once bit, twice shy," Ruby snapped. "Maybe someone ripped her off." She locks her overnight bag in the sitting room. One morning, he easily picked the lock, searched the bag and found only a poorly made fake ID that gave her name as "Barbara Nelson," her age as eighteen, and her residence as Berkeley. Starbright cannot possibly be eighteen, and the blurry photo looks less like her than the girl in the holoid. The scanner picked up half a fingerprint on the doorknob. Then the door banged downstairs and he raced out, barely getting through Ruby's bedroom and down the stairs before Ruby stalked into the living room. "Seen a ghost, man from Mars?" she asked.

The holoid field displays the smudged half-print next to the crisp, inked fingerprints that the Axis left in the Archives. The knuckletop cannot compute a positive identification. Neither can he, studying the whorls of black against the smudges of gray suspended in the slice of blue light.

It makes him want to smash the knuckletop against the wall. Makes him want to smash his *hand* through the wall.

Watch her. That's the best he can do. And *that's* anything but easy. This morning, for instance. Where did they go? Then there's Starbright herself. She's a *girl*. She spends hours in the upstairs bathroom with the door locked. She is painfully self-conscious. She ignores him as though he has grievously offended her. She is sensitive about his surveillance, no matter how casual he tries to be. "What are you looking at?" she demands. "Are you following me?" Exactly. He's not any happier about it than she is.

He keeps searching the Haight-Ashbury for a better match. But till he finds and verifies the Axis, he decides he must, at a minimum, guarantee the safety of this girl till midnight, September 4, 1967.

After midnight, September 4, 1967, the hot dim spot of the previous three months clarified. From jumpy errata and widespread holes, the probabilities collapsed into a timeline documented with data as thick and rich as butter-cream. There were no missing lyrics. Hardcopy survived, the videos didn't blur, holoids could be viewed from start to finish. And after midnight, September 4, 1967, there was evidence that a young woman who is the Axis was living with her parents in Shaker Heights, Ohio. Her father held a party at his dental office that got written up in the Cleveland *Plain Dealer*. The Axis registered for the ninth grade at 2:30 P.M., EST, on September 12. She celebrated her fifteenth birthday on September 24 with a gala dinner for fifteen at Stouffer's Restaurant in downtown Cleveland. Her father gave her a laboratory-grade microscope for her birthday. Her mother gave her a necklace of amethyst and silver beads. The father wrote a check; the mother charged it to the May Company.

But where did the Axis spend that summer? The Archives contained no clue. The family spent a lazy time at home, apparently, settling in at the house they bought in 1966, a ten-year-old Tudor that needed roof work. The Archives contained her chubby-faced seventh-grade photograph from the year before and a photograph of her at eighteen, a mature young woman posing with her three-year-old daughter. No incidents of note took place in Shaker Heights that summer. The Axis made no mark.

Minors didn't carry scannable IDs or have retinal log-ons to family databases. Minors weren't fitted with preliminary telelinks. Minors didn't take EM-Trans all over the world or use the comm. Minors her age didn't even carry a driver's license, since they weren't allowed to drive. And minors didn't possess their own credits in 1967. The Axis didn't acquire her own Visa card till 1978.

The Summer of Love for the girl who is the Axis was a classic dim spot. How hot? It was hard to say. When the Archivists finally targeted her, the hole had burned.

There is one prime piece of evidence, however, that gives him a reasonable probability justifying his watch over this girl. He got a good scan as they sat on the sidewalk in front of the Mystic Eye. The one time he got close enough to press the scanner to Starbright's chest, he got a full subdermal probe yielding a basic readout. Sound heart, good lungs, other functions fine. And the double blip. The distinct double blip echoing off her belly. He almost shouted for joy.

The Axis was pregnant when she registered for the ninth grade on September 12, 1967. The parents were compelled to submit this fact to the record. After a somewhat long pregnancy typical of the breeding patterns of her matrilineal ancestors, the Axis delivered a healthy, six-pound, five-ounce, brown-eyed daughter in the spring of 1968. She named her Jessica.

If Starbright is the Axis, then Starbright must be pregnant when Chiron translates-transmits from September 4, 1967, to September 4, 2467.

And she is, Chi rejoices. She is.

He goes back down to the garden, picks up the shovel, thrusts it deep into the rocky soil in Ruby's small backyard. The physical toil abates some of his frustration. Cabbages go here, carrots there, lettuce and onions in alternate rows. Gardening has always been a meditation for him, though he'd only worked his family's gardens and orchards under their private dome. A pair of butterflies called painted ladies flutter round a clump of thistles.

"You're not cultivating this land?" he had asked Ruby one day, unable to keep the scandalized tone from his voice.

"Don't get snooty with me, sonny. I haven't got time," Ruby had huffed. "Besides, I'm renting."

"That doesn't matter," he said. "What a resource. What a shame. What a waste!"

When he woke the next morning, a long-handled shovel and a bag of live earth lay on the floor next to the couch.

He flings away the rocky dirt. Cucumbers will work, perhaps tomatoes. They can grow right under this gracious sun. Not sure what trouble she'll have with slugs and rabbits, but Ruby shouldn't get deer in the middle of San Francisco. Deer wandered here a century ago, and deer will wander here again. But not in 1967. In two decades, the greenhouse age will begin with a scorching summer. In three decades, a backyard garden in the middle of the city will be an astonishing luxury. The technopolistic plutocracy will dump pollutants into the atmosphere for another century on the grounds that compliance with limits is too expensive. Golden Gate Park will wither in a killing drought. The Haight-Ashbury and the Avenues will burn to the ground in the catastrophic fire of 2129 because water supplies fail. In two centuries, at the height of the brown ages, when the stripped sky is at its worst, when salt water contaminates inland freshwater systems and the sea drowns coasts and deltas, the city of San Francisco will erect a massive dike to stave off the Pacific Ocean. One of the first domes will be installed over this area. The dome will be privately funded and owned by Eurasian cosmicists who will refuse public admission to New Golden Gate Preserve. One hundred fifty billion IBUs, adjusted for True Value, will be spent annually on ecological emergencies, stopgaps, and restorations. And still a million children will die of radiation syndrome in California cities alone. The cosmicist movement, together with the World Ecology Taskforce and the International Bank, will labor to reclaim flooded lowlands and experiment with desalinization of salt plains. Detoxification of agricultural lands, sky-seeding, desert-seeding, and development of a radiation vaccine will be vigorously pursued. Two multinational chemical conglomerates will make restitution to the WET trust fund of fifteen billion IBUs for ecological crimes, but ten other defendants at the World Court will be acquitted by a hung jury. One juror will hang himself the day after the acquittal. And, at last, lethal radiation will be cleansed from the soil, ocean krill will thrive, chlorofluorocarbons in the stratosphere will finally decompose. Trees will bud in this yard again. Flowers will bloom and birds will cheer in New Golden Gate Preserve. DNA reclamationists will work feverishly to restore lost species. Raccoons and rabbits will wander fearlessly in this place, for no people but cosmicist caretakers and their private guests will be allowed. Painted ladies will flutter over thistles, and white-tailed deer will nibble at grass along the brick foundations of vanished Haight Street and around the marble columns of the Portals of the Past.

That's when deer come to this yard again. Only then.

Chiron pauses, leans on the shovel. His head spins. Who is the ghost? These people, who will die centuries before he's born? The awful future that will unfold on this tiny spot of land? Or him?

After a frustrating week of testing his stash of contraband holoids, he finally found another disk he could access on the knuckletop. The tiny red message popped into the blue field:

"Date: 07-07-1967. You may insert Disk 2 now."

"Go, H drive," he said and, in the dead of night while everyone slept, the holoid proceeded to boggle his mind for nearly an hour with details of the future of this street. And at midnight, in the sidebar, the red message again:

"Date: 07-08-1967. You may insert Disk 3 now."

Oh, every child knew the history of the world for the past two and a half millennia. Prehistory, the ancient civilizations, the rise of Christianity, medieval times, European exploration and colonization, and so on. The rise of America, the military-industrial economy, the military episodes, the precipitous rise of technology and the technopolistic plutocracy, the criminalization of hyperindustrial society. The greenhouse age, the population crisis, the adjustments age, the really bad population crisis. The emergence of devolts—an entire mutant population descended from drug addicts, pollution victims, and the poor. The brown ages, the terrible population crisis. Establishment, at last, of the World Population Control Agency, the bitter conflicts and terrorism, the sex police, the Generation-Skipping Law, and so on and so on. A professional telelinker could jack into a telespace program that crunched humanity's history into under thirty minutes, hypertime.

But they never showed him the files on Disks 2 and 3. They never showed him the far changes that flowed from this place and time in such excruciating detail. They never showed him what happened to the street. They never showed him the human faces.

He knew the Luxon Institute for Superluminal Applications believed t-porters should limit their exposure to data required to accomplish the object of the project. He was happy to comply. He had his own life, his personal Now. He didn't *want* to know more. He had authorized access to the file about Leo Gorgon's novel and the exotic HIP merchant, for example, because she was known to shelter pregnant runaways and thus was a probable contact for the Axis. But a t-porter shouldn't become intimate with the target period. A t-porter shouldn't know *too* much about the past.

Why?

Because of the Grandfather Principle and the mandate of nonintervention. For a t-porter might be tempted to affect the past. The temptation was overwhelming, as Chiron now knew. And after the Save Betty Project of '66, the temptation must be resisted, and resisted with uncompromising vigor.

Then why? Why did his skipmother slip him the stash cube?

He was grateful at first, if skeptical. But his gratitude turned sour when he realized she had prioritized and date-coded the holoids, dribbling access to him at random like electronic hide-and-seek. What did Ariel Herbert know? What secret did she keep from everyone?

His sourness soon turned to anger after viewing Disks 2 and 3. The scheming, manipulative witch. "Consider impact before you consider benefit, my son." Mega, prime. The cosmicist injunction resonates with new meaning now. For after viewing the holoids, he is struck from all sides by powerful tides of feeling: rage, despair, deep sadness. They never showed him the faces. Never showed him the future of the street itself.

And loneliness. How he longs to share this awful knowledge with someone. He can't even talk to K-T.

Who is the real ghost?

Temptation. Look how far he's fallen into temptation. Stupid, telling everyone his personal Now is in their future. Insisting upon it like a frustrated child, carving a heart in the sidewalk with his maser. His *maser*. Didn't want to be called a narc. Didn't want to get jerked around. Couldn't think of a decent lie. Prime, Chiron, fucking prime.

He's got two consolations, anyway.

First, spacetime didn't blow up in his face upon violating a Tenet of the Grandfather Principle. The LISA techs never said what really happened when you violated a Tenet. He ponders this, late at night. The collapse of a probability consistent with the timeline wouldn't necessarily destroy this spacetime, would it? And consistent probabilities were allowed in tachyportation to the past, or the Archivists could never get away with injecting a bit of new probability. Even Ariel Herbert would have to admit that. Kick the sand on the beach. Go ahead, do it.

And second, Ruby and Starbright don't believe him. The funny thing is, their disbelief bothers the hell out of him. Their disbelief offends his pride, challenges his self-worth. Back off from it, Chi, he tells himself, don't be a colossal idiot twice. But there it is and won't go away. He resents them for not believing him.

Chiron works in the garden for an hour while Ruby and the girl watch their TV program upstairs. What a luxury, stripped to the waist under the open sky, digging in this virgin earth. The afternoon is as delightfully cool as the wheat fields of Siberia, which Chi visited when he was fifteen.

Sweat beads through his Block, tickling as it trickles down his face. He changed the patch on his thigh yesterday. He's got fifty more patches to last him through the SOL Project. He shouldn't touch his forehead. Don't disturb the Block's fine microderm. Dog-fashion, he shakes his head and arms vigorously, sending off a fine spray. The Block screens UV radiation a hundred times more powerful than this sunshine.

"Say, brother." The voice intrudes, jolting him.

"What do you want?" Chiron says, standing up.

"I want to destroy this inhuman, parasitical capitalist system, brother."

Leo Gorgon leans over the fence. He watches Chiron with interest. As usual, Gorgon's interest is calculating and sly. Chi has watched Gorgon, too. Gorgon is one of those people during the Summer of Love who is more alert, intelligent, and streetwise—not to mention ten years older—than most young people in the Haight-Ashbury. Gorgon turns his edge to his advantage, turns it like you would sharpen a blade. Gorgon and his rap. The ideology of failure is what Gorgon calls it. Money is dead, it's free because it's yours. Gorgon and his circle are trained actors. They are hostile to just about everyone not in their circle. Some deal drugs. Others collect monthly allowances from family trust funds. Chiron has seen the destitute teenage runaways gather around Gorgon, listening raptly.

"So," Gorgon says. "Workin' for the bitch-goddess of Love again?"

"For the joy of it," Chiron says.

"She payin'?"

"Work is its own reward. To give is best."

Gorgon laughs. "You're a Digger, brother."

"I'd like to be."

"At least till you tire of the adventure of poverty an' go back home to your rich daddy's house, eh?" Gorgon says.

Chi wields the shovel.

"Where's Miss Ruby?"

"She's upstairs, watching *Star Trek* with Starbright."

Gorgon nods. He taps a cigarette out of a hardpack, plays it through his fingers. "Say, Bub."

"My name is Chiron, Leo." He rests again from his task.

"Yeah. Say, Bub, I got this truck out front, an' she's got a flat tire." He glances up at the back deck. "To give is best, that's a moral imperative. Yeah. You know I gave out free food to the people for months till the heat shut us down? I know Miss Ruby has got herself a jack somewhere in that storeroom in her garage. You wanna go an' get it for me, Bub?"

Chiron lays the shovel down, strolls over to the fence. He follows Gorgon's glance up to the deck, the kitchen door. An easy mark. From upstairs with the TV on, Ruby would never hear someone breaking in back there. "Why don't you ring the bell and ask her," he says.

Gorgon laughs and slaps his knee. "I'm shuckin' you, man! Just shuckin' you! Ain't no flat tire. Oh, but I got me a truck, all right. An' she's parked at the curb. An' she's ready to roll. She's just waitin' for a young dude like you to take her out on the road. Pick up some chick, do your thing. Why should you work on this beautiful day?"

"Someone's got to do it."

"Nah. No, you don't, brother."

"If *I* don't do it," Chiron says, "who will?"

"This is the Great Society," Gorgon says. "This society is rollin' in its own shit. This is the Society of Surplus, brother. If you don't *want* to work, you shouldn't *have* to work. Especially not for a capitalist pig. What do you say?" He dangles the ignition key.

Chiron takes the key. "I say the Society of Surplus is a shuck. A shuck now, and a shuck later."

"What the fuck?"

"You'll see the Society of Surplus disappear before your very eyes, Leo." Chiron palms the key, manages to pluck Gorgon's unlit cigarette right from his lip, and palms that, too. Ruby is a prime teacher. "In three decades, people will wonder how anyone could have ever talked about a Society of Surplus. The Society of Surplus will disappear, and the bitch of it is, the rich will get much richer, and the poor much poorer. Oh, in time society will have plenty again. In time, people who call themselves cosmicists will finally be wise enough to know that the rich cannot get so rich that the poor starve. And that a surplus is not a surplus, but a gift not to be squandered."

Gorgon turns scarlet. "Gimme my key, you ugly lyin' punk."

Chiron produces the key from Gorgon's left ear, the cigarette from his right ear.

"Fuckin' asshole!" Gorgon stomps back to his truck.

The painted ladies rise from their thistle and flutter away.

GOSSIP, INNUENDO & ALL THE NEWS THAT FITS

That's where we start, man. Now, do it. Now, do it, shit, now, go ahead, drop out now. Go ahead, do it, do it. You doin' what you want to? Uh-huh? *Sure* it's what you want to do? Do what you want to do, right? Can't do what you want to do? Uh-oh. Now things get very real. Go do what you want to do. You tell me you're free, you tell me you're free, man. Yeah. Come on, we're talking about freedom. You tell

me what you can do tomorrow. You tell me what you can do,
what you can get away with.

And then we find it's necessary to bail each other out.

—From interview with Peter Berg in
Voices of the Love Generation, by
Leonard Wolf (Little, Brown and
Company, 1968)

But Chi isn't working for free. He thrusts the shovel. The shovel
stops short. *Clang.* A rock. He's receiving Ruby's charity, her good will,
the benefits of the bounty from her years of hard work.

No, he never thought much of the free-thieves, and he doesn't think
much of Leo Gorgon. This t-port has been no adventure of poverty. It's
been a harrowing nightmare from which he cannot wake.

But Chi is the heir to a cosmicist dynasty and a domed estate in
Sausalito. He has never been poor. And he knows that Gorgon was, is,
and will be. Seven years from now, Gorgon will die in a New York City
subway from a heroin overdose.

And there is nothing Chi can do.

He lets himself into the kitchen, stalks into the living room. Their voices
still murmur upstairs. The third floor is their domain, their little queen-
dom. He literally has to break in to get up there. He starts to go up the
stairs. He hears them laughing. Throwing things! He hears a thump, a
clatter, more laughter. Murmuring. Then silence, thick as a cloud of
jasmine incense.

Women.

Strategy, Chi.

He wishes he could take Starbright away and lock her up somewhere. A cabin in Mendocino, say, or a lodge at Big Sur. Lock her up for
two months, set her loose on September 4. Keep her out of trouble,
protect the fetus, shield them both from disease, the strange drugs and
stranger people lurking about the Haight-Ashbury. It would make things
simple and neat. He could go back to the scene and keep looking for a
closer match. If she turns out not to be the Axis, all he's got is one angry
teenage girl and a kidnapping rap he can step across five centuries to
beat. Ah, temptation.

No. He can't do it, and forget Tenet Three. He can't do it because then she could not possibly be the transcendent smiling girl in the CBS News holoid, could she?

Strategy. Try again. Try some tenderness? His approach of nonintervention has gotten him exactly nowhere. She doesn't even tell him when she's going out. Should he make a pass? He wouldn't touch her, of course. He grimaces. She's not a Neanderthal, no, and not a devolt. But all that hair, sending off a musty odor of fur and dust. Like an animal. She cannot compare to Venus Rising. A rad-vacc lass like Venus Rising smells so fresh and pure. He gets hard, just thinking of her sweet smell.

It wouldn't be anything real. He won't pretend he loves her. Nothing like that. Just a strategy. He can do it. The lasses at school adore him.

After all, it's the Summer of Love. Everyone's in love.

He goes to the half-bath off the living room, hangs his shirt, searches for supplies in his jacket. He surveys himself in the mirror with new eyes. The nutribeads are supposed to give him his required calories. He eats two or three beads a day. But he's bone-thin on nothing but nutribeads, bellyache, and a hit of neurobics when he can't stand the throbbing in his gut any longer. Stomach sunk beneath too-prominent ribs, cheeks gaunt. Rock 'n' roll bones. That's all right, but he could tweak it up a bit. He wraps a filter over the water faucet and fills the washbasin. He sets the maser on red, runs the beam around and through the filtered water. He takes out his scope, scoops a sample on the drinking glass, and peers. Not too bad, no wriggling tails. His cleanser tab yields an odorless, slimy lather. He washes his face and hands and arms, shakes himself dry, then presses a new patch of Block on his thigh. Weird tingling all over his skin, like a million ants scurrying. The Block reactivates the microderm. He makes a decent part down his scalp, combs the hair implants with more care. The SOL Project gave him eyebrows and lashes, too. He surveys these with interest for the first time. He takes out the toothbrush Ruby left for him. He's never used this primitive tool on his teeth since he's got resiliency tweaks and mouth swathe. But the tiny bristles comb the unruly eyebrows quite neatly. He finds a vial of musk oil and dabs some on his wrists. Live dangerously.

He goes to the living room and paces, waiting for them to come down. Still silence, a murmuring, upstairs.

When she first came to Ruby's, the girl stayed in her room for days, resting and watching television. Chiron took those days for himself and journeyed about the city, collecting data for the Archives. San Francisco in 1967 is achingly quaint, barely hinting at the glittering megalopolis that will climb skyward one day. No Embarcadero Eight soars over the shell of Old Downtown. No Cloud View Maze, no Bank of New Hong Kong, no dome over New Golden Gate Preserve. And none of the grassy meadows along the shores, the tree-lined walkways, the malls perched atop bridges, while the EM-Trans and private transport sped through tubes far underground.

This genteel skyline is still humbly shaped more by natural hills and valleys than by humanity's monuments. The largest building, at only fifty-two stories, is the Bank of America on California Street. He has trouble with the ugly concrete, the stench of petroleum-fueled cars. Market Street is torn up to build Bay Area Rapid Transit, the great-great-great-grandfather of the EM-Trans and its net of vacuum tunnels.

On one of his free days, Chi agreed to take a stack of *Berkeley Barb*s to sell at Ghirardelli Square for a scruffy boy who hung around the Mystic Eye. Extraordinary to hold the fresh paper, smell the ink of this vanished resource. He was as thrilled as if he held a new roll of papyrus with hieroglyphs proclaiming daily news about King Tut. He hopped aboard a cable car and took a harrowing, jolting ride down to the wharf. A longhaired gnomish fellow with silver rings on every finger and toe and an unbuttoned shirt revealing a furry chest struck up a wistful conversation in an odd flat, brassy accent. By the end of the ride, the gnomish fellow, who said his name was "Hawwass," was calling Chi "Hansum" and blinking up at him with dazed, dark eyes.

Chi hopped off outside the Buena Vista Bar, jogged across the waterfront, and left the gnomish fellow behind. Newly renovated, Ghirardelli Square was wonderful to behold, fresh brick and cement. The square was an alternate tachyportation site, since it had survived till Chiron's Now and was fitted with a shuttle in the middle of these very same bricks.

Quaint, full of simple joy. And innocent. Yes, that's what he thought. Can't stop thinking. Damn these people for their selfish stupidity, their ravenous self-indulgence. Yet they're ignorant. They have no notion of the hard path ahead.

He paces, impatient. One minute more, and then he'll go upstairs and roust Ruby and the girl out of her room.

The latest *Berkeley Barb* sits on Ruby's coffee table. He takes out a prophylak, punches his fingers into it, leafs through the issue. Mega. If the payload could take the mass, he'd love to translate-transmit a *Barb* with him. A gift for his skipfather.

Leafs and looks and suddenly, on the front page, he sees an item he's never seen before. Data that didn't survive, information lost to the Archives. A box in the lower left corner of a page:

PLEASE CALL—NO STRINGS. The parents of the following have contacted the HIP Switchboard instead of going to the police. If you want to pick up on vibrations from your parents, we have more information. We will not contact your parents unless you give the OK.

Joan Gallagher, Shelly Ballinger, Beatrice Clar, Vicky Martin, Susan May Kearney, Louise Thompson, Cathie Mc-Clellan, Patty Lee Corbin, Ann Thrift, Donna Wells, Joni Dawson, Tereze Miller, Susan Stein, Carlos or Charles Piera, Bobby Meyers, Russ Wendel, Allen Weisberg, Mark Zaentz.

With trembling hands, he tears through the rest of the *Barb*. And there—*there*—in the middle of classified ads, he finds what he is looking for:

GUY WITH LONG RED HAIR who was selling *BARB*s and rode Powell St. cable car. Contact Harris, 14 Charles St., N.Y.C. I love you, handsome.

Ripples of shock shoot up his spine, like when he jacked into telespace for the first time.

The Axis really is here, he thinks.

And then, *So am I.*

Cosmic Mind, it *is* right! The Chief Archivist *was* right. I'm here, I have *always* been here. Centuries before I was born, I was *here*! The ouroboros bites its tail, and I have closed a loop across space and time.

And it's true, he realizes: there is a Cosmic Mind. And we—humanity—form a partnership with the Universal Intelligence. A cocreatorship. For we have witnessed, *and* we have made it so. Time is no linear march of days, but One Day. Always new, always coming forth into Being.

He clatters up the stairs to Ruby's bedroom. He knocks on the door and barges in before they can answer.

Ruby tosses clothes from her closet. Silky shirts with high collars, cotton sarongs in purples and reds, velvet pants. "Don't wear these much anymore either," she says. Two cats bat at the fringe of an embroidered shawl, while three cats lounge on Ruby's bed, gold and blue eyes blinking.

"Where did you go?" he demands.

"Out," Ruby says. "This always was too short on me." She holds up a violet suede skirt. "Should fit you just fine."

"You shouldn't go out without telling me, Starbright," he says.

"Get a load of him," Ruby says.

Half-buttoned into a turquoise dress, Starbright turns and glares at him. "I can go anywhere I want to without telling you, Chiron."

He starts at the sight of her.

No white lipstick. No white stuff around her eyes. No blue lacquered lines. Instead, her cheeks are flushed, her lips stained plum. Her eyes are dark. Her bumpy mod hairstyle is combed out. The bangs that hung halfway over her face are brushed away. The dress nips her waist, the long skirt sweeps over her hips. She looks as though she's shed a layer of flesh.

"What have you done to yourself?" he says, turning the probabilities over in his head.

She shrugs and finishes buttoning the dress.

"What do you think?" Ruby says.

He hesitates. At school, he'd come back with a snide remark. The narcissism of these wasteful people, obsessed with the latest fashion while their world goes down a toxic sewer. White lips, red lips, straight hair, curly hair—who gives a shit? But his retort is stifled by the sudden image of Venus Rising, her dazzling body paint meticulously applied to the curves of her sleek skull.

"Starbright has become beautiful, that's all," Ruby laughs. "Right, am I right?"

There is a new camaraderie between these females that makes him uneasy. Not because women are close, which is common among his peers. Venus Rising has female companions. But because they are excluding him from something, and he cannot begin to guess what.

"Do you have a new name, too?" he asks.

"I'm Starbright," she says, with a toss of her head.

"Come on, man from Mars," Ruby says. "Don't look so grumpy. You want to go out with us? We're going to have some fun."

He starts to smile. Is it just his hope, or has Starbright, in a morning, become a closer match to the girl in the CBS News holoid? Is it possible? After all, he's in a hot dim spot. He has always been here, during the Summer of Love. And so has the Axis, wherever she is.

"What's the occasion?" he asks.

Ruby says, "Today is Goddess Day. Celebrate!"

There is no dissuading them, so they all step out. At least Ruby invited him. Otherwise, he'd have to figure out how to follow them. Ruby makes him wear a wide-brimmed gaucho hat, an irony, since mass-produced beef has been illegal for over a century.

They catch the 24 Divisadero bus northbound to Geary Boulevard and stroll four blocks east to a handsome old auditorium called the Fillmore. A bluesman, Bo Diddley, whom Ruby wants to see, and a psychedelic band, Quicksilver Messenger Service, whom Starbright wants to see, are playing there tonight. Chiron has never heard of these musicians. Two obscure notes lost somewhere in the Archives.

They take a place at the back of the colorful queue.

A young man in a yellow poncho and two braids over each ear drifts among the people, murmuring, "Grass, hash, acid, speed?"

A swarthy man bangs out of a side door. His dark hair is close-cut. A five o'clock shadow shades his chin. He wears a V-neck sweater over a white button-down shirt. He looks like someone's square uncle. He carries a broom and begins to sweep the sidewalk. He carefully sweeps from the start of the queue to the end, litter and dust flying into the gutter. He glances up from time to time, forms silent words with his lips. He appears to be counting the number of people in the crowd. No one pays him any attention. Just the janitor.

"That's Bill Graham," Ruby whispers to Starbright.

"Grass, hash, acid, speed?" the yellow poncho murmurs.

Suddenly two men push past Chiron, shove Ruby out of the way, and seize Starbright's elbows on either side. A squat man with a scarred face and a stovepipe hat set over kinky black hair. A tough skinny guy in purple tie-dye, his black eyes darting back and forth like a reptile watching for insects.

"That's the chick," says the Lizard.

"Hey!" Starbright cries.

Chiron tries to elbow past the man in the stovepipe hat, but Stovepipe's got shoulders like a football player.

"You fuckin' owe us, you stupid chick," Stovepipe says. "We're talkin' seven grand."

"Buzz off, scuzz," Ruby says, but her eyes are wide and her lips are pale.

"You shut up," the Lizard says.

"I don't know what you're talking about," Starbright says.

"Dealin' rat poison as dragon's blood acid, chick," Stovepipe says. "That's what I'm fuckin' talkin' about."

"There must be some mistake," Chiron says. He's got his hand on the maser. "This girl isn't a dealer."

"It's the Man!" Ruby cries.

A black-and-white police car, top light spinning, speeds up to the curb.

Stovepipe and the Lizard vanish in the crowd.

A rusty van with a burned-out tail light slows in front of the police car, bears over to the curb, too. The cop wearily pulls himself from his car. The van's driver hops out, a fellow in a fringed jacket and a feathered hat who jogs with a sprightly step to meet the cop. "Evening, officer," he says with a dazzling smile. "What's the hassle?"

"Could we come back here another night?" Starbright says. Her teeth are chattering.

"You bet," Ruby says. "We'll catch the show another time."

Chi takes Starbright's hand. Her fingers are freezing. He closes his hand around hers. He doesn't even use a prophylak.

Haight is packed. Chiron has never seen the street this insane. Tourists gawk, point cameras, lean on their horns. Crew cut military guys catcall "I love you" and leer at Hells Angels, who show them what a leer really looks like. Gangs of guys in neckties tow gals in beehives, and beer-bellies stare at hoodies lounging on their choppers. Heads and teeny-boppers sit in lotus positions three deep on the sidewalk. The mouse magician promenades.

Several heads run up to the cars with bits of broken mirror and turn the mirrors toward the tourists so that they're looking at their own reflections. Other heads stroll in front of the cars with Brownie cameras and proceed to snap photographs of the occupants. Still others leap on car bumpers, making the cars rock from side to side, or jump onto car hoods and sprint across them.

Chiron walks between Ruby and Starbright. He doesn't like it. The mood borders on hysteria. "We should get out of here."

But the two women are enjoying the scene.

Ruby leans across him and says to the girl, "It's pathetic, isn't it, kid? We're living in the United States of America in *1967*, and we *still* don't have our freedom."

"What freedom do you mean, Ruby?" Chiron asks.

Starbright nods and glances about at all the people. "Maybe I'll see Penny Lane."

"It burns me up," Ruby says. "We've got to challenge the law, show the people how bogus it is."

"What law?" he says.

Half a block up, a pail is thrust from a second-story window and turned over. Red paint splatters down. The crowd roars. People start to push and shove.

Chiron stands with the women on the street curb in front of the Psychedelic Shop, waiting for the light to change. A Day-Glo van and two battered junkers stop dead in the middle of the intersection. Westbound, eastbound, north and south, traffic is gridlocked. Horns blare. Two heads jump on the bumpers of a junker, making the car rock wildly. People cheer and boo.

Two policemen in a squad car pull up to the stalled van.

"The cops are coming!" someone yells.

"Get off the street," a cop says through his loudspeaker. "Get off the street. *Now.* Move onto the sidewalk. *Now.*"

Suddenly sirens drown every sound. Twenty black-and-white police cars materialize from all directions, skidding up onto the sidewalks, going the wrong way down alleys and lanes, jostling past the stalled vehicles. Four paddy wagons follow. Police in riot gear leap out. There must be fifty of them, swinging billy clubs.

A dog is barking.

Someone throws a bottle. It smashes on the concrete, spewing glass on a woman in a fringed buckskin dress.

"Get off the street. *Now.*"

Chiron hooks his elbows around the women's arms and drags them back from the curb. They wrestle against the crowd, till their backs are up against the shop front.

A girl in a long black cape steps back from the crowd. She stands next to Ruby, face hidden by a peaked black hood.

Whistles shriek, people scream. A cop smashes a blond man on the side of his head. The man falls to the street, blood staining his hair.

"Police brutality!" someone yells. "Police fascism!"

The dog is barking frantically.

A woman screams, "Revolution, revolution! Get the cops! Get the cops!"

Suddenly three policemen charge through the wall of people toward Chi and the women, swinging their clubs.

A young man flees before the police, cringing and stumbling. The barking dog leaps next to him. The young man's got a leash wrapped round his hand. He stumbles again. The leash tangles round his ankle. The dog, a black-and-white sheepdog, snarls and yelps as a policeman batters the club across the young man's head and shoulders. The young man yells.

A tall woman in filthy rags steps back from the crowd. Her head is crowned with a 'fro of writhing gray curls. A filmy gray veil hangs over her face. The gray beggar presses herself against the shop front next to Starbright.

One policeman seizes the young man's head in an armlock, while the other smashes the club across his kidneys. The young man drops the leash. His dog leaps at the second policeman. The third policeman raises his arms straight up and slams his club down on top of the dog's skull.

Chiron hears a *crack*.

The dog shrieks.

Starbright screams.

The policeman slams the club again. The dog drops to the sidewalk. The policeman bashes the club across the dog's face, again and again, smashing its eyes, its skull. Blood pours through the dog's fur.

The woman screams, "Revolution! Revolution! Get the cops! Get the cops!"

The dog-killer turns. He sprints after the woman, swinging his club. Unarmed, she tries to run. He aims for her face. "Get the cops!" she screams. *Crack.* The club makes contact with her jaw and teeth. He swings again. *Crack.* Blood streams from her mouth. She sobs. The dog-killer jerks her arm behind her back and hustles her into a paddy wagon.

The gray beggar turns toward Starbright. All Chi can see through the veil is two glowing eyes. Not glowing; how can blackness glow? Darkness, as though the light is being sucked into a vacuum, darkness throbbing with a terrible force.

Starbright clutches his arm, tears streaming. Suddenly she sees the girl in the black cape standing next to Ruby.

"It's the girl with my face!" she screams.

The black hood parts for an instant, and Chi glimpses her. Starbright? The same—but not the same. In an instant, fragments of the girl's face shift, as though a manic strobe light illuminates patches and features, showing sickening, dizzying grimaces. She blinks. Her eyes are tunnels of darkness.

The gray beggar groans, a sound like a rusty door hinge. With great effort, she extends her swaddled arm before them. A band of freezing cold confronts Chi's chest. The rags lift and swirl, though there is no breeze. The girl in the black cape brandishes a knobby staff. The staff shifts and twists like a living thing struggling against invisible bonds. The girl lifts the staff as if it weighs a hundred pounds and struggles to swing it toward Starbright.

For a moment Chi can't move. The sheer pull of the demons' anti-matter feels like falling from a great height.

The three cops feverishly push the crowd back against the Psychedelic Shop. The dog-killer is flushed. His eyes glitter. He charges toward them.

Chiron pulls out the maser. He flicks to blue, runs the beam in front of the gray beggar. No smoke, but a faint blue line like a crack in glass glows for an instant. The beggar falls back. Chi flicks to green, bears the beam down. The tip of the girl's staff bows to the ground.

He shouldn't, but he flicks to yellow and aims at the dog-killer's chest. The dog-killer staggers, as though tackled by an invisible half-back. The chest of his uniform shreds, smoking. He roars with rage and pain.

The crowd screams, "Revolution! Revolution! Get the cops!"

The dog-killer gets to his feet. Ten policemen charge at everyone in front of the Psychedelic Shop.

"Go, go, go!" Chiron lunges, pulling Starbright and Ruby with him. He punches people out of their way. He loses his gaucho hat. They shove through the crowd, heading back to Clayton Street.

Suddenly the girl in the black cape steps out of a telephone pole. Fingers trailing, she extracts herself from the dark wood. Her cape ripples in jagged peaks and strange, curving folds. Black sparks crackle all around her.

The gray beggar kneels beside a fire hydrant. She tugs at her rags, pulling them from the fire hydrant's metal rim. She slowly rises, turning her veiled face to and fro like a radar dish seeking a target. A freezing wind gusts.

"Come on, come on, come on!"

They run.

Blood stains Chiron's boot.

Strawberry
Fields Forever

 Ruby stops dead in her tracks, seizing Chiron by his elbow. He whirls back, dragging Starbright with him.

"What are you *doing*?" she yells. "Where are you *going*?"

"Back to the house," he says, panting. He struggles with her, pulling her down the sidewalk. "We've got to get inside!"

She brakes her heels. "And let those women, those . . . ghouls, *see* us? Find out where we *live*?"

"They won't *see* us. They don't *need* to see us."

"You're crazy!"

"It doesn't matter, Ruby!"

"You bet your ass it matters! We've got to scatter, throw them off our tracks!"

"Listen to me!" The young cat is full of fire, flushed scarlet. Never seen him so wound up, but somehow he isn't panicked like she is. "The Prime Probability has collapsed." He glances all around him, at her, then long and hard at the kid. "The timeline is preserved, spacetime is conserved. But we should get off the street. If we're not in danger, the probabilities are stable. The demons can't come through till there's a hole."

This makes no sense whatsoever. Still, she sees a demented logic in his words. "Are you sure?"

Then he does something so bizarre that he frightens her more than the ghouls. What did he call them? The demons. He untangles his hand from Starbright's hand, raises his right fist to his lips, and whispers, "Katie." For a moment, she thinks he's speaking into a microphone in his ring, contacting a confederate hidden nearby. Like he's a spy, a spy from the Man, of course, come to infiltrate the hip community just like she feared. But then he raises his left hand, cupping his palm behind the ring. A slice of blue light winks on! It isn't a *surface* like looking at a television screen, but an *object* the size and shape of a pulp magazine made entirely of sky-blue light. The slice of sky floats in midair! He whispers, "Katie, calc oh seven, oh nine, sixty-seven," and a long string of tiny numbers and letters dances in the light. He catches her astonished look and pivots a quarter-turn so the back of his hand faces her. Though the slice of blue light seemed bigger than his hand, now she can't see it at all from this angle.

A beat, and he says, "I'm sure."

The whole incident takes less than a minute, but it seems like forever. One of those weird moments when time slows down and down, and you *see.*

Ruby hadn't believed Chi's street-corner lunacy about being from the future, but she forgave him for his wild imagination. She believes in imagination, the wilder, the better. And now? Now she can believe he's from *some*where, and it isn't a hop down the road from her hometown of Marin City.

"The demons are gone," he says. "See for yourself."

She looks, and he's right. Or at least they no longer crouch on the corner of Clayton and Haight, those weird sisters, those hags of doom, spewing mortal fear in their path. For that's what she felt, standing next to the girl in the black cape: arctic air and the intimation that she was going to die. They've vanished into thin air, sure as a C-note on a bad bet.

"You in one piece, kid?" she asks.

Starbright nods. Her face is streaked with tears, but she's no longer weeping. She is taut with anger and urgency. If there were any trace of the darling daughter from the burbs left in her, it is gone for good. "They attacked us," she says in a strangled voice. "They killed an innocent living being."

They; she doesn't mean the demons.

"We've got to get inside, out of sight," Chi insists. "Out of danger."

Ruby is shaking. She never shook before, not one time. Not when the fuzz stuck a flashlight in her face in the doorway of her North Beach pad, not when Roi went on the yen and came after her. Not even when she heard about Doc Clyde and his rose gardening fifteen years ago.

Sweet Isis, blood on Haight Street, right in front of her eyes. How can anyone hold onto a New Explanation when the street is choked with hate and garbage and blood? Tourists, the ugly face of the mob. Not the mob of kids searching for something or the media gang hunting for their sensational story. The squares with their sleazy, mindless, heedless perversity, blocking her street with their junk cars, toting cameras along with their ignorance and their violent energy. As though the hip community is a peep show and the scene a sticky floor on which they can throw their wads of bubble gum and cigarette butts.

Yet it's the hip who get hurt. It's the hip who get beat up and sprayed with broken glass. It's a hip dog who gets bludgeoned to death while he's out for a walk in his own neighborhood.

Before she can figure what to do, Leo Gorgon darts from the alley beside the house two doors down. He takes her by her shoulders. Dark circles shadow his eyes. "Ruby. You were seen in front of the Psych Shop, man. The pigs." He catches his breath, exchanging a poisonous look with Chiron. "The pigs are lookin' for you."

"We didn't do anything!" Starbright says.

"They're lookin' for witnesses," Gorgon says. "They'll take you down to the station. Detain you all night, bad-trip you. Try to get a statement on record that'll disqualify you later. A cover-their-ass gig. You want to go down to the cop shop, Starbright? How about you, Beelzebub?"

"She can't go," Chiron says. "I would go if I could, but I can't."

"Got somethin' to hide, Bub?" Gorgon says.

"Don't we all," Chi spits back.

"I'll go," Ruby says, though dread gathers in her lungs, making it hard to breathe. She's no hero. She has done everything she can to avoid run-ins with the police, stayed free of politics and radical entanglements, not to mention dope. But she won't stand for an atrocity like this, coming down at her own doorstep. "I'll call my lawyer, and I'll go."

"Don't do it, Ruby," Gorgon says. "They don't want a brutality rap. It's bad press. They mean business." He hustles all three of them up against the doorway of the Mystic Eye. "Anyway, why should you? We've had enough of this harassment. Cahill has been on the people's ass for goin' on two years. Right?"

"That's right," Ruby says.

"Well, the Summer of Love is gonna change all that. Ruby, everyone's talkin' on the street. We're movin' fast. We're gonna get a legal action committee together an' go after the pigs. Morley, the mouthpiece over on Franklin Street, he says he wants the gig. Me an' Cowboy made the scene right after you left. We saw the blood, an' we heard the story, but the dog was gone. Everyone was freakin' out, an' nobody saw who took the corpse. The dog's owner got arrested for incitin' to riot. They took him away in a paddy wagon! So we want you fresh as the morning dew. Now, don't hassle with me on this one, Ruby. No statements to the Man till we get our act together, all right?"

She nods.

"Let's split town for the night, all of us. Even you, Bub." Gorgon's vicious look again, but Chiron nods. "People say they're sweepin' the streets for me, too. Pigs are claimin' me an' Cowboy were organizin' a riot, some bullshit like that."

"*Did* you set up that scene?" Ruby says.

"No," he says. She meets Gorgon's eyes and sees, for a rare moment, the sadness in him. "That was some mighty bad theater." For all of his shucks and disingenuous ways, she believes him. "Can you take three riders in that kraut car of yours?" he says. "My truck's got a flat." Sure enough, Gorgon's rickety truck is parked down the block, tilting down to the curb.

"You bet," Ruby says. "I gassed her up this morning."

"Let's do it."

The summer sun sinks into the treetops, one of those gusty amber twilights that seems to take forever. The new moon buds into an arc slim as a cat claw. They walk cautiously through the shadowed alley next to 555 Clayton back to the garage. Chi and Gorgon tug at the garage door.

"You stay here," Ruby says. "Starbright, come with me. We'll just be a minute."

"Get me some Jim Beam, if you've got it," Gorgon calls to her.

She and the kid go to the back gate, find it swinging open.

"Sweet Isis," Ruby moans. "Now what?"

Heart knocking, she climbs the deck stairs. The kid trails after her. But the kitchen door is locked up tight, double-bolted like she told Starbright to do before they left. They go inside. Nothing amiss. Upstairs on her bed, the Siamese cats are curled in a mound of gray and brown fur. The white cats perch on the windowsill, staring at the stirring dusk. Ruby rechecks all the windows and doors, leaves fresh water and food for the cats. No Jim Beam, but she's got a fifth of Wild Turkey in the pantry. Her stomach is rumbling. None of them has had dinner. She packs a loaf of fresh bread, a chunk of sharp New York cheddar, six apples, a couple of carob-almond bars. As an afterthought, she takes two bottles of Napa burgundy, plus a jar of Salvatore Espresso, the only instant coffee that's worthy of human consumption and drinkable black. Paper cups, plastic utensils, a Swiss Army knife, and a corkscrew, that should do it. She goes to the half-bath, gets blankets and pillows, finds a sweater in the coat closet for her and a hand-loomed shawl for Starbright.

Ah, Starbright.

What a tangle, a bittersweet surprise, her feelings about Starbright. Damn near seduced a lily-white teenager from the burbs. Does that make her any different from Stan the Man?

She loves men, of course she loves men, always has, always will. Then what is this fierce rush of tenderness for the kid? Would you seduce a little sister? Or *is* there an eroticism propelling her feeling that she doesn't want to admit? What do you do when someone tells you she loves you and kisses you?

It's the Summer of Love. You kiss her back.

It's crazy, she and the kid. They are ten thousand worlds apart.

Oh, how everyone would love to know when she slipped off her clothes, how they kissed. What ecstasies she gave her. How everyone would love to kneel, outraged and breathless, outside the door, an eye glued to the keyhole.

But it didn't happen that way. Ruby cannot abandon herself so easily. She hates exploitation, and the comparison to Stan the Man leaps instantly to mind. Exploitation is contrary to everything she believes in. You nurture innocence, you respect it. You don't destroy it or mock it or stave off your boredom with it or play with it like a toy, thinking only of your own pleasure. For all their morality-mongering, exploitation is an Establishment game.

Starbright bustles about the dark kitchen, packing their provisions in a canvas bag. "Look at this!" She stoops, picks up a scrap of paper from the floor, and hands it to Ruby.

A crude scrawl.

SHUCKING THE REVOLUTION. WE WILL NOT TOLERATE PEOPLE (HIP OR STRAIGHT) TRANSFORMING OUR TRIP INTO CASH. BE ADVISED.

Ruby exhales, sits for a minute on the kitchen chair. "Some celebration."

"You're not hurting anyone, Ruby," Starbright whispers. She stands behind her, lightly places her hands on Ruby's shoulders. Her touch is electric. "You're offering things and ideas people can't find anywhere else. The Mystic Eye is wonderful. I *love* the Mystic Eye. Who would do this?"

"There are crazy tribes in the Haight-Ashbury these days. You know that, kid. The Diggers, the dealers, the acid mystics, the cultists, the Catholic nuns, the musicians, the politicos, the Panthers, the Krishna devotees, the anarchists, the crazies, the speed freaks, the hip elite, the hoodies, the bikers, even the flower children. They've all got a different agenda. No wonder the Man can get away with beating us up. Or maybe this is from the Man. Who knows."

"Revolution. That's the second time I've heard that word today."

"Uh-huh. You know what we used to say? We used to say the revolution is in your mind. First and foremost, above everything else, you've got to change your mind. 'The personal revolution,' that's what we called it."

"They trying to scare us?"

"Are you scared?"

"Yes!"

"Then their love letter worked, didn't it."

"God. Don't we have enough to be scared of?"

"More than enough." Ruby stands, gets the shawl, and wraps it around Starbright's shoulders. "Let's you and me not be scared anymore. Come on."

She meticulously relocks the back door. She shudders as they cross the yard. Chiron's half-dug garden is turned open like a grave. The demon, the gray beggar woman with a 'fro like hers. It was her, the strange intruder in her yard a few weeks ago. Ruby has no doubt at all. Chilled to the bone, she stands for a moment before she closes and locks the gate.

Her bitter nostalgia about the way things were, her paranoia about the Man, her resentment at being excluded from the Council for a Summer of Love. It all boils up inside her like an astringent herbal brew, a strange brew with the sting of nettle. Boils up and clarifies till she extracts an essence of where she stands. A New Explanation, yes. There *is* a New Explanation, got to be one, somewhere, in some space and time. In the Haight-Ashbury during the Summer of Love? She never thought so. But these are strange and wondrous days, and somehow they've become a catalyst. The New Explanation still hovers, like a half-glimpsed mirage, above a street stained with blood.

The two men wait silently inside the dark garage.

"Where to, Leo?" Ruby says.

"How 'bout Morning Star Ranch?" Gorgon says. "I could use some country air. We can hide out there for the night."

"We're gone," Ruby says.

Gorgon knocks back two fingers of Wild Turkey before they're across the Golden Gate Bridge and slumps in the front seat, snoring. Starbright huddles in one corner of the back seat. Chiron doesn't seem much happier in the other.

Ruby speeds into the dark, northbound. She knows the way. She drove to Morning Star Ranch in May to see a sculptor friend who retreated there to finish his latest masterpiece: a man of car-chrome, with a red garden hose dangling between his shiny legs, clutching a woman made of hammered steel. The drive takes an hour or so. After the first volley of Gorgon's snores, she says, "Tell me true, Chiron Cat's Eye in Draco. What *were* those women? You used another one of your words." She shivers. "You called them demons."

Silence, the thrumming of her wheels. At last he says, "Devolved

Entities Manifested from the Other Now. Yes. That's what we call them: demons." He starts to rub his eyes, then stops. He takes out one of his astringent wipes, meticulously cleans his hands and fingers, rolls the wipe into a ball, and deposits it in his jacket pocket.

"Devolved entities, uh-huh. Tell us about it."

And the elegant lad tells his strange tale.

One day last spring, Chiron and his family were visiting his cousin's penthouse condominium at the peak of Cloud View Maze. Cloud View Maze was a brand-new, self-sufficient, completely recyclable mega complex on top of the Oakland Hills. A breathtaking avonite and steelyn minicity of condos, business and commercial spaces, swimming pools, tennis courts, clubs, restaurants, its own police force and fire protection, fishponds, vegetable and grain gardens, fruit arbors, its own bicycle Path and generators. Sky-seeding was kicking in. The last of the chlorofluorocarbons lofted into the atmosphere before the world ban had decomposed to less than four percent. Radiation levels were dropping. In a grand ceremony, dubbed "Let the Sun Shine In," they'd taken the UV shields down and installed picture windows. On a clear day, without the shields, they could see the parched peaks of the Sierras from his cousin's roof deck. And it was a clear day. Clear as good glass. Mega and prime.

Telespace was up and running. Guests could jack in for a hyperminute on his cousin's workstation if they felt like a quick recreational link or had business to attend to. The pro linkers queued up around the workstation, itching for a cool, clean hit of telespace. Jack up, link in, space out. Cool, tool. You could practically hear the hum of computer-generated reality, feel the vast inner space teeming with a billion billion megabytes of pure intelligence.

Family and friends were celebrating. Everyone was popping neurobics, drinking new wine. A feast of fresh food was laid out. Chiron's skipmother had brought a dozen trout from the family pond at their domed estate in the Sausalito hills. There hadn't been much to celebrate for so long. Mars terraformation was on time and under budget. Population statistics were encouraging. Tachyportation projects and other ME3 experiments were going well at the Luxon Institute for Superluminal Applications. The LISA techs were enthusiastic. A comm pundit had christened these days the New Renaissance.

His cousin was showing off. She'd brought in the first harvest from her roof garden. Guests had brought most of the feast, but there she was, proud as a new skipparent, with her microcorn and cherry tomatoes. And flowers. Practically everyone there was a cosmicist. Her orchids sent them into ecstasies. Someone began projecting hyperpoetry onto the wall holoid.

Down below, people were strolling in and out of the Oakland–San Francisco megalopolis. Along the walkways, through the gardens and meadows planted over the ancient traffic corridors, across the Bay Bridge Mall. The EM-Trans was humming far underground in the vacuum tunnels. Tube traffic in deeper tunnels was slow and go. The skyways were thick with jetcopters, sky shuttles, whirligigs. Ferries docked and departed from the ports or streamed across the sparkling blue bay. Chi could see the gleaming spires of the city, the dome over New Golden Gate Preserve. A debate raged over whether to dismantle the dome, since atmospheric restoration was going so well. Many lobbied to let it be.

Then two things happened so fast that it seemed they occurred at the same time:

> telespace crashed, and
>> a cloud appeared in the western horizon.

"A crash!" someone yelled. "All systems down!" The telelinker slumped over the workstation. Chi's cousin seized her before she fell to the floor, neckjack dangling. The pro linkers crowded about. A system failure? Unheard-of! So much data was generated and exchanged in telespace at any given moment, so much intelligence was linked, that a system failure was as disastrous as a chemical spill or a nuclear accident. Maybe worse. With a thousand power sources backing up the mainframes worldwide, a complete crash of telespace was unheard-of!

A freak accident? Sabotage?

Or a Prime Probability, collapsing out of the timeline?

With all the alarm at his cousin's workstation, Chi hardly noticed when the cloud blew in. At least, he thought it was a cloud. The air was mild. Suddenly, a scorching wind blasted his face. Charcoal plumes billowed out of the west and filled the sky. An acid thunderhead from Mexico, a meteor crashing from outer space?

Chi didn't know what to think!

The wind began to howl. He could see that the cloud wasn't a rain cloud at all, but smoke. A thunderhead of thick, black smoke. Ashes swirled everywhere.

The sky was on fire!

The sun was a blood-red disc behind the burning cloud. He heard a sound in the wind, the scrabbling, scratching noise of a million bits of rubble as they blasted within the awful cloud.

Out of the south, a bolt of lightning cut across the sky. Then, like an afterimage, another bolt cut from the north. Only the bolt was pure black! Like a jagged ebony blade knifing the horizon.

The sky split open.

And they saw the Other Now.

They saw their city, and they saw themselves.

The megalopolis crouched beneath a yellow sky, swirling with old smoke and ash. Buildings still stood in ruins, perhaps from the Great Quake of 2129 or from bombs of an unknown war. The city was falling down, broken with no sign of repair. Gouts of flame flared here and there. Bridges hung slack, decks swaybacked and cracked. Yet, despite the danger, tiny vehicles crawled across them, spewing petroleum smoke. The bay was dead and still, gleaming like a fly's wing with poisonous sludge. A firestorm raged out of control near the very hills they were perched upon. The ocean had eaten away huge chunks of the waterfront and lapped against the curbs of downtown streets. Masses of the tiny vehicles slid through water, wheels spraying brown foam onto the sidewalks.

They saw birds decaying in the dusty brown grass of the parks and malls, flocks of fallen corpses. They saw fish rotting among piles of raw sewage and tangles of plastic on Ocean Beach. The land that would have been New Golden Gate Preserve had no dome. Where the preserve should have stood was a naked salt plain, a radiation desert. A few twisted tree trunks punctuated its desolation. The Portals of the Past stood like gaping teeth in the carcass of wasted land.

And people. People were everywhere. People stacked into crumbling buildings, people huddled in squalor and sickness, people lying before flashing holoids in a mass stupor. Devolts ran through the streets. Along a military perimeter, silent EM-tanks materialized before a horde of ragtag troops and disgorged globes of Melt into their midst. People slept in the open street. Compounds crouched behind barbed wire. Within the compounds, rows of people were impaled on posts, writhing in agony. Rows of bound and hooded prisoners were brought to gallows and summarily hanged.

The great medcenters run by mainframes slid people into bioscan tubes. But instead of scanning their bodies and diagnosing medical treatment, the medcenter scalpels slit stomachs, chests, eyes, and brains. Robotic fingers pulled the incisions wide open, probes guided by artificial intelligence were inserted. Chemicals were secreted or electrical wires with sparking ends pressed down into human flesh.

The holoids that people lay before flashed images of the devolts, the tanks and the troops, the impaled and the hanged, the vivisected. Cunning images so real that the watchers could scarcely tell the difference between what was artificial and the reality howling at their doorstep. And in their confusion and transfixion, the people could not rise.

"We saw ruin and waste and violence. Chaos and misery worse than all the suffering humanity has endured in two millennia," Chiron says. "Then the sky sealed up. And the Vision was gone."

They speed down the highway in silence.

"But," Ruby says at last. "It was . . . just a vision?"

"Well, it wasn't real," he says. "But it *was* real."

Telespace was up and running within sixty seconds. The telelinker came to, dizzy and sick. She lost the file she was working on, along with her lunch, but her link program seemed intact. The sheer size and scale of data lost in that sixty seconds was unknown.

The hole in the sky collapsed and disappeared, leaving charred debris, a jagged conglomerate of radioactive waste, meters wide and kilometers long. The debris floated for weeks over the site where the hole was observed. They sent out jetcopters with nets to retrieve the waste. Tricky stuff. They found antimatter embedded in the scar across the sky.

"The Vision of the Other Now corresponded with the Crash of telespace," Chi says, voice thick with dread. "Corresponded, that is, with the most massive hole in the data ever observed. I saw it with my own eyes."

The Archivists set to work, attempting to restore those missing sixty seconds. The Chief Archivist ordered a complete review of the Archives, especially dim spots that the ferrets had been studying as possible t-port sites.

That's when they identified hot dim spots. And that's when they discovered that data was disappearing *without* a disaster to justify it.

"Over, under, sideways . . ." Chiron sings as if the tune were a dirge.

The Chief Archivist declared a Crisis.

Erroneous events began to occur. Telelinkers who had been jacked in during the Crash fell suddenly ill or suffered freak accidents. The pro linker who had used Chi's cousin's workstation died two days later. She fell in front of an EM-Trans and was killed instantly in a fluke brake failure. A hundred witnesses saw a mysterious ripple at her side. Tunnel comms recorded a shadow, standing suddenly on the track, before the linker was sucked to her death.

"Demons," Ruby says. She swings the BMW west onto Gravenstein Highway, heading for Sebastopol. "Devolved Entities Manifested from the Other Now. Another reality trying to break through into this one?"

"Another reality. Another spacetime, a horrible spacetime," Chiron says. "Starbright. In front of the Psychedelic Shop, you said, 'It's the girl with my face.' Have you seen the demon before?"

"Yes," she whispers. "On Twin Peaks, the morning I got to San Francisco. I almost fell down a cliff."

"Sweet Isis," Ruby mutters. "And I nearly fell down the back stairs the night I saw the intruder in my backyard."

Chiron nods bleakly. "Then the Chief Archivist's theory is correct. Demons can intrude whenever a Prime Probability could collapse out of this timeline."

"Tell it to me without your weird words, man from Mars," Ruby says. "What does that *mean*?"

"When there's a chance something will happen that could change all reality as we know it, the Other Now can intrude. Cosmic Mind." Chi rubs his eyes. "With all the holes in the data documenting your Now, I can't say when that will be."

"But we have nothing to do with the Other Now," Ruby protests. Fear needles up her spine. Her fingertips feel cold. "We have nothing to do with telespace or the Archives or your insane medcenters."

"You've seen it yourself," Chi says with grim satisfaction. "The demons can intrude in *any* spacetime, whenever there's a hot dim spot. And that's what the Summer of Love is: a hot dim spot."

"But what do the demons want with *us*?"

He says, "They want to kill you."

Chiron says a lot of things before Gorgon wakes and Ruby takes the turnoff to Morning Star Ranch. His tone is bitter, contemptuous. The radiation he keeps referring to isn't from a nuclear holocaust or World War Three, but from pollution, of all things. A poisoning of the world will lead to a thinning of the atmosphere, which in turn will lead to an awful leap in the amount of ultraviolet radiation from the sun reaching the

Earth's surface. He tells of other pollutants, toxic chemicals and gases. Nuclear pollutants, too, from power plants and limited nuclear skirmishes. Poison in the rain, poison in the oceans. In the fish, in the birds, in the plants, in the food, in the water, in the soil, in the air.

"You people," he says with such scorn that Ruby shuts her mouth. "Live for today. Don't give a shit about the future. So many of the simple things you take for granted will be gone."

Even if Chiron Cat's Eye in Draco is a pathological liar, Ruby thinks, even if he is, sweet Isis, there is some kind of truth in his monstrous lies. She is stunned to her core.

As though awakened by the quiet, Gorgon grumbles, belches, stretches. "Hey." He reaches over and kneads her neck. "What's happenin', baby?"

She pulls into gravel drive. "We're here."

Grandmother Says: K'an (The Abyss)

The Image: A river flows through a deep ravine. The river does not
    shrink from passing through places of danger, through canyons
    or over waterfalls.
The Oracle: Confronting danger brings success, provided one views
    the situation with clarity and sincerity.
    In the time of danger and difficulty, one must not tarry, but
proceed forward with awareness and courage. Danger must be
analyzed objectively, so that one does not become confused or act
foolishly. Caution: the swimmer who attempts to rescue the drowning
person may also drown.

—Hexagram 29, *The I Ching* or Book of Changes

An hour's drive north of San Francisco, in apple-growing country near Sebastopol along the Russian River, some 30 to 50 country hippies live on a 31-acre tract called Morning Star Ranch. The ranch is owned by Lew Gottlieb, 43, former arranger, composer, and bassist for the folk-singing Limelighters, who has his hippie followers hard at work—rarest of all hippie trips—growing vegetables for the San Francisco Diggers. . . .

That hippies can actually work becomes evident on a tour of the commune's vegetable gardens. Cabbages and turnips, lettuce and onions march in glossy green rows, neatly mulched with redwood sawdust. Hippie girls lounge in the buffalo grass, sewing colorful dresses or studying Navajo sand painting, clad in nothing but beads, bells, and feather headdresses. . . .

The new-found trip of work and responsibility reflected in the Morning Star experiment is perhaps the most hopeful development in the hippie philosophy to date.

> —From "The Hippies," *Time* magazine
> (July 7, 1967)

Ruby pulls up to the barricade that says "Park Here," and slowly drives through the dusty gravel lot. She knows of other country communes. Drop City in Colorado, Strawberry Fields in L.A., the Illustrated Farm in Mendocino, the Brown House in Santa Cruz, Gorda in Big Sur. Morning Star Ranch is the closest and best known in the Haight-Ashbury. The Diggers have posted signs, with directions and a map.

Everyone knows how to get to Morning Star Ranch. Everyone knows anyone can go and stay there. It's free.

Night closes over the countryside. The parking lot is lit by a couple of smudged street lights. Moths whirl and dart in the dim glow.

A squat black woman with graying hair and a stained pantsuit staggers up to the BMW and peers in at Ruby. "Hey sister, hey sister." Her breath reeks of Ripple. "Got any spare change for Bad Annie, sister?"

"Here you go, sister," Ruby says, handing her a quarter. "Go take care of yourself, Bad Annie."

People promptly surround the BMW. A young white girl with a starving face, a bearded man in free-box clothing, a fellow with dirty blond bangs hanging over his face, two black men in tattered suit coats. They plead, palms out. "Spare change? Got any spare change?"

"No," Ruby says, waving them away. "No!"

"Beat it," Gorgon says.

Bad Annie guffaws and lets loose a stream of obscenities. The starving girl turns and vomits spittle on the gravel. The free-box man stalks away. The blond bangs hacks with a racking cough. The two black men weave across the lot to a Volkswagen van pulling up.

Ruby parks in a shadow on the far side of the lot. In the city, darkness hides thieves. Here, darkness may be her friend.

They all pile out of the car. Starbright slings the canvas bag with their provisions over her shoulder. Ruby locks the BMW. This is the second time tonight she's turned a key with a sharp sense of dread.

The four of them cautiously walk across the lot.

"I'm goin' up to the big house," Gorgon says and sprints away. "See if I can find Rainbow."

Ruby seizes Starbright in her left hand, Chiron in her right. The kid and the young cat cling to her like she knows what she's doing. They climb over a steep ridge and down to a small house. Pitched tents, lean-tos, and teepees surround the small house. Pinwheels whirl in the breeze, homemade flags and laundry flap, bizarre sculptures and pottery are strewn about, odd constructions of wood and feathers adorn the roofs and lopsided gables. The scent of rose incense is overpowering. Ruby can see the big house on the next ridge.

They find a square of paved stones around a covered water well. People lounge about the square, some seated in lotus positions. Ruby finds a sheltered spot on the edge of the square where she can get her bearings.

A young fellow with bushy brown hair and a friendly grin comes up to them. "Hi, I'm Marcus Aurelius," he says. "I'm from the Bronx, my ma kicked me out an' I got adopted by some junkies on the Lower East Side. I shot shit when I was twelve an' I love to boost, don't you? I went to juvie for a while an' fifty hotel rooms later I'm in Frisco strung out on horse playing beatnik. Then I dropped LSD. It's like an atomic bomb going off in your head, isn't it? I'm doing acid every day till I become God, aren't you? Hi!"

"Are you hungry?" says a deeply suntanned woman with long gray hair. A silver ring pierces her left nostril. "I'm afraid dinner's over for tonight. But if you go up to the big house, you might find some food."

"We brought our own food," Ruby says.

The gray-haired woman nods, vastly relieved. "We've only got about thirty people working the gardens full-time. But on weekends? We end up feeding like two hundred people."

A barefoot girl in a tattered shift that stops halfway between her knees and her crotch sidles up to Starbright. "Watch out, chick." She speaks through a corner of her mouth without moving her lips, as though her face is half-paralyzed. Her jaw looks askew. "Two Gypsy Jokers beat me up and banged me the first night I got here."

"Didn't anyone help you?" Chiron says.

"Oh yeah," the barefoot girl says. "Some people took me to the hospital, and the doctor gave me shots."

"Didn't anyone call the police?" Starbright says.

People turn at the sound of "police." Their faces twist with anger and fear, hatred and paranoia.

"Shit, no!" says the barefoot girl.

"We would never go to the police," says the grinning, bushy-haired fellow. "We would never, we would never, we would never ever go."

"We can't go to the police," says the gray-haired woman sadly. "They would try to bust us."

Bang bang bang!

Gunshots in the night.

They climb the next ridge to the big house. They find the kitchen. A stench of rot and animal waste assaults them as they step inside. Enough dirty dishes for an army are stacked everywhere. In the half-light, things crawl through the sink.

Chiron looks so unhappy, Ruby wonders if he'll yank out one of his plastic wraps and plaster it over his face.

They find the dining room next. A man sits behind a huge wood table as they walk in. He is lean and muscular, deeply tanned, with wide brown eyes, a large hooked nose, thick, wiry black hair, a bushy beard threaded with gray.

A cat Ruby knows only too well from the Haight-Ashbury, a burly black troublemaker with voodoo eyes who calls himself Mystery, stands before the table with a half dozen other black men. The black men are sweaty and bleary-eyed. They dangle wine bottles in their fingers. Mystery sways, holding himself steady with a grip on the table.

Four men in hip clothes stand on the other side of the table. "These niggers drink and make trouble for everybody," says a shirtless man in beads and jeans. His eyes are bloodshot. He reeks of pot. He sways on his feet, too. "Their heads are going nowhere, man. We want them out."

"Lew," Mystery says, restraining one of his comrades who is ready to take a swing at the shirtless man. "Listen to this racist shit, man. We're the people, man. You always said you would never kick the people out, Lew. Now ain't that true?"

The bearded man is slick with sweat. He rubs his brow and grimaces. He looks as if he's about to weep. "That's true, Mystery. I can't turn away the people," he says to the shirtless man. "I just can't."

"They're the reason we've been served with a cease-and-desist order, Lew," says the shirtless man.

"Listen to this motherfucker," Mystery says to his comrades. "Like the heat is all our fault. The pigs are just after the honky runaways."

"We're trying to create a New Way here!" the shirtless man shouts. "You're all fucked up. Go back to the Fillmore, man."

"Go back to New Jersey," Mystery says and guffaws.

"No, no, no," the bearded man says. "This isn't about one man's way or another man's way. I can't say that one man or another man is wrong. There are no judges here. You are all my guests. You are all my brothers. I cannot turn anyone away from Morning Star Ranch."

The bearded man rises from his chair, shaking his head, kneading his brow, and wanders out of the room. At the door, he turns to Ruby.

"I'm tired," he says.

"Throw them both out," she tells him.

His deep brown eyes are blurred, troubled. "I'm just a musician. I just want to write my symphony."

The bearded man vanishes to some private room.

"This isn't over, you son of a bitch," the shirtless man says.

Mystery grins. "No, it ain't. One night, I'm gonna off you, whitey." He punches his fist into the palm of his hand in front of the shirtless man's face. He and his comrades swig from their bottles and stagger from the room.

"Let's go." Ruby leads Starbright and Chiron out of the big house. "I don't know who all these jokers are. They weren't here when I came up in May. The ones who came to live on the land with Lew must be here somewhere."

They hike in the dark. The cat-claw moon is not much help. A pond here, a huge pine tree there, and Ruby recognizes the path winding through the woods far into the back acres where her sculptor friend had pitched his tent for solitude.

Bang bang bang, in the night.

She stumbles over a log, steps on something squishy that smells moldy. Starbright and Chiron follow, holding hands. Chi takes the canvas bag from the kid and slings it over his shoulder.

At last they come to a clearing and a neat configuration of teepees around a flickering campfire. A freckled woman with a grim look and a mane of disheveled chestnut hair steps out of a teepee, brandishing a shotgun. A chocolate-brown puppy bounds after her, tail wagging furiously. Then Leo Gorgon steps out, zipping up his jeans.

Uh-huh, Ruby thinks, with a pang.

"It's cool, Rainbow," Gorgon says to the freckled woman, laying his hand over the shotgun's barrel. "This is Ruby. And Starbright and Chiron. It's all right. They're cool."

"Is Stewart here?" Ruby asks.

"Stewart left in June," Rainbow says. "Left his sculpture, too."

Sure enough, in the flickering light, Ruby can see the car-chrome man clutching his hammered-steel lover. The red hose dangling between his legs is limp. Stewart had always wanted to install the work somewhere with running water handy. There's no plumbing here.

People duck out of the teepees. Men with hair to their waists and beards trailing down their chests. A woman with a baby suckling at her breast, other women in long dresses or jeans. Some of them carry rifles or handguns, too.

They sit around the campfire, to which Rainbow adds wood. "Raisin, come here, Raisin." The brown puppy frolics, bounding from person to person for a pat or a kiss. Rainbow hangs a huge iron pot on a tripod over the fire.

Ruby passes around the bottle of Napa burgundy. No one drinks except a fellow with Einstein hair who shares the bottle with her. She gives him the other bottle she brought. She passes around the loaf of bread, the cheese, apples, and carob bars. All is promptly devoured before she and Starbright get any. Ruby is very hungry. She and the kid watch wistfully. Chiron is impassive. The people of the teepees eat ravenously. They are all so thin, a patina of grime over their faces and hands, clothing more fragile than the wings of the moths circling round the campfire.

Rainbow rises and takes the lid off the pot. Steam rises from a fragrant, bubbling stew. She dishes hot stew into wood bowls, giving the first servings to Ruby, Starbright, and Chiron. The stew is mostly brown rice, with a few diced onions, carrots, and zucchini. Not spicy enough for

Ruby, but fresh and good. Just about anything would taste good now. Chi places his bowl on the grass for Raisin. The puppy practically inhales the stew, snuffling and sneezing from the steam.

"We had to send Misty and Pink to the hospital," Rainbow says to Gorgon. "Hepatitis. I guess we screwed up, digging the shit ditch so close. Flies were landing on the food. We dug a new outhouse downwind, though, and fifty feet out. Plus, I got a lid for the stew pot."

A man brings out a guitar, begins to strum. The tart, herbal scent of marijuana blows over the campsite. Several people get up and dance in the shadows. A woman sits down next to Ruby and Starbright. She takes out a piece of white cotton onto which she has embroidered a peacock. She has sewn human eyes on every green and blue feather.

Starbright smiles, but she is watchful, silent, glancing over her shoulder now and then. A long day. Raisin leaps into her lap, but she's too tired to give the puppy much attention.

Chiron is inscrutable, but he cocks his head, listening. More gunshots?

Their paranoia is catching. Ruby stands. "We'd best be off," she says. Better to find a roadside rest stop, sleep in the car. The energy here is too weird.

"No, let's stay a while," Gorgon says. He is stoned. He can't take his eyes off Rainbow.

"You stay, Leo." Ruby picks up the canvas bag and brushes off her skirt. "We're gone."

Rainbow comes up and wraps her arms around her, planting a kiss on her cheek. "Thank you for bringing the food and the wine and your good vibes," she says. Her eyes are bottomless, filled with sorrow. "It was beautiful of you to visit us. We have so few good vibes anymore."

Ruby nods.

"Did you know we've got a garden out back?" Rainbow says. She finds a small kerosene lamp. "I'd love to show you. The cabbages are beautiful."

In lamplight under the cat-claw moon, Ruby goes out back with Rainbow and the puppy to see their garden.

And she's right. The cabbages are beautiful.

July 27, 1967

Rumors

10

Dedicated to
the One I Love

Susan lounges with Cyn on the grass in the Panhandle, watching out for cop cars. She takes a mauve chalk from her box of pastels and draws two eyes on the sidewalk. The pigs have been busting sidewalk chalk artists on the charge of defacing public property, not to mention sweeping hip girls off the street on suspicion of being runaways. It's strange and exciting to feel like an outlaw for drawing chalk pictures on the sidewalk.

"Did you hear the rumor about the concentration camps?" she says.

Cyn, the barefoot blond from Texas, shakes her head.

"They say it's happening in Tule Lake and Arizona and Oklahoma,"

Susan says. "The FBI and the Defense Department are doing it. This building contractor came to a priest for confession. He was all in a panic. He confessed they hired his company to refurbish World War Two detention centers as concentration camps. They wanted it done right away. They'll be able to detain up to forty thousand people. Protesters and hippies and anyone cool. We'll all be arrested if there's a National Security Emergency this summer."

"I believe it," says Cyn. She's got a whispery drawl and ends every sentence as though it's a question. She gazes at Susan's handiwork with her palms lying open on her skinny knees. Cyn never looks anyone in the eye, not even Susan.

Susan loves to draw eyes, though she remembers only too well when she turned twelve and she was afraid to look in people's eyes. Eyes seemed too personal, too revealing. The meekest checkout clerk at the grocery store used to scare her. It was Daddy who knocked her aversion to eyes out of her one day. He was yelling about something or other, his face right in her face. She could smell his bad breath. "*Look* at me when I'm talking to you," is what her father said. She did. And that's when she learned how to look someone in the eye and not let him see her soul.

She makes her trademark star-pupils and abundant lashes. Twiggy eyes. Goddess eyes. This is dedicated to the One-Eye Love. Real-Eyes. Ideal-Eyes. Crystal-Eyes; groovy! Oh, little i, who peeks at me, what do U see? Over the Summer of Love, she has developed a new view of eyes.

The morning commuters in their business suits and big finned cars stream downtown. The sky is the color of a dove's wing, the air chilly and damp. Susan feels good lounging in the grass, drawing on the sidewalk. How good to wonder about things, even if they may or may not be happening. She never got to wonder in school. She was always busy memorizing. She feels free, even though she owns no more than an overnight bag and less than fifty dollars, not counting the hundred bucks Stan the Man still owes her. Where did all her money go? Eating out, concerts, cool things. Still, she's freer than the commuters scurrying off to their jobs where someone with bad breath will probably yell in their faces about something or other.

"I heard the Vietcong got cannons hidden in North Beach," Cyn says.

Susan laughs. "I don't know about that. I mean, people can barely hide a nickel bag from the Man, let alone hide cannons in North Beach."

"Maybe so. They say some night the Vietcong's gonna bomb downtown, though."

"Know what else?" Susan says. "I heard the CIA is putting rat poison in street acid. They want to kill the heads."

"I heard the CIA killed President Kennedy," Cyn says.

"If they can kill the president," Susan says, "they sure can kill the heads if they got a mind to."

Cyn nods. "I heard some bikers took over Morning Star Ranch and are rapin' the chicks."

"Oh," Susan says. "Well, *that's* true."

She leans over her drawing, a little sore in the middle. She woke with a cramp and a rush of dampness. Delighted for the first time in her life to see her period.

Chiron sits apart from them, resting his back against a tree trunk. He watches her, smiling when she glances his way. Susan thinks this is very enlightened of him, withdrawing like he does. Letting her do what she wants to do, rap with people, but always being there, watching. His eyebrows and lashes are as strawberry-red as his hair. She's never seen anyone with hair on his face so perfectly matched to the hair on his head. She feels funky and crude beside him. He's so . . . *perfect.*

As luck would have it, Mr. True-Blue Eyes doesn't see *every*thing. She can sneak a couple dexies past him. Pop, down the hatch. No problem, and why not. She caught him snorting something out on the deck. A neurobic, he called it. He didn't offer to share it with her. Harmless, he said. If it was so harmless, how come he didn't offer to share it with her? The real problem is that dexies are getting harder to score, since the taste on the street is running to crystal, meth. Stuff you have to shoot with a hypodermic needle. She gets queasy just thinking about it. She hated when the doctor gave her penicillin shots for her earaches. Needles are gross, no thanks. It's a shame. She loves those dexies. Easier on the stomach than ten cups of coffee, and so fine in the mind, clear as glass.

She doesn't mind Chiron watching her anymore. For one thing, he suddenly started being cool. Smiling, always helpful. But he doesn't put the make on her, which makes him easy to be around and also makes her wonder. She finds herself taking his hand before he takes hers, letting him look down her blouse, or bumping into him accidentally. It's really stupid. She's never spent so much time with a guy who stays so . . . *good.*

Chiron is forever muttering to himself and gazing at the palm of his hand. She's seen the blue light. So has Ruby. Ruby says Chi might be a spy, after all, like in *Goldfinger*, which she and Nance saw when they snuck in the back door at the Cedar Center Theater and which devastated them both. Nance painted her whole hand with gold enamel before her skin began to itch and she got an awful rash. Susan isn't sure what Chiron's mission could possibly be. What in the Haight-Ashbury would attract the likes of James Bond? Well, aside from half-naked girls. Chiron tries to peek at the blue light when he thinks she's not looking, but then he gets so absorbed in it, only an idiot wouldn't notice.

When she asked about his ring and why he keeps whispering at it, he stalled at first, then told her that the ring is a calculator and a computer, with some kind of drive. Typical Chiron shuck. Susan knows computers are as big as a whole room. And calculators? Ruby's calculating machine is as heavy as a sack of potatoes and not much less bulky. He says he's calculating the probabilities, searching the files for a Prime Probability. He reminds her of Professor Zoom, searching for the Final Expression to his equation proving God equals a hit of blotter. Only Chiron's Prime Probability has nothing to do with God. It has to do with demons.

The girl with her face. A Devolved Entity Manifested from the Other Now? A demon that wants to *off* her? It's like the rumors of concentration camps. So weird she can't believe it, and so plausible she can't afford to disbelieve it.

But what can she *do* about it?

"Don't die," Chiron tells her grimly. "Be ready, always. You've got to survive, Starbright."

But it isn't cops-and-robbers, a tangible *thing* she can stab with a knife or shoot with a gun. The demons are like greenhouse pollutants, Chi says, unpredictable, uncontrollable, poison blowing in the wind. Like ultraviolet radiation piercing through holes in the ozone layer of the upper stratosphere. Susan never thought about ultraviolet radiation, much less worried about it piercing through the ozone. What is ozone, anyway?

Don't die. Survive. Be ready, always. It's terrifying and exhausting. Anyway, she *is* going to die someday. That's one thing she's come to understand and accept over the Summer of Love. How can she be ready, always? Ready how? Ready for what?

"What is the demon trying to do when it comes near me?" she asked him.

"Didn't it pull you toward the edge of the cliff?" he said.

"Yeah," she said slowly.

"And didn't it try to push you toward the dog-killer in front of the Psychedelic Shop?"

"Yes!"

He nods. "Even worse, it's trying to touch you."

More Chiron shuck. He is weird about touching and not touching. He never touches anything without punching his hand through the plastic wrap he calls a prophylak. She is so used to him flailing his hand around, she hardly notices anymore. He's a lot like some of the crazies she's seen on Haight, Chi and his hand thing. He hardly ever touches her, except in extreme moments. And, even then, he's usually got a prophylak on. She loves to seize his bare hand and watch him squirm.

"What happens if the demon touches me?" she asked.

"The demon is antimatter," he said.

"So?"

"Well! The demon is your analog from the Other Now. If the demon touches you, the matter-antimatter annihilation exchange will trigger, and spacetime as we know it will be destroyed. Not to mention you and me."

God! This revelation both frightened and angered her, like the time she found out about the atomic bomb. *She* didn't make the atomic bomb. *She* didn't ask to be chased by a demon.

"But what should I do if the demon gets close?" she said, panicking.

"I'll counter its energy with the maser. The blue and green beams deflected their movements in front of the Psych Shop. But if the demon gets close enough to touch you, I'll use purple. Believe me, I won't think twice."

"And purple is similar to the Dead Stop near-annihilation exchange used in the ME3 Event." She was good at memorizing, but she had no idea what that was supposed to mean.

He gave her the look. Only his look wasn't dirty. "That's right. Theoretically, the purple beam will collapse the demon back into its own spacetime."

"I thought you don't completely understand how purple works."

"We don't. We've tested it in this spacetime, of course. But we can't say exactly how it'll work in contact with the Other Now. But . . . Don't worry about it, Starbright."

Don't worry about it. Right. His tone was so ominous, like when her parents talked about the arms race and the balance of terror, that she shut up about the purple beam.

"Why me?" she asked at last. This question has haunted her since the night they drove to Morning Star Ranch.

"You're important," he simply said. "In your Now. And in mine."

That was cool. Ruby said the same thing, too. But Chi didn't mean it the same way Ruby did. In her Now and in his? But *everyone's* important somehow, aren't they? The question keeps haunting her. *Why me?*

It's hard to know what to believe.

Like rumors on this foggy morning.

There's a rumor that STP is far out and the Establishment media is just creating scare stories saying STP will kill you. The Alchemist says Serenity, Tranquility, and Peace is a sacrament.

There's a rumor that brushing your teeth with clover prevents cavities. But no one has figured out how to get the grass stains off.

There's a rumor that the corpse of the sheepdog beaten to death in front of the Psychedelic Shop was stolen by aliens. It might as well have been, since the legal action committee that was supposed to challenge the police has dematerialized, too.

There's a rumor that the Swedish have invented a pill that gives a woman an abortion with no risk, no pain, no humiliating social retribution, and no need to consult doctors, the district attorney, husbands, lovers, fathers, or brothers. But the FDA won't let the Swedish pill into the United States.

There are rumors that black people are rioting in the Bronx, in Harlem, in Miami, in Toledo, in Memphis, in Cairo, Illinois. There are rumors that the police are going to use the riots to kill thousands of black people in the ghettos.

The riots in Newark, New Jersey, and Detroit, Michigan, are not rumors, they are real. Stokely Carmichael says the black people are going to fight to the death.

Charlie Artman, with his necklace of chicken leg bones and a huge wood ankh, strolls up to Susan and Cyn. "The Haight-Ashbury's gonna burn, baby. Get off the street by ten tonight." Cowboy, Leo Gorgon's pal, jogs by and drops a Communication Company mimeograph into Susan's lap. The mimeograph feels thick, like the paper has fur, and stinks of chemicals.

Susan picks up the mimeograph and reads:

BROTHERS:

An Important Notice for Your Safety and Survival.

Sorry to bring you down, but this is about the riots our black brothers have planned for the city tonight. There isn't much hope they won't occur.

We can expect vast looting, which means that people will be treating all stores as free stores. Some people will be setting fires, usually after a store has been emptied. Police and later National Guard and federal troops will come into all riot areas by the thousands, armed with rifles, machine guns, and tanks. Curfew means if they see you they will bust you, and if you run, they will shoot you.

There is more, but Susan doesn't have the heart to read it. She tosses the Communication Company mimeograph on the grass. Chiron carefully picks it up and tucks it in his pocket.

"Uh-oh, here comes the Baptist," Cyn says. She chews her thumb. She gnaws a bit of nail free from one side, seizes the bit in her teeth, and pulls a strip across the whole top of her thumb. Cyn's fingertips are a bloody mess. Susan can't watch. She wishes she could slap Cyn, but she doesn't know her well enough. Cyn is moody. One minute she'll be talking to you like a normal person, then the next she's staring off into space, or yelling, getting tearful and angry about something but you're not sure what. Cyn would be really beautiful if she weren't so dirty and down-and-out. Photographers are always stealing snapshots of her, her white-blond hair, angelic face, big dark eyes. Cyn will never make it back to Texas. But, Susan thinks, that's okay. Cyn says her mother is crazy.

Four young black men in leather jackets and bandannas tied round enormous 'fros stroll up Oak Street. One spots Cyn, waves his comrades over. Chi gets to his feet, but they leave Susan alone, acknowledging his claim to her. They surround Cyn.

"C'mere, li'l bitch," the Baptist says. His hands twitch, suggesting the violence in them. The Baptist takes Cyn behind a tree and shoves her to her knees.

Susan draws a woman's face on the sidewalk to go with the eyes.

The three young black men stand over her, tense and watchful. She wishes Chiron would do something, but he just stands and stares. She hears the Baptist's zipper. There is nothing she can do.

The Baptist struts from behind the tree, grinning. He and his comrades saunter away.

Cyn crawls out onto the grass on her hands and knees. She retches, wipes her mouth.

A cop car turns the corner at Cole Street.

Cyn rises. In one swift motion, she's gone.

WEATHER REPORT

In 1967, climatologists have started monitoring other substances besides carbon that are being injected into the atmosphere. All manner of exotic gases are showing up, including chlorofluorocarbons—CFCs or Freons—which are used in refrigerators, spray cans, and air-conditioning systems. CFCs will linger in the atmosphere for over 110 years, drifting up through the troposphere into the high stratosphere. Other exotic gases released by the industrial nations include methane, carbon monoxide, nitrous oxide, and nitric oxide. Some of these gases will linger in the atmosphere for 125 years and longer.

o

Dear *Barb:*
Listen, it can also happen in a quiet apartment in the afternoon. Yesterday I was sitting at home listening to music, feeling calm and peaceful, all alone. I got up to

answer a knock on the door. A young man, on the pretext of asking questions about "friends next door," observed that I was alone and pushed me back inside the apartment. He held me up against the wall, covered my mouth to keep me from making any unseemly commotion, and, gesturing toward a knife on the kitchen table, allowed as how he would make some unforgettable incisions on my body if I didn't keep my trap shut. Each time I made an effort to talk to him he threatened me again. He got what he was after—a fuck he called it—although I'm afraid it wasn't a very good one.

I have not told the police about it. Every member of the police department I have encountered during my stay in San Francisco has been nearly as surly and intractable as my rapist friend, because I look like a hippie. Each time I attempted to explain myself I was rebuffed or threatened.

From this experience I am tempted to draw an odd analogy: under stress, neither the policeman nor the rapist allows an opportunity for rational communication. Each one relies on violence to make his impression. This is not an accident but, rather, evidence of a widespread sickness. When will violence stop long enough for communication to begin? On second thought, perhaps I am doing the police department a grave disservice in not attempting to put them in contact with the rapist. Maybe, with just a little mind-bending, that rapist would make a damned good cop, and both could swagger together, true soul brothers, under the many-colored cloak of Fascism.

In the meantime, when you come to San Francisco wear flowers in your hair by all means (I shall be wearing some tonight) but don't forget to take a course in karate on the side—till the day such defenses are no longer necessary.

Yours, With Love.

—From Letters to the Editor, *Berkeley
Barb*, Vol. 4, No. 23, Issue 95 (June 9–15, 1967)

The cop car speeds across Oak Street, sliding over to the curb where Susan sits.

"Chi?" she says.

He's got her box of pastels and her purse. He seizes her elbow, hauls her to her feet, hustles her in front of him.

They dart behind the trees and run through the park. Whatever you do, flower child, don't get busted by the Man.

Susan sees the van on the other side of the Panhandle. The funky Volkswagen van covered with blue clouds. Before she can take off into the park again, the voice reaches out and hooks her.

"Seek new life, new civilizations." Just the facts, ma'am, and a chuckle like the pull of a saw through wood. "Trixie, hey Trixie, which way, Trixie?"

"My name is Starbright, Arnold."

"Don't call me names."

"Don't call me Trixie."

"Where the hell've you been, Starbright?"

He crooks his elbow round her neck, gives her a nutcracker hug. Professor Zoom's eyes are shiny for a moment. He has painted bands of black, blue, yellow, and red around each eye like an archery target. His lank hair sticks out in a deranged hairdo. If it's possible for him to be thinner, he is. Instead of the baggy, grass-stained jeans, he wears tight hip-huggers with flaring bell-bottoms that emphasize his spidery thighs.

"Hi, Professor Zoom," she says. She kisses him on the cheek. After all, he is the first person who ever sensibly discussed death with her. "You look wild. I missed you."

"Emotions are the lowest form of consciousness, Starbright. Beware the lurching lunatic, the churning robot gone berserk."

Susan leans out of his hug and studies him. "Did you find the Final Expression to your equation, Professor Zoom? *Does* God equal a hit of blotter?"

He looks away. "Alas, anon, I need fuel to stoke the fires of genius. And my cupboard is bare. We endure difficult times." He looks at her. "There's a serious shortage of acid these days, in case you haven't noticed. I'm dropping yellow flats, blue dots, that speed shit, you know. I'm even doing psychedelic dreams. Man, that's desperation."

"What are psychedelic dreams?"

"Mostly smack, sweet pretty pussy." His look grows intense. "Got any acid?"

"No. And don't call me a pussy, Professor Zoom." Susan cranes her neck at the van. She doesn't see Stella or Fawn. A new crowd of caterpillar-eyed girls poses around the van. They look tougher, dirtier, meaner than the old crowd, tending more toward leather and chains than velvet and lace.

"Say hey. Professor Zoom. Check it out. Foxy lady. It *is* foxy lady, isn't it? My little flower child."

The mountain man, oh Stan. His eyes, his mouth, his lean body. He's so beautiful.

"You're looking fine." He bends to kiss her.

She pulls away, like any sensible person would flinch from the edge of a sharp knife.

He stands there, looking her up and down in that teasing way of his. If he's troubled by her recoil, he gives no sign. But he doesn't try to seize her, press her to him, thread his fingers over her ribs. He doesn't try to kiss her despite her recoil.

She's relieved and wounded. It's really stupid, but she wishes he would try to kiss her anyway.

Kid, she can just hear Ruby say, don't you take shit from *anyone*. She pulls herself up tall the way Ruby does when she means business.

"I need to get my hundred dollars back," she says, looking straight into his face, exercising her new view of eyes over the eyes that once mesmerized her.

"Flower child, I don't know what you mean."

"I mean the hundred dollars I lent you for the dragon's blood deal."

"Say hey. Dirty David said he saw you at the hip lawyer's office. He said you were asking about some kind of legal aid. Is that true, Starbright?" His eyes are infused with concern.

"The hundred-dollar bill you took from me," she says, wavering before his misdirection, but not for long. "Did you know that Stovepipe and the Lizard are looking for you? They said the dragon's blood was no good. They said it was rat poison. They want their seven grand back, Stan."

"Are you in some kind of trouble, Starbright?" His eyes grow hard, his tone harder. "Or are you turning state's evidence on me?"

"I told them I don't have any seven grand," she lies, refusing to back down. "Me, I just want my hundred dollars." She's appalled. He won't even *listen*. All he cares about is his trip!

Chiron stands to the side like he usually does. But when Starbright walks away and Stan starts to follow, Chi steps in his path. Not in a biker-bully way, but he steps, deliberately and firmly, proclaiming with an unsmiling face that Stan is not to follow her. Chiron may be slimmer than Stan, but he's taller by nearly two inches. Scowling, Stan stops.

Susan catches her breath. Chiron, the five-hundred-year wonder, guarding her path!

She goes to the Double Barrel Boogie Band's van and peers inside. Chi hovers behind her, peering in, too.

Lady May sits hunched and cross-legged in the back of the van. The glittery pink boa she clips in her hair flashes in the thin light. She wears the same leather vest over nothing but her skin and jeans. Cords of muscle entwine the bones of her bare arms. Her ribs are as prominent as girders. A leather band is wound round her left arm below her lightning bolt tattoo. She grips one end in her teeth, the other in her right fist. She pulls the band so tightly, Susan can see it cut into the spare flesh of Lady May's arm.

A girl sits in front of Lady May with her back turned to Susan. Dark spiky hair cut as short as a boy's, she also sits cross-legged, thighs jutting like delicate wings. She wears a halter top tied over her bony spine. She is doing something, fiddling with something, that Lady May watches with ravenous eyes. The van reeks of matches, Lebanese hash, plum incense.

Lady May looks up, sees Susan and Chiron. "Sst!" Bending over, bare waist thin as a rail, hissing and glittery-eyed with her wild mop of hair, Lady May reminds Susan of a snake. Like in Kipling's "Riki-Tiki-Tavi," a rainbow-scaled cobra with her hood spread.

The dark-haired girl takes what she's got in her hands, calmly slides it under the blanket next to her, and blows out the match. She turns her face. Susan can see her profile, lips pursed over the trail of smoke, the curve of her cheek, her unmistakable pert nose.

"Penny Lane!" Susan shrieks.

Nance hops out of the van.

"Starbright!" she screams.

She throws her arms around Susan. They hug, jump up and down, dance, rock back and forth, pull each other's hair, pound each other's shoulders. Susan kisses Nance's cheek. Nance plants a long kiss right on Susan's mouth.

Nance, oh Nance!

Nance the elf at seven on her bike with training wheels, red, white, and blue crepe-paper streamers taped to her handlebars for the Fourth of July. Jones and Stein, they sat in the back in second grade, traded erasers, cribbed answers, passed notes back and forth declaring their love for each other. Nance the thief, stealing a box of Milk Duds—which really were duds—when they went to see *The Time Machine*. Nance the explorer at nine, making a tunnel in the snowdrift the plow had left behind, wiggling through like a fearless mole. Nance the daredevil at ten, climbing the old ironwood tree in Cheryl Rubinstein's front yard, the first to jump from the big branch fifteen feet up, laughing though she broke her ankle and Susan had to carry her home. Nance the rebel at twelve, talking Susan into taking out Mom's Mustang when Susan's parents were in France. Nance the hip chick at thirteen, showing up at Cheryl's party dressed all in black, *Let's Boogie Boogie* tucked under her arm. Nance cajoling a joint out of her cousin Don. And Nance the whirling dervish in Susan's recreation room, twirling to *Rubber Soul* blasting on the stereo, moving her hips like a belly dancer.

"Star light, star bright," Susan sings. "First star I see tonight . . ."

"Wish I may, wish I might," Nance sings back. "Have the wish I wish . . ."

"Toooo—night," they sing together.

Like Jiminy Cricket, with his own wishing song, in *Pinocchio*. They scream and shriek with laughter and hug again.

"You grew your hair, Starbright," Nance says.

"You cut your hair, Penny Lane," Susan says.

Nance wipes the tears from Susan's face.

Then she winks.

They do not blow each other's cover, even now, standing in the Haight-Ashbury during the Summer of Love, two thousand miles and two thousand lifetimes from Cleveland. That's what Nance's wink means. Without a moment's hesitation, they use the names Nance chose for them. Susan can see how proud Nance is that she is playing the game. They have always played the game. Like the time they took the Rapid Transit downtown. They had just seen *A Hard Day's Night* and they drifted into a long, loud conversation in thick British accents that were completely phony. Nance said something like, "Bewt'ful dye, inn't it?" Then Susan said, "Oh, but the ah is puhfectly frrrresh." Pretty soon, they managed to fool a proper old lady in a pillbox hat. Stewdents abroohd, you see, fancy free and ohff to discovah Amuhdica. They charmed her into taking them to high tea at Stouffer's where the desserts are so good. Nance ordered a pudding *and* a cake. And never once did they blow each other's cover. They carried on their masquerade till the proper old lady bid them a fond good-bye and tucked a five-dollar bill into each girl's pocket. They screamed about it for weeks. "Nawncee." "Yes, Suzahnnah." "Might I have anothah crrrrumpet and a spot of Uhl Gway?" "Of cawse, my dahling."

Oh, dig it, it was so cool. Pretending to be someone else. With a completely different life. An exciting life in a faraway place. Since they were little, wishing on the first star of the evening, they both understood this: the most exciting game in life is to invent yourself.

Yes! Invent yourself. It makes sense, Susan thinks, hugging her best friend, that they should meet again in the Haight-Ashbury during the Summer of Love.

"Like wow," Nance says. She checks her out. Susan feels a blush of pleasure bloom in her cheeks. "You look groovy, sweetheart." She pronounces it *shweethawt.* "Get-ting rahthah slim, ahn't we?"

"God, Penny Lane," Susan says, gazing at her in wonder. "You're thinner than ever."

It's true. Nance has always had a tight, athletic body, though she ate ice cream and burgers in huge quantities. But Nance never ridiculed Susan for getting breasts and hips. Nance sided with her when Susan's mother thought her breasts were too fat and forced her on the hard-boiled egg diet. Nance has always stood up for Susan against the whole world.

Nance hooks her arm through Susan's and takes her to the new crowd of caterpillar-eyed girls. "This is Starbright, my best friend. Starbright is one of the smartest chicks I know. Plus, she's an Artist. I remember how you used to draw," Nance says doubtfully. "You're still drawing, aren't you, Starbright?"

"On the sidewalk," Susan says proudly, pleased Nance remembers her silly sketches with Prismacolor pencils knickknacked from Mr. Rosenstein's art supply store. "Plus I drew a six-foot Isis in the Mystic Eye."

"The big chick on the wall in the witch shop?" one of the caterpillar-eyed girls says. "That is so far out!"

"That's my Starbright," Nance says authoritatively. "Starbright has always been brilliant. Plus, her family's rich."

Suddenly *every*one is looking at her, including Stan the Man.

Rich. Nance knows Susan's family isn't rich. Susan's family is disgustingly middle-class. Over the years, Susan has told Nance all about Daddy, the way he moans over the bills, doles out allowances to Susan and her mother, groans over how much gas his Cadillac guzzles. They are certainly not rich compared to their new neighbors. Susan feels ashamed at how poor she is compared to their new neighbors. She longs for the old neighborhood, where girlfriends like Nance didn't put her down for being a dentist's daughter.

For a weird moment, though—in one of those over-under-sideways-down insights she keeps stumbling upon during the Summer of Love—she suddenly sees herself through society's eyes. Her father is a professional with his own practice, while Nance's stepfather works in some office for someone else doing who knows what. Susan's parents left the cookie-cutter developments of South Euclid for the tree-lined avenues of Shaker Heights, only slightly less prefab, perhaps, but enormously more prestigious.

How easy for Susan to be self-denigrating, to put down her father's hard-won victories from the other side of privilege. Her forced separation from Nance stings anew. The way her father forbade her to see Nance strikes her as incredibly stupid. Yet, right or wrong, she can suddenly see why. Her father is ambitious. His ambition extends to his daughter. By comparison—and doesn't the Establishment always compare?—Nance's stepfather is not as successful as Susan's father. And his lack extends to his daughter.

Gross. But she can see why.

No wonder she and Nance wanted to get away as fast as they could. What do their fathers have to do with them?

They drift from the crowd, Nance's arm crooked round Susan's neck in a hammerlock reminiscent of Professor Zoom. They sit together on the grass fronting Fell Street.

"When did you get here?" Nance says.

"In time for the Celebration of the Summer Solstice," Susan says. "Got your postcard."

"Were my parents looking for me?"

"Sure. They came to our house." Whoops, that's a sore spot, that Susan moved away to a new house. "But I didn't tell them anything, Penny Lane," she says in a rush. "I swear."

"You didn't tell them where I was?" Suddenly, Nance isn't smiling. Her face becomes somber. Susan can see lines etched in Nance's young face.

"I didn't even talk to them, actually. My father, you know Daddy, he kind of kept me away from them."

Nance pauses. "I knew I could depend on you." She sucks in her breath. "So you got that dumb postcard, huh?"

"Sure! The postcard is what brought me here, Penny Lane."

"No! Really?"

Susan giggles, confiding like they used to. "I hid it, but Mom found it. They got so pissed! Daddy made me burn it."

"Your father made you burn my postcard?" Nance says.

" 'That little tramp, that no-good so-and-so,' " Susan says in a masculine voice. " 'I never want you talking to her again.' Can you believe it?"

"Your father called me a tramp?"

"And then he said I was stupid when I told him you were my best friend."

"Your father called me a no-good so-and-so?"

"*Stupid.* He knows I'm in the ninety-eighth percentile."

"You've always been the smart one, Starbright," Nance says. Her eyes glisten unexpectedly. Her voice quavers.

"I left that night."

Nance stares off into space the way Cyn does.

"Oh, Penny Lane," Susan says. "You know what a jerk my father is. He's the one who's stupid."

"Yeah." Nance chews on her thumbnail. She won't look at Susan.

Suddenly, Susan knows she has done something terribly, irretrievably wrong. But she isn't sure exactly what or how to undo it.

A cop car slides past the corner of Divisadero and Fell Street.

"Where are you crashing?" Nance says, pulling up, glancing about warily.

"With the lady who owns the Mystic Eye."

"Ruby A. Maverick?"

"Yes!"

"Isn't that just like you, Starbright. Nothing but the best."

Nance stands, brushing off her jeans. Stan the Man strides up and throws his arm around Nance's shoulder. Nance looks at him with a sensual grin. Susan turns away, controlling the trembling in her lip as best she can. Nance, with Stan the Man?

Suddenly Chi is there.

"Is this your old man?" Nance says. She gives Chiron such a lustful glance up and down that Stan frowns, a glimmer of competitive malice in his eye. Nance steps away from Stan's proprietary embrace.

"This is Chiron Cat's Eye in Draco," Susan says.

"Like wow," Nance says and wiggles her hips, blinking up at Chi. She smiles at Susan with approval. "He's a fine one, Starbright."

That Nance, she's so silly. She's treating Susan's companion like the guys on Haight Street treat other guys' ladies. Susan laughs. No wonder people have always thought Nance is crazy. Nance the daredevil, Nance the rebel. Nance has always carried on her very own personal revolution.

The cop car cruises Baker Street.

They scatter like criminals, like Vietcong smuggling cannons into North Beach. The Double Barrel Boogie Band's entourage climbs into the van.

Suddenly Susan is afraid again.

But Chiron is there. Chi is always there.

"I'll call you at the Mystic Eye," Nance shouts as the van pulls away.

"Call me! Call me! Call me, Penny Lane!"

Susan starts to dart into the park again. But Chi catches her, slows her to a walk, throws his arm over her shoulder. They calmly walk down Fell Street, staring straight ahead.

The cop car passes.

And Susan sees the squat man in the stovepipe hat with his psychedelic reptile friend. They're walking straight toward her and Chi, deep in conversation. The dealers! Stovepipe and the Lizard!

Neither Ruby nor Chiron ever questioned her about the confrontation in front of the Fillmore Auditorium. She never offered an explanation.

It's too embarrassing.

Chi spots them, too.

The dealers look up and see *them*. Their eyes light with a cold gleam of recognition.

"You know those men," Chi demands. "Don't you?"

"He made me," she says helplessly.

A bus pulls up to the stop ten feet in front of them.

"Got fifteen cents?" Chi says. He's got his coins ready.

They run and jump aboard the bus like it's a getaway car in *Bonnie and Clyde*. It's strange and exciting to feel like an outlaw for walking down the street with Chiron. Except for the painful hammering in her heart.

11

Sunshine Superman

 Chiron shoves her onto the bus, hustles her down the aisle. The doors flip shut, then open again.

Stovepipe and the Lizard climb up the stairs as the bus takes off, lurching down Fell Street. The driver detains them while Stovepipe searches his pockets for the fare.

The bus is packed with sleepy-eyed people taking up all the seats, standing in the aisle. Chi pushes Starbright around them. A grizzled old man in a shabby raincoat leers at her. "Hippie whore," the old man says and spits on her jacket. She whirls, eyes wide, mouth gaping. Chi navigates her around him. "Pig," he snarls at the old man. "Hippie scum," he snarls back.

Chi pulls the bell-cord. The bus careens into the next stop. The back doors flip open. He pushes her down the stairs, clatters after, catches her before she pitches forward on the sidewalk.

"God, Chi!" she yells.

"Sorry! You okay?" At her nod, he wraps his arm around her. They dash across the street.

The doors close. The bus lumbers away, then stops in half a block. Stovepipe and the Lizard stumble out, get their bearings, look up and down the street. The Lizard points.

An eastbound bus pulls up at the stop two steps away. Chi can hear the dealers' boot heels ringing on the pavement as they sprint across the street.

"Go, go, go!" He tosses her up, dashes in.

The bus takes off toward downtown. She falls against him. He seizes the handrail and steadies them both. She digs deep in her purse for more dimes, drops them into the change box with trembling hands.

He guides her back to a seat. They're both breathing hard and shaking. He doesn't even think to take out a prophylak as he pulls her against his chest.

She snuggles like a needy child. Then, rebellious, she struggles free of his unexpected embrace.

Damn! Those dealers again! He tries to recall the incident in front of the Fillmore. That was before the cop killed the dog and the demons manifested. What did they say to her? Something about dragon's blood? Seven thousand dollars? He thought it was a case of mistaken identity. Why *are* they after her?

Each day of the Summer of Love is so dense with data, he has trouble keeping track of all the events. What an irony! A hot dim spot, glutted with information! And it's odd. He sees a pattern unfolding. In little more than a month, the Summer of Love has changed from innocence to knowingness to anger and disillusionment.

Or is it just him? What's next?

He feels like his stomach is bouncing up his throat. The seat is a sheath of vinyl barely concealing wire springs. The bus has no brain. It is hand-driven by a tough old guy with Aztec cheekbones and a toothpick tucked in his lip. She takes the window seat. She always insists on the window seat, and he always lets her take it, even though he wouldn't mind sitting next to the window himself. Like every adolescent who insists on testing limits, the way a bird needs to fly, she takes advantage of him every chance she gets. He suppresses his annoyance, but it is by no means easy, since she annoys him every other minute. To give is best, he reminds himself. How easy to believe in cosmicist platitudes when everyone else does, too.

She peers back down the road with such alarm that he leans over her shoulder and looks, too.

Stovepipe and the Lizard are nowhere in sight. Lost them. Who made her? Do what?

She takes out a rumpled Kleenex and dabs the spittle off her jacket. Then she presses her cheek to the smeary window, suddenly moody.

He lays a hand on her shoulder. She presses harder, like a cat moving in the opposite direction of where you want her to go.

"Don't do that, Starbright," he says. For a modern person with basic scientific knowledge at her disposal, she cultivates a pathetic indifference to the elementary rules of cleanliness. Why doesn't she know better? It bothers the hell out of him.

"Don't do what?" she demands.

He tries to pull her back from the window, but she glares at him.

"You're not my daddy, you know." She trots out the pout she uses whenever she's displeased with him.

Exasperated, he whips out his scope. "See for yourself." He adjusts the focus—a mere 10× will show enough scum to turn anyone's stomach —and hands the scope to her. She examines the scope, sniffs the metal, rubs her fingers down its length, and peeks through the wrong end before she finally turns the lens toward the window glass. Her open mouth and shocked silence are good enough for him.

"Gross, huh?" he says, using her favorite word. "You see that? That's bacteria. Bacteria and crap from other people. It can make you sick."

"So what," she mumbles. And then, *"You're* sick." She coughs, but he knows she's faking. She hands the scope back, surreptitiously wiping her cheek with the back of her hand.

He starts to pull out one of his wipes for her, then stops. He pockets the scope. Another violation of Tenet Seven, no doubt, applying a modern technology in the past. Since he made the decision to get closer to the girl, he finds himself bumping up against the Tenets at every turn. The more deeply he gets involved, the more difficult observing the mandate of nonintervention becomes. It angers him. How easy to spout the Tenets of the Grandfather Principle from the comfortable boardroom of the Luxon Institute for Superluminal Applications. Anger and disillusionment; what's next, indeed.

Between the HIP Switchboard notice in the *Barb* and Starbright's resemblance—not perfect, not complete, but close—to the girl in the CBS News holoid, the probabilities that she truly is the Axis have skyrocketed. They are probably better than ninety percent. Sometimes he still walks his loop through the Haight-Ashbury. Sometimes he tries to pick up more of her fingerprints with the scanner and compare them with the prints in his file. Most of the time, though, he tries to stay close to her. Watch her. Protect her.

For she's the target of a demon. That alone is enough to enlist his surveillance. And that alone would be persuasive evidence that she is the one capable of collapsing a Prime Probability out of the timeline, but for another awful fact. Ruby A. Maverick is targeted by a demon, too. The Chief Archivist's theory is not only correct, but more correct than she bargained for. Do other people in the past for whom the data was disappearing in this hot dim spot have analogs that can manifest from the Other Now? In Ruby's case, yes. But who else? A million people could pass through the Haight-Ashbury during the Summer of Love. Are there other demons, too?

He can't guard them both. He consulted K-T. The knuckletop calculated that Ruby's ability to survive was significantly greater. Besides, the Axis—the one whom the Archivists first identified as capable of collapsing the timeline—is a longhaired girl. So he follows Starbright, everywhere.

He's gone every damn place with her. She took him back to the Fillmore Auditorium and to the Avalon Ballroom, too. He's heard the Butterfield Blues Band, Country Joe and the Fish, the Yardbirds. The music is deafening. He likes to stand at the foot of the stage, tapping his toe, while Starbright dances by herself. Her dancing is dramatic. Gesticulating arms, undulating hips, bobbing head, flying hair. He can just see Venus Rising's eyes get big. *You* went to the Fillmore Auditorium *and* the Avalon Ballroom? It's like saying he attended the first Surrealists' Ball. The high point, so far, was the Yardbirds concert they attended two days ago. With a rush of joy, he heard with his own ears every word of, "Over, Under, Sideways, Down." Live! Prime!

Ruby calls the knuckletop his magic ring, but to Chiron, *this* is like magic. Data that disappeared *exists* again! Because *he* is here to observe it, remember it, record it in the Archives once more. A shiver went up his spine. *He* is restoring the data! And the SOL Project—never less than crucial—has taken on whole new levels of meaning. Consider impact before you consider benefit, his skipmother said. Is his impact negative, neutral, or positive? He makes an impact merely by *being* here. His impact *is*. That's all he can know.

He also took Starbright downtown to the "Joint Show," an opening for psychedelic poster artists at the Moore Gallery. Everyone who's anyone was there: Wes Wilson, Stanley Mouse, Victor Moscoso, Rick Griffin, Kelly. Socialites from Pacific Heights showed up in diamond chokers, paisley satin jumpsuits, and Mercedes-Benzes. Starbright showed up with a pad filled with her pastel drawings. She wanted to show her work to Rick Griffin, who is her favorite. But she couldn't even get close. A photographer stepped up just as she was opening her drawing pad and said, "Clear the chicks out of here." He commenced snapping photos of the artists.

She cried as they left.

Chi hadn't been happy about it, either. "Did you see any women artists at that show?" he pointed out to comfort her. "How about women journalists writing articles for the *Barb* or the *Oracle*? Or women playwrights or women filmmakers? Hardly any women poets? Or women shop owners? Have you noticed how special Ruby is? How the other HIP merchants are always putting her down, even though she's got the most successful shop on the block? What about women lawyers or women doctors? Where are the women political leaders? You know, the hip rhetoric talks about the equality of the brothers, Starbright. But I don't see much equality for the sisters. Oh, I see women's bodies and teenagers with their unlicensed babies. I see hipsters and hoodies and bikers hassling you and Cyn. But I don't see women's minds. I don't see women's works."

He wondered, in passing, if he was violating Tenet Three. He was supposed to protect her, not politicize her. At the time, though, he didn't give a shit about Tenet Three.

"But *you* can change all that, Starbright," he told her. "It's going to take someone like you."

He didn't know if he had comforted her or not, but she stopped crying at once and brooded somberly all the way home.

They ride the bus to the end of the line. Lost Stovepipe and the

Lizard, at least for now. The fog lifts, burning off. With the sun, she's suddenly in a better mood. She bubbles, spilling over. "Penny Lane! Chi, I found her, I finally found her! God!"

He cannot help but smile. As much as she annoys him, she surprises him, too. He doesn't love her. No. No, love has nothing to do with it. But Starbright has her charms.

"Is Penny Lane from Cleveland, too?" he says casually.

She frowns and ignores him. Bad move, but always worth a try. This is a sticking point between them. She is *Starbright*. She is *Here*. She is *Now*. Why does he need to know more? If she is surprised at his guesses about her—her hometown, her parents, her real name—she never shows a sign. She has made no slip, permitted no chance remark to betray her.

Could *he* withstand the pressure to tell all? Obviously not. After t-port training and indoctrination into the Tenets, he spilled his true identity at the first opportunity.

There is, of course, a probability that her hostile stare means Starbright isn't the Axis at all. Yes, an inescapable probability. He doesn't want to think about it.

"She's balling Stan the Man, don't you think so? Didn't it seem like it? I'm not jealous or anything, but I don't like that. Penny Lane is smart, but she might not know about him, what he's really like. *I* didn't know what he was really like. Do you think I should tell her about him?"

He shrugs.

"I mean, I feel weird about it. But I *love* her, I don't want her to get hurt."

But Chi can't think about Penny Lane. "How do those dealers know you, Starbright?" he says.

She sighs. "Stan made me deliver some acid. Well, he said it was acid. They were the connection. They weren't even sure who he is. God. I was really stupid." Her face falls.

"Well, he manipulated you, Starbright."

"He did, he really did. Plus, he took a hundred dollars from me."

"Really!"

She looks away. "I mean, I lent it to him. He's supposed to pay me back." But her lip trembles.

A twinge of guilt needles him. Is he manipulating Starbright, too? She is tough about some things, but otherwise she's so open, so eager to please. What a gap between young-teen and twenty-one. Chi and his peers consider themselves infants at twenty-one. They've got more than a hundred years ahead of them. They try not to get old too soon. Yet as fast as this girl wants to grow up, she's still so young and vulnerable.

He takes out the Communication Company mimeograph that Cowboy gave her.

> The riot may last as long as a week. Your problems in this
> state of war in the streets include not getting killed or
> stomped, having enough food, getting somewhere else alive
> if your house burns down, and not getting arrested.

The riots in Detroit and Newark are front-page news. It saddens and frightens him to witness how long racism and poverty persist. Will persist.

He doesn't like it. Four black hoodies. Big-time dealers who think Starbright is part of a burn. And a race riot in the Haight-Ashbury? But violence is contrary to everything hip people like Ruby believe in.

He doesn't have to calculate those probabilities.

"Let's not go back to the scene if those dealers are hanging around Haight Street today," he says. "Okay?"

"Okay!"

He takes Starbright by the hand. They catch the next bus across the bridge to Sausalito.

GOSSIP, INNUENDO & ALL THE NEWS THAT FITS

Q: Did you have a long relationship [with the father]?

SANDRA: No, he doesn't even know. I just wanted the baby. I wanted a choice of colors. I could have had green, pink, Chinese, anything. And I said, "What color do I want?" Why not blend the races? All this hypocrisy and prejudice. It should all be a blending. The races should mix with no fear, no hatred. When this tension is gone, just think how much more beautiful things will be.

So guess what I did?

It was a really shitty hotel area of New York. I was serving beer in one of those clubs to get money to get back to San Francisco. And I knew it was time to get pregnant. So I was walking around, looking around. And I looked at all the faces and I said, is there anybody there I want to make a baby for me? And I could tell right away, there was no face. There [was] no face for my baby. . . . It's funny because people would say, "Oh, how shocking," but it isn't really shocking at all. It's the same thing as if a college girl wanted to get pregnant by the football captain or something. It's the same thing, only this was a different trip. So I [went] looking at the guy [who was] washing, and the guy turns around and he had a beautiful brown face, full at the temples—like a wood carved face—beautiful to look at, and I said, that's the one.

> —From interview with Sandra Butler,
> *Voices of the Love Generation,* by
> Leonard Wolf (Little, Brown and
> Company, 1968)

The shoreline below Sausalito is astonishing. Bridgeway Avenue is an overland road with ground traffic, not the romantic canal set off by a sea breakwall on one side, extravagant piers and clubs and casinos on the other. Blue-gray water laps low against chaotic chunks of slate. Greenish-red rock crabs crawl along the waterline like tourists. The wind is sweet and salty.

They sit together on a flat gray boulder and gaze at the city skyline across the Bay.

He searches the hills behind him, sees only a few small houses here and there, pink and yellow and blue. The place high above Bridgeway where the towers and domes of his family's estate will stand is a tossing patch of undistinguished greenery. Great Victorian estates once stood upon these hills at the turn of this century. Great domed estates will stand here centuries later. But in 1967, Sausalito is like a young girl with flowers in her hair.

He catches her studying him. "I've never known anyone named Chiron Cat's Eye in Draco," she says, sipping her Coke. "Is that your street name or do you have a real name?"

He laughs at her mockery of his question. "That's my real name."

"Does it mean something?"

He nods. "Chiron is an asteroid. Not in the Jovian asteroid belt, but between Saturn and Uranus. Way out there. Might be a far-system terraforming project some century. The asteroid is named for Chiron, the centaur. That's a half-horse, half-man. A myth from the ancient Greeks. His symbol is a key."

"A key?" She eyes him suspiciously.

"A key." He thinks a minute. "Not a kilo of grass. Like this." He takes his house key to 555 Clayton and scratches on a rock.

"Oh, a key." She takes out her house key, too, and scratches one of her strange eyes with a star for a pupil. "Hey, let me borrow your maser."

"Nope."

"Please."

"Uh-uh."

"I bet I can carve this rock with it. Please, please, please?" she whines.

"Can't do it, Starbright. Against the Tenets."

"You and your Tenets." The pout. "I saw you. You carved the sidewalk, just like that."

"I can't let you touch my tools."

"Then you hold the maser, and I'll guide your hand."

He cannot believe he is doing this. He takes out the maser. She places her hand over his and, after a few preliminary doodles, like a dancer leading the couple in a waltz, she draws.

"Wow!" she says when they're done. "You really *can* carve with this thing!"

"Put your hand on mine," he says, not to be outdone. She does. Now he leads. Next to her flower, he draws.

She shrieks with laughter. A fellow on a sailboat anchored offshore looks up from swabbing his deck to see what's going on. Chi pockets the maser.

"You make me crazy, Starbright. That's a serious Tenet Seven violation."

"Oh, so what."

"So what. What if I disappeared and your hair turned green after that little stunt? Hmm?"

"Is reality that easy to change just 'cause we drew some silly pictures on the rocks?"

In her uncanny naive way, she has hit upon one of the big questions, like a child asking what happens when we die. He has no answer. The LISA techs have no answer. He gazes at the rocks, wondering himself. *Kick the beach, go ahead, do it.* "Sometimes the probabilities collapse into the timeline," he says unhappily. "Sometimes they don't."

She nods, satisfied, and tips her paper cup, getting a mouthful of ice. She chews. "You're always asking questions about me. What about you, Chi? Who are you, really?"

He shrugs. Damn SOL Project, he didn't ask for this.

"See, you don't want to tell me, either," she teases.

For a moment he shakes with the impulse to let her have it, vent his rage at what her people will do to the Earth and to the future. No, Chi, he tells himself. Don't rage against Starbright. Not her. She crunches her ice, watching him with open curiosity. He cringes at the crunching sound. He can practically see her tooth enamel cracking and chipping. She doesn't have a resiliency tweak, let alone mouth swathe.

"I'm just a student," he says at last.

"Really?"

"Sure. Like you. Well, a little ahead of you. I was about to take my doctorate in medical modeling, with a pro link application, before I was drafted for the SOL Project."

"The SOL Project?"

"The Summer of Love."

Cosmic Mind, how distant his own day seems. Of his Now, but so far away from it. Not of this Now, but growing closer. The discrepancy is painful. Sometimes he wonders if he'll ever leave the past. As of July 27, 1967, the probabilities of his successful translation-transmission to 2467 are no more than sixty-six percent.

"What does that mean, pro link? Like golf, or something? You're like Arnold Palmer?"

He laughs. "Pro link means I'm professionally rigged for telelink. Most of my modeling experiments are conducted in telespace."

"Telespace?"

It's prime, the mega thing. Telespace, he tells her, is a four-dimensional, computer-generated reality maintained by mainframes, vast banks of them. Telespace: the aggregated correlation of a hundred million minds worldwide. A super net, a hyper-reality. You entered telespace by jacking in your telelink—equipment and programming installed in early childhood.

"Installed?" Starbright says warily.

With utter carelessness, he sweeps the long red hair implants aside, takes off the synskin patch at the base of his skull, and, in broad daylight, shows her his neckjack.

"God," she whispers, staring at the aperture, the cortical wiring rippling up his spine into his neck, diving here and there into his skull. He knows what it looks like. A fine piece of surgery, a web of wetware. Venus Rising has felt him there before.

"Go ahead," he says. "You can touch me."

She does. "What's it like?"

"Telespace?" he says. "It's a rush! A clean sweep of amber burning through your Being. You *are* the amber, the juice. Pure. You're real. More real than out-of-link could ever be. You become part of the Universal Intelligence, you see. You can access huge memories if you want to. You can go Macro and view the whole universe. Or you can go Micro and view the whole universe." He laughs. "And it is so fast, Starbright. Man, you zoom! You work at speeds and in ways you never thought possible. Jack up, link in, space out!"

She squints at him, crunching ice in her teeth. "Sounds like LSD."

He is taken aback. "That's ridiculous!"

"No, it really does." She looks surprised at his annoyance. "I've tripped, too, you know."

"I'm talking about telespace!"

"That's cool." She stretches her legs over the rocks, lobs a stone into the waves. She gives him a sidelong glance. "So what else are you not telling me? Do you have a girlfriend somewhere?"

A lass, somewhen. Venus Rising. The very thought of her makes him smile unlike he's been moved to smile in too many days. "I have a girlfriend, yes."

Starbright gazes out to sea. Her lip trembles. "What's her name?"

"Venus Rising," he says. "For the first star of the evening."

"The first star of the evening! My name means the first star of the evening, too." She wraps a lock of hair round her finger and bites the ends. "What's she like?"

Venus Rising. Exquisite is the word. A tall lass, nearly as tall as he. Reed-slender with graceful bones, her jack on the left of her neck, skin the color of fine white-gold. They met on a bicycle Path and donated two giftdays together the week after. Both rigged for professional telelink, they soon put their fine minds and prime hardware to a delicious use.

Free-link.

"Venus Rising was the one who discovered we could tinker with the standard neckjack and interface directly, booted only through a palmtop minidisk. Forget access codes and monitors and utility surveillance. There are no secrets in public telespace. We discovered the private side of link." He chuckles. "Free-link. It's illegal."

She frowns, but he is so caught up in the sweet recollection of free-linking with Venus Rising that he pays little attention. "Can you get busted?" she says.

"Hell, yes! Generating unauthorized private telespace outside the mainframes? That's first-degree link-abuse."

"Then why do it?"

"Because," he says, "it's so exquisite! The applications are enormous. But we went straight to making love. Link to link, Starbright. Mind to mind, fantasy to fantasy. When she wants me to touch her, I *know*. And she *knows,* and she loops her pleasure back to me, directly into my pleasure center. We can overlay illusions to optical perception or, even better, surrender optics to telespace simulation. She can be anything for me. I can be anything for her. I can be a . . . a cat or a bull or a woman or another man. Whatever she wants."

Starbright blushes scarlet. She opens her mouth and shuts it. "Why would you want to be a woman?"

"For the ecstasy!" He smiles at Starbright's pout. He pats her hand. "Maybe you'll understand someday."

"No, I understand. I'm not a virgin, you know."

"I know," he says. Careful, Chi. Their relationship is fragile enough.

"What color is her hair?" she persists.

"She doesn't have hair."

"*What?*"

"She's bald. Like me."

"You're not bald!"

"Yes. Yes, I am."

In 2446, the year of Chi's birth, a million children died in California cities alone of the dreadful collection of symptoms known as radiation syndrome. Not just among devolts, exdomers, day laborers, the poor, the middle classes. Upper-class children attending schools and camps under public domes fell ill. And children of the rich who lived under private domes, who had always been protected from the sun, who ate food grown in private gardens and fish raised in private ponds, who had drunk filtered water; *they* fell ill. No one could shield babies and young children from the vast poisons of the world. Certain toxins and types of radiation caused massive cellular breakdown, leading to inevitable, painful death.

"The technopolistic plutocracy ignored the problem for decades," Chiron says. "Everyone was caught up in the population crisis. People advocated nonintervention with death. No one cared about the grief of the poor. No one wanted to come out and say so, but the poor were generally considered most responsible for the population crisis in the first place."

The radiation vaccine—the rad-vacc—was a vaccine in the sense that it was a preparation of an attenuated infective agent used to produce an active artificial immunity. The infective agent consisted of a microdose of the deadly toxins and certain radioactive substances. The vaccine portion was boosted by a nanotechnological application of smart robocells that escorted the microdose about the body and imported mini-microdoses to a strategic number of cells.

"Look, we were pushing hard for negative growth. But, even so, the next generation had to live. I remember how my skipmother monitored everything I ate or drank. Everywhere I went, everything I touched. I felt like an invalid. And I remember when the first safe dose of the rad-vacc was announced. I was five years old. Anyone could get it free! The lines went three times around our school. They handed out doses of rad-vacc in nutricubes. Everyone wanted to take it."

Chiron unbuttons his cuff, rolls up his shirt sleeve. He shows Starbright his arm. He pulls his jeans up over the ankle of his Beatle boot, shows her his leg. She runs her fingertips over his smooth, ivory skin. He remembers Ruby's astonished look. Starbright's face is hard to read.

"There was a side effect, you see," he says. "For children under age ten. Had to do with the robocells' importation of the mini-microdose to cells at the epidermal level. The dose had to be stronger there, more intensive. Well, we all went bald, top to bottom."

"I'm sorry," Starbright whispers.

He pulls his jeans leg down, rolls back his cuff. "Don't be. It was a miracle! The rad-vacc saved millions of lives and freed us from the domes. Anyone older than ten who took the first rad-vacc wasn't affected. They've improved it since. Doesn't cause baldness in young children anymore."

"But what's this?" She touches his long red hair.

"Implants! Oh, we can get implants. Just like you and your friends in the Haight-Ashbury can get haircuts. We choose not to, just like you don't want to cut your hair. Me and my friends, we're the cool tools who are nude. As you say, we dig it. Starbright, bald is *beautiful*!"

She stares at him, openmouthed.

In what other day has the youth of the world so joyfully celebrated baldness? What other youth has made baldness a statement of their generation?

"Bald is prime!" he declares. "When something is especially pleasing? We say, 'It's nude.' There's nothing like pure skin to make you pay attention to every muscle, every curve, every pore. Nude is mega, Starbright!"

"Then you . . . walk around with no clothes?"

"Oh, no. We like headgear. Hats and scarves, all manner of accoutrements. Head-painting is in. Venus Rising paints her entire skull, works the designs down her forehead, around her eyes and cheeks, down her neck. You should see her chrysanthemum design. Pink petals on top. Stems curling around her ears. Leaves falling over her shoulders. You should see her clouds and lightning design, it's extraordinary. Or her tidepool and fish. Or her feathers and birds. And body-painting? You should see her body-painting!"

But he has struck another nerve. Starbright frowns again, furrowing her brow.

"Would Venus Rising like my drawings?" she asks shyly.

He breaks from his reverie. Ah, Venus Rising. "Sure she would."

"Would Venus Rising like the drawing of Isis I did for the Mystic Eye?"

"Sure."

"Do *you* like it?"

"Your Isis drawing is very good, Starbright. You have talent. More talent than you know."

A swift glance, pooled with tears. "You really think so?"

"Well, you could use some training. You made the neck too long. It's disproportional."

"That's just what my mother says! My drawings are disproportional." The pout deepens.

He grits his teeth. Wrong answer. "The drawing of Isis is very nice, but her neck is too long. You want me to tell you the truth, don't you? You should study anatomy. It would help you."

"I know all the bones in the human ear."

"That's a start."

"That's just stupid memorization." She whispers, "You like bald women."

"Well," he says. "I guess I don't think of it that way."

Then, trembling, she says, "You don't mind my hair?"

"I'm getting used to it."

This is not the right answer, at all. She snuffles, wipes her nose under the guise of pushing back a stray curl.

"What I mean is," he says, struggling for words. "What I mean is, your hair is fine, Starbright."

Still not good enough. A tear escapes the corner of her eye. She turns her back to him.

Women! Do they ever change? I want you to want me, but I'm not sure if I want you. That's the game this young woman is playing with him.

He wants to laugh. He longs to tell her not to worry about him. She has her whole life ahead of her. A life without him.

Who are you, Starbright? Are you truly the Axis?

For he found Disk 4 last night. He searched the contraband holoids, testing for access over and over, while he raged at his skipmother and wondered for the hundredth time why she decided to torture him like this. He tested and retested the crystal slivers till after midnight when the H drive engaged and the tiny red message he'd been waiting for popped up in the field of blue:

"07-27-1967. You may insert Disk 4 now."

He doesn't laugh. He strokes the back of Starbright's bowed head and recalls what he saw on Disk 4.

You have nice hair, Starbright, for hair. But, if you truly are the Axis, one day you'll cut your long, soft curls. One day you'll get gray. If you're the Axis, you will change in ways you cannot know. But your tears will stay with you. After your first daughter is born, you will win the high school senior prize, along with the National Merit Scholarship Award, and the Archives will finally contain another image of you. You will discover an affinity for science, and you will struggle with amphetamine abuse. After your years at Columbia University and Harvard Medical School and postdoctoral work in immunology, you will still draw romantic pictures of goddesses. After the first marriage and a difficult divorce, a challenging second marriage and another daughter and a son, you will still cry at the sight of someone dying and just as swiftly at a beautiful kitten. If you're the Axis, they will think you are impossibly eccentric when you lobby against the use of animals in medical research, but they will never doubt your brilliance. You will not return to San Francisco except to visit your daughter, who will go to Stanford University. After twenty years of watching men and women suffer and die from an awful wasting disease, you will cry at the age of fifty-five when your life's work, the DNA mutation experiment, fails. But seven years later, when your daughter wins the Nobel Prize for the AIDS cure, and she thanks you for the inspiration you always gave her, up on the podium, in front of all those people, you will cry while they give you a standing ovation.

If you're the Axis.

Gulls wheel and cry in the sky above.

That's what he longs to tell her. You have fine hair and a pretty young body and a quick intelligence. But never lose your gentle heart, Starbright. That's your most precious gift.

But of course he cannot say any of this. If she *is* the Axis, he cannot reveal her future. Tenet Six, of course. Anyway, who would want to know? Conserve at least this last illusion of free will.

And if Starbright is just another longhaired girl who ran away to the Haight-Ashbury for the Summer of Love, the life of the Axis will mean nothing to her.

He says nothing. He strokes her hair, her wavy, light brown hair. He has never felt such a profound ache in his heart.

Then, in a flash, he realizes: If Starbright *is* the Axis, he need not tell her. She will fulfill her destiny as surely as the sun rises.

If she, and the daughter she carries, survive this hot dim spot.

He is struck with overwhelming tenderness for her, this lush, pouting girl with tears in her brown eyes, who may play such an important role in history one day. Upon whose life the conservation of spacetime as he knows it depends. He takes her limp hand, kisses her fingertips. She looks up, startled. Another tear spills. He kisses that, too, and wraps his arms around her. He catches his breath for a moment against the furry scent of her hair, the saltiness of her body. Then he relaxes and allows the smell of her, the feel of her, to drift into him.

In another fit of shyness, she stiffens, pulls away from him. This spacetime includes her tears, too. Her thoughts and her feelings are as much a part of this Now as the gulls wheeling above. Why is she sad?

She is as elusive as dreams or whispered words, the half-remembered rumors of childhood.

12

A Whiter Shade
of Pale

 Ruby is ready for the riot before nightfall. She packs most of the Mystic Eye's inventory into three dozen cardboard boxes. She and Morgana lug the boxes out back and stack them in the garage. Come eight-thirty, as clouds blow in from the ocean and dusk spreads out from the hills, the two women sit on the front steps, sipping apple juice and fanning themselves, soaked with sweat and paranoia.

" 'To smash something is the ghetto's chronic need.' James Baldwin wrote that in *Notes of a Native Son*. He was talking about the Harlem riot in August '43," Ruby says. "Sweet Isis, I was younger than a flower child in August '43."

"The Haight-Ashbury isn't a ghetto," Morgana says.

"Sure it is," Ruby says. "The Hashberry is the Love Ghetto."

They laugh, but the sound rings hollow.

A flatbed truck rolls by, packed with rolled-up Persian carpets, three-foot-high brass water pipes, black lights the size of baseball bats. The grim driver waves. Some HIP merchants are moving their best goods out of the neighborhood till the riot is done or the rumors blow over, whichever comes last. Mnasidika and the Print Mint have sent out the word that any hip person who has no place to sleep can get off the street tonight and stay in their deserted shops.

A haystack of plywood planks sits at Ruby's feet. She intends to board up her front windows before it gets dark. The windows will cost five hundred bucks apiece to replace, not to mention the damage if people get in and tear the place up. All her beautiful shelves and cases and counters, crafted by hand. Five years' worth of work.

H. Rap Brown says violence is as American as cherry pie. What if they start fires, like in Watts in '65? Like in Detroit last week?

She doesn't want to think about it. Just take care of business. Got her bankbooks and business records, her photograph albums and psychedelic posters, the jewelry her mother left her plus the cats' five pet carriers, waiting by the kitchen door. What else can she carry in the BMW if they set her place on fire? Not much more. Take only the most important things.

Ruby wipes her brow with a handkerchief, throws the sopping cloth down with disgust. She picks up a book from the stack she left on the stoop. Anna Riva's *Secrets of Magical Seals*. She pores through it again, searching for some practical magic. The book depicts all manner of marks and symbols: Solomon's seals, signs of the Goetia, voodoo vèvès. A vèvè is a decorative design that incorporates shapes and images symbolizing supernatural forces. Voodooists draw vèvès to invoke the supernatural forces, press them into service, put them to work. Far out. Ruby finds the vèvè for Legba. Legba is the protector of doorways, a guardian against thieves. Yes. She takes a scarlet chalk that Starbright left behind and very carefully draws the vèvè on the sidewalk in front of the Mystic Eye.

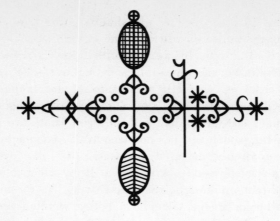

Where is Starbright? She needs an artist now.

"We're conducting a ceremony at my house tonight to invoke Bune," Morgana says. "He's one of the Goetia. We were going to sacrifice a dove, but everyone voted against it. We decided we shouldn't kill an innocent being." She says this as matter-of-factly as if she told Ruby they're baking banana bread tonight.

Morgana is a tall, sturdy woman with a mane of curly hair and a full Celtic face. She's a witch. She lives in the House of Magick, a commune of women on Baker Street. Some strange things go on there, that's the rumor. Everyone loves a good rumor, preferably with sex. So many rumors floating around, the weirder, the better. But the women from the House of Magick don't seem all that strange. Morgana works the drawer for Ruby some afternoons. So does Bettina. They are scrupulously honest. Anne-Marie conducts tarot readings in the back of the shop on Thursdays. Ishbette casts astrological charts on Fridays. They buy magic candles and incense, exotic jewelry, Indian saris in saffron and teal. Ruby gives them a big discount.

And that's how Ruby has always regarded the women at the House of Magick. The hired help, contractors on a percentage, or good regular customers. She never thought one way or another about their lifestyle. Whomever they sleep with is their business. It's uncool to indulge in rumors.

But what about her? What about her lifestyle? What about her feelings toward Starbright?

Is she discovering at the age of thirty-five she is not who she thought she was? What a time to find out, during the Summer of Love.

Why, she could find herself one girlfriend or three. She could join a group of swingers. She could call someone straight out of the classified ads and taste the forbidden fruit any night. No one in the neighborhood would think less of her. No one would even be shocked.

But, no. That's not her way. All right, so she did the Beat scene. So she wrote nasty poetry and ate peyote. Slept with white cats, black cats, took the purple people eater to her bed. She loved the Beat scene because the Beat scene accepted her, welcomed her mongrel pedigree. Yet she never saw herself as a frivolous person, even then. Or impulsive. Well, maybe a little impulsive. But not heedless. She has always been firmly in the driver's seat. In control.

This is all different, an alien thing. This challenges her very identity. Does she think less of herself? Or more? Is *she* shocked? For she is drawn to the kid, yes, and the kid is drawn to her. Starbright adores her, hugs her and kisses her. But this girl's love isn't carnal. The kid is like a kitten climbing onto her lap, seeking warmth and a scratch under the chin. And Ruby? For the first time in her life, she doesn't feel in control. She looks in the mirror and doesn't know herself.

Is it possible to have a romantic relationship without sex? Or is she being cheated?

"Bune, Bune. Which seal is that? Let me see." Ruby takes *The Lesser Key of Solomon: Goetia, the Book of Evil Spirits* from Morgana's hands. This is a rare book. You can't find this book just anywhere. People used to be burned at the stake for possessing a book like this. Fortunately, Sergeant Billy Dillon doesn't care about books. Just herbs.

These magic seals—strange little drawings inside circles—are used in ceremonies by magicians to summon the Goetia, spirits of the infernal regions. Ruby studies the seal. Bune is the Twenty-sixth Spirit, appearing in the form of a Dragon with three heads, a Dog, a Gryphon, and a Man. Bune governs thirty Legions of Spirits. So if you could appease Bune, perhaps you could stop the riot. That makes sense. The seal is complex, with swooping loops and glyphs.

She sighs. She's too tired to draw that. "Thanks, Morgana. You've done enough. Better go home and lock your doors."

"I will," Morgana says and squeezes her shoulder. "Listen, Ruby. I feel that everything will be all right. Venus is in Virgo. That's a peaceful place to be."

"Yes, but the moon is in Aries," Ruby snaps. "That means violence in the subconscious mind of the world."

"Maybe so," Morgana says. She hurries away before Ruby can apologize for being blunt.

Ruby throws down *The Lesser Key of Solomon.* She hauls herself to her feet, bends her aching back to the stack of lumber. She gets her hammer, bites on a couple of nails, and takes up a plywood plank. Damn, but she's tired. Forget it, get that hammer pounding. Evil spirits aren't summoned by this ancient text. Violence isn't in the moon. The vèvè drawn in chalk on the sidewalk won't help her.

No, the evil is *here*, in only too human form. On the streets of San Francisco, during the Summer of Love.

Or will Devolved Entities Manifested from the Other Now be let loose tonight?

She is worried sick. Where is Starbright?

Leo Gorgon pulls into the driveway in his ragtag truck, hops out. With the kid! She and Chiron slide out the other side. Chiron offers his hand to help her down, but she ignores him. She is flushed with sunburn.

"Uh-huh," Ruby says, glaring at them as she pounds the last nail in the last plank. "Just in time for dinner. And the curfew."

"Look who I picked up hitchhikin' on Market Street," Gorgon says.

"We were not hitchhiking," Starbright says.

"We were waiting for the bus," Chiron says.

"And where did we go today?" Ruby says.

"Sausalito," they say together.

"Nice work, Ruby," Gorgon says, jutting his chin at the boarded-up windows. "Say, I got this hole that needs fixin'. I don't suppose you could swing my way."

"I'll swing your way," Ruby says and swipes the hammer at his head, only half in jest. Gorgon doesn't come around like he used to. When he does stop by for an afternoon tryst, his harangues against HIP merchants have gotten more vicious. He has actually started calling her a whore, which she will not tolerate.

He seizes her hand, takes the hammer away, and flings it to the sidewalk. The hammer crashes, gouging the center of Chi's delicate heart.

"Damn you, Leo," she says and lets him kiss her. His kiss is rough, exciting. He smells of sex and patchouli oil, a scent Ruby never wears.

She pulls away.

"Ready for the revolution?" Gorgon grins. He hands her a Communication Company mimeograph.

She reads:

Within the black people's mind, they will be fighting a
revolution. If you hamper them in any way, you will be their
enemy. During the riot, the only help they want from you is
your gun. If not that, get the fuck out of their way!

"Did you write this, Leo?" Ruby says, sweet as poison.

He nods proudly. "Me an' Cowboy musta passed out a thousand of 'em today."

"Got it all on good authority, did you?" she says.

"Well." He hesitates. "It's what we heard, anyway."

"Do you have any notion what you're doing?" She finds herself shouting. "You're starting *rumors,* Gorgon!"

"But it's true! The Fillmore's gonna blow tonight."

"Says *who*? Who asked *you*?"

"Wow," Starbright says, staring at the vèvè on the sidewalk. "What is *that*?"

Before Ruby can tell her about Legba and voodoo vèvès, Papa Al, the burly hipster who volunteers at the Free Clinic, comes tearing around the corner of Haight and Clayton. They all turn and stare. Papa Al clatters up the clinic's stairs, bursts in the front door, bursts back out again with four scruffy boys in tow. One boy has got his wrist in a cast.

"We need more people!" Papa Al shouts, hustling the boys before him. The boys scatter in every direction, footsteps ringing in the empty street. "Go get more people!"

"What's going on, Papa Al?" Ruby calls to him.

"I saw dozens of spades, man! Dozens of spades with shopping bags full of knives!"

"Full of knives! Where?"

"Comin' from the Fillmore, man!"

Dr. David Smith races down the stairs. "Papa Al," he says reasonably, "we can't close the clinic. I've got patients here tonight."

"You've got to close it down!" Papa Al shouts.

"What if people get hurt?" Dr. Smith glances about, his face taut with apprehension. "What if people need medical attention?"

With one hand, Papa Al pulls out a thirty-eight caliber revolver. With the other hand, he pulls out a Colt forty-five. He pushes past Dr. Smith and sprints up the stairs, waving the guns. In a flash, he's out again, dragging two young men. Each young man holds a fire ax. They stand at either side of the door, wide-eyed and tense, axes held high like Roman guards in a B movie.

Papa Al positions himself halfway down the stairs, brandishing his guns.

Now Teddybear, Papa Al's sidekick, races around the corner.

"I seen carloads of spades with machine guns!" he yells. "They're comin'!"

Ruby retrieves her hammer and the rest of her wood, and hurries inside the shop. Starbright and the men follow. She triple-locks the front door and hammers two planks, crisscrossed, on the inside. She peers out her peephole.

The street is so empty and silent and dark, Ruby finds herself missing the carnival crowd she used to curse.

Grandmother Says: Lu (Treading on the Tail of the Tiger)

The Image: The sky is above, the lake below. This is the placement
of the elements. When vapor lifts from the lake, however, it rises
to the sky and makes rain. The tiger has a temper when he is
hungry.

The Oracle: One who is humble seeking advancement among the
powerful is permitted to rise when the principle of placement of
the elements is observed.

When universal equality does not exist, class struggle takes
place. One who is in a lower position advances through the
accomplishment of worthy goals, the righting of injustices, strength,
quality, and perseverance. Beware, however, if the lake rises above
the sky. Beware if the tiger turns to bite.

—Hexagram 10, *The I Ching* or Book of Changes

Dear *Barb:*
I was raised in segregated schools and never knew individual Negroes
till, at age 17, I was arrested with black college students in a CORE
lunch counter sit-in. It was easy to relate to the acculturated middle-
class Negro students who then (1960) led the civil rights movement.
But I was surprised in summer '63 as a voter registration worker in
the black ghetto of a small Southern town to find I had nothing much
to say to uneducated working-class Negroes. Worse yet, when I moved
into Harlem, my neighbors were hostile, shouted "Whitey, go home"
when I walked the street, causing me to move back to the East Village
after only 2 or 3 weeks. . . .

At first I felt indignant: "I'm not prejudiced, so why should
Negroes discriminate against me?" I've probably done more for Negro
rights than most of them. When criticized by the nationalists, I still

feel the temptation to ask how many times they have gone to jail for black freedom (compared to my 5 or 6). . . .

But my indignation is unjustified. Negroes believed in racial equality and brotherhood for 300 years. Did we love them back?

Moral for white hippies: we must expect to "pay dues" for our position in life, just as the Negro does.

We can hardly expect to be loved.

Signed,
J.P.

—From Letters to the Editor
  Berkeley Barb, Vol. 5, No. 1, Issue
  99 (July 7–13, 1967)

Dig it:

The underground is buzzing with rumors, some of which Ruby knows are true. At the International Congress on the Dialectics of Liberation in London, Stokely Carmichael announced that color is a state of mind. If black people choose to be white, he said, they should be shot like any other white person.

They say Jimi Hendrix's father is black and his mother is a full-blooded Cherokee. Jimi told reporters, "I don't *feel* black. I feel the music."

Would Stokely Carmichael have Jimi Hendrix shot?

The Black Panthers are exciting and handsome in their berets, leather jackets, bandoliers of bullets crisscrossed over their strapping chests. The white revolutionary boys are especially excited by the Black Panthers. The latest fashion statement on Haight Street is berets, leather jackets, bandoliers of bullets crisscrossed over strapping chests.

But what about the young black hustlers Ruby sees stalking about the Haight-Ashbury? The street spades, that's what they're called. She sees them rapping their kill-whitey rhetoric, working the crime angle, hitting on hip women of any color, or all of the above. Who is telling these young men to go to school, become lawyers and doctors? Pool their resources, own businesses, elect their own political leaders? Build up their community, not tear things down. Who is telling them? Martin Luther King tells them, Whitney Young tells them. But Dr. King and Dr. Young don't wear handsome black berets, leather jackets, exciting bandoliers of bullets crisscrossed over their chests.

Gorgon goes back outside to pull his truck into Ruby's driveway. Starbright sits on the couch in the living room, surrounded by the cats, anxiously studying the Communication Company mimeograph.

"You don't need to read that," Ruby says to the kid.

"I already saw it today."

"Confusing, isn't it?" she says.

The kid nods.

Ruby sits next to her on the couch. "Don't be confused," Ruby says. "This riot thing? This talk of shooting whitey, and the revolutionary boys running around, all excited by the prospect of a street fight? The whole damn thing; it's a shuck. A shuck, you hear me?"

Guilt brims in Starbright's big brown eyes.

Ruby pats her hand. "This is just the sort of stupidity that the personal revolution will not abide. Aggression and violence are Establishment games. The revolutionaries will tell you love is weak, but they're wrong, Starbright. They're wrong, isn't that true, man from Mars?" Ruby says to Chiron. "Things will be different in the future. We'll cut the crap. We'll achieve a society based on opportunity and merit and deeds. People will be recognized for their intelligence and talent and hard work. People will be honored for their good will and their good hearts. For *love*. Whether you are white, black, tangerine, or green. That's the way the future will be. Right, am I right?"

But Chi is silent.

Gorgon clatters up the back stairs, hauling the tin of gasoline from his truck.

"Where do you think you're going with that?" Ruby says.

Gorgon says nothing. He goes into the kitchen, rattles her trash can, comes out with four empty wine bottles.

"Your love shuck is bullshit," Gorgon says.

"Maybe," Ruby says. "And maybe not. Violence and destruction definitely are bullshit."

He goes to the half-bath, pulls a pillowcase from her linen closet, and rips it to strips. "You can't change things without tearin' em' down."

"Leo!" Ruby screams, scattering the cats.

But he's gone. Out the kitchen door and up the back stairs, to the roof.

The moon in Aries is a scythe in the sky. From the roof, Ruby can see Papa Al and Teddybear conferring on the stairs of the Free Clinic. A cluster of terrified patients in pajamas gather about the front door.

The two guards lean their axes on the ground, but their stance is still tense.

"What's goin' on, man?" Gorgon calls to them, leaning over the gutter and gingerbread trim. He's filled the wine bottles with gasoline, stuffed strips of the torn pillowcase in their necks, spilled a box of kitchen matches.

"We called Chocolate George," Teddybear yells up. "The Hells Angels say they're gonna come and kick some black ass, man!"

Starbright hovers behind her.

"Get back," Ruby says, pressing her arm against the kid's chest.

A shimmer of ebony deeper than the night sky ripples across the roof. The gutter begins to rattle, like an earthquake striking.

Starbright hovers behind her again.

"I told you, get *back*!" Ruby turns and pushes her by the shoulders, like she is pushing away the feelings the kid has stirred in her. The kid stumbles backward, face twisted with surprise, and falls on her butt. Ruby does not go and comfort her.

"Chi," Ruby calls in a ragged whisper. He crouches by her side at once. "What's happening? Things are getting strange, can't you see it? What's going on?"

Chiron whispers, "Katie" at his magic ring, whispers other things that make no sense. He cups the slice of blue light in his palm. The light flickers eerily in the darkness. "Ruby," he finally says. "I've checked three times. I've got no record in the files of a race riot in the Haight-Ashbury during the Summer of Love. No record at all."

"What do you mean? What are you saying?"

"The riot is a probability." He whispers, "Katie, off." The blue light disappears. His eyes are puzzled, anguished. "But it doesn't have to happen, Ruby. I'm telling you, it doesn't have to happen!"

She stares at him, his face impossibly pale and baby-smooth. He used to look so innocent to her, but not anymore. Not so innocent and not so familiar. *Who are you*, she thinks for the thousandth time. *What are you*, Chiron Cat's Eye in Draco? And in a white rabbit flip of reality, it occurs to her that this elegant lad really could be a tachyporter from 2467. Suddenly, this makes more sense to her than what is happening on Haight Street tonight.

It doesn't have to happen.

She nods at him, then creeps across the roof to Gorgon. Gorgon's four Molotov cocktails are arranged before him in a semicircle.

Two drunks, one black and one white, stagger down Clayton Street. They walk arm in arm, yodeling, "Wild thang; you make my heart sang." They cannot carry a tune to save their lives.

For a moment, a huge, hollow-eyed face presses out of the whole wall of the house across the street, a gaping skull as big as the moon. Then disappears. Waves throb through the wall as though it's made of liquid.

"Gorgon," Ruby says, but she cannot catch his eye. He stares down at the street. "Who you gonna trash, huh? Your black brothers? Your black brothers, isn't that what you white revolutionary boys call them?"

"No," he says in a low voice, caressing the neck of a bottle with his fingers. "These are for the pigs, man."

The rooftop shivers, shaking as though the building is falling down.

"The pigs, uh-huh. And what good does that do for your black brothers if trash the pigs? What good does it do for *them,* man?"

He will not look at her. He breathes hard. "Capitalist pig, with your witch shit an' your love shuck." He spits. "What do you know about the revolution?"

She seizes his elbow. "I know this, sonny. I know it isn't *your* revolution."

He still won't look.

"*You're* not the one who will get hurt by this!"

He turns at last.

"You accuse me of selling out the revolution. You call me an opportunist. But that's exactly what you are. No, you don't care about money. Money isn't kicks for you. The *revolution* is kicks for you, Gorgon!"

His eyes flash fire.

"Right, am I right?" she says, heart pounding in her throat. "Just kicks, damn it!"

Gravel sweeps across the roof in a gust.

Gorgon plucks the rags out of the bottles and scatters their contents. He clatters down the stairs, leaving the stink of gasoline behind. Black glass shimmers in the moonlight.

Gorgon's truck is gone by the time they get downstairs.

It's over. Sweet Isis, her time with him is over, just as strangely as it began. Not likely she'll ever see Gorgon again. Just some cat she used to know during the Summer of Love. They will pass on the street like strangers.

But she still has to wait out this dreadful night. What to do?

"Sweet Isis," she says, "I'm hungry." Ravenous, in fact. Best thing she can think of to settle that sharp, empty feeling of another lover leaving her is a bottle of wine and hot food. She uncorks a crisp chenin blanc at once. "You kids eat dinner?"

"You know I can't eat, Ruby," Chi reminds her. He finally did show her his nutritional necklace one day when she remarked how much shorter it looked. He actually *eats* the *beads*—nutribeads, he calls them —which she thought was hilarious. He sternly lectured her for a good hour about contamination in food that a t-porter like himself cannot expose himself to. Right. He is so gaunt she can practically see what he will look like dead. He doesn't sound very convinced himself.

"I can't eat, either," Starbright says, plucking at her ribs through her gauze shirt. Since the abortion, the kid has become nearly as thin as the magazine models she studies so intently. Ruby wonders if she's dropping speed. She gives Ruby a hurt, soulful look. "You *pushed* me, Ruby."

She would love to throw her arms round the kid and give her a hug and a kiss, but no. No. Cool it with the hugs-and-kisses thing. The kid hardly knows what she wants, let alone what she's doing half the time. Ruby remembers being that age, filled with raging, ambiguous passions.

She shrugs. "Well, I'm cooking. You two watch the front window. See if anything is happening out there."

She has been so busy getting ready for the riot that she hasn't had time to go to the market. Her cupboard is practically bare. And all these dire warnings about stocking up on food for a state of siege. Nothing but bits and scraps in the fridge.

Six warped heels of bread, wheat, rye, and five-grain. She slices each heel lengthwise, slathers the bread-fingers with safflower butter, sprinkles on garlic powder, and puts them under a low broiler.

Got some eggs, and that's about it. She cracks them into a bowl, beats till they're frothy with a palmful of parsley, black pepper, sea salt, oregano. Stirs in the dollop of leftover salsa, thick and spiced with cayenne. Gets out her two cast-iron skillets. Ma said cook with iron 'cause it's good for the blood.

She coats the bottom of the first skillet with olive oil. What else does she have? A couple of baby carrots from the garden Chi planted. A medium red onion, two wilted scallions. Half a bell pepper that has seen better days, but it's not rotten. She peels the lonely half clove of garlic. Everything gets diced with a sharp knife. The moon in Aries is good for cutting, but watch your fingers. She heats the skillet on high, tosses everything in. Soon the scent of frying onions and toasted bread fills the kitchen. She quickly dices two tomatoes and a zucchini, another harvest from her garden. Black olives, a handful of garlic-packed mushrooms, the last golden pepperoncini left in the jar. In they go. Juice pops. She turns the vegetables over, puts on the lid, and turns the heat down.

She plunks a chunk of safflower butter in the second skillet and drizzles it with Japanese chili-sesame oil. Licks oil off her finger; that's hot! Turns the burner on high till the butter foams and tosses in the egg mixture. She scoops the eggs and flips them till they're half-cooked. In the meantime, the vegetable ragout is steaming. She adds more garlic, more garlic, more garlic. At last, she folds the vegetables through the eggs. She covers the skillet, turns the heat down.

What else has she got? A last dusting of Parmesan. In it goes, soaking up juice like a sponge, plumping with surprising flavors. A quarter of cheddar, a finger of Swiss, a cube of Gruyère. She dices bits and pieces of cheeses. Salvador Dali once said Jesus is cheese. In you go, Jesus. She turns her broiler on high. When it's good and hot, she takes the top off the skillet and places her concoction under the broiler for exactly fifty-three seconds, no more and no less.

Chiron and Starbright hover around the kitchen. Cheese bubbles, herbs release their odors. Humble eggs transmute into an exotica. Garlic bread-fingers toast to perfection. The cats gather, too, trilling and purring. They know what's good.

"A little bit of everything," Ruby says. "My Summer of Love spicy eggs. I'm glad no one wants to eat. More for me."

Eleven o'clock. Everything is still quiet, deserted.

Morgana phones. "The S Squad is sweeping the street tonight." The S Squad is the city's special police force, operating for the express purpose of closing hippie gathering spots in the Haight-Ashbury. "A big bust at 615 Cole Street," Morgana says. A friend of hers made her one permitted phone call to the House of Magick. "It's all on suspicion. The Man's got nothing but a flushing toilet."

Hippie gathering spots? Suspicion? Ruby pours herself another glass of wine and works out their story. Chiron is the son of a friend of

Ruby's deceased mother who now lives in Paris, and Starbright is Chi's cousin from the East Coast. They turn the music off, the lights down, and devour Ruby's Summer of Love eggs and toast.

It's the first time Ruby has seen Chiron eat food. He packs it away, like a skinny six-foot-four cat in his twenties should eat. Nutribeads, right. That's better, she thinks, pleased at his ecstatic expression over her makeshift meal. The kid wolfs hers down, too. "Wow," she keeps saying. "It's not Swanson's frozen Salisbury steak."

Ruby peers out the living room window. Papa Al, Teddybear, and a cadre of patients still stand guard at the clinic. But now they lounge on the steps, smoking, passing a bottle around. A cop car glides down Haight. The Hells Angels haven't shown up, for which Ruby breathes a sigh of relief. She likes the big cat with the fur hat, Chocolate George. Chocolate has a righteous reputation. He actually drinks chocolate milk instead of beer. But the rest of them? She dreads the sight of hogs and colors. The Angels are notorious for hating blacks, Jews, women, anyone not white, the police, other bikers, and each other. They are not people you want to have partying at your doorstep.

"I can't believe I ate that." Chi rubs his stomach, sipping the wine Ruby pressed on him. "I think I'm getting heartburn."

"You get heartburn?" Starbright says skeptically. The kid's tone is belligerent, a mood Ruby picked up earlier when she refused Chi's hand from the truck. Why? Chi has never excited more than a tolerant smile from her, much less anger.

"I think I'm getting it now," he says.

"Oh, I thought you were different," the kid says.

"Never ate real bird eggs before," he says. "Only the cultured stuff."

"You can't just turn off some switch?" the kid persists in a hostile tone.

"What's this? You can switch off heartburn in the future?" Ruby says. She's feels all right, considering. She sits in her rocking chair. Alana, the Angora, and Sita, the sealpoint queen, settle on her lap. Luna, the bluepoint, balances on her knee. Her boys, Ara and Rama, crouch around her ankles. The cats don't care for spicy eggs, but they devoured the bits of melted cheese over toast that Ruby fixed for them.

Chi shakes his head, a warning in his eyes. But the kid won't stop.

"He *is* different, Ruby. He showed me this afternoon. Didn't you, Chiron?"

He gives her a stony look.

Starbright says, "Yeah! He's got this thing like an electric plug, only it's real tiny. Right in the back of his neck. In his *skin*! It's gross. And he's got a girlfriend. You never told me you had a girlfriend," she says to him. To Ruby, "He's got this girlfriend who walks around naked all the time, and *she's* got a plug in her neck, too. He says they plug wires into their brains and telelink—isn't that what you call it, Chi? They *link* into a place that a computer makes called telespace."

"Plug your brain into a computer!" Ruby says. "What kind of science fiction nightmare is that?"

"The hardware enters at the base of the skull," Chi says brusquely. "The interior wetware interfaces with the arachnoid membrane in the brain, then connects at strategic points in various lobes."

"Sweet Isis, that sounds awful!"

"It isn't awful," Chi says, flushing. "Telespace is a miracle! It's a quantum leap in technology. The use of telelink is comparable to when people first mastered electricity, manufactured light bulbs, and safely lit the night. Or first understood bacteria, how microscopic organisms can kill us, and how to medicate against them. Or developed the internal combustion engine, the invention of automobiles and airplanes and rockets. Or discovered the silicon chip. In a decade, your calculating machine will be a laughable antique, Ruby."

"Not so fast," Ruby says. "I have *fought* for my calculating machine."

"Telespace, and our ability to interface via telelink, has made possible the mastery of data so vast you can't conceive of it. Made that mastery possible at speeds you can't imagine. Jack up, link in, space out. The ability to analyze ten thousand years of Archives was what made tachyportation to the past possible. Our ability to construct and implement in telespace the thought experiments of theoretical physics using link programs enabled physicists to overcome the hypothetical rest-mass dilemma. Enabled us to develop the ME3 Event to translate-transmit matter to energy and back, and apply tachyportation." He sits back with his glass of wine, haughty and arrogant and disgusted with them both. "You can't possibly know," he says.

"When I first came to the Haight-Ashbury," Starbright says, "I realized all sort of things about my life. The way my life was before the Summer of Love. School, and my parents, and everything. And you know what I kept thinking about? You know what I flashed on when I was tripping?"

Chiron won't answer, so Ruby says, "What's that, kid?"

"I flashed on a photograph in my biology textbook of a monkey used in a sleep experiment. They stuck wires into its skull and connected the wires to a machine that monitored its brain waves. Some kids in my class thought it was funny, but I didn't think it was funny at all. That's what I thought of today when I touched your neck, Chi. When you told me you and your girlfriend have wires plugged in your necks that are hooked up to a computer."

He sputters. "That's ridiculous!"

"I thought of the monkey," the kid says.

"That's reactionary! I've explained everything telespace can do. Telespace frees us. And telespace gives us pleasure."

"Pleasure?" Ruby says.

"My lass and I free-link," he says. "We each can access directly in to the other's pleasure center."

"My biology textbook said they did other experiments," Starbright says. "They plugged the wires into the monkey's pleasure center, too. They pushed a button and sent electricity there, and the monkey got a rush. Then they let the monkey push the button by itself. It pushed the button over and over. It wouldn't eat or sleep anymore. It just kept pushing the button." She goes and sits at Ruby's feet, hooking her elbow over Ruby's knee. "The monkey died."

Chi shakes his head, pours another glass of wine for himself, goes to the front window, and stares out.

Ruby reaches down in spite of herself and tangles her fingers in Starbright's hair. The kid is onto something.

"You talk about the cosmicists, Chi," Ruby says. "How far out they are. Do cosmicists link into telespace, too?"

"Of course. I'm a cosmicist."

"Uh-huh. And what does it mean to be a cosmicist?"

"We believe in the Cosmic Mind," he says. "In the cocreatorship of reality by humanity and Universal Intelligence. We believe in assuming responsibility for each individual's actions because each action affects all spacetime. To give is best. Live responsibly or die. That's what we believe."

"You also keep mentioning how rich you are."

"We've been responsible about consumption," he says.

"That's a principle in the hip community, too," Ruby says. "Free yourself from the consumer culture."

That stops him for a minute. "The cosmicists have launched major projects, like the Mars terraformation, by saving funds and investing them over decades. Over *centuries*," he says. "President Mitsui outlawed deficit spending to finance public works in the United States in 2093 and worked for two decades after that to restructure and establish an International Bank system based on True Value."

"But you're privileged," Ruby insists. She recalls the killing looks he and Gorgon have exchanged. "Fishponds in the Sausalito hills? Domed estates? Hmm?"

"Not all cosmicists are rich," he says, but his tone is defensive. "But all cosmicists have restructured their values from what you know. They have learned the genuine desire to benefit the world. They put aside self-interest and greed. They believe in opportunities for all people. And they have taught the people these new values, too."

"Put aside greed," Ruby says, trying to sort out Chi's rhetoric from whatever the truth may be. "But you don't say you give it all up. You don't even want to tell me there is no more racism or poverty in the future. Do you."

He is silent.

"Well, do you?"

"Life by definition is greedy, hungry, self-indulgent. Pleasure seeks pleasure. Life can't be self-sacrificing, not totally. Death is the only true sacrifice." Chiron sighs. "No, we have no intention of dissolving our family fortune. Yes, we expect a return on our investments. No one has given away a family fortune since Buddha." He stands and paces. "Come on, Ruby. You own the Mystic Eye. You—of all the people I've met in the Haight-Ashbury—you believe in success. Isn't that so? I've seen you work twelve hours a day. I've heard you argue many times with Leo Gorgon about incentive and free enterprise. And the future, Ruby, will prove you right."

"Maybe you know that, but I don't," she says. "Maybe Gorgon's got a point, too. Selling trinkets to the flower children? What good is that? How am I contributing to the betterment of society?"

"You're opening people's minds, Ruby," Starbright cries.

"That's right," Chi says. "Whether it's wearing a pretty flower or a skull and crossbones. Reading the Bible or studying the *Bhagavad-Gita.* You're showing people they have a choice, Ruby. The Mystic Eye gives people a choice."

"You offered me a choice on the roof," Ruby says. "I could have picked up one of Gorgon's Molotov cocktails and flung it to the street with my own hand."

"But you didn't."

"But I could have."

"But you didn't. And as of the moment you didn't," he says, "you never could have. Not in this spacetime. The probability that you would throw a Molotov cocktail has collapsed into the timeline. And our spacetime is conserved."

"Wait, wait. After your rap about the Grandfather Principle, and Tenet this and Tenet that, what you're saying is you tachyporters allow that the past may not be what you thought it was," Ruby says. "So the timeline you keep talking about is some kind of *process.*"

Starbright's mouth falls open.

Ruby astounds even herself. "Right, am I right?"

He smiles, but there's ice in his eyes. "We could never have developed tachyonic translation-transmission without allowing for *some* continuous cocreatorship between humanity and the Cosmic Mind. There are always bits of probability collapsing into the timeline. Cosmicist philosophy supports that notion."

"Sweet Isis!" Ruby cries and claps her hands. "I don't *believe* it!" The cats look up, then go back to their napping. She lowers her voice. "I can't do *this,* no, no, no. I can't do *that.* The Grandfather Principle, you know."

"It's not *that* chaotic," Chi says quickly. "The mandate of nonintervention and the Tenets have a sound purpose. If a probability collapses *out* of the timeline, we're in trouble. That's why the Luxon Institute for Superluminal Applications invested fifty million IBUs into the SOL Project. To preserve the timeline during this hot dim spot. To conserve spacetime."

"I don't get it," Starbright says. She leans her cheek against Ruby's knee. "How can reality be probable?"

"Well, in quantum physics," Chi says, "reality is a set of probabilities. We see them as constantly collapsing into the timeline. The theory goes back to Schrödinger's cat."

"You mentioned that once before," Ruby says, stroking Luna. The bluepoint purrs and gazes at her with sapphire eyes. "Whose cat?"

"Schrödinger's cat," he says. "That's twentieth-century physics. The Heisenberg uncertainty principle is from your Now, not mine. Our probability analysis stems from the notion that at every moment reality is manifesting to us, and also branching off into an infinity of unmanifested probabilities. Our cocreatorship as the observer is part of the probability. That's why it's so hard for the Archivists to reduce reality to a one hundred percent probability." He laughs sourly. "And why it's so easy to find dim spots."

"But what does that have to do with a cat?" Starbright says, scratching Ara's chin. Ara yawns. Rotten-shrimp breath wafts from his mouth.

"Phew!" Ruby and Starbright say together and laugh. Ara looks pleased.

"Schrödinger's cat is another thought experiment," Chiron says. "A cat is placed in a box. A device is inside the box that releases a lethal gas that will kill the cat. A random event, like the radioactive decay of an atom, determines whether the gas is released or not. No one knows if the cat is alive or dead till they open the box and look. Till someone looks, the cat is alive and dead at the same time. This illustrates the bizarre and contradictory nature of probable reality."

Ruby sits bolt upright. Starbright moans and pulls Ara into her lap.

"What?" Ruby says in her sweet-as-poison voice.

"I didn't make it up!" The cats stare at Chiron, blue and gold eyes blazing. "A physicist, Erwin Schrödinger, proposed the thought experiment in 1935."

"Nineteen thirty-five, uh-huh. And what nationality was Erwin Schrödinger?"

Chi rubs his forehead. "He was Austrian."

"Achtung! Sehr gut, Beelzebub!"

"I know, it's crude," Chi says. "I never thought much about the way thought experiments were expressed till I met you, Ruby." He is abashed.

"Crude!" Ruby says, furious.

"All the Schrödinger's cat thought experiment does is demonstrate how spacetime exists as a set of probabilities that can be mutually exclusive till we observe a probability collapsing into the timeline."

"No, what you're talking about is a gas chamber," Ruby says. "A real experiment to design how to make a gas chamber. Right, am I right, Herr Chiron?"

"I don't know," Chi says helplessly. "It's just a metaphor. A scientific convention. Common parlance. The techs still refer to it."

"Common parlance," Ruby says. "Starbright, didn't you tell me you're half Jewish?"

"Daddy's Jewish," she says. "And my mother's Catholic. Guess Hitler could have gassed either side of my family."

"Cool," Ruby says. "Tell you what, Chi. Forget gassing a cat when you translate-transmit to your Now in our future. Tell your techs to put Starbright in the box and wait for the random event to release the gas. Is she alive? Is she dead? Have we gassed the pussy? What a groovy thought experiment, demonstrating the probable nature of reality!"

"I'm sorry," he whispers.

"You bet your ass you're sorry," Ruby says and stands, scattering the cats. "If you remember one thing to tell your techs in the future, you remember I told you this, Chiron Cat's Eye in Draco. Told you once and I'll tell you again. Dig it: the way you think about things shapes the way your reality is."

"I *will* remember," he declares, eyes flashing.

"Liberate Schrödinger's cat!" Starbright cries and raises her fist.

He raises his fist, too. "Liberate Schrödinger's cat!"

The tiny Angora with gold eyes and plumy white fur arches and mews. Alana is hungry again.

Ruby goes down to the shop, checks her locks, peers out the peephole. Still nothing but Papa Al and Teddybear and a pack of longhaired boys. They're laughing, toking. It's good to see laughing people out there. Let them toke. For the first time in her life, she shivers when she thinks about the future.

So peaceful and quiet. When was the last time the street was so quiet at midnight? She hates this, being barricaded in her own place. She gets the hammer, pulls out the nails, takes down the plywood planks. She unlocks her door and steps outside. The air is fresh, tinged with sandalwood incense.

Then suddenly it's happening.

A flatbed truck careens around the corner of Clayton and Haight. A gang of twenty crammed in back. A truckful of shouting black people!

Sweet Isis! Do they have shopping bags full of knives? Do they have carloads of machine guns?

They shout, "Love and peace! Love and peace, sister!"

They're throwing things off the truck.

Bricks, stones, Molotov cocktails?

They're tossing flowers onto the street. A long-stemmed carnation lands at Ruby's feet.

August 8, 1967

Inquest for the Ungrateful Dead

13

Are You

Experienced?

 Susan sees the headlines all along Hayes Street as she hurries
to meet Nance at the Blue Unicorn Café. Can't miss them, in
every newspaper box:

HIPPIE DRUG MURDERS
SYNDICATE "MOVES IN"

But when she slides into the seat across from them, she finds Nance
and Professor Zoom are unimpressed.

"If you've ever lived in the Village," Professor Zoom says, studying the swirls of cream in his coffee, "you're just seeing the Village all over again. It's the same old shit. I, for one, am vastly displeased. I mean, I left New York to get away from that crap."

"I thought you were at Yale," Susan says. "Isn't that in Connecticut?"

"Connecticut, New York," he says, with a withering glance. "It's all the same old shit." He actually looks at her for the first time since she sat down. He moves and speaks as if he's in slow motion, suspended in some inner place, more self-absorbed than he used to be. Three-quarters comatose, instead of half. Before she can wrest a glimmer of recognition from him, his eyes flick back to his coffee cup, staring as though the chipped ceramic is an artifact of fantastic complexity.

Five days ago, John Kent Carter, also known as Jacob King or Shob Carter, was found in an apartment furnished with nothing but a mattress on the floor. The mewing of a cat trapped in the apartment brought a neighbor. The cat had walked across the roof and slunk into Shob's window. The apartment's walls were covered with psychedelic sunbursts, rainbows, and his blood. Shob had been stabbed twelve times. His right arm was gone, cleanly severed above the elbow. Shob had been known to handcuff the briefcase in which he kept his cash to his right wrist. Earlier last week, his girlfriend had helped him count out three thousand, three hundred dollars. The police found no money in the apartment. Shob called himself an unemployed flutist, but everyone knows he dealt LSD.

Two days ago, William Edward Thomas, also known as Superspade, was found zipped into a sleeping bag that had snagged on the cliff below Point Reyes Lighthouse. He had been shot in the back of the head. The corpse was three days old. Superspade had been known to carry fifty thousand dollars in cash. Some said Superspade dealt acid, some said he only dealt grass. Some said Superspade and Shob were making a deal. Everyone says each had been approached by the Syndicate and ordered to get organized or get dead.

"Starbright's never lived in the Village," Nance says, inhaling her third Kool as though mentholated smoke is desperately required for her proper respiration. "Have you, sweetheart?"

"No, I haven't, Penny Lane," Susan says. "And neither have you."

"Starbright has never even been to New York, or anywhere, really."

"I have so been to New York. On the way to France for Christmas."

"On the way to France for Christmas." Nance mimes being impressed, wide eyes, open mouth. "You mean Daddy took you along this time?"

Susan studies her coffee cup.

"Being chauffeured around with Daddy doesn't count," Nance proclaims. "I mean, you've never been on your own, sweetheart."

This is one of Nance's new affectations, calling everyone sweetheart with her weird pronunciation *shweethawt*. She says everything in a phony accent, accompanied with a cunning wink. Her shocking crew cut is bleached ivory-white. She makes strange movements with her hands. She looks as though she's been dipped in lacquer and turned hard and shiny.

What did Susan expect? That they could be best friends again? That they could take things up the way they were before Susan's father forced their separation? Maybe so; why not? Or if not exactly the same, then a new friendship, maybe crazier, more daring and fun now that they are both on their own.

But she chased after Nance for nearly two weeks, never finding her at the Double Barrel house, or there, but too spaced out to come to the phone. Yes, she had expectations. She expected the old spark, the excitement of their first meeting on the Panhandle. Or at least a warm nostalgia, like looking at family photographs together.

Abandon expectations, oh ye who run away to the Haight-Ashbury. Nothing is real, reality is nothing.

She hadn't expected to see Professor Zoom with Nance this morning, either. Nor had she expected *his* bleached white hair, kohl-lined eyes, pancake-powdered skin. He and Nance look so *weird*, even by Haight-Ashbury standards. Like vampires or ghouls. Professor Zoom's ice-cold aloofness instantly adds another undercurrent of tension between her and Nance.

She hates this. Everything is wrong. She doesn't want things with Nance to be wrong anymore. Try, Susan. "Wow, it's scary about Shob and Superspade, huh?"

Nance shrugs, squeezes her lips into a sardonic little smile, and raises her eyebrows at Professor Zoom, excluding Susan from her reaction. Nance has always been dramatic. With fingers as fragile as fish bones, she hands her Kool to him with the familiarity of a lover. "Starbright scares easily. Don't you, Starbright?" she says in that awful phony voice.

The big news this morning, and the reason for the lurid newspaper headlines, is that Eddy, also known as Shank, was arrested outside Sebastopol. Shank is a well-known Haightian with a predilection for acid, speed, and choppers. He was caught driving to Morning Star Ranch. The black '62 Volkswagen bug with STP decals on the doors belonged to Shob. A right arm was found by police in the back seat. The arm was wrapped in a black-and-red suede cloth. In a fit of squeamishness, the newspapers don't want to say the arm also belonged to Shob. Shank didn't want to say, either. He told police, "I'm very, very hazy about that arm."

"Shank was involved in a burn," Professor Zoom says, taking the Kool from Nance and studying the smoke eddying from its tip. "That's what it is, sweet pretty pussies. When a burn comes down, shit comes down."

Susan shivers and sips her coffee. She never drank coffee in the morning before. That was her parents' prerogative. Now she can't imagine how she ever managed to wake up without it. The caffeine blooms in her head like a half-cap of dexie. She feels like she's been asleep her whole life, as though reality was like watching television.

This is real. This is as real as it gets. She *knew* Superspade. A tall, handsome black dude, he lived two doors down on Clayton with a series of pretty young white women. Susan always thought Superspade had style, with his leather jumpsuits and his button, "Faster Than a Speeding Mind." And she *knew* Shob. He was always on Haight or at the Avalon Ballroom. A pixie-faced guy, sweetly aging at twenty-five with his handlebar mustache and a receding hairline. His button said, "America Is Going to Pot."

She shouldn't feel sad Shob and Superspade are dead. Shob and Superspade were bad. They were drug dealers. But, she thinks, recalling her Econ class, people want to buy pot and acid and speed. They are screaming for it. There is—what did her teacher call it?—a consumer demand. Shob and Superspade were supplying the demand. You could say they were capitalists, entrepreneurs. Isn't that the American way?

Susan doesn't know. It's like everyone has been infected by the virus from the planet Psi 2000. The virus from Psi 2000 releases people's deep repressions. Susan watched the *Star Trek* rerun of "The Naked Time" with growing horror. The virus makes people act as if they were shooting crystal, the dope easiest to score these days. Mr. Spock weeps over his mother, crewman Tormolen dies of despair, Nurse Chapel wants to go to bed with Captain Kirk. And Mr. Sulu—sweet Mr. Sulu with his flat, pockmarked cheeks—Mr. Sulu threatens everyone with a fencing foil! It reminds her so much of the mood in the Haight-Ashbury that she turns the TV off before the Captain, Mr. Spock, and Scotty can save the ship from being sucked down into Psi 2000. She knows they save the *Enterprise*. They always do.

The question is, can *this* starship be saved?

She doesn't have to take this shit from Nance and Professor Zoom. She scrapes back her chair and stands. "I think you're right, Professor Zoom." She reaches over, plucks the Kool from his fingers, and drags on it, willing herself not to choke. Nance knows she never was a smoker. Nance does another little drama, My *my*. Susan flings the Kool into the overflowing ashtray. "I think Shank was involved in a burn, too. Did you know Stan the Man was involved in a burn? The dragon's blood was rat poison. He burned Stovepipe and the Lizard for seven grand, you know that, don't you? Plus he still owes me a hundred bucks for my time and trouble."

Nance stares at her.

"You tell Stan I want my hundred bucks back, Professor Zoom. You know what I heard? I heard when a burn comes down, shit comes down. Now, where did I hear that?" She slings the woven bag Ruby gave her over the shoulder of her high-collared shirt.

Nance shakes her head and grins, that sly look of appreciation Susan used to know. For a moment, her eyes twinkle at Susan, a look that always gave her courage.

"Dig it, Arnold. You take care of it for me with Stan the Man," Susan says. "And I told you not to call me a pussy."

Professor Zoom scrapes back his chair. He's gone.

"Far out, Starbright," Nance says. "You have passed the acid test." She pats the chair. "Don't go, sweetheart."

Susan sits.

"Stan burned some dealers?"

She nods. In all the crazy times she had with Professor Zoom, they never shared a smoke with such intimacy. She swigs her coffee, burning her tongue. "Are you balling him, too?"

Nance laughs. "Sweetheart," she says, suddenly full of flirt. She strokes Susan's hand with her fingertips. "Who am I not balling?"

WEATHER REPORT

In the sixties, systematic measurements of methane have
begun for the first time. The atmosphere's methane content
is particularly worrisome because it is rising at a much
faster rate than carbon dioxide and is extremely toxic.
Studies show that the methane increase over the centuries
parallels the swelling of the human population, a logical
connection since methane is produced through the
rumination of cattle, which service an exploding consumer
demand for meat and dairy products, and through increased
rice paddy cultivation. During the ice ages, methane was
present in the atmosphere at roughly three hundred parts
per billion. During interglacial periods, the level doubled.
Now we can measure methane in the atmosphere at one
thousand, eight hundred parts per billion and climbing.

o

The blues life is a mystique. And the blues-life mystique is
that if you want to do anything, you have to lose your arm.
You have to pay a lot of dues, to live full out—full out, not
far out—as you can, if the cost is in dues. The only people
that can do it are oppressed, the hard-kick seekers who
laid down the patterns of extreme beauty for this
civilization. . . . They're all people who got burned for
what they did, being repressed beyond recourse. Don't you
know what that means? People who lived it were essentially

oppressed beyond action. To be oppressed without recourse is the blues life.

—From interview with Peter Berg,
Voices of the Love Generation, by
Leonard Wolf (Little, Brown and
Company, 1968)

Susan loves the Blue Unicorn. It's one of her favorite coffeehouses. You can curl up on the swayback sofa with a friend, use the chessboards and sewing kits, read the books lying about. There's no jukebox like in Bob's Big Boy. Instead, there's a funky old off-tune piano that anyone can play, and people do, mostly badly but sometimes pretty well. The owner of the Blue Unicorn is one of those grizzled Beat types who believes coffee is the supreme drug of enlightenment and has a soft spot for hip chicks. Susan always promptly pays for one cup, and he always gives her two refills.

Nance sits down with her second cup and says, "I panhandled George Harrison yesterday."

"You mean—*George Harrison?*"

"Yeah! We were hanging out on Hippie Hill. Some doo was going around and the Pied Piper was playing his guitar. This dude strolled up. He was wearing heart-shaped glasses and flowered bell-bottoms and a button that said 'I'm the Head of My Community.' He walked up to the Piper and said, 'Can I borrow your guitar, man?' The Piper is cool, he said sure, and the dude riffed into 'Norwegian Wood.' And pretty soon everyone's screaming, 'It's George Harrison, it's George Harrison!' "

"Wow!" Susan hangs on every word. *George Harrison*—their idol—*here*! In the Haight-Ashbury? "No shuck?"

"No shuck." Nance pulls on her Kool. "I would have fucked him in a second, but that bucktooth wife of his was tagging along. Is she ugly, or what? So I panhandled him instead."

Susan gulps her coffee, goes up to the counter, comes back with another cup. A newspaper is folded on the next table. When she turns it over, sure enough, beneath "Hippie Drug Murders" is a photograph of George Harrison in heart-shaped glasses.

Fuck him? Fuck George Harrison? Suddenly Susan is inexplicably offended. His wife, Patti Boyd Harrison, is one of the skinny, longhaired blonds in *Life* and *Seventeen*. She is the ideal of beauty everyone adores.

What makes Nance, a girl from Cleveland with a freaky crew cut, think George Harrison would want to have sex with her?

"Is Marilyn still around?" This is a mean question, and Susan knows it. She taps out a Kool from Nance's pack, strikes a match, and flexes her fingers, trying out Nance's hand gestures.

"Who's Marilyn?" Nance coldly tosses back the question.

"That girl from Mill Valley. Stan the Man was balling her."

"I don't know who Marilyn is. I don't give a shit."

Susan studies her. "Well! Stan's not someone you can depend on, you know. If you're balling him. If you're . . . in love with him." Susan tries out Nance's shrug.

"Sweetheart, I haven't depended on anyone since 1960. I mean, Stan. Say hey, he's good in bed, and he's got good dope, but I'm not hung up on him. It's a freaking never-ending party at the house. So many cool people, and music. Always music. It's a beautiful scene." She slaps Susan's knee. "Well, you know. Zoom tells me you lived there a while."

"Yeah, I know."

Zoom. Isn't that just like Nance? Forget Professor. He's just Zoom.

And Susan can't help it. A pang of envy strikes her. The party, the never-ending party where you don't have to worry about the Syndicate or the Vietnam War. Forget whether spades from the Fillmore are going to burn the place down, or whether some guy you thought you were falling in love with is plugging into his electric lady friend back home in the future. Or even worry very much about the death of two of the brothers. Ten dealers have replaced Shob and Superspade, so what. It feels good not to give a shit.

And she threw it all away, her connection to the Double Barrel house, to the never-ending party. For what? Her chaste little room, her chaste little crush on Ruby. Ruby; forbidding her to watch TV unless she's watching a science fiction program, switching *off* the TV when she walks into Susan's room to talk. What kind of Nazi is she, anyway? And Chiron. There's a freak. To think she was starting to fall for him before he told her about Venus Rising. The curve of her skull, her head-painting, having sex while they link into each other's neckjack. God! Oh, he tries to act cool. He still follows her around like a lost puppy. But she stays away. Gets away from him as best she can.

So what about the demon. Be ready, always? Then she's ready. Let the demon come. Let the demon try to touch her. She doesn't trust

Chiron's ability to stave off the demon any more than she trusts the government's ability to stave off a nuclear war. Survive? Far out; she's surviving. Blow her up, blow her down. Go on, do it, do it.

"*Are* you in love with Stan the Man?" she says.

"I love everybody, sweetheart," Nance says.

"You don't care if he balls other girls?"

"Love isn't the possession of someone's body. Anyway, love is shit."

"Love is the highest consciousness we can attain."

Nance howls with laughter, tears spurting from her eyes. The other patrons in the café turn. Susan's cheeks burn.

Nance calms herself. "Are you in love with that red-haired dude?" she asks sardonically.

"Not anymore."

"There! You see? Can I have him if you're done?" Nance digs in her ratty handbag, takes out an eyeliner pencil and a compact, fixes her eye makeup.

Susan can't finish her coffee. She pushes the cup away.

"How's tricks at the Mystic Eye?" Nance says, gripping the cap of the eyeliner in her teeth. "I heard Ruby Maverick is down on dope."

"That's true."

"So you're not smoking, or anything?"

"Not around Ruby," Susan implies, not lying.

"What a square." Nance studies her face, then snaps the compact shut. "Still, I'd like to meet her."

"Meet Ruby?"

"Yeah." The shrug. "I'd like to rap with her about the trip that was done to her."

Susan drags on the Kool. The smoke makes her head spin. "The trip?"

"Well, her cousin was a junkie."

"I know. She told me."

"Then you must know he raped her. He was going cold turkey, that's what Stan the Man says. And the cousin, he raped Ruby. She was like nineteen or twenty."

The shock is like touching a frayed electrical wire. Susan drags on the Kool again.

"That's how junk is, you know?" Nance says. Fake-cool of a new kid on the street. Susan's seen it before. "When you're shooting shit, you lie back and dig it. But when you come down, you go crazy and wild. Crystal is just the opposite, isn't that strange? When you're shooting shit, you go crazy and wild. But when you come down, you lie back and die. Anyway, I'd like to talk to her about it."

Susan nods. The question hovers like a cloud, dark and foreboding, before she gets the nerve to ask. "Why?"

Nance rolls her eyes and tokes her Kool. " 'Cause of my stepfather. Stepfather, huh. I mean Andy. Handy Andy, my new daddy-o. You know."

"Know *what*?"

"Christ, Starbright. He started doing me when I was seven. My mother was out, God knows where, and he came to my bedroom. He gave me a kiss goodnight, and then a little feel goodnight, and another kiss goodnight, and then his hands were down my pants, and then he did me. He's been doing me off and on ever since. Oh, he beats up Paul, but Handy Andy saves the very best for me, sweetheart. That's why I had to leave. My mother is so stupid. She wouldn't believe me, and even if she did, she wouldn't do anything about it. I mean, I got my period. What if I got pregnant? My ass would be grass!"

"Oh, Penny Lane," Susan whispers.

"I thought you knew."

"You never told me."

Nance rubbing her crotch back and forth on the nub of her bicycle seat. Nance making angels in the snow, pumping her slim little pelvis up and down as she swept her legs back and forth to make the snow-angel's skirt. Nance leaping from the old ironwood tree in front of Cheryl Rubinstein's house, shouting, "I want to die! I want to die!" Nance swigging a bottle of cough medicine as Susan sped Mom's Mustang round the block. Nance throwing up ice cream and burgers in the bathroom. Nance cajoling a joint out of her cousin Don, whispering in his ear. And Nance whirling in front of Susan's father, smiling at him as she moved her hips like a belly dancer. Daddy had frowned. Susan thought he was unfair. She still does.

"Don't cry, sweetheart. Really, I thought you knew," Nance says. "That Starbright, she's the smart one." Nance scoots her chair next to Susan's, throws her arm over Susan's shoulders. "Poor Starbright," she croons. "Daddy called her stupid for being friends with that tramp, that no-good so-and-so. But Starbright knows Daddy knows she's smart. Who is Starbright fooling? That Starbright, she's so sensitive. Mom and Daddy fight sometimes, and they're not very nice, but they're not divorced, they would never do that, I mean, what would the neighbors think? Little Starbright, Mom thinks her breasts are too fat, but Starbright'll get new clothes for the ninth grade, won't she?"

"Stop it," Susan says, recoiling.

"Oh, and Grandpa died. He loved Starbright more than anyone, but he died anyway, and Mom and Daddy couldn't handle it, and Starbright was sad. And Daddy? Daddy works so hard, he doesn't have time for Starbright except when he's taking her to France for Christmas, poor thing."

"I said stop it."

"Poor Starbright can't be seen with her lowbrow friends from dirty, old, common South Euclid. Daddy listens in on her phone conversations and grounds her when she's naughty. Starbright has to move to Shaker Heights and go to school with the rich kids, only—surprise!—now she's one, too. Pretty Starbright won't have to work at Mr. Rosenstein's art supply store anymore, will she, sweetheart?"

"I said stop it, Penny Lane!"

"That's what I said, too!" Nance mimes surprise. "When Handy Andy came to my bedroom? I said, Don't. Stop! Don't. Stop! Don't, stop, don't stop, don't stop." She rocks with that awful laughter.

"I've got to go." Susan gets ready to run this time.

"Oh, I'm shucking you. Wait, wait. Please?"

"No!" Her voice sticks in her throat like chalk across sandpaper. "I've really got to be somewhere."

"Hey. What a reunion." Moist eyes, a trembling lip. "Don't you love me anymore, Starbright?" Quavering voice. Dramatic Nance.

Susan hesitates.

"Look, I've got a joint," she says brightly. She opens her purse, shows the fat, hand-rolled cigarette tucked inside. She switches instantly to a flirty look. "Have a joint with me, sweetheart. For old times' sake."

No pot-smoking is allowed in the Blue Unicorn Café, so Susan and Nance take the joint to the toilet. They crowd into a narrow stall. Susan stares down at the toilet bowl. The place is clean, but the porcelain is old, stained tobacco brown. Someone has thrown in several cigarette butts with bright lipstick on the filters. The sides of the stall are covered with graffiti.

Nance tucks the whole joint into her mouth, pulls it over her tongue and through her lips, making the paper damp. She lights it, drags and hands it to Susan. Susan takes the joint. She never did like grass that much. She tokes, but she lets the smoke out right away. As usual, the grass makes her eyes and throat instantly sore. She begins to shiver.

She hands the joint back to Nance, but Nance holds up her palm and commands, "Take another hit."

"That's okay." She presses the joint into Nance's fingers. "You know, I think I'm allergic to this stuff." The grass slides through her consciousness, rearranging things. Righteous shit, as Professor Zoom would say. Suddenly she is claustrophobic in the stall. Paranoid. She doesn't want to be here. The graffiti swirls. She doesn't want to look at Nance. Nance looms before her, a bristling gaunt stranger who, with her white hair and deep lines in her powdered forehead, looks much older than her fourteen years. Susan feels trapped in a metal box with an alien being whose intentions are unclear. She can feel Nance breathing, hears the rustle of her clothes as she raises the joint to her lips and hands it to Susan again.

Susan won't take it. "I like speed better."

Nance shrugs, finishing the joint herself. She blows the smoke in Susan's face with a sly smile. Susan stands there, paralyzed.

"You're mad at me, huh?" Nance says at last.

Her words resonate, spinning off implications. Emotions tangle. All the times they had together flash before Susan's eyes, but nothing is like what she wants to remember. "I don't know what you mean."

"Well, don't be."

"I'm not mad at you, Penny Lane."

"You're the only person in the whole world I don't want mad at me, Starbright."

The sorrow in her voice almost makes Susan weep. Nance Jones, the pretty little dark-haired girl from Cleveland. But the edge of mockery, the sarcasm in her voice, makes it seem as if Susan has betrayed her, too, along with everyone else in the world.

Nance unzips her jeans. "Got to pee. All that coffee."

Susan reaches for the bolt on the stall door, but Nance says, "Stay." She pulls down her jeans. She wears no panties. Her thighs look like those pictures you see of people in Asia who are starving to death. She sits on the seat, stands again. Now Susan sees the dark scarlet rash beginning at the middle of her thighs and dappling her pelvis up to her belly button. She turns to pull up her jeans. The scarlet blotches stain her bony buttocks, too.

Susan has not smoked grass in so long that, for a moment, she doubts her perception. A hallucination, a trick of the light? She stares. Nance grins, raises her eyebrows, and shrugs.

"Gross, huh? Just a dose of the clap."

"You better go to the Free Clinic and get some medicine!"

"Oh, it looks worse than it is. Anyway, they're too wasted to notice. They usually want to do it in the dark."

"They?"

"The tricks, sweetheart. The tricks. The guys who want to do it for money."

"What are you *talking* about?"

"I'm talking about survival, Susan. Don't give me that look. I never had a gig like you at Mr. Rosenstein's art supply store. I had no bread when I split. I just had to get away from Handy Andy as soon as I could. Did you fly to San Francisco? Pan Am or United? Not me, sweetheart. I hitchhiked. Inch by inch, mile by mile." She smiles. "It was an experience. 'Are you experienced?' " She hums the riff from the Jimi Hendrix tune.

Susan knocks the bolt back and stumbles out of the stall. She goes to the sink, turns on the water, stares at the rivulets swirling in the basin. The chrome of the faucet is smudged with greasy fingerprints. Same for the hot and cold water knobs, and the plunger on the soap dispenser. She thinks of the bus window, looking through Chiron's scope. She pulls down a paper towel, wraps the towel over the soap dispenser plunger, and squirts a ton of soap into her palm. She washes her hands, turning soap and hot water over and around her fingers. She goes to turn off the water, stares again at the greasy fingerprints on the hot and cold knobs. The patchwork of smudges looks like the rash on Nance's crotch. She can practically see bacteria swarming on the knobs. And it strikes her, one of those lightning flashes that the Summer of Love can bring you and you forget again instantly, but she holds it in her mind, holds it carefully: *that's* what Chiron means. About doorknobs and bongs passed around. His clean thing, his prophylaks. Suddenly it all makes sense. She takes another paper towel, turns the water knob off, and takes another towel to dry her hands. The thought of touching anything in this toilet with her bare hands makes her ill.

Nance bangs out of the stall. "If you ever want to party, you let me know, sweetheart. There is plenty of bread to be scored during the Summer of Love. I'd love to turn you on."

"That's not my scene," Susan says bluntly. Who in the Haight-Ashbury can argue with that?

"Sure," Nance says. "It's not your scene. I mean, why should you party with a no-good so-and-so? Why should you hang out with a trampy girl like me?"

"Cool it, Penny Lane."

"Always first class for Starbright. Fly to San Francisco, find a place to stay with Ruby Maverick. You don't need to turn tricks. You've got plenty of money, right?"

"I don't have plenty of money. Stan the Man owes me a hundred bucks. He stole it from me for the dragon's blood deal."

"That's really true?"

"You bet your ass."

They stare at each other in the mirror over the sink.

"Tell you what." Nance bends, pulls up her jeans, pulls something from her boot. A twenty-dollar bill. "I was saving this for a bag of shit, but I'm going to give it to you."

"No," Susan says. "It's not your responsibility."

"My postcard brought you here. It *is* my responsibility." She savors the word. She cocks her head at Susan as though she's discovered a new way to get at her.

"Penny Lane, no. Forget it."

Her eyes darken. She juts out her chin. "Don't tell me to forget it. Don't tell me I'm not responsible."

Everything has twisted around. Does Nance need to feel Susan is in her debt? This strikes Susan as absolutely fair. She *is* in Nance's debt. "You're right. If it weren't for you, Penny Lane, I wouldn't be here at all."

"Plus, I named you, sweetheart."

"That's true, you really did. You named me as surely as my parents once named me."

Nance is triumphant. "I'll get the rest of that money for you, sweetheart. I'll get it somehow."

Susan's hands are finally clean, but she's got to touch the door handle to get out of here. She wraps a paper towel over her hand like Chi would wrap a prophylak.

"And if you ever need a place to stay, sweetheart, you let me know." Nance seizes her shoulders and kisses her on the mouth. "You were the one thing I could care about all those years. I love you, Starbright. I've always loved you."

And Susan loves her, too. She has always loved Nance. Loved her like a sister. A weird feeling rises in her throat. She breaks away. As she plunges through the door, she turns back for a moment.

Hollow cheeks, hollow eyes, white hair, and the body of a child. Nance is a puzzle, an optical illusion. Is she a fair young girl looking into a mirror, or a monstrous crone with death on her face?

Which are you, Nance?

14

Piece of

My Heart

 Chiron stalks the streets, searching for her. The news of hippie drug murders is nothing compared to the darkness in his heart.

Strategy, Chi. Thought he could play with a young girl's heart. Starbright. So easy to win. So easy to lose.

He doesn't give a damn about the arrest of Shank, who is a loud-mouthed freak, always wasted and on the make. As for the Syndicate moving in, what do these people expect? Because they rap about peace and love, they can deal drugs freely? Anytime there's bread to be scored in a hustle, mobsters will make the scene sooner or later.

That's why President Mitsui decriminalized all drugs in 2093 and instituted the registration system, regulating the ingestion of everything from nicotine to heroin. The system took decades to become fully operational and was challenged during the brown ages on more than one occasion. But tax revenues in the very first year financed the start-up of educational and detox programs that went hand in hand with registration. Reallocation of resources from an inefficient and sometimes corrupt criminal justice sector to the private civil sector, from the black market economy to legitimate business made accountable to government regulation, proved so successful and reasonable that Chi finds it hard to believe American policy was so shortsighted for so long. Cosmicists always supported President Mitsui's registration system.

And Chi has always supported cosmicism. Of course! He's a survivor of the world's tragedies of the past half-millennium, a student of history with twenty-twenty hindsight. One of the superior few who finally understand how to live fairly on the Earth. Cosmicists dethroned technology, wrested it free of the technopolistic plutocracy, and humbled it before True Value. Cosmicists subjected technology to grace. Applied it as a tool to advance life, not as a means to exploit unsustainable growth and concentrate wealth. If humanity cocreates reality with the Cosmic Mind, then humanity must live responsibly or die.

Yet two women from this ancient day who know nothing of these things have managed to undermine, first, the fundamental of tachyportation to the past, and then—as if that's not enough—the fundamental of probable reality theory that supports the feasibility of tachyportation to the past. The Grandfather Principle and Schrödinger's cat. Are these ugly symptoms, then, of a moral disease corrupting the very root of tachyportation itself?

He hated Ruby, at first. She was the traitor, the looter of his belief. She laughed at his nutribeads, and then she tempted him. She deliberately set out to sway him from the path he was required to follow. The policy under which he was expected to live for a mere seventy-six days. A policy imposed for his own good. He cannot eat the food or drink the wine of this day. Salmonellae, shigellae, microbial toxins; any of these could kill him. But with the scent of frying onions and buttered toast, she broke his will. And then—when he was prime, when he was heavy with food and slow with contentment, in one stroke—*the way you think about things shapes the way your reality is*—she broke his belief.

What does that make the Archivists, the Luxon Institute for Superluminal Applications, his skipparents, himself? Virtual murderers of grandfathers? Theoretical Nazis cackling over their gas chambers, conducting some awful experiment to see if a cat is alive or dead, like tossing naked concentration camp prisoners into tubs of ice water to see how long human beings can endure cold before they freeze to death?

But it's absurd, irrational, emotional! Physicists down the ages have toasted these chestnuts. Students and writers have swigged new wine and made jokes, devised clever conundrums over the fundamentals. Who ever questioned their form, their expression? The fundamentals weren't literal. Murder your own grandfather; it's just a thought experiment. Is the cat alive or dead; it's just a metaphor.

He feels like a shattered man. Starbright's tears and Ruby's anger make sense to him, in spite of how badly he wants to rationalize their reactions away.

Dizzy, disoriented, like another bout of tachyonic lag. He feels like the song about warm San Francisco nights—which are actually quite chilly—about how walls move, and minds do, too. Shadows ripple, moonlight blinds him. Walls bulge strangely as though the buildings are breathing. Sidewalks shimmer. His questions of but a week ago take on a deeply ominous tone. If Starbright has an analog from the Other Now, and Ruby A. Maverick does, too, can either encounter a Prime Probability and collapse the timeline out of this spacetime? *Or who else?* Who else in the Haight-Ashbury during the Summer of Love possesses that awful power?

Suddenly, he feels confused about the object of the SOL Project. "K-T," he whispers, hungry for probabilities. But the knuckletop spews out tiny red alphanumerics that make no sense. Be ready, always; that's what the knuckletop says. Watch for Prime Probabilities. Watch for demons. Of course, of course. Why does K-T's readout leave him feeling so uneasy? Is he becoming paranoid? The hysterical gaiety of the street scene fails to enchant him anymore. The costumes and dazed smiles are a gaudy mask concealing a sick face. The mouse magician is insane.

Yet the Summer of Love parties on. Young runaways arrive every day. The Doors, the Young Rascals, Buffalo Springfield play the Fillmore. The Diggers have started providing free food in the Panhandle again after a hiatus of nearly six months. Leo Gorgon is so busy with the free feeds that he doesn't come around to the Mystic Eye anymore. Or maybe his confrontation with Ruby on the roof broke apart whatever they had. Chi isn't sure, but he's glad Gorgon's gone.

Five hundred people gather every sunset in front of the Psychedelic

Shop. They march from Haight Street to Hippie Hill, chanting, ringing bells, clanging cymbals, tooting flutes, strumming guitars. They carry sticks of incense, a silk-screened banner of a scarlet phoenix rising from a conflagration, and torches. They call themselves The Flame, dedicated to preserving the spirit of the Haight-Ashbury.

Can he sustain his outrage against these people?

No. The shattered man can barely sustain his self-respect.

He followed The Flame into the park, strode beyond Hippie Hill down John F. Kennedy Drive to the Portals of the Past. He examined the marble column with disbelief and despair. There's no glyph. No glyph.

And there is no peace at 555 Clayton Street. Starbright avoids him. Ruby has turned cold since the night of the riot that never happened. He was always the aloof one. Now she holds herself from him in a way she never did before. She shoos her precious cats upstairs to sleep with her instead of allowing them to drape themselves all over him and the couch. He wakes up shivering in the night without those damn cats, who generate a lot of body heat. He finds himself feeding them, changing their water and litter, even combing them for fleas in a silent apology.

But Ruby doesn't see this, or, if she does, she gives no sign. He never realized how much he took strength from her smile. How much he took for granted her ready generosity till she withdrew from him. She does not evict him from her house. But in a thousand small ways, she evicts him from her sympathy. One night, very late, after viewing Disks 2 and 3 again, he found himself nearly weeping. And all his anger at how Ruby tempted him, all his outrage at how she shattered his belief, dissolves at last into a desire to appease her.

And win Starbright again. He can't keep following her at a distance. He can't keep searching for her every time she escapes him on the street.

How can he prove he's not some monster from the future with a jack in his neck? How can he prove his sincerity? Prove all of cosmicism's sincerity? His violation of the Tenets and the mandate of nonintervention pale next to what he believes has become his moral imperative: They have to believe in the future he has translated-transmitted across five centuries to conserve. They have to.

How can he make things right?

Chiron jogs across the intersection of Clayton and Fell Street. He's already searched Haight Street from Broderick to Stanyan, looping east down Oak along the south side of the Panhandle. Cyn sits on the grass under the eucalyptus trees with some people. A handsome young black man Chi has never seen before in a black leather jacket and a black beret sits next to her, watching her intently. Cyn's hand rests lightly on the young man's knee. "We saw her crossin' the Panhandle an hour ago," Cyn calls to him. He proceeds north on Clayton, pauses at the corner of Hayes.

Nothing, no one. Damn it! "She's making me crazy," he mutters to himself.

He doesn't love Starbright. No, love's got nothing to do with it. He feels like an idiot. At twenty-one, shouldn't he know better? Indulging in sweet memories of Venus Rising at the expense of exciting the jealousy of a teenage girl. Yes, a pretty girl. All the pretty women of the Summer of Love, with their sloe eyes and their bare feet and their bodies through translucent cotton. They're all making him crazy. In truth, Venus Rising can't help him just now.

There!

There! Crossing the block on Hayes Street, a flash of light brown hair in the wind. Her bobbing head, the way she strides down the street. He would know her walk anywhere.

He sprints after her. She spots him and takes off, heading east on Hayes. She ducks south round the corner at Ashbury, flies down the block, dashes across Fell without looking. He dodges oncoming traffic, nearly colliding with a flower-spattered van. The driver honks, flips the bird. She flees across the Panhandle, the soles of her boots flipping up behind her knees. The speed of her flight shocks him.

He catches her at the corner of Haight and Ashbury, where the Tuesday afternoon crowd slows them both down. He seizes her wrist.

"Damn it, Starbright," he says, panting. "This isn't a game!"

"Yes, it is," she says. "You're nothing but games, Chiron Cat's Eye in Draco. I don't know what the demons want. I don't know what *you* want. Except that you're all using me for some game."

"No! I don't believe in using anyone. Cosmicists don't believe—"

"Oh, you and your cosmicists! You and your awful thought experiments. You're using me, you're using Ruby. You tell me I'm important, and everything depends on me, and then you treat me like I'm just . . . some . . . girl."

She's deeply flushed. Her eyes look bloodshot. He takes her shoulders, won't let go when she tries to twist away. "*I'm* the one being used in a game, Starbright. You and Ruby, you've taught me things I didn't want to know. But . . ." He searches for the right words. The right words are so important to her. "I'm glad I know what I know from you and Ruby. It *does* make a difference. In your Now, and in mine."

She flinches, but says nothing.

"You *are* important. And that's true, it's not a game. I can't harm you, or let any harm come to you."

"Because you would look bad in front of your cosmicist friends."

"Because I care about you."

She is trembling, but she does not try to dart away.

He takes out a wipe, blots the sweat from her forehead, smooths her hair with his fingers. "Star light, star bright, first star I see tonight. That's you, and only you," he says. "The first star of the evening: Starbright."

She tosses her head. She squints up at him. "You're full of it, Chi." But a grin twists her mouth. It's like high stratospheric clouds. How long since he's seen her smile?

The crowd jostles all about them, but he doesn't notice. Someone bumps into him, a very tall, slim, mannish woman with a strawberry-blond mod hairdo and pale ivory skin. She looks like that famous Irish fashion model. She taps Starbright on the shoulder. "I say, love," she says in a brogue. "Could you tell me where the Psychedelic Shop is at?"

"Down the block," Starbright says, turning to point. Suddenly, she sees something over her shoulder. She whirls. "Look, look!"

She darts across the intersection. The Irish lass follows, striding after her on the other side of the street.

Chiron jogs after them both. Damn it, Starbright, he starts to shout, can't you stand still for one minute. But the words stall in his throat.

He sees a small knot of people, kids crossing the intersection. The backs of heads, all that sun-spangled hair blowing in the wind. He sees the cameraman walking ahead of the crowd, the producer gesturing, the sound boom and a microphone with the logo: CBS News.

Cosmic Mind!

He darts across the street, pursuing the group. There, in the center! The clean-shaven profile of an older man, his sandy hair and distinguished face. Starbright squeezes into the crowd behind the man's shoulder. Her hair lifts in the breeze. They march across the intersection of Haight and Ashbury. As Chi catches up, he sees the man glance down at a small boy walking beside him and say, ". . . the hippie capital of the world."

It all looks so different from behind the scenes!

He cannot see Starbright's face, just a sliver of her profile. She stands behind the sandy-haired man, tall and slim and cocky in her high-collared shirt and woven shoulder bag. She nods her head at the camera, a quick bob, that's all. He can see only the corner of her haunting smile. The cameraman beams at her, the producer nods back, the sound man looks like he is having trouble with the microphone.

And Chi is so excited—one hundred percent! one hundred percent! one hundred percent!—that he exclaims in a voice thick with wonder and joy, "Beautiful!"

The sandy-haired man says, "I'm Harry Reasoner."

Transcendence.

When space and time slow down and hover, a convergence of light and consciousness.

When the One Day that is spacetime shows its true face.

When the moment flees, and you have only the memory.

When you say, I *knew* it. I *knew* it!

But you never did know. Because human consciousness knows time as a forward-moving experience.

You only *know* after time has passed.

She is jumping up and down, shouting, "Wow! Wow! Am I going to be on TV?"

He grins, proud as a new skipfather. The girl in the holoid, one hundred percent! Now, if only he can get positive identification that she is in fact the Axis, he can translate-transmit to 2467 in peace.

Starbright takes his joy at face value. "Am I? Do you think I am?"

"I think you're going to be on TV," he tells her.

"Did I look all right? Was my hair okay?"

"You looked beautiful. Your hair was beautiful."

She prances down the street. He follows. She stops in front of the Pall Mall Cocktail Lounge. An emaciated man crouches, shaking and babbling, next to a free box filled with shredded bedding. The emaciated man pulls his pants down, then up, then crawls to the other side of the free box, and sits.

Love Burgers is jammed with kids munching twenty-five-cent lovewiches. At the street curb, an entrepreneur has set up a small cart with a grill. The entrepreneur dispenses his own love burgers on spongy white buns. Red, yellow, and green jars of ketchup, mustard, and pickle relish rest, open-topped, in a rack along the side of the cart. The scent of grilling beef is thick and greasy. To Chi, it smells like burning bodies. Dogs prowl about the entrepreneur's cart with hopeful eyes. Flies buzz.

Starbright steps up, pays her quarter, and steps out of the sidewalk traffic to eat her prize.

Suddenly Chi isn't smiling. "Stop!" he says.

"What?"

"Don't eat that. I'll get you something else."

"Chi, I got stoned at the Blue Unicorn. I'm starving."

"I'm telling you, don't eat that."

"I've got the munchies. Mmm." She opens her mouth.

He seizes her wrist. "Beef is full of fat. Aren't you worried about staying slim?"

"But I haven't eaten a thing all day."

"It's not good for you, Starbright. There's this fat in the meat called cholesterol. It can clog up your arteries and give you a heart attack."

"Oh, only old men like my father get heart attacks."

"No! Everyone is affected by cholesterol, Starbright."

"One burger isn't going to kill me."

"Listen to me! One day most beef will be grown on South American rain forest lands, and the forests will be cut down, which will reduce the amount of oxygen released into the atmosphere, not to mention destroying a precious and unexplored ecosystem. The cattle produce methane, which is a greenhouse gas, besides being a terrible pollutant. Plus, they consume huge amounts of grain and water, resources that human beings could eat. Yet the cattle will produce only a small amount of protein in return. The taste for beef will screw up the use of resources so badly that the commercial beef industry will be banned! Mass-produced beef has been illegal for over a century!"

She stares at him with her bloodshot eyes. "Are you crazy?"

"I've never tasted beef," he says.

"Well, here, take a bite, it's really good."

"No!" he says, repulsed. He tries another tack. "This was once an animal. I thought you loved animals."

"I do! Animals are high spiritual beings."

"That cow was raised in misery and murdered in misery for the piece of meat in your hand, Starbright." He thinks again. "Murdered, like Shob and Superspade."

"God, you are gross!" She struggles with the grease dripping through the waxed paper. "I just want to eat a burger! What is wrong with you?"

"All right," he says. "Forget all that. I want you to look. Look at this."

He whips out his scope and adjusts the focus. He plucks the top half of the bun off the burger.

"Hey!" she cries.

In the scope's viewer, he can see the strings of fat like a ropy web connecting the bits of meat. He swings the scope over the bun. Ah, yes. On top of the bun is a sprinkling of moist brown chunks. He increases the magnification. When the focus is right, he hands the scope to her. "Look here. And here. You were going to eat that. See?"

"Yeah," she says slowly.

He points to the lunch cart, the flies, the emaciated man crouched next to the free box. The waste that the emaciated man left on the other side of the free box. The flies. The flies. Landing here, landing there. A huge black fly with a sheen of green lands on the grill, commences flicking its front legs over its face.

"Look," he whispers in her ear. "See that one? See his busy legs? Now look. Look!"

As the entrepreneur scrapes another burger off the grill, and plunks down a fresh pink patty, the fly takes off. Chi points to its flight with his finger, follows the trajectory down to the sidewalk. The fly lands on the other side of the free box, buzzes up when someone walks by, and heads back to the lunch cart. The fly lights on the pile of buns, on the jars of garnishes, on the grill, on the pink meat.

Furious, she slaps the scope back into the palm of his hand. She replaces the bun on top of the burger, sets the burger in its waxed paper on top of a mailbox. A scruffy young boy sees the burger and seizes it. He devours the sandwich in three bites.

Starbright stalks away.

Chiron smiles, filled with joy.

If Starbright *is* the young Axis, he can't tell her what she'll do with her life.

"Starbright, wait," he calls to her.

But he can take the time to show her what she needs to know.

GOSSIP, INNUENDO & ALL
THE NEWS THAT FITS

I have a teenage son. But equally important was the fact
that the Clinic provided me with an outlet for my idealism.
What excited me most was that we were trying to evolve a
new and badly needed approach to community health
problems, providing services to one dispossessed minority
which should be afforded to all. The approach was never
finalized, because we were in a constant state of flux and
had to respond to new crises every day. But our adaptability
was intentional. We wanted to answer the needs of our
patients as they, their problems, and their abuse patterns
changed. . . .

We observed scurvy, pellagra, colitis, appendicitis,
acute hemorrhoids due to anal intercourse. Measles,
ringworm, mononucleosis, strep throat, influenza, pleurisy.
Trench mouth, lip cancers, inflamed cavities of the teeth,
impacted wisdom teeth. That was just in an ordinary day.

—From David E. Smith, M.D.,
   and John Luce, *Love Needs Care* (Little,
   Brown and Company, 1968)

She yells and protests and digs in her heels, but Chiron won't let
Starbright go.

He drags her up the stairway at 558 Clayton and into the Haight-
Ashbury Free Clinic. The clinic is packed with the usual crowd. Old
hipsters in cracked leather, sad winos in stained suits, bikers in colors
and chains. Young black women from the Fillmore in housecoats and

plastic shoes with their unlicensed babies, hip white women from the Haight-Ashbury in headbands and bare feet with *their* unlicensed babies. Young men in various states of madness and disrepair.

It's not a place Chiron likes to be, but he has visited the clinic just about every day since June 21. He knows his way around. After all, he's getting his doctorate in medical modeling. He can't jack into telespace, but he can observe this Now well enough.

Starbright's eyes widen.

The place is in pandemonium.

Nurse Peggy and Miss Laurel are shouting.

A man hangs from the exposed beam in the ceiling of the reception area. He dangles, choking and flailing. Dr. Smith balances precariously on a chair, trying to hold up the hanging man against gravity. Dr. Reddick steadies the chair. Papa Al and Teddybear and two Hells Angels pull the hanging man by his ankles, helping gravity along quite nicely. They are trying to pull the hanging man down with the noose still looped about his neck.

"Cool it, Theo!" Dr. Smith cries.

"I'll rip his fuckin' head off," says one of the Hells Angels.

"Crazy son of a . . ." Dr. Reddick mutters.

"Aaaagggh," the hanging man says. He wears a white clinic coat.

A young woman, holding nothing but a paper towel over her body, peeks bashfully from behind a partition.

"What's happening, Nurse Peggy?" Chi says.

"Oh, hell, he's not a real doctor." Nurse Peggy frowns at the hanging man. "Jesus, it's embarrassing. This doesn't usually happen. We've got interns from all the med schools coming through here like it's a train station. But this guy. Papa Al and Teddybear and Skin and Theo caught this guy giving a gyn exam to Theo's lady. He had the coat on and everything. I guess she's got a problem. I'm real sorry."

Nurse Peggy runs to help Dr. Smith take the hanging man down. Chiron promptly seizes caps, surgical masks, and clinic coats, hands the clothing to Starbright, takes a clipboard, and sets off into the clinic. When they are out of sight of the hanging man, they slip on the clothing. He motions for her to hold up her hands. He applies prophylaks over them like tossing tinsel on a Christmas tree.

"Do I have to do this?" she pleads. "I don't really want to do this."

Chi punches prophylaks over his own hands. "You have to do this."

They find a young man lying on a stretcher, waiting for an ambulance to San Francisco General Hospital. His face and dazed eyes are bright yellow. Though he's strapped to the stretcher, he curls his legs to his chest in a fetal position. His face twists in unspeakable pain.

"Jaundice," Chi whispers. "Infection and destruction of the liver. Probably from serum hepatitis. He's probably going to die."

"How?" she whispers back, horrified.

"Sharing a dirty needle."

They find a room filled with people coughing, sneezing, wheezing, spitting. A man Chi recognizes as the guy with the eyes spits into a cup.

"Respiratory infection," he whispers to Starbright. "Could be bronchitis, aggravated by pot smoking."

A grizzled man lies in the corner. His breath rests lightly on the top of his chest. "Advanced pneumonia. He could die, too," Chi whispers.

He trains his scope on the patients' fingers, the coffee cups, the floor. He focuses the view till, even against the variegated backgrounds, she can see the crawling, pulsing life there, the bacteria and toxins from human beings.

She looks. And looks.

They peek into an examination cubicle. A young man lies naked on the table, waiting for a doctor. His skin is riddled with half-moons of rash. Red nodules extrude from his joints. Chi focuses the scope, finding a patch below the young man's belly button. At $5\times$ magnification, an alien landscape. On every hair of the young man's crotch is a crab louse, its head buried into the skin next to the hair follicle.

He hands the scope to Starbright. She blushes scarlet, but she takes a long time looking.

A blond girl thinner than Cyn lies on a stretcher in the hall. She is waiting for an ambulance, too. Her unconscious face is like a crone's, a living skull. Her arms and legs are like sticks. Her abdomen is swollen, bloated as big as a watermelon. "Kwashiorkor," Chi whispers. "A nutrition-deficiency syndrome observed in chronic alcoholics and weaning infants in famine areas." Chi gently lifts the sleeve of the girl's hospital gown. The soft interior of her arm is pocked with black-and-blue bruises. "Junkie," he says.

Starbright nods briskly.

They wander through the clinic. A wild-eyed man is backed into a corner. Dr. Dernberg tries to coax the man with a cup of hydrogen peroxide. "Just sip a bit, rinse your mouth," Dr. Dernberg says. The man shakes his head, baring his teeth in a grotesque grin. His gums are bleeding. Two of his front teeth are withered brown stumps. He shrieks when Dr. Dernberg reaches to examine him.

Two young boys are retching in the toilets. Chiron closes the door against the stench.

"That's what could have happened to you if you ate that burger," he whispers to her. "Probably e. coli. There are two sets of symptoms, one that mimics cholera and one that mimics dysentery. Take your pick. The organism is spread by contaminated, improperly cooked food. It could kill you. A Prime Probability, Starbright. Dig it?"

She presses her fingers to the base of her throat. "Dig it."

They visit patients in one row of cots stricken with gonorrhea, syphilis, condyloma acuminata, trichomoniasis, other infectious diseases of the genitourinary tract.

"Love, love, love," Chi whispers.

In another row of cots, patients lie with gunshot wounds, broken bones in casts, knife slashes, razor cuts, great patches of abraded skin.

"Hate, hate, hate," she whispers back.

They tour back to the reception area. The hanging man is down from the rafters.

A woman with her hair in half a dozen lopsided braids stumbles up the stairs. She babbles and shrieks, "He fuck he fuck he fuck he fuck!" She weaves, swoops, claws at the walls. Her eyes roll and stare. The braided woman fixes upon Starbright. She leaps across the room, tries to tear the surgical mask off Starbright's face. Dr. Smith and Nurse Peggy restrain the braided woman. She wears a backpack slung over her shoulders. Nurse Peggy eases off the backpack. Inside is a tiny girl, no more than three months old. The baby chokes and gasps for air.

Miss Laurel gets on the phone, dispatching another ambulance.

"What is it?" Starbright whispers.

"Could be meningitis," Miss Laurel says, barking the clinic's address into the phone. "Hello, Mission Emergency?"

The baby girl has big brown eyes.

"Bye, everyone!" Chiron takes off his mask, cap, and gown. He tries not to be too cheerful in the face of all this misery, but he can barely contain his glee.

Starbright frowns as she takes off her mask and gown. She shakes her head, lost in thought, peeling off the prophylaks with the unconscious precision of a surgeon. She fixes him with a baleful stare.

"What do you think of the Free Clinic, Starbright?" he says as they climb down the stairs and cross Clayton to the Mystic Eye.

"Do you think it was right that we looked at all those poor people without their permission or anything?"

He's surprised for a moment. But he shouldn't be. Medical ethics will be a major issue to the Axis one day. If Starbright really *is* Susan Stein.

"Yes," he says. "I think it was all right. But what do you think?" he insists.

"I think you're mean."

"How am I mean?"

"Just when I'm starting to think you're cool again, you make me see that."

"The Free Clinic is a beautiful thing, Starbright. The American system of medical care will come back to this idea one day. You'll see. Well," he says sadly. "It may be a while before the priorities are sorted out about medical care. Maybe you won't see." He shuts his mouth, but still. Still, he is pleased. His skipmother said, consider impact before you consider benefit. And he has. He has.

"It's gross," she says somberly. "Being *alive*. The human body is not designed very well at all. It really upsets me. All those pores and tubes. The skin is so weak. God! It's gross!"

"Then redesign the human body," he says. "Go ahead, I dare you."

"Maybe I will, just 'cause you're gross," she says and sprints across the street. "But," she yells at him, "I'm *still* hungry!"

She glances back at him, flashing eyes, flying hair, and he can see that she's changed.

She's *changed*!

For a moment he's scared. Has *he* wrought this change? Has *he* changed all spacetime? Done the dangerous deed forbidden to a t-porter to the past?

Or has he only nudged the probabilities? Gently, gently.

No, he never was the tall, pale, red-haired person in the background of the CBS News holoid. But he *did* say, "Beautiful!"

Then he has always run across the street to her. He has always taken her hand.

15

Over Under

Sideways Down

 When Ruby goes downtown to the San Francisco Gun Exchange to buy herself a pistol, she sees four Haightians she knows there.

The gun exchange is stockpiled with weapons on racks from the floor to the twenty-foot ceiling. Revolvers, pistols, rifles. Semiautomatics of every description and combat automatics, too. Hunting knives, daggers in leather cases, aristocratic fencing swords, curved sabers fit for barbarian marauders. A hard-bitten clientele slouches at the counters like regulars at a local bar, chatting, smoking, checking it out.

The pock-faced white cat watches her turn the medium-frame Beretta over and around and says, with a gap-toothed leer, "Whaddaya want this piece for, lady?"

She aims her best glare at him. "Gonna off me some pigeons, now what do you think?"

She hefts the pistol. James Bond carries a Beretta. Stan the Man always fancied himself a hip James Bond. He went to see *Goldfinger* four times. Ruby cannot tolerate James Bond, who is more of a bumbling idiot than the publicity machine would have you believe, as is only fitting for a booze-soaked womanizer. But if a Beretta is good enough for James Bond, it is good enough for Ruby A. Maverick. The pistol is heavy, a dead weight. Plastic and anodized steel would be cheaper, but the wal-nut grip with a shiny nickel barrel looks classy. Sort of elegant. Almost makes her feel all right about buying a gun.

She goes back to the cashier, and damn if she doesn't see Luther and his latest lady, Peter, and Jerry lined up in the queue. She hardly knows Luther's lady, a voluptuous girl with runaway eyes and strings of gooey brown hair plastered over her cheeks. She gawks at the wares as though a rifle is going to hop down and blast her all by itself. The three cats Ruby knows only too well. Two are HIP merchants of recent vintage, the third a speed dealer with a hog shop for cover. Ruby doesn't say hello. Neither do they. They each pay their bill and hurry out.

But the neighborly pull overcomes this uncharacteristic shyness. As Ruby leaves the gun exchange, she finds the quartet lingering on the sidewalk outside.

"Shob and Superspade got everybody spooked," Peter says out of the corner of his mouth to no one in particular. With his Stetson, mut-tonchops, and pointy-toed boots, he's a cosmic cowboy with a habit of staring at the clouds whenever he is supposed to be carrying on a conversation with a human being.

"I'm freaked out by the Syndicate thing," Luther says.

"Fuck the Syndicate like my shop my shop my shop got ripped off last night, man," Jerry says. "Last *night*." He's a wiry little cat in a sleeveless shirt, skulls and screaming eagles tattooed on his arms. "Like the second time this week, 'n the third time in a month, 'n the pigs don't give a shit give a shit. Wasn't no Syndicate did that, man. Was some fuckin' little speed speed speed freak over-ampin', man, over-ampin'."

"Don't see how you can bitch about that, ol' Jere," Luther drawls. "Karmic compensation, y'know." Luther is one of the boys invited to sit on the Council for a Summer of Love. He's got the guru trip bad. Wears all white, from his beaded suede headband to his ivory leather boots. Uh-huh, Ruby thinks, holy animal skins. But she keeps her mouth shut.

"Karmic compensation, shit," Jerry says. "I deal it, I ain't payin' payin' payin' for it, too, man. Ain't gonna tolerate ain't gonna put *up* with no more rip-offs." Jerry pulls out a cheap, mean-looking revolver from his paper bag and spins the barrel, demonstrating his intent. "How 'bout you, Ruby?"

She shows them her Beretta.

Luther whistles. "You always got fine taste, Ruby."

"Why, thank you, Luther," she says, sweet as poison. She knows through the grapevine that Luther has called her a nigger and a bitch behind her back. He's always been jealous of her financial acumen. Why is she not surprised? Luther tokes most of his profits, and, guru that he is, turns on his friends as well, friends being defined as whoever is cool in the tribal echelons of the Haight-Ashbury and whomever he is having sex with. Never has much bread for small matters like his employees' salaries or the quality of his inventory or the Swiss abortion for his last lady, let alone donating to the Free Clinic. "Anybody looks cross-eyed at me, baby," she tells them. *"Blam blam blam!"*

They all laugh, but the sound rings untrue, like the clapper in the cracked bell of freedom. It's the Summer of Love, and graffiti is stenciled in red paint on the sidewalk in front of the Bank of America on Haight Street.

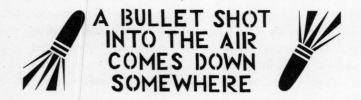

A BULLET SHOT INTO THE AIR COMES DOWN SOMEWHERE

And hip people who celebrate the infinite holiness of life are buying guns.

The *Berkeley Barb* has fastidiously avoided coverage of the murders of Shob and Superspade and declined to report the arrest of Shank, opting instead for polemics about Black Power and dreadful essays about the superiority of the hip mystique, complete with a goggle-eyed celebration of how hippie chicks like to fuck. The Establishment media, however, has covered each new scandal with barely concealed glee. But if Shank killed Shob and cut off his arm, what does that have to do with the Syndicate? When the Establishment media jumps into the rumor game, watch out.

Rumors of the Syndicate moving in have haunted HIP merchants in other ways. Who is pulling the strings behind the Straight Theater lease, for example? Ruby is as concerned about this bit of news as the reports of escalating burglaries. If the lease goes through, a consortium of investors will control six major storefronts, extending from the theater to the hardware store next to the I/Thou Coffee House. The prospective landlords have informed the merchants they will increase the rents by double and a half, plus seven percent of gross. Rumor says the owner of three North Beach strip clubs is calling the shots, but the front man for the investors says it's hip money. Now everyone is worrying about where the money is coming from. Who gives a shit? If it's hip or Mob or Daffy Duck, *some*one wants to rip off the HIP merchants, those evil opportunists of the Love Revolution. Double and a half, plus seven percent? Greed is greed, all right? We're gone come autumn, everyone's saying. The hip community is bust. And if Mrs. Andretti doubles the rent or demands a cut of gross, Ruby will shut down the Mystic Eye, too, fare thee well my own true love.

Dig it:

You want to know why the Establishment media is so pleased with all this lousy news? Why they salivate over each and every gory detail, parade headlines about the murders of two dope dealers who don't amount to a hill of beans while thousands of young men are dying in Vietnam? Because this kind of news means the hip community is as bad as they always said. It means the New Explanation is as corrupt in its soul as the rest of the morally bankrupt world, maybe more so, due to false pretenses. The personal revolution can assert no valid ideals, can provide no guidance to the disaffected youth of America, can offer no alternatives. The hip community has failed. They have failed.

Fog rolls in, casting a cold shroud over the street. Luther is a bigot and a woman-hater, Jerry is a speed pusher, Peter is just plain weird. Ruby doesn't really like any of them. She owes them nothing.

She says, "Want a ride?"

Luther's lady digs into her handbag, pulls out a black and pink abalone shell, and presents it to Ruby with a shy smile. Luther takes off his headband. Jerry slips her a plastic baggie with a couple of hits, which she promptly dumps in the gutter. Peter actually looks at her and says, "Gee, thanks," and she notices for the first time that he's cross-eyed.

They all pile in, and Ruby takes them home.

Grandmother Says: Ku (Decay)

The Image: The wind blows low on the mountain. When the wind blows low, it is thrown back and spoils the vegetation. But if the wind rises, it dispels the despoliation.

The Oracle: Work on what has decayed brings supreme success. It furthers one to undertake great tasks, but great tasks take time and patience.

What has been spoiled through the fault of humanity can be made good again through humanity's work. Corruption occurs not due to immutable fate, but by the abuse of human freedom, indifference, and inertia. Ascertain the causes of corruption; thus begin with deliberation. Ascertain whether the new way brings renewal; thus examine your path after you have embarked upon it.

—Hexagram 18, *The I Ching* or Book of Changes

Some say those that live by the gun die by the gun—others say let's get high—

Mafia is a state of mind anyone can slip and fall into—Just try getting rich or selling just enough dope to stay alive, after all we have to stay high—

MAFIA IS A STATE OF MIND—LET GO OF IT!

Whenever we attach value or worth or wealth to any external

object whether gold or dope or property or country, that object in the pursuit of happiness becomes an object of contention more important than the human mind that is the original source of all wealth or value. . . .

Dope has no effect at all—it is valueless. . . .

Do not buy or sell dope anymore! Let's tell our friends not to buy or sell dope anymore—Let's detach ourselves from that material value —Plant dope and give away all you can reap—Tell all big dope dealers that their Mafia consciousness—fear, guns, knives, precautionary paranoia strategies, fantasies and dreams and seeming realities will disappear—if they give away in small lots for free distribution all their drugs and then detach themselves from dope consciousness by not buying or selling or making dope.

CONSCIOUSNESS—GODHEAD—LOVE ARE THE GOALS. . . .

For JOHN KENT CARTER and WILLIAM EDWARD SUPERSPADE THOMAS our brothers who lived in fear and died from fear may their consciousness return to bodies that will not want for anyTHING but the beauty and joy of their part in the great dance.

> —From "IN MEMORIAM: For Superspade and John
> Carter," Allen Cohen, *The San Francisco Oracle*, Vol. 1,
> No. 9 (Aug. 1967)

Broken glass. Bits of it scattered on the deck, a hole in the window. That's what Ruby sees first. Then the kitchen door cracked open like a wound.

Sweet Isis! Her heart leaps. For a moment, she feels like she's floating. Superstitions she always held about owning a gun—if you get one, you'll attract bad energy and sure as shit you'll end up having to use it—leap to mind, instantly proving their truth. She draws the Beretta, hands shaking so hard she couldn't hit the side of a barn. She swings the door open, cursing the squeak she never got around to oiling, and creeps inside.

A man bends over her turntable in the living room, plucking plugs from the wall socket. On the floor, by his feet, lies the disconnected amplifier, plus one of her speakers.

"I've got a gun!" she says. "So you can stop what you're doing right now, sonny, and turn around, nice and slow."

The man turns. Gorgon's face is a mask, deadpan, dead. A scrap of paper falls from his hand to the floor like a dry leaf.

"Leo!"

She stares. And it dawns on her: she knows that look, knows the grim purpose chiseled in crystallized flesh. She looks at his arms, but his jacket sleeves go to his wrists. She can't see his tracks. Doesn't matter. She *knows*. And it's terrible, like a death and a grieving. Not Gorgon, she thinks.

Uh-huh, Gorgon.

She pulls herself up all her nearly six feet. "What do you think you're doing, Leo?"

"I'm liberatin' your stereo for the revolution."

"*What* revolution?"

He shrugs. "You can only be free if you live outside the private property premise of this shitty country. If you participate in that, you can't change anythin'. You can't change yourself."

"What are you changing by stealing my stereo, Leo?"

He shrugs again. "The love shuck changes nothin'. We must destroy the United States of America."

"My father died for the United States of America. My father was Cherokee."

"Then he died for nothin'. He was a stupid redskin who died for a shuck."

"Don't you call my pa stupid!"

"You understand nothin' of the dialectics of liberation. *You're* one of the oppressors."

"Oppressor, uh-huh. I got me a business, sonny. Thanks to my ma and my pa and working hard, I got my own little piece of free enterprise. That's not oppression. That's success."

"Oh, you got yours," he says sardonically. "You got yours, Ruby A. Maverick."

Without taking her eyes off him, she stoops and retrieves the scrap of paper he dropped.

SHUCKING THE REVOLUTION.
YOU WILL PAY, CAPITALIST PIG.
BE ADVISED.

"You!" Her head suddenly throbs in syncopation to the pounding of her heart. "Taking me to bed, and messing with my head." She is too disgusted to summon outrage. "*Why?*"

"Why? Because you *are*. You *are* a capitalist pig, with your kraut car an' your metaphysics shuck an' your bank account."

"I'm putting up a runaway and a tourist in my home for free. I'm feeding people, I donate to the Free Clinic, I—"

"Fuck your charity. You're not *changin'* things with your charity, man. You say you're not Standard Oil, but you're wrong. I've seen your trip with my own eyes, *that's* why. You're no different, that's why. When the revolution comes, I'll be after you with a gun." He grins. "You'll be the first one I off."

She's speechless for one of the rare moments of her life. Her head spins. She thinks of Chiron and his self-righteous cosmicists with their domes and gardens, their sky-seeding and telespace. Their anger at the past.

Do the Leo Gorgons of the world tear down the system for the good of the people? In 1967? By 2467?

No. Somewhere, in between all these polarities, there has got to be a New Explanation. Do the cosmicists possess it? Maybe, maybe not. But they're still searching for new values after five hundred years.

She shakes with fury. "Right now, *I* got the gun, and your revolution is a shuck, Leo Gorgon. Get out of my house."

He eyes the gun, eyes her. Can he take it from her, will he try? But no, he's got the shakes. Sweat beads on his forehead. From his habit, not from fear.

He goes, banging the back door.

She stands, stunned, in her shadowed living room. Her cats slide out of the shadows where they've been hiding and wrap themselves around her ankles.

She lifts the Beretta. So strange to see her hand gripping this alien scrap of metal, knuckles taut. The nickel gleams. Only then does she realize she never loaded the magazine. The gun is empty, a husk, without the means to its end.

Capitalist pig. After their afternoons in her sun-dappled bed. After her with a gun. Broken glass, broken door. A door she opened to him freely with her own hand.

Junk does that. Junk is a forge. You enter the fire and come out twisted.

Her sense of violation is so complete that another door opens to another room. The shadows stretch lengthwise. A room she's kept shut, a past she's locked away. T-porting in her memory, images of ancient light flash faster than a heartbeat.

He stands before her, big as life. Long dead.

Roi.

Her skinny girl-arm was insubstantial next to his when they pushed back their sleeves and compared. She had envied his skin. Like chocolate, coffee, blackjack toffee, walnut wood drenched in lemon oil. Good things, fragrant and rich.

But Roi had laughed at her, slapped her fingers away. Already bitter at age nine, he was far wiser than she could know at six. "You practically white, girl. You got no nose." He had tweaked it, making her giggle. "You an angel, Ruby. You blessed."

But she didn't see her blessing when her father was killed at Pearl Harbor in '41, and her mother signed up for crash courses in welding and shipyard skills at Tamalpais High School in Mill Valley. Ma went to work at Marinship, clocking overtime and Saturdays, burying her grief in the great battleships like the asbestos she installed in their inner works. It was the last time before the Summer of Love that Ruby recalled being confused. Canned peas and potted meat left out for her dinner when she came home from school 'cause Ma was working. A pall of dread cast over everyone.

She remembered sitting by the engine room one Saturday morning, waiting for Ma. You couldn't call it playing. She huddled outside the door with a Superman comic book and tried to understand the ache in her heart. Why Pa wasn't coming home. Why Ma sat with a bottle when she finally came home, face slack and numb. Ruby remembered that engine room clear as day. She had peeked through the window in the door. And it looked like it was snowing inside that damn room! A sight a girl from Marin City could identify only from *Nanook of the North* or Chaplin's *The Gold Rush*. There stood her mother and her coworkers. Four women of color, trim and purposeful in their white overalls, white bandannas wrapped round their dark hair. They had bold brows and cheekbones, lips like exotic fruit. They were haughty toward the other Marinship workers. Asbestos installation was a plum job compared to welding or painting. It was clean and easy on the bones. Her mother and her coworkers were quick and efficient, deft with their hands. They pushed the asbestos up, panting, mouths open as they worked, catching the white flakes on their tongues like children gobbling a new snowfall.

Roi's mother took her brother's death worse than Ma. When the notice came he was gone, Aunt Clarice took to drink. She spiraled down a well of despair and never came up. Clarice and Roi lived in Hunter's Point, another huge black ghetto spawned by the war and its temporary industries, its greed for cheap labor. Hunter's Point was nothing like Marin City, though, another disadvantage Cousin Roi came to hold against Ruby. Worse than the Fillmore or Oakland, Hunter's Point fell idle at the end of the war. If you could, you got out. If you couldn't, you got down.

You blessed, Roi told her. In time, she came to see it.

Ma did well at Marinship. She learned how to tell her coworkers what the boss wanted them to do. When the shipyard shut down, she was offered work at the steel company that took over. Ma took shorthand at night, learned how to use a dictaphone, bought a black '47 Ford, and commuted to the gleaming corporate offices in the city. Ruby never thought of them as middle class. That was something white folks were, not her and Ma. Still, her mother bought her the new fashions and put money away for her college education, while Aunt Clarice and Cousin Roi moved from a modest house in Hunter's Point to a modest apartment, to a lousy apartment, to a dive.

Daughter of a working single mother in the late forties, Ruby grew up fast. She suffered acute shame for not having a father. Everyone had a father. Children borrowed much of who they were from their fathers. The doctor's daughter was bossy and vain, the office clerk's son was meek and obedient. "You be you, Ruby," her mother told her when she came home in tears one day. But, at the time, that wasn't good enough. "All right," Ma said. "Your pa was a hero. You're the daughter of a hero."

Ruby was admitted to the prestigious local women's school, Mills College. In time, Ma took a lover, Mr. Ben, a bearded bohemian cat who lived in Berkeley and talked about a spiritual philosophy called Zen. Dig it: she was blessed.

But Cousin Roi was not blessed. Ma didn't approve of Clarice and her dissolute ways. Years went by, Ruby didn't see that side of the family, and Roi grew up wild and mean. When she was in her freshman year, reading James Joyce and *Galaxy* and listening to Mr. Ben and his hip-bop talk, Roi was out of school. Way out. Doing the junkie scene with a gangster lean. She was nineteen when she saw him again. A Fourth of July family picnic at Lake Merritt was a halfhearted affair, tense with unspoken accusations and stored-up grief. From the start, Ma was clucking her tongue. It shocked Ruby to see how dark Roi had become, not his skin. She felt the meanness coming off him like a cold wind, the bravado he assumed before junk began to wear him down. There is no mistaking that look of death.

Yet his darkness and his danger seduced her totally. In a blinding knife-stroke, she knew she loved him.

They began to rendezvous in San Francisco, since Ma had forbidden her to see him. He was sardonic, with an edge of wit. He squired her into tinselly downtown bars that checked his ID, not hers. He was cool, carved in ebony, cast in high-fire basaltic clay. In their first days together, he kept a leash on his habit and boasted of his control. In their next days together, he began to call horse *she,* talked all the time about *her.* Like the drug was a fickle woman—instead of a bag of shit—tugging at his heart.

Ruby was twenty, for her a haughty and imperious age. She read Sartre at school, Beat poetry and *If* at home, and warily followed news accounts of the civil rights movement in the South. She fell in with the Berkeley crowd, the North Beach crowd. She got tired of tinselly downtown bars.

One night, she attained an enlightenment. Cousin Roi was beyond changing, she decided, and so was she. She knew she could never tolerate the gangster life, let alone surrender to junk. She confessed to her mother, who told her in no uncertain terms to break it off. She hadn't really rebelled against Ma, just disagreed with her. She didn't disagree anymore.

The day she broke it off Roi was on the yen. Grim purpose chiseled in crystallized flesh. That deadpan look, already dead. Wanting *her.* Needing *her.* Do anything for *her.* And in his shadow-striped room in Hunter's Point, he got crazy. Bad-crazy. Incest never crossed Ruby's mind. Only how much she once wanted him, and he refused to touch her, his pretty cousin. And how much she now wanted to leave his room and never come back. He was rough, but that was all right. What she hated most was that he was too damn late.

Ruby shuts this t-port down, slowing the tachyons of recalled light and shadows to the rhythm of her heart. Shut it down, sweet Isis. Shut it down.

Roi died a day, maybe two days, later. They found him on the third day. His death was banal. An OD in an alley with a pin of bad shit behind his knee.

In the end, it wasn't so bad that they were first cousins, forbidden to each other. It was bad he'd fallen to junk, but, in grief, she found herself forgiving that, too. No, what was bad—*really* bad—was that she got pregnant. What was worse, it was 1952, and she went to Doc Clyde for an afternoon of rose gardening.

"Ah, Roi," she whispers, guilt so sharp it still carves her heart. Afternoon shadows merge with night. "Does anyone ever really change anyone?"

She could not have Roi's baby. Not another child without a father. Not the child of a father who was never a hero. Not a child when she was twenty with her whole life before her. Not the child of a rape.

These are strange and wondrous days, she sniffs. Her daughter would have been fourteen going on fifteen during the Summer of Love.

She is sitting in the dark when Starbright and Chiron clatter in and flick on the lights. They are arguing about something, how human skin is designed, if she hears them correctly, which makes absolutely no sense to her. The youngsters have been estranged from each other for over a week, but now they move together with an easy grace. Peace restored apparently, Starbright cautious, Chiron eager. Their reconciliation makes her feel better instantly.

"Oh, Ruby!" Starbright cries. "Are you all right?"

The stereo equipment, the look on her face. Ruby slips the Beretta into her pocket.

"God!" Starbright drops to her feet and hugs Ruby's knees, nestling her head on Ruby's lap.

Ruby cherishes the gesture, but it is too charged with meaning and too confusing. Does she yearn for her lost daughter, or lust for an unknown lover?

Pushing the girl away, she comes to a decision. She doesn't have to decide that question right now. It's the Summer of Love. It's all right to wonder who you are. She smiles at Starbright's puzzled look and brushes a lock of hair behind the kid's ear. "It's all right. I'm fine." She waves at the equipment on the floor. "Leo Gorgon paid us a visit."

Chiron shrugs off his leather jacket and sets about restoring the equipment to her shelves.

"Leo?" Starbright says.

"Uh-huh. Something about liberating my stereo for the revolution."

Starbright sits on the floor, snuggles up to Ruby's feet, and takes Alana and Luna into her lap. The cats purr and preen. Stubborn girl, just like Ruby used to be. All right. Ruby lets her stay.

Chi breaks from his task and sits on the couch, watching the kid and the cats, face downcast. He heaves a great sigh. They have not sat together like this for some time.

He says, "Listen."

"No, no," Ruby says. "I don't want to listen. I don't want to hear about the terrible mistakes we'll make."

The elegant lad squirms in his Beatle boots. "But, Ruby."

"But, nothing. I don't want to hear about our guilt. I know how selfish people are. Even the hip community is sick with violence and greed. Murders over dope. A stereo for the revolution. You and your cosmicists are right to think you're better. We're wasteful, we're stupid. But, dig it. Gary Snyder, the Zen poet, is saying the same thing. You don't have an exclusive on the bullshit of 1967, sonny."

"Please listen," he says.

"No, we don't give a shit about ourselves, much less about the future. You're right, man from Mars. You are right to be pissed at us. I would be, in your pretty boots. Holes in the sky, everything poisoned, the adjustments age, the brown ages. I don't blame you, Chi. I really don't. No, I envy your superior view. I envy your genius and your perfect skin. I envy that you know so much, that you can look at us and know we are worse than we can even imagine."

"Don't envy me," he says. "You're the one who's shown me how little *we* know. I need *you*. I need you to believe in the future. To believe in us, the people of the future."

"You're mad at us," Starbright whispers. "You hate us."

"No! We don't hate you. And we're not superior. We can claim no more genius than what you possess. Listen," he says painfully. "We've made mistakes, too. We made a terrible mistake. It was called the Save Betty Project."

It was 2466, and a robust woman of sixty-four in the prime of life named J. Betty Turner was deeply involved in the development of tachyportation projects for the Luxon Institute for Superluminal Applications. Dr. Turner was a probability physicist with sublime telespace expertise, one of the first to explore systematically the potential of t-porting. She was there when tachyportation was applied to the Mars terraformation. She interviewed the laborers who paradoxed. When everyone—including Betty—was too ecstatic about the new technology, Betty proceeded cautiously according to sound cosmicist principles. Consider impact before you consider benefit. Don't intervene, even when you think it's for the Great Good. She helped develop the Tenets of the Grandfather Principle. She was a key adviser to the Chief Archivist and one of Ariel Herbert's best friends.

Betty was a great lass. As a cosmicist, she tithed twenty percent of her income to LISA research and the WET trust fund. She loved hummingbirds. She had single-handedly funded the restoration of twenty premillennium species and supported their habitat in New Golden Gate Preserve. Everyone loved her, including Chi. She had this laugh, full-bellied and sardonic, and she let him sniff her neurobics when he was ten.

Since Betty started on the ground floor of tachyportation, she felt she had a right to try the technology herself. She had a right, and she had a reason. An old sorrow, a secret that had haunted her for fifty years. When she was a child of fourteen—a spoiled cosmicist child, she was the first to admit—she was given a whirligig with which she had an accident. She had been flying downtown. In the proper skyway, yes, but she was barely old enough to fly and giddy with her new toy. A breeze tilted the whirligig. She didn't know how to stabilize it, and she struck an old devolt woman in the chest with her blades, killing the woman instantly. If only she had pulled up. If only she had flown a different skyway. If only the old devolt woman had stepped back from the curb by half a stride at that precise moment, Betty would not have killed her.

But none of those probabilities manifested. She killed an old woman when she was fourteen years old. The accident haunted and depressed her, gave her nightmares for fifty years.

Betty requested a t-port to the day of the accident. At last, she had a chance to make things right. If changing one small, sad moment didn't matter, why couldn't Betty translate-transmit to that day and pull the old woman off the street curb, out of harm's way?

The Archivists set to work. The accident had occurred only fifty years before, but, as usual, the Archives were dim. So many devolts wandered downtown. The old woman had no identification. Her body had been whisked off to the morgue. No one claimed her, no one mourned her, no one sued the Turner family for wrongful death. Nothing happened. The accident was inconsequential, except in Betty's mind. If she couldn't avoid the guilt of the past fifty years, she could at least find peace of mind for her next seventy years.

Betty wanted to do it. She *needed* to do it. So they set up a tachyonic shuttle at Ghirardelli Square, and Betty crossed over. The t-port was to last but seven hours in the past. Plenty of time for Betty to get downtown, find the accident scene, pull the devolt away from the blades, and get back to the t-shuttle. She took two nutribeads, full identification, a stack of prophylaks and wipes.

Seven hours later, they waited for J. Betty Turner at Ghirardelli Square. The Chief Archivist and her ferrets, Ariel Herbert, the LISA techs. They stood with their supersmart knuckletops, arrays of calcite crystals, an artillery of photon guns, banks of microframes, the half-moon of imploders. The awesome dish of the macrofusion chronometer hummed softly. They stood, whispering and waiting, pleased they had done the right thing. They had used the new technology for a harmless purpose. They popped the corks on seven bottles of champagne. A humane and beautiful purpose.

But Betty did not step back.

"Human consciousness knows time as a forward-moving experience," Chiron says with a sigh. "A successful tachyportation works because it's an OTL. An Open Time Loop. Look."

He whispers, "Katie" to his magic ring. The slice of blue light pops up in his palm. This time, instead of trying to conceal it from Ruby, Chi turns the blue light so she can see it plainly and whispers more things to his ring.

Floating in the middle of the light, Ruby and the kid see a drawing made of glowing red lines.

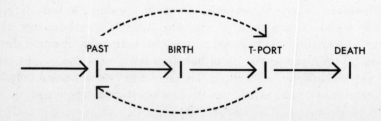

"An OTL," he says, "works with the timeline because the t-porter keeps moving forward. It's an illusion, of course, but that's how we see it. Time moves forward."

"What about memory?" Ruby says.

"Memory is the conservator of consciousness. A survival mechanism. Memory preserves information to enable you to move forward."

"What about a transcendental moment? What about cosmic consciousness?"

"That's not a normal mode of perception. If you functioned with cosmic consciousness, you'd see your whole life from birth to death, before and beyond, and none of this would matter." He whispers to the ring again. "I'm talking about everyday consciousness. Because we normally know time as a forward-moving experience, the great danger, the terrible danger, for any t-porter, is death in the past."

Now the arrows and lines rearrange themselves in the blue light, and another drawing appears.

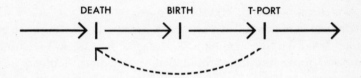

DEATH   BIRTH   T-PORT

"This is a CTL. A Closed Time Loop. When a t-porter is caught in a CTL, he is born in his personal Now, translates-transmits to the past, dies, is born in his personal Now, translates-transmits to the past, dies." He rubs his forehead. "And so on and so on. Forever."

They realized J. Betty Turner was caught in a CTL the moment she failed to cross over the t-shuttle at Ghirardelli Square. The Chief Archivist was mortified. She fired her number one ferret, promoted her number two ferret, and sent him and a staff of fifty to recheck the data. They discovered the day of the accident was hot and violent. Several armed robberies were reported along Montgomery Street that afternoon. The old woman who young Betty thought was a devolt could have been anyone. A t-porter roughed up and stripped of her identification. Perhaps disoriented, even disfigured, from a bad beating. The overworked police could have placed a person without proper ID in the public morgue. And no one would have claimed her, no one would have mourned her, no one would have pursued her cause.

"She was caught in a CTL within her personal past," Chi says. "This is what Betty went through."

"Katie, off," he whispers and snaps his hand shut. The blue light disappears.

"So she killed herself," Ruby whispers, "and she had to keep killing herself, living out the guilt, and going back to die, over and over."

Chi nods. "The Save Betty Project won instant support. Everyone acknowledged—and Betty herself would have agreed—that they could not change the fact of her death. What they could change, though, was *when*. When, in the timeline. They could save Betty from the CTL by bringing her through the t-shuttle to die in her personal Now."

"But that's beautiful!" Starbright says.

"Oh, we were careful. We sent a t-porter to the day of the accident. He stole her from the ambulance, dragged her back to Ghirardelli Square, and translated-transmitted before she died of blood loss and lacerations to her lungs. She looked like an old devolt woman by then. But she died in her Now. She died in peace, never to return to that awful past. The Chief Archivist was so happy. My skipmother cried for weeks."

He falls silent.

"You did the right thing," Ruby says gently. "How is that a mistake, then?"

He takes a breath. "No one knows how a CTL forms. A CTL has no beginning and no end. Theoretically, a CTL exists forever. And theoretically, there is no escape from a CTL. But we helped Betty escape. We broke the CTL. And at the moment we broke it, the probability of *when* Betty would die *in the timeline* collapsed out of this spacetime. We tore a hole in spacetime. The technology of tachyportation polluted all reality."

"Tore a hole!" Ruby says.

"Oh, some people believe the ME3 Event itself is responsible. It's driven by the Dead-Stop annihilation exchange, after all. I mean, we've been playing with antimatter."

"That's what the demons are made of!" Starbright says.

He nods grimly. "With the technology of telespace, we can back up the whole Archives. After the Vision of the Other Now and the Chief Archivist's order for a complete review of the Archives, the ferrets could compare the number of available bytes at each backup and figure out when the data began disappearing. It started with song lyrics. The lyrics vanished after the Save Betty Project succeeded."

"Polluted all reality," Ruby muses.

"We brought the Crisis upon ourselves," Chi says. "And we brought the Crisis upon you."

Like all young cats, he doesn't want to admit his people were wrong. She goes to the couch and hugs him, anyway. Starbright comes and throws her arms around them both.

"Cosmic Mind," he says, "we didn't mean to."

The tension breaks, and Ruby finds herself tumbled on the couch in a heap of crisscrossed limbs. Chi is in the middle, Starbright on the left, Ruby on the right.

"I forgive you, man from Mars," Ruby says. "I forgive you future people. On one condition."

"What's that?" His look of relief clouds.

"That you have to forgive us, too. It's a two-way street, this reality game, isn't that what you said? Human consciousness knows time as a forward-moving experience, but that's an illusion. That's not the true nature of reality. Right, am I right?"

"Yes," he says, warily. "Now is always Now. The One Day always is."

"The One Day, uh-huh. Then when you translate-transmit to your Now, Chiron Cat's Eye in Draco, you tell everyone. You tell them we need your forgiveness as much as you need ours."

He nods gravely.

Ruby laughs. "Well, don't look so blue! This is beautiful! It's Cosmic Mind Day! Let's celebrate. Kid, go get that sherry."

Starbright goes to the kitchen, but she pops back into the living room too soon. Her eyes are wide.

Two shadows follow her. Ruby sits up, Chi does, too, and she sees the switchblade before she sees their faces. Stovepipe and the Lizard.

"Back door," Starbright whispers. "Smashed open."

Stovepipe flicks his gaze around the room. "Some pad. So this is how you blew our seven grand?"

A quick dart. The Lizard wraps his arm round Starbright's waist, dangling the switchblade in front of her face. "You got lots of friends on the street. They know where you live."

"Maser's in my pocket," Chi says casually to Ruby. His jacket lies crumpled across the room by the stereo shelves where he left it.

"You shut up," the Lizard says.

"This kid is not a dealer," Ruby says. "We are not dealers!"

"When he says shut up, shut up," Stovepipe says.

"She was just a runner for Stan the Man," Chi says to Stovepipe. "She had nothing to do with the deal."

Ruby stares at him, astonished, then at Starbright, horrified. "You *did* pass dope to these jokers?"

Starbright nods, terrified, but resolute. "Stan used me," she says to Stovepipe. "He ripped me off for bread, too."

"That's right," Chi says. Sweat pops out of his brow. "I've been after Stan for weeks. You think you're pissed."

Stovepipe trades a look with the Lizard. The Lizard jerks the edge of the switchblade against the kid's throat. She whimpers.

The pieces of the puzzle fall into place. "Then Stan the Man is the one you want," Ruby says coolly. She stands. "Don't you know who Stan is? He's the manager of the Double Barrel Boogie Band. They've got a house. Stan's always got dope and cash around there. You want your money and your revenge, you go to the Double Barrel house."

Stovepipe nods, but the Lizard says, "I don't dig this, man. They gotta be taught a lesson. Them and their friends. Nobody fucks with us."

"Haw," Stovepipe chuckles.

The Lizard tightens the knife. Starbright closes her eyes.

Ruby swings the Beretta from one pocket, swings the magazine from the other pocket. In one stroke, she clips in the magazine and points the barrel at the Lizard's face. "Let her go, brother, or I'll blow your head off."

"Haw, haw," Stovepipe guffaws. "She's a love shucker. She won't shoot," he says to the Lizard. "Go ahead, teach the stupid chick a lesson."

Ruby fires. The bullet nicks the Lizard's ear, which instantly blossoms with blood. He makes no sound, but he drops the switchblade and claps his hand to the side of his head. Ruby suddenly understands the graffiti stenciled in red paint on the sidewalk in front of the Bank of America. A bullet shot in the air comes down somewhere. You bet your ass, baby.

Chi scrambles across the room for his jacket, the maser.

Stovepipe scoops up the switchblade, seizes the Lizard by his elbow, hustles him out the kitchen door.

Ruby chases after them.

They clatter down the back stairs, disappear into the night. Police sirens wail, bongo drums beat.

A woman shouts, "It's hard, it's hard, it's so damn hard!"

Chi comes and touches her shoulder.

The damp night makes her throat sore. But will Ruby ever stop shouting?

August 28, 1967

Chocolate George's Wake

16

Penny Lane

 Badger and the Cat clink cans of Coors and chugalug their beers in one great swallow. Foam streams from their mouths, drenching their beards, dappling their denim vests that say Hells Angels on the back. "Get *down*, sumbitch!" Badger tosses his can over his shoulder. The Cat crushes his can in his fist. They each reach for another from the tub of ice at the back of the funeral parlor, pop the tops with a church key, and guzzle.

Susan claps her hands and cheers. Chiron folds his arms over his chest and scowls. She loves it when he gets hassled about funky old 1967. She threads her hand through the crook of his arm and finds his hand. He wears no prophylak, ha!

"We're talking about political struggle," she whispers as they stand at the back of the Daphne Funeral Home behind a hundred Hells Angels in colors, with their old ladies in leather and ratted hairdos. "We've *got* to go to Chocolate's wake!"

After the private funeral service for Charles George Hendricks, Jr., also known as Chocolate George, there will be a wake at Lindley Meadow. The Grateful Dead, Big Brother and the Holding Company, and the Double Barrel Boogie Band are playing. It will be a scene. The last big scene of the Summer of Love.

Susan got invited to Chocolate George's private funeral due to her chalk drawing on the corner of Haight and Shrader. She had been practicing drawing hands for two weeks after Ruby bought her *Gray's Anatomy* and was finally getting them right, thumb and all, when they heard the news about Chocolate Friday morning. She went down to the street next to the spot where Chocolate died and drew a portrait of him as best she could recall. His beard, dark eyes, fur hat. She drew him astride a horse with wings, one hand holding the reins, the other extended in a peace sign. As an afterthought, she drew motorcycle wheels where the horse's hooves would be, which ended up looking weird. Hairy Harry, one of Chocolate's best brothers, saw her there, squatting on the sidewalk, putting the finishing touches on her masterpiece.

The day after that, Sonny Barger, president of the California chapter, rumbled by on his hog as she and Chi strolled in the park. He threw a wad of paper at her and sped away.

"Political struggle, my ass," Chiron whispers back. He's so tall the Angels don't try to bully him. But his hand is ice-cold in hers. "That's revolutionary-for-the-weekend shuck, Starbright, and you know it. Don't get radical with me."

He glares at the barbarian horde. Just like Chi. Oh, a shiver goes down her spine, too, standing in a funeral parlor with a hundred Hells Angels. The air seems thicker around them. They bend the light, like demons from *this* Now. They are ripe with funk, adorned with Nazi swastikas and storm trooper helmets, boasting great unkempt beards and an attitude.

At the front of the funeral parlor, Chocolate George lies in state, white as wax, as noble in his repose as a Cossack prince. His fur hat covers his shattered skull where he hit the pavement of Haight Street after colliding with a tourist's car at one in the morning. His jacket is pinned above him on the coffin's open lid. Quarts of his namesake and favorite drink—chocolate milk—line the inside of the casket. His wife sits in the front pew, her bowed head covered by a black lace mantilla. His seven children—Chocolate had seven kids!—sit behind a screen that shields them from the rest of the congregation.

"Revolutionary shuck," she says. "You sound like Ruby."

"It's not political struggle. It's a party. A Hells Angels party. We don't have to go. I don't think it's cool. It could be dangerous! You want to run into Stovepipe and the Lizard again? That's just the sort of scene they'd make."

"Look, Parks and Recreation tried to ban free music in the park," Susan says. "We should go to show our support. The ban is like an attack on the Haight-Ashbury. An attack on our right to be free." It's strange and exciting to feel like an outlaw for wanting to dance in the park.

"Your right to be free," he says sarcastically. "What about the interests of the people who live by the park? See, every time you talk about your freedom, you have to consider the freedom of the person next to you." His whisper gets so loud that an Angel lady standing next to them in her leather bra, jeans, and cowboy boots gives him a poisonous look. "You should have your freedom, I agree," he says, lowering his voice. "But not to the extent that you harm the interests of the next person. There's got to be a balance. The cosmicists . . ."

"Chi, this is the last free concert of the Summer of Love," Susan says. "I want to hear the Dead. I want to hear Big Brother. I even want to hear the Double Barrel Boogie Band. I haven't heard them play in ages. Besides, Penny Lane might be there. I need to see her."

Since their meeting at the Blue Unicorn Café, Nance has avoided her completely. Her promise to get back the rest of Susan's money was forgotten. But Susan doesn't care about the money. She cares about the way things have turned out. Nance was the reason she ran away to the

Haight-Ashbury. Nance was the spark, the inspiration. And she's seen her but twice during the Summer of Love.

Just one more time. If she could just see Nance one more time, maybe she could make something right out of the bad feeling between them.

Chi refuses to meet her pleading eyes. "Oh, cool," she says, pouting. She kicks at the hem of the long, black velvet dress she bought at Mnasidika with her last twenty bucks. The twenty bucks, she realizes with a twinge of guilt, that Nance gave her at the Blue Unicorn. "I'll go by myself. I'm not afraid."

But she knows her threat is empty. She goes nowhere without Chiron. Not till the hot dim spot closes and no more Prime Probabilities can collapse. He says the dim spot will close any day now. But till the dim spot closes, she's in constant danger. The nearer they come to the closing, the more dangerous things become.

Susan finally *feels* the truth of it. She doesn't question Chi's rap or try to avoid him anymore. Chi has stepped up his watch. His paranoia is catching. He even stands outside the upstairs bathroom when she bathes. "You okay?" he calls from time to time. "I'm okay," she calls back through her toothbrush or in the shower. He curls up on blankets outside her locked door. Ruby raises her eyebrows, but says nothing. It's really weird, Susan knows, but she doesn't complain.

She's convinced. Reality could shake loose any moment. A hole in spacetime, caused by pollution from tachyportation in the far future, could let in the Other Now. And the demon is coming for *her*.

Sometimes she thinks she sees the girl with her face. If she chokes on a crumb, the demon could step out of the wall. If she slips on the stairs, the demon could slide beside her. If she doesn't look both ways four times before she crosses the street, the demon could leap from the concrete and push her over the threshold of death. It's eerie. The world is not the solid place she used to know.

But what about the night Stovepipe and the Lizard broke into 555 Clayton and held a switchblade to her throat? Why didn't the demons come then?

"Ruby had a gun," Chi said, not meeting her eyes. Meaning he's trying to sound like he knows, but he's not really sure. "We know from the Archives that a lot of local people were buying guns because of the murders of Shob and Superspade, the rising rate of burglaries, and general apprehension. So Ruby was part of the trend, you see. Her personal action contributed to a macro effect. Theoretical probability physics supports the notion that probabilities are reduced in the presence of a macro." He laughed bitterly. "I was exploring the effect of macros in my doctoral thesis on the growth trends of liver clones before I got drafted for the SOL Project."

"He held a knife to my throat! I felt the blade!"

"Yes, but because of the macro, the event didn't generate enough uncertainty to create a Prime Probability and attract your demon. Even though the Lizard seemed threatening."

"*Seemed* threatening! I was scared shitless!"

He had patted her hand. "Let me tell you a story. One time I saw a podbot race. A field of twelve, really beautiful craftwork. A titanium sphere with two dozen hoofed legs sticking out in every direction. A one-legged hopper with a foot like a giant duck. Couple of quadpods, one built like a unicorn, the other a chimera. The sun shone through the dome, making shadows. What a race! The sphere and the unicorn were neck and neck. Something like neck and neck, anyway. But just before the finish line, a flagpole on the railing cast a shadow across the track. And the sphere leapt over that shadow! Its perceptuals thought the shadow was a real thing. It leapt and it stumbled and it lost by a nose. Something like a nose. I'll never forget that, Starbright. It leapt over a shadow, and it lost the race." He shook his head. "Lost me a couple IBUs, too."

But Susan got angry. "A switchblade at my jugular vein is not a shadow, Chiron!"

"But it was, Starbright. Given the probabilities in that macro, the switchblade was just like that shadow."

What is just a shadow, Susan wonders, and what will really slit your throat?

Sonny Barger strides to the front of the funeral parlor and stands beside the coffin. He gestures for silence. He holds up a book, squints at the pages. "See, I'm gonna rap about the future," Barger says. He consults the book. "The outlaw of a fat society, man, is the dude of the future."

"Tell it, Sonny!"

"What they call the rugged individualist is the cat who is our next hero."

"Hero . . . in, man!"

"Gimme crystal or gimme meth."

"Dig Caesar, dig Napoleon," Barger says. "Dig Alexander the Great, man."

"Great balls o' fire!"

"Ball me, baby!"

"These cats were outlaws," Barger says. "They like took over and ruled the fucking world, man."

"Right," Chiron whispers. "A scheming politician, a voracious general, and a brutal conqueror."

"Ssh!" Susan and the Angel lady hiss at him together.

"So wherever you are now, brother George," Barger says, "ramble on, man. Ramble on."

"Chocolate was cool," Susan whispers to Chi. "He never hurt anyone. He volunteered at the Recreation Center for the Handicapped, that's what I heard."

"Volunteered for twelve years," the Angel lady snarls. "Handing out volleyballs. He loved them little kids. Never laid a hand on 'em."

Sonny Barger turns, bends over the coffin, and kisses Chocolate George's face. The funeral parlor falls silent. Then, with scattered grumbling and nervous giggling, no tears but a lot of grim mouths and hard eyes, the Angels and their ladies file past the coffin. Some touch or kiss the corpse. Some deposit things inside the coffin. When Susan and Chi file by to pay their respects, she sees joints and tabs and pints of Wild Turkey next to the quarts of chocolate milk, flowers, a switchblade, and a pair of brass knuckles. She remembers the barbarian in the fur hat who sat next to Professor Zoom on the first day of the Summer of Love and sang to her, "First there is Starbright." She tucks her tribute in the coffin, too: a milk-chocolate kiss.

The mile-long phalanx of Harley-Davidson motorcycles follows the hearse out to Cypress Lawn Memorial Park. There they bury Chocolate George with a priest and everything, then parade back to San Francisco. With a huge growling racket, the hogs wind up and down Dolores Street past ancient palm trees and frightened old ladies peeking through Spanish lace curtains.

Susan sits on Chi's lap in the front seat of the Diggers' green truck. Gorgon's pal Cowboy is driving. The back of the truck is filled with shaved ice and what looks like a thousand cans of beer. By the time they get to Golden Gate Park, a thousand people or more are milling about the gentle hills.

One hill is staked out by Hells Angels, Gypsy Jokers, Vagabonds, Nomads, Cossacks, Satan's Slaves, Misfits, and Saints' Executioners. Angel ladies pass around a tambourine, gathering coins for a beer run. On the other hill linger the hip folk in their own version of colors. Toking, tripping, tooting flutes, lighting sticks of incense, shaking their bells. The Diggers and other tribal chiefs are there. Charlie Artman, the Hun, A.J., Slim Jim, Luther, Teddybear, Rockin' Johnny. Susan and Chi stroll up Hippie Hill.

Badger and the Cat seize fists of ice from the back of the Digger truck and pelt each other with snowballs, which melt under the August sun. Soon a dozen Gypsy Jokers have joined the fracas. Beer is shaken and spewed from cans, punches are thrown. Two cops stop, get out, and loiter at the back of their car, surveying the scene through their sunglasses. The tension is as thick as the sweet smoke wafting from Hippie Hill. Susan squeezes Chi's hand so hard he says, "You're hurting me!"

The Grateful Dead ride in atop an Avis truck. Big Brother shows up. And, there, the blue clouds of the Double Barrel Boogie Band's van. The Dead plugs in. An electric guitar shrieks, drums roll, a cymbal crashes, trailing off in a sound like waves on a beach. People turn, mesmerized. The snowball fight stops. People start to dance.

A voice booms over the loudspeaker, "Heads up! We've got . . . uh . . . We hear there is Sonoma Gold under the big tree. And, uh, our brothers and sisters at the Purple Haze House say they are laying hits on anyone who knows the magic word. That scene is happening in front of the Double Barrel Boogie Band stage. For your information, the magic word is . . . uh . . ." A deafening crackle of feedback.

Someone shouts, "The magic word is *buzz*."

Excitement prickles up Susan's back. She's not afraid. No, she's filled with that sense of magic and destiny she has only felt in the Haight-Ashbury. The last free concert of the Summer of Love. And despite the death and ugliness of the past month, the scene manifests this afternoon in all its gorgeous, insane glory. A fitting tribute for Chocolate George, who they say manned the corral for lost children at the first Human Be-In. That was Chocolate's myth. A rebel who drank chocolate milk. The outlaw who loved kids.

"Chocolate's death is like the soul of the Haight-Ashbury dying," she says to Chi.

But he nods absently. He looks warily about. His hand is tucked into his jacket pocket where he keeps the maser. She sighs. There's no point in telling him to ease up and dig it. She breaks away from his grasp, wanders over to the bands, not bothering to see if he's following. This meadow is a few steps away from where she stood two months ago. Two months! It feels like five hundred years.

"Say hey. Foxy lady. Beautiful in black today," says Stan the Man. Oh Stan, the mountain man, so beautiful. But Susan knows he's older than Ruby. To her, he's just a dirty old man conning young women, a Don Juan whose sleight of hand isn't very good once you've seen his tricks.

"Where's Penny Lane?" she says.

"Don't I get a hello?" he says.

Big Brother turns microphones on, amps whine. Janis Joplin launches into "Didn't He Ramble."

"I need to see her, Stan." She tries to peek into the back of the Double Barrel's van.

He blocks her view. "My, my. The flower child is a child no longer."

No one's inside the van. "Do you know where she's staying?"

"Not a child, and not with child. At least, not anymore." He seizes her by the waist and, in an astonishing imitation of that other dirty old man, Mr. Rosenstein in his art supply store, he presses his palm on her stomach, down low. "That's what you were doing when Dirty David saw you, isn't it?"

"I don't know what you mean."

"I had to make sure you weren't turning state's evidence. So I turned Larry on. Clerking in a law office is such a drag. You had an abortion, didn't you?"

She twists away. "It's not your business."

He seizes her wrist. "Yeah, it is. It is my business. You were carrying my child, weren't you, Starbright?" She won't answer, but she can't hide her face. "Why didn't you tell me?"

"Why should I? It was my decision."

"But I would have wanted to share in that decision."

"Oh? You want children?"

"No."

"You would marry me and support me while I finish high school?"

"No, I don't think I would. But I feel this sense of . . ." He gazes away and his eyes pool. "This sadness. Like here was this life we made together. With joy, in celebration. And that life, that human being, never happened."

"I don't want to hear this! You rip me off for a hundred dollars. You deceive me."

"You've deceived me."

"You break my heart, and then you cry—*cry*—over something you wouldn't give a damn about even if you did know!"

A tear lingers at the corner of his eye. "That baby was a part of me, too."

"But *I* would have had to raise that baby. You can't possibly know *my* pain!"

She turns and runs, crashing headlong into Chiron hurrying toward her.

Chi catches her wrists. "Starbright! What's happened? Are you all right?"

Stan strides up behind her. "She's all right," he says to Chiron. "Here." He shoves a wad of crumpled twenty-dollar bills in her hand. "Here's your bread, Starbright."

"Forget it. I don't want your money!"

"Take it." His voice is harsh. "Your girlfriend, Penny Lane, or whatever she's calling herself these days, she's at the house with Professor Zoom. I don't think she wants to see you." He wipes the tear from his eye and touches his wet fingertip to her cheek. "Say hey, flower child. Be cool."

He stalks away.

Dogs snarl and yip. A knot of Hells Angels bend and cluster. Fists rise and fall. A spate of laughter, and the Angels ramble on. A barefoot man lies crumpled in the mud, blood smeared in his long hair and beard.

"Bye bye, Chocolate, bye bye," Janis wails up on the Big Brother stage. "Bye bye, Chocolate, bye bye."

WEATHER REPORT
Ecology Sucks!

It sucks the life out of social reform. It sucks the energy out of campus movements. It sucks the irritants out of capitalism. It sucks change out of politics. It sucks reason out of thought. . . .

The movement to save spaceship Earth from extinction is so infinitely reasonable that it's difficult to find any opposition to it. The planet . . . has become such an obnoxious open sewer that every sane person, regardless of age or political persuasion, is convinced a remedy must be found before it's too late.

But the issue is so blinding that no one is asking the questions that must be asked. No one is taking the time to understand fully what it is they are lending their support to. . . .

It is madness to believe that an unresponsive government and corrupt economic system will or can save the Earth. Just as it is madness to participate in a popular ecology movement that is endorsed by the very people who make the movement necessary.

> —From "Ecology and/or The Police
>   State," *Earth Read-Out* (Mar, 1970)

Dear Editor:
I love dogs, and when I saw two huge dogs beating up on one mercilessly, I "lashed out" with a nylon jacket and successfully broke the fight up, preventing anyone in the crowd from getting hurt, as well as the small dog. I was chased and beaten for this by the owner of the dog and his friends, the Hells Angels. . . Will you please do me a favor and print this letter. Thank you.
JD (I request that my name be withheld from the paper, thank you again.)

> —From "Sadder 'N Hell, Angel,"
>   *Berkeley Barb*, Vol. 5, No. 9, Issue
>   108 (Sept. 8–14, 1967)

The sense of magic and destiny flees. Her last concert of the Summer of Love is marred forever. Susan wipes Stan's tear from her cheek and tells Chiron she wants to go, which pleases him enormously. They hike through the park back to Haight Street. Evening brings a chill and an ominous feeling.

Susan turns up the block. So strange to see the Double Barrel house again. She has avoided this street for two months. Rain drizzles. The block is deserted. Their footsteps echo up the front stairway.

The house is trashed worse than before. Instead of a noisy throng of laughing, cavorting people, the living room is empty, silent but for the erratic tick-tock of a junkyard clock. The scent of incense and dope smoke cannot conceal a stench like rotting meat and excrement.

Susan gags.

Chi covers his mouth and nose. "Something dead in here."

Suddenly Dirty David bursts out of a back room. He waves a sawed-off shotgun. He shakes so badly, the barrel swings wildly about. "Who's there?" he calls in a hoarse voice. "Who's there?"

"Dirty David!" Susan cries. "It's just me and my friend!"

Dirty David got his nickname due to his taste for pornography, not his personal hygiene. Now his meticulous mod clothes are ragged and torn, stained with grime and what looks like dried blood. He always was a fine-featured, almost delicate, man. But now he looks emaciated and nearly as pale as Chiron. He narrows his eyes. "Who the fuck are you?"

"It's Starbright, Dirty David. Don't you remember me? And this is my friend, Chiron. Don't worry, he's cool."

Dirty David stares, a glimmer of recognition flickering in his eyes and dying out. "What are you doing here, what do you want?"

"Dirty David, I've got to see Penny Lane."

"Penny Lane. There's no Penny Lane here." A spasm courses through him, making his limbs twitch all over.

"Let's go," Chi whispers.

"No, I've got to find her!" She turns to Dirty David. "You know, my friend from back East. Short dark hair, dark eyes, very slim. Actually, her hair was white the last time I saw her. Stan the Man told me she's here with Professor Zoom."

"Oh, you mean Crinky." Dirty David laughs. "They're upstairs. They're all upstairs." He squints at them again. "Say, you got any reds or yellow jackets?"

Chiron pops a blue bead off one of his necklaces, holds it up between his thumb and forefinger. "Break it in half like this, see? And sniff." He tosses the bead on the coffee table.

Dirty David scrambles for it. He seizes the bead in his trembling hands, breaks and sniffs it. "Ooh," he groans. He collapses on the floor in less than a second, spilling the shotgun, which goes off with a soul-splitting *bang*. Plaster flies off the wall.

Susan ducks, paralyzed for a moment, teeth chattering.

Chiron takes out a prophylak, takes the gun, and stashes it behind the swayback sofa. "Just a knockerblocker," he whispers to her questioning look. "It won't harm him."

"Oh wow," she says, not bothering to hide her sarcasm. "Isn't that against one of your Tenets?"

"He'll calm down, get some rest," Chi says. "Won't remember a thing, except that it was good shit and where can he get more."

"Right. We always want to know where we can get more."

He kicks at the husk of the bead on the floor. "Vegetable plastic," he muses. "It'll decompose. In this mess, no one will notice."

"I believe you're becoming a revolutionary, Chi."

"You make me crazy, Starbright," he says with a quick grin.

They hurry up the stairs. Deep silence on the second floor. Clothes, sleeping bags, rumpled sheets strewn about. They cautiously climb to the third floor.

"Hey," Susan calls out. "P-Penny Lane? Are you here? Where are you?"

A door bursts open, and a skull with a pink boa clipped to its hair peers out.

She jumps. "God! L-Lady May?"

Lady May stares.

"It's St-Starbright. This is my friend Chiron. You met him on the Panhandle, remember? We're cool, okay? We're cool. Lady May, where's my friend? Where's Penny Lane?"

Like a ghost, Lady May slips back into the room.

A pounding rises in Susan's head. She can't swallow. She tips her forefinger to the door and pushes.

The door swings open.

They're sprawled on a mattress on the littered floor. Lady May wearily lowers herself next to Nance. They wear nothing but bikini briefs, including Professor Zoom. Flickering light comes from candles.

Candles everywhere, on the floor, lining the windowsill, all over the top of a chest of drawers that's the room's only furniture.

In the smoky candlelight, they look like corpses, refugees from life. The room is stifling, the air thick with the stench of burning wax and matches, Kool Menthols, a rancid sweat, a strange decay.

"Hey, Trixie, Trixie," Professor Zoom drawls. "Which way, Trixie?"

Chi whips out a handful of prophylaks, carefully arranges a seat for Susan on the floor, then another for himself. He does not bother to conceal his movements.

Nance watches with cavernous eyes before she bursts into a cackle. "What the fuck?"

"Protection," he says grimly, staring at her. She laughs again, but a throb steals into her cold mirth.

Susan is struck dumb. She doesn't know where to begin. She sees the glint of glass, the gleam of steel. Syringes lying everywhere, everywhere. At last, she says to Professor Zoom, "Which way, Arnold? Out of here. You've got to get out of here."

"There is no way out, sweet pretty pussy," he says and chuckles. He picks up a kit lying on the floor next to the mattress. "No exit, and I don't mean Sartre."

White powder everywhere, bags of it, piles of it. She says to Nance, "Penny Lane, what are you doing?"

"Drop that stupid Penny Lane, Starbright." She says Susan's street name with exaggerated sarcasm. She sings, "Crystal meth is up my nose and up my ass." She cackles again, an awful sound. "My name is Crinky."

"Crinky. Is that from *Sergeant Pepper* or *Revolver?*"

"Fuck *Sergeant Pepper.* Fuck the Beatles."

"Oh, I wish I could," Lady May howls. "I bet they are popping some righteous shit!"

"I don't like 'Crinky,' " Susan says. "It's stupid."

"Oh, and Starbright knows what's stupid," Nance says to Lady May, caressing her thigh. "That Starbright, she's the smart one, sweetheart. She's in the ninety-eighth percentile."

"What does 'Crinky' mean?" Susan says angrily.

"Splash, grease, rhythm, meth, crystal, speed, crink," Professor Zoom says. He holds up his hand, dangling a needle in his fingers. "Splash, grease, rhythm, meth, crystal, speed, crink, crink, crink. Crink is crank. Crank is crink. Crinky loves crank. You dig?"

With a look of slow deliberation, Nance takes the needle from him, leans forward into the candlelight. She extends her arm. Needle punctures tatter her forearm. An abscess the size of a walnut bulges from the inner bend of her elbow. She extends her skinny leg. A blood vessel is visible from her knee to her crotch, etched dark in her skin like a fine tattoo. She plunges the works behind her ankle. Her pupils flutter beneath her lids. A little shriek pops from her lips. Then she grins at them, transformed, gleaming, demonic.

"You've got blood poisoning, Penny Lane," Chiron says flatly. "If you don't go to a hospital at once, you're going to die."

"Oh," Nance says like a child disappointed by a gift.

"We're all gonna die," Lady May says reasonably.

Nance smiles slyly. "Look how Starbright is shocked at us."

"No," Susan says and shakes her head. "I'm not shocked."

"Then here, sweetheart." She offers the works. "I thought you said you like speed. Come here."

"I just like dexies," Susan whispers.

"Come on, sweetheart. Dexies are chickenshit. Let me fix you." A caricature of that sly, flirty look distorts Nance's face. "I'd love to turn you on."

Suddenly Professor Zoom blurts, "Alackaday and anon, Trixie! I found the Final Expression to my equation. Not in the clouds. Not in the stars. Not in the pattern of a spiderweb. I found the Final Expression here, in this crystal palace. Do you want to know what the Final Expression is?"

"Sure, Professor Zoom," Susan says.

"LSD is a hoax, that's the Final Expression! There is no Illumination. There is no key. There is no New Consciousness. Nothing! No God! Buddha and Jesus are myths, do you understand, *myths*. There is only the Great Motor. The Great Rotor Motor, grinding, grinding, grinding your mind. The Great Rotor Motor!" He bursts into tears and guffaws at the same time. "No one will be saved!"

Lady May pries the kit from Nance's fingers, rigs it up, tenderly shoots Professor Zoom in the back of his thigh.

"Shut up, Zoom. He's really lost it," Nance says to Susan. "We saw you on TV, Starbright. Last week, isn't that right, sweetheart?" She tussles playfully with Lady May for the needle.

Lady May rigs the kit again and fixes herself. Sobbing gently, Professor Zoom lays his head across Nance's bare thighs.

"On TV?" Susan says. "*I* was on TV?"

"The CBS News Special. With Harry Reasoner, sweetheart. Man, is he an ass. He doesn't know the first thing about the way life is in the Haight-Ashbury. Don't tell me you didn't see it."

"I don't watch TV so much anymore," Susan says, but her heart quickens another beat.

Nance sniggers. "Listen to this! She doesn't shoot shit, she doesn't watch TV. I bet she doesn't ball anymore, either."

"Neither do we, little love of my valley, o pin in my heart," says Professor Zoom, sniffling and stroking her knees. "We just jack off the spike."

"We figured it was the CBS News Special that brought that pig rooting around here," Nance says shrilly. "Looking for you, Starbright."

"What pig?" Chiron says.

"Some dude sent by her parents, like a private investigator or something. What a drag! Freaked us out." Nance coughs. She flicks her graceful hand at Lady May, gesturing with irritation for the pack of Kool Menthols lying on the mattress. "Isn't that just like Starbright. Mom and Daddy want you back home," she says, lighting a Kool, tossing the match in an overflowing ashtray. "Isn't that sweet? Why, that's so damn sweet, I forgot to puke."

"Listen to me, Penny Lane," Susan says. "Your stepfather and your mother came to my house. They wanted to know what happened. They wanted to know where you went. They were worried about you, too!"

"But you didn't tell them, sweetheart," Nance says like she's reminding a stupid child to watch her manners.

"No, I didn't. I thought that was the right thing to do. I thought that was what you wanted. But they were looking for you. They were, and you can go back home." Susan pulls out the wad of twenties Stan gave her. "Go home. You can work things out. I'll help you, I swear it. I will never let you down again. Please, Nance, you don't need this shit."

"Nance, who's Nance? You still don't get it, do you, Starbright?" Nance snorts. Professor Zoom starts to weep again. Lady May looks like she's about to weep, too. But Nance is as hard and glittering as the crystal. "I called my parents. I called Handy Andy and my mom. I *called* them. I called *them*. *I* called them."

Susan shakes her head at Chi. She doesn't get it, she doesn't understand. Nance is over-amping, she isn't making sense.

Chiron looks behind him. Boot heels clatter up the stairs.

"I thought you were the smart one, Starbright," Nance says. "They told me they have no daughter."

She is an elf, an explorer, a daredevil, a rebel, a whirling dervish. A junkie, a needle freak, a speed freak. A child, leaping from the old ironwood tree.

The Summer of Love did not corrupt this child.

You did, Mr. and Mrs. Jones.

Stovepipe and the Lizard burst into the crystal palace. Chi pulls Susan to her feet.

"Stan the Man?" Stovepipe cries, face twisted with rage. "We want our fuckin' bread, an' we want it now!"

"I'm Zoom!" Professor Zoom cries. "Stan's with the band!"

The Lizard kicks at discarded kits and plastic bags, the ashtrays and candles. Crystal spews into the air like dust.

"He sure as shit ain't here, so knock it off, man!" Lady May cries, rousing herself. She stands and totters across the floor, tries to restrain the Lizard's fury.

The Lizard flashes his switchblade.

Lady May screams. "He cut me!" Goggle-eyed, she holds up the bright gash across her arm.

Susan swings her purse at the Lizard, kicks and tears at him. Chi seizes her, hustles her out of the room. She shouts, protests, tries to twist away. But his hands are firm, she forgot how strong he is. He forces her down the stairs and out the front door to the street gray with rain.

A window on the third floor suddenly flares with light. Glass shatters. Screams, people choking.

Nance thrusts her head through the window. "Fire! Fire! There's a fire!"

"Fire!" Susan takes up the cry. Neighbors come to their windows. "Call the cops! There's a fire!"

Smoke billows, flames leap.

She tries to run back inside, but Chi stops her.

"Chi," she cries. "She was my best friend."

"I can't let you in there, Starbright." His face is anguished, but unrelenting. "This could be a Prime Probability. It's too dangerous!"

"Then you go!"

He shakes his head. "I can't leave you."

"I'll stay right here, I promise. You've got to go, get her out of there. Please! Please! I'm begging you!"

He clatters back up the stairs and darts inside as fire trucks pull up in a blaze of lights and wailing sirens. Cop cars careen around the block.

Susan cringes. A pig, a private investigator, looking for her? She hates the idea of being tracked down, of being busted by the Man. Maybe going to jail for the night, who knows. She drifts into the gathering crowd, hiding from the cops.

Cyn stands in the crowd, arm in arm with a handsome young black man in a beret and leather jacket. There's the cat with the skull and the guy with the eyes and the elderbeard. The crowd swells. The air thickens, the lovely scent of burning wood ruined by too much smoke. Ashes spark, whirling like fireflies. The green Digger truck pulls up. Susan spots the sharp profile of Leo Gorgon. Hells Angels rumble in on their hogs, cutting through the crowd. Firemen dash up and down the front stairs, hoisting hoses inside. A ladder angles up from the fire truck. Men scramble, leaning the ladder against the house. Police are barking, "Get back, get back!" More sirens wail as flames burst through the roof of the Double Barrel house like an evil, flickering crown.

A tall, slim man with red hair and a brown leather jacket steps out of the crowd and gazes up at the awful spectacle. "Chiron!" she cries. She pushes past people and runs to him, as glad to see him back so soon as she's frightened for Nance. "Oh Chi, did you get her out of there?"

The man turns, hair swinging like ropes of skin. She recoils from his bitter cold. His pale face is alive, crawling with little bits and pieces that wiggle and squirm like maggots on a corpse. His eyes are pools of darkness.

God, she's sick!

Stomach churning, she presses her fingers to her throat. She stumbles away from him, backing into the crowd. Groping, confused, suddenly she staggers into the arms of the gray beggar woman. The beggar embraces her, clutching her to a moist breast stinking of garbage and rot. She strikes out with her fists. It's like punching the scum at the bottom of a pond.

But she breaks away. The demon can't hold her!

"Yes!" she shouts. The demons that don't correspond to *her* can't hold her! They can't kill *her* with their touch!

A wind like ice and sulphur strikes her skin. She whirls and finds she's staring eye to eye at the girl with her face. The demon looms a handsbreadth away, but Susan resists, struggling back against the force pulling her in.

Black, they're both in black, black blowing all around them. The demon's face shifts, splintering into a thousand leers and scowls and sneers. Susan's head spins. No one should ever see such dreadful expressions, let alone on your own face. The demon raises her hand, extending the knob of her staff.

The force seizes her, tears at her.

Susan ducks. Duck and cover! Isn't that what they tell you to do if the Commies drop an atomic bomb on your house? Ducking, she breaks loose from the terrible force.

She runs, she runs, she runs.

17

Light My Fire

An inferno! The crystal palace is engulfed by the time Chiron gets back upstairs. Flames leap from the walls. Smoke surges in black curls. The Vision of the Other Now rears up in his memory, the stench of forests burning and charred flesh. Dread beats in his chest, his eyes sting. A lurid din of crackling and popping fills his ears.

Shit! This is a wood house, maybe fifty years old. No fire system, no miniframe monitor, no sprinklers autohooked to the local reservoir. A shake-shingled roof. He can't believe it. These people live in a damn tinderbox!

Chi pulls out a filter, clamps the square of SemiPerm over his nose and mouth. The filter instantly adheres to his skin, leaving his hands free. He inhales lightly, experimenting. Sooty, thick, but he can breathe all right so long as the fire doesn't eat all the oxygen.

The skinny fellow Starbright calls Professor Zoom lies at the head of the steps like a naked bundle of bones, holding his throat, hacking, tears streaming down his face.

"Starbright's friend!" Chiron shouts in his ear. "Did she get out?"

Professor Zoom clamps his hands to his scalp and claws at his limp hair, digs at his cheeks. He's got crank bugs, a shivering of nerves and muscles under the skin, creating the sensation of crawling insects. A common symptom of heavy methamphetamine abuse. His fingernails draw blood.

Chi shakes him, but he claws at himself and moans.

Chi dashes to the door. Fire darts at him like a living thing, nearly singeing him. Can't see a thing! He steps back, pulls out his scope, peers through the macro end, clicks the infrared lens on. Nothing. Mega, Chi. He shouldn't be here, shouldn't be doing this! He suddenly realizes with another part of his mind—how well the LISA techs have brainwashed him—that this is a violation of Tenet Three. Regardless of Starbright's love for Penny Lane, he cannot—should not—try to save her. Penny Lane is on her own.

He left Starbright on her own, down on the street.

Get out of here, Chi!

He shakes off a queasy feeling. For a moment, in the awful heat, his skin feels like a thousand tiny insects are crawling and wiggling all over him. His very own crank bugs. Disgusted and confused, he brushes his hand over his face, dislodging the filter. He chokes, stumbling back to the stairs.

"Did she get out?" he shouts again, seizing Professor Zoom's hands. "Is Penny Lane okay?"

"The bed," Professor Zoom says, staring helplessly up at him. "The mattress just . . . lit up!"

"What about the others?"

"The dealers split, but Lady May. They cut Lady May. And Crinky." Professor Zoom pulls Chiron's face to his. His eyes are glazed with horror. "It just . . . lit up! I heard her screaming, oh shit. I never heard her screaming before, do you understand? I heard her screaming!"

"Let's go!"

Chiron slings the fellow's arm over his shoulders and drags him downstairs. Firemen race in. A young man in ambulance whites takes Professor Zoom outside. Chiron finds Dirty David snoring peacefully on the floor. He hands the slumbering body to another ambulance attendant. He dashes back upstairs to the second floor, unwilling to accept Professor Zoom's story. Startled, rumpled people stumble down, clutching sleeping bags, hot plates, bongo drums, clothing, a whining puppy, a puckered aloe vera in a terra cotta pot.

"Have you seen Crinky? Have you seen Penny Lane?" he asks them. "The speed freak on the third floor?" But they glare at him angrily and push past him, or stare with wide, frightened eyes, uncomprehending. So many people crashing in this place, he had no idea.

A fireman yells, "Get out *now*!" He runs down to the street. The Man is everywhere. Police cars with their lights spinning, fire engines frantic with activity. News reporters with their photographers in tow, film crews with booms and microphones. The cops have got their billy clubs out and brandish them at the media people as much as at the sightseers.

A crowd has gathered, robed, feathered, beaded, spangled, stoned. Some people gape at the flaming house with tearful, horrified eyes. The mouse magician solemnly rings his brass bell and extends his skull-topped wand as if his invocation will stop the conflagration. Others giggle and smile, or stare, mouths dropped in a permanent "Wow!" There—a couple of greasy hoodies, and there—two street spades. They snake through the crowd, hands darting into jacket pockets, seizing bags. A young woman in purple yells, "Stop, thief!" but no one heeds her. Hells Angels and Gypsy Jokers straddle growling hogs, their ladies splayed behind them.

And at the corner where the steps meet the sidewalk, where Chi told her to wait, wait for him no matter what, there is no one.

No one.

Starbright's gone.

GOSSIP, INNUENDO & ALL
THE NEWS THAT FITS

Dear Editor:

I don't know the Angels personally and the wake for
Chocolate George is the first time I've photographed them at
close range. Perhaps my feelings would be modified if I did
have intimate contact with one of their "articulate"
spokesmen. Somehow, I doubt it. It seems likely that the
inner man is revealed by his external actions and the
actions of the Angels are all too evident.

     During this particular afternoon in the park, I talked
with a number of girls who seemed to believe that the Hells
Angels are beautiful people. Well, I don't know the hangups
these girls have, but I do know the Hells Angels are not
beautiful people. They are, collectively, a group of misfits
and assorted morons who, at any given time, are one step
away from violence and who will kick the shit out of anyone
who happens to displease them (hippies included). . . .

     I am confused by the hippie–Hells Angels alliance
when the fundamental concepts of each group would seem
not to coincide.

Signed,
H.S.

—From Letters to the Editor,
   Berkeley Barb, Vol. 5, No. 10, Issue
   109 (Sept. 15–21, 1967)

Chiron pushes through the crowd. "Do you know Starbright? Have
you seen Starbright? I've got to find her, have you seen her?"

    The owner of the I/Thou Coffee House pats him on the shoulder,
saying, "No, man, I haven't seen her." A man in a robe and a crown of
flowers says, "Fuck off, I'm God." Some people stare blankly like they've
never seen him before, though they have seen his face nearly every day
over the Summer of Love. Dr. David Smith comes striding up, clad in his
white clinic coat, carrying his black leather bag. Everyone draws near
the fire like moths, with little purpose or sympathy.

    Chi knows these faces, he thinks with a pang, but he knows nothing of *who* these people truly are. Where did they come from, where will they go? What is that vast spacetime inside their minds? What *do* they believe in? Is he any closer to the truth of the Haight-Ashbury during the Summer of Love? What special revelation will he have for the Archives? Fifty million International Bank Units, and he still knows nothing?

But that was never the object of the SOL Project. To understand. The object was to protect the Axis, preserve the timeline, conserve all spacetime as they know it. Rage swells in his throat. Fifty million IBUs to preserve the timeline, and nothing more. And under Tenet Three, he's not even allowed to pull a girl from a burning house.

The way you think about things shapes the way your reality is. For people like Starbright and Ruby A. Maverick, the Summer of Love has meant shaking up reality as they know it. Rejecting conformity, rejecting prejudice and blind consumerism and the way things are supposed to be. Making things different. Breaking loose from spacetime itself.

How dare the Luxon Institute for Superluminal Applications translate-transmit him across five hundred years to preserve their notion of the timeline? The LISA techs, the Archivists, the smug cosmicists with their centuries of accumulated wealth. They considered themselves the vanguard of human civilization. They believed in their superiority. But they hadn't changed enough. They hadn't even begun their personal revolution. Not if they still spoke about the mandate of nonintervention in a metaphor about murdering your grandfather or the probable nature of reality in a thought experiment in which a cat is killed in a gas chamber.

And *that* is the truth he knows from Starbright and Ruby. *That* is the special revelation he can bring back.

He looks around at the jostling crowd. Anger burns in him. He sees strangers, people he's never seen on the street before, not even after the thousands of people he saw on his loops through Haight Street. Tourists, squares, gawkers with their cameras. Do they give a shit about this house burning down?

"Why don't you move on?" He finds he's shouting. "Why don't you get the fuck out of here and let the fire department do its work?"

A guy nearly bald beneath his crew cut catcalls, "Dirty hippie," and throws a fake punch at him.

Chiron throws a real punch back, connecting with the guy's square jaw. "I said move on, you son of a bitch!"

The crew cut's buddies leap on Chi. Punches pummel his ribs.

Half a dozen Hells Angels suddenly materialize like a hulking wall of denim and clanking chains.

"Heads up, man," the Cat says mildly. Close up, the Cat's face is deeply furrowed across his forehead, around his eyes, from his nose to his mouth. He must be pushing forty. Chiron sees an Air Force patch on the Cat's jacket. "Korea, '52." The Cat grins.

The crew cut slams into Chi. He tastes blood. He plants his knuckles in an eye, feels nose cartilage crunch. Damn, it feels good! He swings like a freaking barbarian, all his rage and frustration finding targets at the end of his fists. Shake up reality, *whack!* Disrupt spacetime as we know it, *pow!*

The Cat plucks the crew cut from Chiron's grasp and tosses him at Badger.

A silver BMW Sports Coupe inches down the block. "Chiron!" Ruby leans out the window. "Have you lost all your marbles? Where's Starbright?"

He ducks from the fight, buzzing with adrenaline, heaving for breath. He sprints to Ruby's car, tears open the door, hops inside, panting and bloody.

"Uh-huh, gone crazy." She shakes her head. "I can't believe it. The man from Mars, rumbling with the Angels. How's your magic ring doing?"

"Shit!" He examines the knuckletop. A couple of dark spots spatter the housing. "K-T." A *beep*, and the holoid field pops into his palm. "It's okay." He grins sheepishly. "Guess I lost my head."

Ruby nods, glancing at him inscrutably. "Stan the Man came by the Mystic Eye. I don't know what the kid did to him, but he's splitting town. He said it's 'cause of her. Me, I think Stovepipe and the Lizard have finally got his number." She clucks her tongue. "Stan did one thing right, though. He told me you and Starbright were going to the house, looking for her girlfriend. I guess he didn't have to do that." She sighs and leans out the car window again. Leans back and fixes him with a dangerous stare. "So what happened? Where is she?"

"Not in there," he says miserably. "That's for sure."

"You don't sound glad." She peers out again. "Sweet Isis! I haven't seen a fire like that in twenty years." Ferocious eyes, getting more and more alarmed. "Where *is* she, Chi?"

"I don't know."

"*You don't know?*"

"She begged me to get Penny Lane out of there. I told her to wait. Wait, no matter what. By the time I got out, she was gone."

"I thought you told us these are the last days before the hot dim spot closes."

"Yeah." He hangs his head. "The house, the fire. I'm sure it's a Prime Probability."

"Then why the hell did you leave her, you little shit?"

"I don't know! I screwed up, okay? It all happened so fast!"

And his anger heats up about a hundred degrees, along with another bad feeling. As though an unseen force is pushing him. He can almost feel probabilities collapsing like evil dominoes, toppling in a direction he cannot control, heading into a dark destiny.

"Ruby, help me," he cries. "We've got to find her!"

"All right, all right." Ruby steers the car through the crowd. "Someone must have seen her."

The crowd grows thicker still. Fights break out here and there, pushing and jostling. Hells Angels, Satan's Slaves, Misfits everywhere. Is a riot brewing?

Suddenly, Chi spots Cyn with the handsome young black man in his beret and leather jacket. "Cyn!" He motions them over to the car. Despite the young man's militant demeanor, Chi sees at once how he holds Cyn, his arm protectively gripping her frail shoulders. Her fearful look is not inspired by him, but by the burning house, the restless crowd. Cyn's man regards the world around her with angry vigilance.

"Have you seen Starbright?" Chiron says, feeling relieved about little Cyn for the first time.

She nods, points. "We saw her runnin' down Haight to the park, Chiron."

Cyn's man nods and leans into Chi's window. "Brother, a chick runnin' through the park, nobody there but her and a pack of hoodies? You know damn well she's gonna get banged. I heard about a chick who got banged in the park. They had to do some operation on her, and she is no longer a woman. I mean they had to cut out her female parts, or somethin'. The Man said, 'Well, she was a hippie, she must've had VD, she must've been a whore.' That's bullshit. I don't dig it, brother."

"She was runnin' like crazy," Cyn says. "Like there was somethin' chasin' her, Chi. But as far as we could see, she was all alone. Isn't that weird?"

"Anybody ever try to fuck with my lady," says Cyn's man, "I'd off him. Brother, you better go find your lady. *Now*."

Chi searches the shadows as Ruby speeds down Kezar Drive into Golden Gate Park. Stragglers from Chocolate George's wake stalk in the dark. The rumble of engines splits the night. Bikers joyride their choppers down every lane, hooting with drunken laughter. Trees toss in the sea breeze. Eerie shapes ripple across the wet grass. Light rain silvers through street lights.

The park is alive, shivering. The ground seems to swell and lurch. Branches swing against the wind, instead of into it. The darkness slithers, black serpentine shapes coiling, then dissolving into nothing again.

Chiron feels sick. He has tried so hard. Stayed with her, stayed by her side nearly every moment all these days, even when he was unsure of her. Done his duty. His cosmicist duty.

And now she's gone. Impossibly gone, like a coin slipping through Ruby's sleight of hand, vanished into the night.

Ruby brakes the BMW, tires squealing. She pulls to the side of the road. "Get out! We're never going to find her this way."

Ruby brandishes her Beretta.

Chiron tucks the maser in his palm.

They dart down a twisting path into the park, confront a fork in the road. They take the left turnoff and run. Lindley Meadow, Hippie Hill, the Sharon Building, the Carousel. Five miles of parkland stretches down to the sea, a maze of trails in every direction.

"Damn it!" Sweat pours down Chi's face, even though he's shivering.

"Let's go to the fuzz," Ruby says. Her voice is harsh. She heaves for breath. "I'm no athlete, sonny."

"You go back to the car, I'll keep looking. I'm the one who blew it."

"Spare me, Chi." Ruby takes his shoulders. "Listen. This is no time for your guilt trip, all right? You can't search the whole park by yourself. Let's go to the police."

"You think the cops will help us?"

"We've got to try! It's the best we can do. Get an APB on her. She once told me her father was a doctor or a dentist, something like that. We'll tell them she's the daughter of some bigwig back East."

"I heard her parents may have a private investigator looking for her," he says. "That might help."

"Cool. I can deal with the heat if you can. We can't find her alone."

She sweeps her arms at the vast trees, the dark lawns, the labyrinthine paths. "It's too damn big!"

They jog back toward Kezar Drive, take the fork toward Alvord Lake Bridge. They stride beneath the road through a stonework tunnel, a City Works engineering project. The tunnel was built to look like a cave with rough rock walls, stalactites hanging from the roof, stalagmites jutting from the pavement.

Suddenly, there they are at the end of the tunnel.

Six hoodies. Not Hells Angels or Gypsy Jokers with colors to identify who they are, from what chapter, what hometown. Just cheap hoodies, puny and anonymous, pissed at the world and raring to pick on someone not their size.

And *her.*

Starbright crouches at the center of their circle, her eyes and mouth dark pools of terror. Her black velvet gown is torn down from the shoulder.

Without a moment's hesitation or a word of warning, Ruby fires. Her bullet nearly ricochets off the toes of the hoodie with his switchblade out. He yells, flings his blade into the duck pond on the other end of the tunnel, and lopes away like a beaten dog.

"Cosmic Mind, Ruby!" Chiron shouts, drawing his maser. He shoots a green beam, sending a shower of sparks across the concrete. "I thought you believed in peace. Can't you wait till we see the whites of their eyes?"

"If I can see his face, sonny," she yells, "I can shoot him in the forehead!"

The other hoodies scatter. A couple head toward Haight Street. A couple charge at Chi and Ruby, staring wild-eyed at his maser, sprinting past them into the dark.

Chiron leaps to Starbright's side. "Damn you, Starbright! I told you to wait!" He hooks his hand over her shoulder. "I'm not going to lose you again!"

Ruby joins them, hugging Starbright, pulling up the girl's torn bodice. She tucks the Beretta in her shoulder bag. "Let's get out of here, kid."

They turn, start up the hill to Stanyan Street.

But the walls of the tunnel rumble and sway. A sound swells like the long, low roar of the surf at night. The stalactites quiver. Bits of rock break loose and tumble. The roar gets louder. And louder. The ground shakes like the start of a big earthquake. Stones in the bridgework crack and fall. The huge eucalyptus trees sway and groan, leaves rain upon the swelling ground.

The girl in the black cape suddenly stands before Chi, her knobbed staff planted in both hands before her. For a moment, she looks just like Starbright in her long black dress, the smooth young face of a pretty girl with dark eyes and long tawny hair. But a hole pops open in the middle of her forehead. A net of cracks instantly spreads from the hole, fanning over her face. The face shatters, skin and flesh bursting off like she's exploded from inside. A bloody skull stares at him, exposed eyeballs held inside bone sockets by milky spiderwebs crawling with shiny black widows. A scorpion poises between her gaping jaws, stinger curled like a tongue.

He yells to Starbright and Ruby, "Get behind me!"

The gray beggar woman stands before Starbright, tall and gaunt, her 'fro and features a ghastly caricature of Ruby. Her curly hair begins to slither and hiss. Black snakes blink beady eyes at the end of each strand, mouths gaping, curved fangs glinting like needles, yellow tongues darting. The beggar stinks of decay. Her rags fall away, peeled off by a huge wind, till her gray-skinned body is naked. Revealing sores, raw skin, mottled rashes, open wounds, exposed bones. Her flesh rots and falls, piece by piece. The demon howls. Strange internal organs pulse between her ribs, a throbbing heart tinged green as rotten meat, wriggling strings of veins, intestines unraveling in mucus and watery excrement. A skeleton dripping with putrefaction looms before Starbright, crowned by the mass of hissing snakes.

Chi thumbs the maser to purple, the antimatter beam.

"Leave us!" he yells and aims.

Paralyzed. He's suddenly paralyzed.

For an entity appears before Ruby. An entity Chiron has never seen before: a tall, slim man with flaming red hair, dead-white skin, sapphire incandescence leaping from his eyes.

Him!

Chiron faces his demon. But this Now is not his Now!

How can there be a demon of *him*?

And his question strikes him like a blow: Who else in the Haight-Ashbury during the Summer of Love disappeared into this hot dim spot?

He is here now. And always was.

The demon smiles. Each of his teeth is a tiny face exactly like Chi's, and each face smiles, revealing more teeth, and each face smiles again, and again, and again. Faces form in his cheeks, his forehead, in the swinging strings of his hair. No rotting limbs, no putrid entrails, no serpents. Just *him,* Chiron Cat's Eye in Draco, over and over and over. He's never really *seen* himself before. His awful face. His awful power.

For whom else did the data disappear?

He feels wasted, plucked out of himself and flung across an abyss.

Gigantic cracks split the concrete. The walls yawn open. The cave shatters. The world falls away.

A huge wind sucks him and the women through a yawning aperture. Gleaming panels surround them like the hull of a machine. Black sparks spit and crackle.

They are flung upon a gray plain.

Ashen clouds roil about them. A storm thunders. The sky burns sickly yellow. A stench fills Chi's nose and mouth, making him gag. Rotting flesh, forests destroyed by fire, sulphur, smog, toxic chemicals.

Chi seizes Starbright with one hand, Ruby with the other, as he staggers in the tempest. The wind whips Starbright off her feet, levitating her, buffeting her like a black flag. Ruby drops precipitously as though the ground won't hold her. Chi is nearly ripped in two, but he holds on, *he's* the Axis, refusing to let them go.

Viscous red seeps from the horizon till the sky roils with bright blood. The sickly sweet smell of blood fills the air.

Suddenly, they perch atop a needle of rock.

A burning valley lies below. Ruined cities choke the valley. A man writhes in agony upon a huge plate while hyenas tear out his stomach and devour him alive. A pack of howling chimeras lope after children dressed in rags. Gargoyles lead a screaming woman to a gigantic noose, hang her, and ravage her corpse. Flapping vultures crouch on gut-strewn fields, flesh dangling from their long, dripping beaks. A masked robot plugged into a giant mainframe operates a guillotine, hacking off the heads of handcuffed prisoners, the stained blade rising and falling every twenty seconds exactly.

Black lightning knifes the sky.

The three demons surround them, snarling and hissing.

The demon with Starbright's face swings her staff at Chi. The Ruby demon wraps her stripped hand round Starbright's wrist. The Chiron demon folds Ruby into a ghastly embrace.

Chiron ducks, knocks the demon's staff away. He raises the maser.

But Starbright seizes him.

"No!" she cries. "Chi, don't!"

The needle of rock begins to shake, tilting crazily back and forth like a pitching ship.

He aims, but Starbright wrestles with him, throwing him off. With sudden strength, she turns the maser toward her own stomach.

"Stop it!" he cries, bewildered. "This is the only way, what I was sent here for!"

"Don't do it!" she shouts.

Ruby A. Maverick seizes his other hand, and for a terrible moment, he is convinced *they* are demons, and everything, everything—the Summer of Love, his mission to protect the Axis, the LISA techs, his own skipparents—is a monstrous hoax.

"Why are you stopping me?" he yells, anguished.

Starbright shouts into his ear, "You told us your people don't really know what the purple beam does."

"It counteracts antimatter! We're surrounded by antimatter! It's the only way we can get out of here!"

"But how do you know for sure? You told us you don't know exactly what'll happen if you use purple in contact with the Other Now!"

And she's right. They're not just in contact with the Other Now. They're trapped *inside* it!

"But it's all we've got to defend ourselves!" he says.

"But it's like the atomic bomb," Starbright says. "It's like the balance of terror. What if *you* destroy *everything*?"

They shake, tilt, barely keeping a foothold on the needle of rock.

"She's right," Ruby shouts. "The scientists thought there was a chance they could set the sky on fire when they dropped the atomic bomb. A chance they could have destroyed the whole world along with Japan. But they dropped it anyway!"

The Starbright demon strikes his kneecaps with her staff. Chi reels. The horde below them shrieks and groans.

"You're crazy!" he yells. "I can't think about that now!"

"You have to," Starbright pleads. "Look at your cosmicists. You thought you could do something good by saving Betty. But you couldn't,

Chi. You couldn't." Tears stream down her face. "Don't use the purple beam," she says. "I'll die if I have to."

"You can't die, Starbright! I can't let you die!"

She slaps him. "You can't tell me what to do, Chiron!"

The Ruby demon darts her hand of bloody bone and seizes a lock of Starbright's hair, dragging her out of Chi's grasp to the edge of the precipice.

Who else possesses the power to collapse the Prime Probability?

Him.

"Then what can we do?" he cries, regaining his grip on her arm, dragging her back.

"You said the touch of my demon could kill me," Starbright says. "But I touched Ruby's demon, and I touched *your* demon. And their touch didn't kill me!"

"*Their* touch didn't kill *her*," Ruby shouts. "Understand?"

"Then join hands!" Chi commands. "Starbright, take Ruby's hand!"

The three of them stand back-to-back, each gripping the other's hand, facing the demons and the Other Now.

"Let's touch *them*," Starbright shouts. "Let's touch them *together*!"

The Chiron demon snaps at him like a rabid dog. Chi can hear the demon's teeth *click*, sending shivers of nausea through him.

The Starbright demon beats him with her knobbed staff, raining blows on top of his skull. He can feel the bright pain, wetness pouring down his forehead.

The Ruby demon rakes her nails across his face. The razor edge of bone cuts deep into his cheek.

Together, he and Starbright and Ruby extend their interlocking fingers. No demon can touch only the one of them to which it is the killing analog.

They are intermingled.

Mixed and blended.

They are united.

"Let's sing!" Starbright says in a quavering voice. And in a thin soprano she sings the refrain from "All You Need Is Love."

Ruby starts to wail, "All you need is love."

Chiron bellows, "All you need is love."

18

With a Little Help from My Friends

The bloodstained sky turns black, the ghastly howling dies, and Ruby stands back-to-back and hand in hand with Chiron and the kid beneath Alvord Lake Bridge. They're singing tunes from *Sergeant Pepper's Lonely Hearts Club Band* to moths flapping round fake stalactites, wailing as though their very souls depend on it.

A buzzing feeling chases all over Ruby's skin like she's strolled through a wall of electricity. She shivers, reluctant to look down at herself for fear her flesh will split and fall from her bones, piece by bloody piece. Her mouth tastes metallic, her stomach turns somersaults. Only the knuckle-crunching grip of the young folks' hands in hers gives a clue that this is *real*.

She's *alive*. She's *here*.

How long did they stand on that needle of rock, gazing at Hell itself? Five hundred years? Or but a moment?

The gash the demon slashed in Chi's cheek is gone. The bloody patch of hair torn loose from the kid's scalp is restored. The bite wounds on her own arms are healed.

"Sweet Isis," she moans. She shakes her hands loose from theirs, leans up against the wall. "Not even when we got loaded on peyote tea have I ever seen what I just saw."

"Cosmic Mind," Chiron mutters, dazed. "Could that have been the secret loop?"

"The secret loop?" Ruby gasps.

Starbright kneels down on the sidewalk, clasping her stomach.

"The loop, snaking way beyond human sight," he says. "The secret loop no one could have foreseen. That I was lured here, to this moment. To this Prime Probability. To the three of us here, on this day."

"But why?" Starbright says.

"To use the purple beam and collapse the Prime Probability out of the timeline. *Destroy* our spacetime, instead of conserve it. Oh," he groans and grips his forehead.

Ruby shakes her head. "Well, you didn't use the purple beam. And the atomic bomb didn't set the whole sky on fire, either."

Hells Angels amble down from Stanyan Street. No one else is on the path. Their leather boots tromp on the pavement, their chains and swastikas clank, they trade talk in low growls. The stink of sweat and booze and pot surrounds them like swamp gas. As they come upon Ruby, Starbright, and Chi in the dimly lit tunnel beneath Alvord Lake Bridge, their bleary eyes gleam. They grin, five gap-toothed leers guaranteed to make your heart beat faster.

Ruby draws her Beretta.

Chiron whips the maser from his jacket pocket, clicks the setting to green.

"Hairy Harry," the kid calls out in a high, clear voice. "Hey, it's me. It's Starbright."

"Cool it," Hairy Harry says, eyeing Ruby's pistol, holding his hands up.

"We don't want any hassle, Hairy Harry," Ruby says, aiming for his stomach.

"We ain't hasslin' with the chick who drew Chocolate, man. We just want to take a piss in the woods."

And the Angels ramble on like a herd of clanking, shuffling, grumbling beasts.

Grandmother Says: Ta Ch'u (Integrity)

The Image: Heaven within the mountain. The dragon hides in his glen. The treasures within are the most precious.

The Oracle: Even great and difficult undertakings succeed when one approaches them with integrity.

An accumulation of pebbles results in a mountain.

The study of great deeds and principles of the past strengthens and elevates character. Such study should not be pursued merely to acquire knowledge, however. One should strive to apply the great principles of the past to the future.

—Hexagram 26, *The I Ching* or Book of Changes

A basic premise of the hippies is that all things are that which they are and have their own beauty and meaning. Before being able to determine what they are, careful and intimate contact is considered a prerequisite.

With respect to the Hells Angels, the same principle is involved. They are our fellow men and all men are basically beautiful. If they do not appear to be so, or do not act in that way, the hippie way is to beam love and not hatred.

By beaming love, the hope is there may be enough left over to be absorbed by others.

What hippie would condone violence? Yet, which of us hath not also sinned? We are not out to make excuses for anyone, whether hippie or Angel. At the same time we cannot carelessly put them down.

If the hippies choose to weave a web of love around the oft-condemned Angels, who can say categorically that they are wrong? Has any other group gotten along better with the Angels? Have the police who have matched force by force? Or other citizens who have beamed hate?

We can only hope that some day it will no longer be thought necessary to use violent means to achieve good. Maybe the hippie insight will help us arrive at that day.

—From "How High on What Beam Can
    You Get?" *Berkeley Barb*, Vol. 5, No.
    10, Issue 109 (Sept. 15–21, 1967)

They find Ruby's car on Kezar Drive and head back to Haight Street. The crowd has cleared. Two ambulances are parked in front of the Double Barrel house. A harsh light fills the inside of an ambulance. Ruby can see two bodies covered head to toe with sheets, lying strapped on stretchers. Doctors and emergency attendants swarm all over the place, but they're not in any hurry to take the bodies away.

Professor Zoom leans against the doors of the ambulance, a blanket wrapped round his shoulders.

Starbright jumps out of the car. "Professor Zoom! It's Professor Zoom!"

Ruby sets the parking brake, opens her door, and steps out, leaning over the roof of the car.

Starbright takes Professor Zoom's hands, but he stares at her, limp, uncomprehending. "Is Penny Lane okay? Crinky, Professor Zoom?" She shouts in his face as though he's deaf, which he does a fair job of miming. "Is Crinky okay?"

Chiron jumps out behind her as Professor Zoom slowly shakes his head. "Crinky has gone to God, Starbright." He stares at Chiron. "Didn't he tell you?"

She screams, drops his hands, peers into the ambulance. Her face twists with horror. She turns to Chiron, purple with fury. "You! You didn't even try, did you? Not supposed to help anyone, not supposed to help! You didn't even *try*!" She pounces on him, punching and slapping. "Oh, I hate you! I hate you!"

"I did try!" he yells, shielding his face from her blows. He catches one flailing wrist, then the other.

"I don't believe you!"

"All right, I can't lie to you, Starbright. I thought about Tenet Three. Damn right, I thought about it. I *have* to!"

"Tenet Three," she says, disgusted. "You're *worse* than my father who treated her like she was bad when he should have helped her. You're *worse* than her stepfather who raped her. You let her *die*!"

Professor Zoom pats her shoulder. "No, no, Starbright. He did try," he says quietly. "He ran up the stairs. He ran into the crystal palace. But he got there too late. The crystal palace was already gone. Truly, verily, it was already gone."

Starbright shakes her head, unwilling to believe.

"I was *there*," Professor Zoom says. "I saw. *I* could have pulled Crinky out of the crystal palace."

"Why didn't you?"

"You know," he says, with a perplexed look. "I just didn't think of it."

The kid jumps into the car and buries her face in her hands. Chiron gets in beside her.

"Arnold," Ruby says, studying Professor Zoom over the roof of the car. "Get out of the Haight-Ashbury. This place is no good for you anymore. Go back to Yale. Finish your damn philosophy degree."

"You know, I never did go to Yale." He chuckles like the pull of a saw through bone. "I dropped out of high school, man. The closest I ever got to Yale was the time I hitchhiked through Greenwich Village, trying to score some dope."

Ruby's cats climb all over Starbright as she sits weeping, cross-legged on the couch. Alana rests her paws on Starbright's chest and licks her cheek, while Luna purrs like a little panther and rubs her whiskers on Starbright's knee. Sita climbs into her lap, while Rama and Ara perch somberly on the back of the couch, two sapphire-eyed sentinels.

Ruby doesn't know what to say. No, wrong. There are a thousand and one things she could say, and none of them seem right. How she felt when they told her about Pa at Pearl Harbor and the day they found Roi in the alley. How she felt when Ma told her she was dying of lung cancer, but the company had sponsored a study showing asbestos was safe for shipyard workers. Ma's death at age fifty—fifteen short years from how old Ruby is now—had angered her beyond anything she had ever felt. Angered her all the way to a lawyer's office and to the library, where she found a University of Michigan study that came to the disturbing conclusion that breathing asbestos could kill you. Yet after the grave was dug, and the settlement was tucked in her bank account, Ruby couldn't shake the feeling of unfinished business, unrighted wrongs. That engine room, clear as day. Maybe that was the worst part of losing her mother. That somehow she should have told Ma to get out of that engine room.

Chiron sits on the floor by the fireplace, distancing himself. Is he pleased they survived this Hell brought by the future? Or dismayed he didn't do enough? Not enough for Starbright, anyway. Ruby cannot read his somber face.

"It's all my fault," Starbright says between sobs. "If only I wasn't so stupid. I could have done something. I should have saved Penny Lane."

"No," Ruby says. She sits, takes the kid in her arms. "Listen. You got nothing to do with it, Starbright. You were kids. You were friends, and you loved each other. But that little girl you loved was lost to you a long time ago."

But the kid shakes her head. "I want to die, too."

Chiron raises his hand to his lips and whispers, "Katie." A *beep*, and he plays around with his magic ring, whispering dates and times. The slice of blue light pops up between his face and his palm like it always does. The sight of him sitting on the floor in his perfect jeans and beads and boots with a piece of light dancing in his hand is damn near as strange as anything Ruby has ever seen.

He smiles. "It's over. The knuckletop computes that there are no more Prime Probabilities tonight. We're clear."

"I don't give a shit," Starbright sniffs.

His eyes widen. He sighs and shakes his head. "Starbright," he says gently. "I tried to get Penny Lane out of the crystal palace. Her death is a terrible thing, I know. But her death . . . How can I say this? Her death isn't . . . significant. Her death doesn't affect the timeline."

"Yes, it does," Starbright says, wiping the tears from her cheeks with both hands. Her face hardens with anger. "Because *she, her death*— affects *me*."

Chiron aims a look of appeal at Ruby.

Ruby shrugs. "Kid's got a point."

"Why should I care about your spacetime?" Starbright says. "You've told us over and over how badly we're screwing up the Earth.

How mad you are at us. And me, I'm supposed to be important somehow? Just the fact that I make it through the Summer of Love preserves your whole future?"

"Yes!" he says. "We must live responsibly or—"

"You say you want to liberate Schrödinger's cat. But you're not doing it. You're just letting her live *this* time. I'm like the cat who survives in your gas chamber *this* time. Do I prove how smart you are five hundred years from now? Do I make sure you get your domed estate in Sausalito? How nice for you!" Starbright stands, scattering the cats. "Why should I give a damn about your future?"

"It's your future, too," Chi says quietly.

"My future, too," Starbright says sarcastically.

"The future for all of us!" he says.

"So *you* say," Ruby says.

He studies them with an inscrutable look. Then he stands. "All right," he says. "Consider impact before you consider benefit. Maybe this will make an impact."

He carefully takes down three of Ruby's framed Rick Griffin posters, exposing the wall.

"*Now* what's he up to?" Ruby mutters to the kid.

"This," Chi says, fiddling with something. He aims his magic ring at the wall. "Is a holoid field."

The slice of blue light, which has always been the size of a pulp magazine every time Ruby caught a glimpse of it, suddenly appears in the middle of the room. It's as big as the whole wall! A glowing red message pops into the blue:

"Date: 08-28-1967. You may insert Disk 5 now."

"Sweet Isis." Ruby goes to the holoid field, walks in front of it, next to it. The field is perhaps three feet in depth, floating a foot off the floor. Like a chunk of the sky! She walks through the space between the holoid field and the wall to the other side. Her distorted shadow ripples through the field like on a movie screen when someone walks in front of the projector. The letters and numbers are three-dimensional, as brilliant red as garnets, and as big as her knee to her ankle. She can see every angle of them, the crisp red edges.

"And this," Chiron says, "is a holoid."

He takes a tiny cube from his pocket, opens the lid. He plucks out a crystal sliver. "Let me show you." He tucks the sliver into a tiny slot in the bezel of his magic ring. "A bit of the future. *Our* future."

A tall, slim woman materializes in the middle of the blue light. She's clad in elegant, precise clothes. Her hair falls in dusky waves. Her distinctive face is grave. Her hands gesture gracefully, sending a sparkle from gemstones in the rings on her long, slim fingers. She appears no more than thirty-five, but her bearing and demeanor seem older. Her dark eyes search before her, glinting with the force of her personality.

Ruby sinks into the couch. Starbright instinctively seizes her and huddles against her like a child. The woman hovers a foot off the floor in the middle of Ruby's living room, gazing straight at them.

"Hello," Ruby whispers, just in case she can hear.

Chiron sits, staring raptly at the holoid.

"My fellow Americans," the woman says in a thrilling contralto voice. "As we celebrate the close of the third century, and embark upon the fourth century of our great nation, we face more difficult challenges than we have ever faced before. And we must meet those challenges with solutions. Not easy solutions, but hard ones. Solutions aimed toward the future. Toward relieving our present suffering, surely, but also aimed toward our heirs and the destiny of this planet. Not merely the short-sighted quick fixes of previous administrations who sought power and personal aggrandizement at the expense of the future and abused the power of the media to propagandize when they hardly understood their own rhetoric. We need long-term solutions. Solutions that will work now *and* tomorrow.

"For we must accept the responsibility of a cocreatorship. The cocreatorship of our world with the Cosmic Mind, the Universal Intelligence that truly has graced us with this small blue globe. I believe in the Great Good of the Cosmic Mind, my friends, my neighbors, and my colleagues. And I believe we must devote our lives, each and every one of us, during each day on this Earth, to the furtherance of the Great Good.

"I don't intend to define for you what Good is. No one can do that. But I can tell you what I personally believe. I believe the Good is love. Kindness, joy, creativity. And work, placing the impact of our actions before our own self-interest, before even our own benefit. The Great Good must serve our fellow Americans, yes. But also our fellow human beings all over the planet, our fellow creatures, and the Earth itself.

"But this does not serve *our* Good, my worthy opponent says. We must think of ourselves first, we must draw the line. But I ask you, where can we draw lines when the whole planet suffers?

"In the rebel days before our great nation was formed, when our ancestors fought against governmental oppression and tyranny, a colony —later our sister state of New Hampshire—had a motto, a slogan, a rallying cry. That cry was 'Live Free or Die.' As we plunge into our fourth century, we must rally to a new cry. I propose we must 'Live Responsibly or Die.' "

A vast applause fills the living room.

"It's a campaign speech!" Starbright whispers.

"You're right," Ruby whispers back. "Who is she?" she asks Chi.

"That's Lia Mitsui, the first woman president of the United States. Won the election in 2092, assumed office in 2093," Chiron says in a tone matching his rapt gaze. "President Mitsui is generally credited as the founder of cosmicism. She was the first person to attain a mass following and gain enormous political power who articulated the fundamentals of cosmicism. From those fundamentals stemmed a massive shift in values, especially during the 2200s at the height of the brown ages. People broke away from consumeristic-passive-self-interest to contributistic-activist-universalist-interest. To give is best, that's what we say."

"Not *these* days, sonny," Ruby says.

"It took three hundred years after President Mitsui gave her speech." He shrugs. "Major changes in values historically have taken a couple of centuries before they manifest as mature philosophies, spawn institutions, and gain power through the work of their advocates."

"So she never saw people practice cosmicism in her time?" Ruby says. "How sad!"

"Only in a limited way," he says.

The woman hovers in the field of blue light for a moment, then disappears. She reappears in a scarlet robe with swooping sleeves. She stands, arm in arm, with a slim Oriental man, slightly shorter than she is, dressed in a suit of luminous black silk. They smile and blink, as though the light is too bright. Ruby jumps again. The illusion that this handsome couple actually stands before her is unnerving.

"Lia married Yoshio Mitsui, a Japanese billionaire in the electronics and media industries," Chi says. "Their partnership was viewed as a sort of royal marriage. She took his surname as a gesture of respect. Relations between our two countries were repaired after decades of damaging economic competition. Yoshio was one of the first great billionaire cosmicists. He donated huge sums to the free medical clinics."

"Free clinics!" Starbright says. "Like the Haight-Ashbury Free Clinic?"

"Yes, but these clinics were endowed with the latest technologies. Anyone could get care. Oh, private medicine specializing in exotic techniques, nontherapeutic gene tweaking, stuff like that, that's still around. But the free clinic network proved crucial during the brown ages. At that point, basic health care included detox for pollution poisoning and radiation sickness, treatment for skin cancer and cataracts. Things like that."

"Because we screwed things up," Starbright says darkly.

He hesitates. "I'm telling you a lot of good things will happen, too, Starbright."

The couple vanishes. The wall of blue light glows.

President Mitsui appears briefly again. Her forehead is wrinkled, her shoulders stoop, her proud figure is thinner. "I have had joys in my life and disappointments, too, my children," she says. Her voice quavers. "I am still fearful for our Earth. You must carry on the Good in all ways, great and small. Be new. Always come forth into Being."

"This is Lia a month before she died. She was ninety-five," Chi says. "She survived three assassination attempts and twenty years as the Chief Executive Officer of the International Bank. I think she got more done at the International Bank, paving the way to the True Value system. Programs she set up led eventually to the World Birth Control Organization. We call them the sex police." He laughs without mirth. "She organized and funded the World Ecology Taskforce as early as 2102. WET later exposed the petroleum conspiracy, which engaged in systematic terrorism and discrimination against new energy-source developments for decades. WET was instrumental in the movement to decentralize the technopolistic plutocracy, which was responsible for military adventures for three centuries. President Mitsui," he says proudly, "was my great-great-great-great-, and a couple of more greats, grandmother."

Ruby whistles. Starbright stares.

The blue field flickers. Brilliant red letters appear:

"Date: 08-28-1967. You may insert Disk 6 now."

Another woman springs into the light, so full of life and energy it's hard to believe she's not real. She sits in the lotus position in the middle of an extraordinary sculpture. The woman is a fanciful young version of President Mitsui. Her waist-length hair is dyed every color of the rainbow, matching her costume of beads, bells, flowers, flowing ribbons of silk. The sculpture in which she reclines is a giant bird's nest, perhaps ten feet in diameter, made of tiny strips of different-colored woods, poised upon a gigantic carved tree branch. A round mattress, fitted within the bed, is covered with a quilt stitched and pieced to resemble the twigs and bits of down inside a bird's nest. The young woman fans herself with an enormous feather and grins at them with a naughty look.

"Everybody needs a nest, don't you think so, babies? Hi! I'm Pearl Mitsui. I'm nesting. Hee, hee, hee!" She struggles to regain her composure. "Lookit. This here is a genuine handmade sculpture-bed crafted by some folks in my company, Back to the Hands. A team of twenty-five international craft workers helped design and execute this concept, which was dreamed up by yours truly." She giggles again. "I'll be honest. This sculpture will set you back seven hundred and fifty thousand boo."

"International Bank Units," Chi whispers. "IBUs. Boo."

"Which puts the thing into very few hands, I know, I know, I *know*. That's why we donated one Nest to the Back to the Hands Museum in San Francisco, and you can reserve a night to sleep on it there if you want. For free!" Pearl shakes her head and leans toward them. Ruby and the kid lean back. "The notion we're devoted to—me and my cousin Michael Robbins in Los Angeles and Pat Moore-Eisen in New York and the New International Craft Guild in Berlin and MicroHands in Tokyo and a lot of other folks—is a return to True Value in the arts and crafts. A return to craft in everyday objects. We reject the mass-production-mass-obsolescence thing! MicroHands is crafting a first generation of knuckletops, we're making furniture in San Francisco, and the Craft Guild is making the Solar Chariot in Berlin. That's a handmade car. It's gorgeous and runs on sun like a dream. It'll set you back three million boo."

She laughs, another high-pitched giggle. Starbright joins in.

"The point is," Pearl says. "We've got millions of people—billions! —these days with vision and skill and talent and not enough work to go around. Not enough work *in the super-mass-production thing*, that is. Everyone's been saying for two centuries that we've got to adapt, learn to deal with postindustrial society. But we're not dealing with *post*industrial society. We're dealing with *hyper*industrial society and the devaluation of individual talent and skill. So what we're saying to people is, no, you don't *have* to fit in with the super-mass-production thing, which produces degraded goods, shit our great-grandmothers would have thrown back in the bin. We're saying we don't like the products of the hyperindustrial technopolistic plutocracy. We want craft back, even if it costs a bit more.

'Cause craft connects you to the Cosmic Mind, to your fellow human beings, to *beauty*. And craft *lasts*." Pearl sighs. "Anyway, here's the Nest." She waves her feather. "Dig it, babies." She disappears.

"Sweet Isis," Ruby says. "She's hip!"

Chiron laughs. "She was the biggest kook of the family, that's for sure. It's like having Andy Warhol as your uncle. Pearl was gene-tweaked, so she lived well into her hundreds. She devoted her whole life to the international handcraft movement, which has lasted till my day."

A series of tall, slim men clad in suits, jumpsuits, or shirts and jeans, stride swiftly through the field of blue.

"Let's party," Ruby mutters.

"That's Jason Behrens, a geneticist working with microbots whose combined therapy techniques preceded development of the radiation vaccine," Chiron says, pointing. "That's Thomas Mitsui, a mathematician active in the World Birth Control Organization. He predicted a global population of twelve billion six months before the census-takers proved it.

"That's Mars Herbert, who married Calliope Mitsui in 2350." A lovely, strawberry-haired woman briefly materializes in the blue field. An extremely tall, slim man lingers in the holoid, his pale, aquiline profile turned yearningly to where she disappeared. "Mars was a world-modeler with one of the first telelinks. He did much of his work in telespace. He and Calliope started the practice of giftdays.

"Mars set up the bicycle Paths. This fellow in China invented the BikeBat, a battery that recharged from the energy generated by a person riding a bike. But the BikeBat had limited efficiency, so you needed to recharge it with a two-hour bike ride just to get fifteen minutes of light from an ordinary lamp. Mars took the BikeBat, improved efficiency by routing the energy instead of storing it, and set up Paths in domed public preserves. The bikes are connected to a wire over the Path."

"Like the trolleys on Market Street?" Ruby says.

He nods. "People go and ride for however long they want to. Their physical exercise generates electricity into the Path. The bikes monitor the energy generated, and the biker gets utility credits equal to that energy. The Path is so efficient, people who bike a couple times a week can pay for their whole utility bill."

"Sounds like we should be doing that *tomorrow*," Ruby says.

Chiron turns to her with a troubled look. "Funny, isn't it? Look at your science fantasies in 1967. You'd think we'd be whizzing around the galaxies by the 2400s. But we're not. We're not even close to those ancient dreams. We've only begun to develop outer space, with the Mars terraformation, and inner space, through telespace." He shakes his head. "Dreams cost. Dreams require sacrifice and saving over generations. The notion that you might never see or enjoy the fruits of your own frugality was a radical notion in President Mitsui's day, especially at the start of the brown ages. I guess that's why people tried to assassinate her."

"We want results," Ruby says. "And we want them *now*."

"I accept True Value," Chi says, but he sighs. "I expect to live to a hundred and forty years or more. Yet maybe I'll never see the results of work I do in my lifetime. But my heirs will. And that's good enough. It's got to be."

And as night turns into dawn, Chi shows Ruby the wonders of the future. The great domes, the megalopolises. The EM-Trans, a system of trains levitated by huge magnets that travel a thousand miles an hour in subterranean vacuum tunnels. Gene tweaking, the medcenters. Telespace, tachyportation. Many wonders.

And things people decided *not* to do. When the damage to the stratosphere was the worst they'd ever seen, some scientists wanted to build enormous lasers on mountaintops to blast the sky or pump tons of toxic chemicals into the atmosphere, hoping the chemicals would recombine into ozone. Guided by cosmicism, people decided to do nothing. They hid under domes, they invented Block. They argued, they debated, they harassed the technopolistic plutocracy for decades. They gridlocked on the issue while the Earth slowly healed. By the 2300s, the cosmicist scientific community finally determined that sky-seeding would work or at least not do very much harm.

"And sky-seeding *does* work," Chi says. "The rad-vacc *does* work. Telespace *does* work. Even the purple beam on the maser, when used in this spacetime, *does* work. Tachyportation, applied under the mandate of nonintervention, *does* work. Everywhere, in ways great and small, the future *does* work. We've survived."

Birds begin their early morning ecstasies. Ruby's cats stir, leaping onto windowsills, meowing in the kitchen, demanding their breakfast. Starbright snores against Ruby's shoulder.

Chiron whispers to his magic ring. The blue light shrinks, folds into a pinpoint, and disappears.

Ruby yawns. "Your family album. Right, Chi?"

He glances at her with bleary eyes. "Parts of it."

"Beautiful. What an amazing family. Lia Mitsui, her granddaughter Pearl, Mars and Calliope. So talented and beautiful. So brilliant and fortunate."

"We've suffered, too," he says wearily. "We've all suffered in our struggle against the near-death of the Earth."

"Ah, but you and your family are not devolts or day laborers on the street."

"No, we're not." He laughs dryly. "I probably wouldn't be here otherwise."

"So this future you've shown us is selective, isn't it?"

"Everything is selective." He chuckles. "You're a tough nut, Ruby A. Maverick. President Mitsui would like you. She'd probably make you her Minister of Propaganda."

Ruby laughs, pleased in spite of herself. What a night. "So you wanted to give us hope. You wanted to give the kid hope."

Starbright's sleeping face is still stained with her grief.

"Do you think I gave her hope?"

"I hope so," Ruby says.

"And you?"

"Man from Mars, I abandoned hope a thousand lifetimes ago."

"I don't believe you."

She shrugs.

His face falls. Not enough of a cheerleader for him? What the hell.

She disentangles herself from the kid when suddenly he whips out his maser. He aims that thing at her cats, all her beautiful cats gathered around the fridge.

He aims and fires before she can scream.

Red light strikes them, bathing the whole kitchen in scarlet for a moment.

"What are you *doing*?"

The cats blink at Ruby's yell.

Starbright starts awake, crying, "Nance? Nance?"

"Those fucking fleas are driving me crazy," he says, scratching at his ankle. "Don't worry. It's just the microlevel beam. Oh, I know. I'll catch hell under at least two Tenets. Affecting the past, using a modern technology. But you know what? I don't give a damn." He aims the maser at his ankles and shoots the red beam through his socks.

"You little shit!" Ruby yells.

Alana flops on her butt, scratches at her chin. Black specks fly from her plumy white fur. Luna does her calisthenics, a clawed hind foot deftly raised to her shoulder blade. She scratches, and fleas fall out dead.

Ruby roars at him, laughing, waking up the neighborhood.

Chi looks around. "Guess I didn't blow up all spacetime this time, either." He tucks the maser away. "Dig it, Ruby: the future *will* liberate Schrödinger's cat!"

September 4, 1967

A New Moon in Virgo

Hello Goodbye

Susan wakes to the sound of rain on the roof. The skylight is as gray as her foreboding mood. Chiron told her he's leaving tonight.

And *she's* got to leave, too. How can she? How can she leave the Haight-Ashbury and Ruby to go back to her parents in Cleveland? She has never stopped loving Ruby. She's only starting to love Chi.

Oh, why does the Summer of Love have to end?

She shivers. It's cold outside.

Cold. Cleveland will be freezing in two months.

She twirls a lock of her hair, bites the split ends and spits them out, a habit she hasn't indulged in for over two months. Twirl, bite, spit. She thinks of Cyn's ragged fingernails.

Cyn married the handsome young black man, who is the son of a prosperous saloon-owner in Oakland. Eli's father told Eli to take off his Black Panther gear and put on a bartender's apron if he's got a child on the way. Eli does. Cyn is pregnant, a grown-up woman at sixteen. Her fingernails have grown long and strong. She'd even polished them pink, Susan noticed, as she admired Cyn's diamond wedding ring.

Susan takes another lock of hair. She has to go back to high school. Twirl, bite, spit.

The private investigator found her at 555 Clayton the day after Nance died. He questioned Susan for nearly an hour. The private investigator turns out to be the guy in the military cap. A rustler, that's what Ruby calls him. Susan promised the PI she would contact her parents herself if he didn't turn her in. "Groovy," the PI said. "I always thought you were a foxy lady."

Nance's body was so badly burned that the coroner had to match her dental records at twelve years old—her parents hadn't sent her to the dentist for two years—to the jawbone left in the charred corpse the firemen retrieved from the crystal palace. Susan heard the stepfather declined to collect the remains of his daughter, while the mother had taken Nance's brother and moved in with her aunt.

Professor Zoom walked out of the psychiatric ward at San Francisco General Hospital, never to be seen or heard from again. Stan the Man left town the night of the fire, destination unknown. The Double Barrel Boogie Band failed to return to the wreckage of their house when authorities discovered a fake name had been signed on the lease and the rent was six months overdue. Leo Gorgon went back to New York City. Papa Al was identified in the *Berkeley Barb* as a speed pusher recruiting dealers at the Haight-Ashbury Free Medical Clinic, and later as a rip-off, a dealer who turns in other dealers for protection from the Man. Teddybear split to Mexico. Dr. David Smith struggles on at the clinic, with more patients and less money than ever. Hairy Harry and the Hells Angels took their hogs out for a ride to Miami, Florida. Stovepipe was found in Richmond behind a bar called The Pony, wrists and ankles bound, four bullets in the back of his head. The Lizard's photograph can be seen in the stack of Wanted posters in the post office. The mouse magician promenades forlornly down Haight Street, ringing his bell and waving his skull-topped wand, but only on Saturdays.

The woman Susan knew only as Lady May could not be identified. The burned remains of whoever Lady May was were placed in a box and filed in the morgue under Jane Doe.

Susan packs her overnight bag. She carefully wraps two hundred green-and-white dexies that she scored with the money Stan gave her. She tucks them beneath her high-collared shirt in an inside zippered pocket.

Late morning slips into lunchtime. Susan goes down to the kitchen. Chiron lounges about the table with Ruby. He doesn't have to pack. He came with nothing but the clothes on his back, which look and smell as fresh as the day she first saw him.

"I'm becoming a grup," she complains, sliding into a chair.

"A grup?" Ruby says.

"Yeah, a grup. Like in 'Miri,' on *Star Trek*. All the flower children who came to the Haight-Ashbury, we're like the three-hundred-year-old children living on Miri's planet. Now that we've got to go home, it's like losing our childhood. Losing the innocence of the Haight-Ashbury."

"Innocence." Ruby dices scallions, zucchini, Roma tomatoes fresh from the garden Chi dug in her backyard. "I can think of a lot of words for the Haight-Ashbury, kid, but innocence isn't one of them."

"But it *is* innocent, Ruby. And when we go back to the soulless burbs, we're all going to contract some terrible wasting disease that will rot us into madness and death, just exactly like the children who come of age on Miri's planet."

"Starbright," Ruby says. "Life is not one big *Star Trek* metaphor."

"Yes, it is," Susan says gloomily. "It is to me."

Ruby is more cheerful than usual. Is she glad they're finally leaving her in peace? Did Ruby ever love her, really?

"I don't think Starbright is becoming a grup quite yet, do you, Chi?" Ruby says, winking at him.

He shrugs, preoccupied with his magic ring.

"Madness and death," Susan says. "Madness and death."

Ruby drizzles olive oil in her iron skillet, tosses in the fresh vegetables, heaps on garlic and herbs.

Chiron projects the blue light into the palm of his hand, whispering Katie this and Katie that. Seen this small, the holoid field looks as ordinary as an old boot. He looks troubled, though everything seems as stupidly right as it should be to Susan.

"You talk to that thing more than you talk to me," she shucks him.

"When are you going to call your parents?" he says.

"God."

"You promised."

"I know, but—"

"But nothing."

"I'm . . . I'm scared!"

"Scared why?"

"I don't know what to say!"

"Try 'hi,' " Ruby says, spooning her ragout over angel hair noodles. She sprinkles on grated cheese. The scent of garlic fills the kitchen.

"You don't know my father."

"Uh-huh, I don't," Ruby says, sliding steaming bowls to her and Chi and sitting down before her own. "But you do, kid. And you're lucky you do."

"Lucky!" Susan says. "How am I lucky?"

"You've got a father," Ruby says through a mouthful of noodles. "You *know* him. You'll probably know him for many more years." At her puzzled look, Ruby adds, "My pa died at Pearl Harbor. A war hero, huh. He was my daddy, and nobody could compare. He was tall and handsome and smarter than Einstein. I was nine when he died. Sometimes I wonder what he would think about things. The civil rights movement. My shop. Me." She glances out the window and shrugs. And Susan sees for the first time how that movement of Ruby's shoulder is like rolling off a weight that keeps rolling right back on. "Missed my pa ever since. So you call up your father," she says, blinking back the slickness in her eyes. "And be glad you've got him, no matter what a pain in the ass you think he is. Isn't that right, Chi? You going home to your pa?"

"No," he says curtly. "I never knew my father, either. Or my mother."

Susan and Ruby look at him, openmouthed.

"You're an orphan, Chi?" Susan says. "You never told me you're an orphan."

"Oh, I've got skipparents. Abraxis and Ariel Herbert."

"But . . . do you know who your parents were?"

"Sure. My parents were Mars Herbert and Calliope Mitsui. Ah, she of the slanting blue eyes, golden skin, strawberry hair." He shakes his head and laughs in his mirthless way. "Calliope chose my name: Chiron Cat's Eye in Draco. How Calliope loved fanciful, mythological things."

"But—" Susan struggles with her recollection of the holoids he showed them. The lean, aquiline-faced man, the lovely woman. "Wasn't Mars a world-modeler with one of the first telelinks? The bike Paths? Didn't you say that was the mid-2300s?"

"Yes."

"But you're only twenty-one!"

And he gives them such a haunted, sorrowful look that Susan pushes her bowl of food away and folds her hands.

The population had reached twelve billion. Even the wealthy hiding beneath their private domes couldn't escape the impact of twelve billion human beings on this small Earth.

The strain was evident everywhere, from ozone holes to ocean sludge. People had been talking about the population crisis for decades, for centuries. The People's Republic of China, first under Communist rule and then under Socialist-Confucianist rule, imposed a one-child policy, with limited success. Most Western nations only grudgingly permitted birth control and abortion. Lia Mitsui raised the issue of population control at the International Bank in the early 2100s. The World Birth Control Organization commenced operations soon after. But these movements were educational and voluntary, not mandatory. No nation had enforced a sane population control policy.

People struggled with the deep belief in the sacredness of birth. Children were considered a source of wealth, emotional and economic. Some nations suspected America and the European community of ulterior motives, the imperialism implicit in controlling another's population. By the time people could speak about mandatory population control in a rational way, it was too late.

Population growth is exponential, a pyramid with an ever-expanding base. And people were living into their hundreds by the 2100s. Despite new viruses and pollution poisoning and famine, human life flourished. Despite suicide cults in the megalopolises and unprecedented murder rates and international pirate gangs, human life surged.

Something radical had to be done. By the 2200s, the World Birth Control Organization *required* birth control, *required* abortion if the mother wanted one. The sex police enforced these requirements worldwide. But with exponential growth, it wasn't enough. The base of the pyramid kept expanding.

Among practicing cosmicists, voluntary childlessness was another common way of giving back to the Earth, by restraint and nonconsumption. But when Calliope Mitsui proposed the notion of mandating child-lessness to WBCO, she met with outraged resistance even among cosmicists. Charges of genetic fascism flew. No one wanted to give up the right to pass on genes to another generation. No one wanted to forfeit the possibility of producing another genius or saint. Most of all, no one wanted to be left without heirs.

Enforced childlessness was the only way. But they had to compromise on the heirs issue.

The World Birth Control Organization convened an international meeting and passed the Generation-Skipping Law. The plan was this: Randomly chosen couples all over the world would have their genetic material—sperm and eggs—harvested and frozen by cryopreservation, a freezing technique that had been mastered centuries ago. From their harvest, they could create and choose their child. Skipparents would be arranged for the child, typically from other family members. These skipparents would be youthful members of a younger generation, chosen late in the birth parents' lives. After the birth parents died and a statutory period had passed, their child would be birthed either in the lab or by implantation in the skipmother and raised by the skipparents.

Then another random pool of couples would be chosen to skip a generation.

A huge bureaucracy and a network of mainframes were devoted to the complex law and its myriad tasks. The first two billion couples to skip were chosen. Their children were harvested and skipparents arranged. And for the first time in centuries, the population remained the same. The same, not more!

"The goal is to reduce our numbers to six billion and fewer, which was the last time people had a reasonable quality of life," Chiron says.

"So," Ruby says. "Calliope and Mars were chosen in the first pool of couples who had to skip?"

"Oh, no. They were good cosmicists. They volunteered," Chiron says, unable to conceal his bitterness. "You know, sometimes I feel I know them through the holoids they left for me. And don't get me wrong, I love my skipparents. They certainly cherish me. But sometimes I feel this . . . sadness. Like I've lost something that I can never get back. Or like I'm longing for something that I've never had and never can have."

"So you never met your parents . . . *at all*?" Susan says.

"They died," he says, "twenty years before I was born."

* * *

"Hi," Susan says into the telephone. Silence, a sputter of static. Her hand shakes so hard that the mouthpiece bumps against her lower teeth. "It's me."

A long, deep sigh. A snuffle. Noises knocking in the background. Her mother's voice. Then the clatter of the phone in the den being picked up. A second breath, a second breathlessness.

"Hi, it's you," her father says. "Do you have any idea what you have put us through, young lady?"

God. Her heart pounds in her throat. She braces herself.

"Where are you now?" her mother says shrilly.

A nervous giggle spills from her mouth. "I'm . . . ah . . . well, I'm in San Francisco. It's really far out, you should see it, ha ha ha."

"Any idea at all?"

"Are you all right, dear?"

"I'm okay, Mom. I know you're pissed at me, but—"

"Pissed. Pissed. Pissed is not the word, young lady."

"Susan, don't you use that kind of language with your father."

"Gloria, I think you better—"

"Or when you're talking—"

"Get off the phone, Gloria, and let me handle—"

"Just because she's calling doesn't mean . . . Susan, just because you're calling doesn't mean you can get away—"

"Let me handle this, damn it, Gloria!"

Her parents' tangling voices almost make her laugh out loud. Then she instantly gets furious. She has not seen them or spoken to them in over two months.

"This is so typical," she says. "You haven't changed one bit. I can't *stand* the way you hassle over every fucking thing. That's the reason I left. Why can't you just *talk* to me?"

Shocked silence.

She hears a *click*. Her mother hangs up the phone in the den.

"If you can't *talk* to me, Dad, I'm going to hang up, okay?"

Her father sighs. "Don't hang up, Susan."

"Then *stop* it!"

He sighs again, a bone-weary sigh. "You've got to start school next week. I want you back here *now*."

"I ran out of money. I don't have enough for a ticket."

"I'll buy the ticket. It'll be waiting at the airport."

"What if I don't want to come back?"

"You don't want to come back?"

"I don't know. Why should I?"

A pause, another snuffle. It suddenly occurs to her that her father is crying. "Because we love you, Susan."

"You do?"

Now *she* is crying, and this makes her mad, because she swore she wouldn't, no matter what. She wipes her nose on the back of her hand. Ruby looks up from across the kitchen table and tosses her a napkin.

"Of course we do. You know we do."

"Maybe I don't know. Nance died, Dad."

"I know." More silence, muffled sighs. "So. I'm not Daddy anymore?"

"I'm not a little girl anymore."

He thinks that over. "Tell you what," her father says. "Your mother and I are going to get on a plane and meet you in San Francisco."

"You don't have to do that."

"Yes. Yes, I think we do. We can talk on the way back."

He takes down Ruby's number, hangs up, and calls her right back. They are coming out on Pan Am flight 524, to arrive twenty minutes after midnight tonight. He wants to pick her up wherever she is, but she chickens out on that one, and asks Ruby if she could drive her to the airport. Ruby nods.

"We saw you on TV," her father says. "I couldn't believe my eyes."

"Oh, I heard 'The Hippie Temptation' was awful. Harry Reasoner doesn't know the first thing about the way life is in the Haight-Ashbury."

"Your mother thinks you've gotten too thin."

"She would."

He clears his throat. "Susan, you didn't . . . you wouldn't . . . did you . . . um. Did you take any of that LSD drug they're talking about?"

That LSD drug? *Which* LSD drug? Owsley white lightning, or purple double barrels, or dragon's blood? She doesn't know which LSD he means.

"No," she implies, not lying. His huge sigh of relief makes the implication worthwhile. "Listen, Dad. Don't ever call me stupid again."

"I know you're not stupid, Susan. You're in the ninety-eighth percentile. I'm proud of you. You're one of the smartest kids in your school."

"Because the Summer of Love hasn't been stupid. This has been the most amazing summer I've ever had in my life."

* * *

Chiron takes the dark, oblong stone from his jacket pocket and places it on the kitchen table. He stares into Susan's eyes so intently she fidgets with the last of her lunch. Ruby whisks the bowls away.

"Starbright," he says. "Will you place the fingers of your right hand against the scanner?"

"Yes," she says. Thumb, too.

"Left hand?"

She does the same.

"Starbright, will you please tell me your true and legal name?"

"My name is Susan Stein."

"How old are you?"

"I'm . . . going on fifteen." She blushes at Ruby's look of surprise. "I'm fourteen years old."

He heaves a great sigh and wipes his forehead. "Prime. That's mega. Do you have any identification you could show me to confirm that you are Susan Stein?"

She digs deep into her purse, finds the fake ID and throws it on the table. Digs deeper into the secret place where the lining is torn. She takes out the embossed plastic card. "It doesn't have my picture, though."

Ruby picks up the card. "A library card! You *do* read books, Starbright!"

"Of course I read books!"

"You turn off that damn devil box," Ruby says, shaking her finger, "and read more books!"

"That's fine," Chi says, running one end of the scanner over the face of Susan's library card. "Now one last thing. I'm going to press the scanner to your chest, right here, on your sternum. You'll feel a prick, okay?"

He tenderly presses the stone to her breastbone. She feels the prick again, like the touch of a tiny needle.

"*Oh, no!*" he shouts.

Susan screams.

The cats scatter.

"No, no, *no!*" Suddenly he tears at his hair like a madman, hyperventilating, shaking the scanner, rereading the data again and again.

He lunges for Susan. She ducks. He lunges again. He seizes her, presses the stone to her chest.

Ruby tears him off her. "Sweet Isis, Chiron! What has gotten into you?"

He collapses in a chair. Sweat pours down his face. He stares at Susan with haunted eyes. "You're not pregnant!"

Susan and Ruby look at each other, astonished and wary.

"Well, of course she's not pregnant," Ruby says angrily. "Why should she be?"

"But you *were* pregnant." He leaps to his feet, lunges for her again. "You were pregnant about a month ago, weren't you? *Weren't* you?"

Susan burns scarlet. "Y-yes, but it was Stan the Man's, and I didn't want it, I couldn't have it. I didn't want it, and I couldn't have it, and that's that!"

"This is none of your business," Ruby says.

"It *is* my business! You've got to tell me what happened."

"I-I-I had an abortion."

"An abortion!"

"Dig it, man from Mars, it's very simple," Ruby says coldly. "This woman is fourteen years old. She is not married, and it wasn't likely she'd be marrying the SOB who knocked her up. He is gone with the wind now, huh. She was less than two weeks pregnant. She didn't want to identify herself, and anyway the new law is shit. She's a minor, and she would have needed consent from her parents. So I took her to a doctor who does D and Cs, all right? We talked it over, and why the hell do you *care*?"

"She *can't* have an abortion!"

Ruby seizes Chiron by his collar. *"Yes—she—can,"* she says in his face. "She can, and she did. All women should have the right to choose. I thought you just got through telling us that you and your people, your World Birth Control Organization and your sex police, *enforce* that right."

"We do, but—"

She shakes him. "But nothing, sonny. Because I'll tell you what happens when women don't have a choice. When they are made into criminals? When their doctors are made into criminals? They will go and get an abortion anyway. And if something goes wrong, if they get a little problem called puerperal sepsis, if they get infected and go into shock, if they are afraid to get treatment because they will be branded a criminal, they can die. And if they don't die, if they are so lucky that they do not die, they may never be able to have children again. Not even if they want to. Because puerperal sepsis can make you *sterile*." She releases him, goes to the kitchen sink, and turns her back to them. In a low, trembling voice, she says, "Did me."

WEATHER REPORT

Fifth Estate: What effect do you think ecology-oriented poets like Gary Snyder and Diane di Prima are having on the people as far as changing things go?

Allen Ginsberg: I don't like the phrase 'the people.' Who the fuck is the people? I keep bridling over this political terminology. Who is the people? What does that mean?

Fifth Estate: Well, the people who are capable of changing things or setting the world straight, because the trees certainly can't do it by themselves.

Allen Ginsberg: The trees are the only ones who are getting the world straight. They're the ones who are producing the oxygen we are consuming, the trees are like the oxygen factories of the atmosphere. The trees are our biggest allies. If the enemy is the materialistic, consumer-oriented, predatory, acquisitive, capitalistic, manufacturing society which is consuming all our natural resources at a suicidal rate, our natural allies in this battle for survival are the trees and the grass.

—From interview with Allen Ginsberg,
  The Fifth Estate (Oct. 15, 1969)

The recent abortion test case is "helping to establish in people's minds that the present abortion laws have to go," Pat McGinnis of the Society for Humane Abortion told the

Barb this week. The Society plans to test a new case
soon. . . .

"Not one therapeutic abortion has been passed by the
San Francisco County Hospital," she said.

—From "Winners Ready to Test New
Law," *Berkeley Barb*, Vol. 5, No. 1,
Issue 99 (July 7–13, 1967)

Susan presses her face into Ruby's back between her shoulders,
wraps her arms round her waist.

"It's all right, kid," Ruby says. "I've had time to deal with what
happened fifteen years ago. It's old news in 1967."

Susan always thought of Ruby as powerful, so strong. Pressed
against her back, she can hear Ruby's breath, her beating heart, can feel
her long, slim bones. And, for the first time, Susan sees how fragile Ruby
is. Vulnerable and mortal.

"God, Ruby," she whispers.

"No! Don't cry." Ruby turns and hugs her. "It's been an amazing
summer for me, too. I've learned something from the Summer of Love.
Learned something; or maybe I just remembered something I always
knew. That we *do* have choices. All sorts of choices. It's going to be all
right, because it's *got* to be all right. We carry on."

But Chi looks drained. He shakes his head at the scanner, rereading the data. "Listen," he says.

"No, we're not going to listen, sonny," Ruby snaps. "I don't want to
hear any more claptrap about how she can't do it."

He shakes his head, pale and drawn. "Susan Stein *has* to be pregnant before I translate-transmit to 2467. If she isn't, I've failed. The
object of the SOL Project has failed. And I don't know what will happen
to our spacetime. I don't know what will happen to me. After all we've
been through with the demons, maybe *this* is the secret loop that subverts
everything." He sits, defeated.

"Oh, Chi." Susan goes to his side and kneels. "Maybe I'll get
pregnant someday with a man I love. Why must I be pregnant now?"

"Because Susan Stein will give birth to a child in late spring of
1968."

"Oh," she cries, all her fantasies rushing back. "I would want a
little girl."

"You *do* have a little girl."

"I would name her Jessica."

His eyes widen. "You *do* name her Jessica."

"I would want her to have brown eyes and blond hair. Oh, a little girl."

He stares.

Ruby sits next to him and pats his shoulder. "Chi," she says gently. "Are you telling us you *know* what Starbright's future is supposed to be?"

He nods. He goes to the living room, takes down the Rick Griffin posters. He projects the blue light again, as big as the wall. Red letters say:

"Date: 09-04-1967. You may insert Disk 7 now."

He inserts a crystal sliver into his magic ring.

"My skipmother smuggled these holoid disks into the back pocket of my Levi's before I translated-transmitted to this day," he says. "It's subversive, what she did. The holoids contain amazing data. Oh, some data I already knew about. But some data I'd never seen before. Data I wasn't supposed to know." He smiles wanly. "Ariel prioritized and date-coded the holoids. Man, was I pissed."

The blue field dissolves. The street signs at the corner of Haight Street and Ashbury pop up! People mill about. In the background, a slim girl in a high-collared shirt confers with a tall, pale redhead. The girl darts across the street, gaining her place behind the shoulder of a sandy-haired man. The girl's hair lifts, she brushes it from her face. And she smiles, a radiant smile, an enigmatic smile. The sandy-haired man says, "I'm Harry Reasoner."

Susan screams.

She stares at the girl with her face smiling back at her. "Wow! Is that *me*?"

Ruby laughs. "That's you, kid."

"What else do you know about me?" Susan says to Chi, struck with anxiety.

"Just know this," he says quietly.

A young woman materializes in the blue light. Her face is pale, tired-looking. She is self-possessed and very serious. Her hair is pulled back and clipped at her neck. A blond toddler of three sits on her lap. Susan stares. An eerie feeling filters through her, making her shiver.

"I can't show you your life or your family's life," Chi says. "But know this. You have children, your children have children. And those children have children."

The holoid of Susan and young Jessica disappears too soon.

Another mother and her child replace them. The mother stands in profile, watching a dusky-haired girl with the legs of a dancer, a distinctive face, flashing eyes.

"One of the children has a daughter," Chiron says, nodding at the holoid. "Her name is Lia Hawke. When she is forty, she marries a Japanese billionaire named Yoshio Mitsui."

Susan is suddenly aware her heart is pounding.

"Then Starbright," Ruby says carefully, "is the great-great-grandmother of the first woman president of the United States."

"Yes," Chi says.

He whispers to his magic ring. The holoids and the blue field disappear. The living room darkens. The autumn sun flees into the west. A chill settles in. Ruby rises and stacks wood in the fireplace.

Susan's heart pounds harder.

"Then Starbright," Ruby says carefully again, striking a match, "is the great-great-great-great-, and a couple more greats, grandmother of *you*."

20

Brown-Eyed Girl

 Pop eyes and slack jaw, Starbright stares at him like an R. Crumb sketch out of Zap Comix. Chiron can practically see splotches of sweat and exclamation points leaping from her brow. Can't tell if she's furious, delighted, or just plain horrified. But he knows the feeling of pure shock because it's rushing through him, too.

"Why didn't you tell me?" she finally says.

He studies the toes of his boots, speechless.

"Why didn't you tell me! Why didn't you *tell* me!"

"I couldn't."

She doesn't believe him, of course. Won't believe he never knew Lia Mitsui was the daughter of Charles Hawke, who was the son of Geneva

Robbins-Hawke, who was the daughter of Michael Robbins, who was the son of Jessica Stein-Robbins, who was born Jessica Stein in late spring of 1968.

But he didn't know.

Why should he? He is the great-great-great-, and a couple more greats, grandson of the first woman president of the United States. Chief executive officer of the International Bank, founding mother of cosmicism, a woman who singlehandedly placed a semblance of order on a hundred years of chaos that came down during the adjustments age. A woman who set the tone for generations to come. Lia Hawke was the daughter of a wealthy, educated couple in northern California, that's all he knew. All other forebears were insignificant to him. They simply had not existed. Who could compare to President Mitsui?

He feels like a dupe. What a chump! Consider impact before you consider benefit. Was this Ariel Herbert's secret? A terrible secret. A woman's secret. Now what?

All spacetime will change if Susan Stein dies during the Summer of Love. All spacetime will change if Susan Stein isn't pregnant as of 11:59 P.M. on September 4, 1967, when he must translate-transmit to September 4, 2467. Will he be twelve hours and ten minutes late? Who gives a damn?

He recalls the note on Disk 4: "Daughter of the Axis born slightly underweight. Place probable Axis under strict surveillance for health risks."

Now he sees that little Jessica will be delivered a month early.

"Why did you make me love you?" she demands. "If you're my . . . my . . ."

"Grandson," Ruby says in her sweet-as-poison voice.

"I didn't know," he says. "I swear it, Starbright. I mean, I don't look anything like you, do I? After so many generations, and five hundred years."

"Go with me *everywhere,* and hold my hand, and make me fall in love with you?"

"Dig it, Chiron," Ruby says, laughing. "The kid's in love with you."

"You are?" he asks Starbright quietly, incredulously. He intended to encourage her crush on him, of course. It made placing her under surveillance that much easier. Easier on *him.*

But she's just a girl. A young woman, he corrects himself, a smart young woman, but very young, too young to love anyone. Too young, and with too much hair.

"You've got a lot of nerve!" She stomps around the living room. "You . . . bastard! You *played* with me. *God!*"

"Simmer down, Starbright," Ruby says. "I wouldn't mind listening to you rant and rave at him for at least another hour. And Chi, I'd love to watch you cringe and grovel and beg her forgiveness for at least that long. But if what you say is true," she gestures to the spot where he projected the holoids, "and preserving spacetime rests on Starbright fulfilling her destiny, then tell me this. What are you going to do about it?"

"Me?"

"Well, who else, sonny? You going to run down to the street and find some fine cat to knock her up?"

"Knock me up!" Starbright cries. "I just got out of being pregnant. No, I won't! I can't stand this!" She darts up the stairs to the sitting room and slams the door.

Chi waits for the lock to click. It clicks. Then unclicks.

"Sweet Isis," Ruby says. "You'd better hurry, Chi." She goes to the front window, peers out into the evening. "Only I don't see anyone, let alone a man Starbright would want. Why, I haven't seen the streets this empty since the night there was supposed to be a riot. Everyone has gone home."

He looks out, and Ruby's right. The corner of Clayton and Haight is deserted.

He is utterly defeated. "I've failed," he whispers, sick at heart.

Ruby lights a candle and hands it to him with a smile. "Listen. You say your skipmother did this subversive thing. She deduced something from the Archives, hmm? But she knew you're a good cosmicist. You would never violate the Tenets unless there was a *really* good reason. Right, am I right? So go do your duty, sonny. Or should I say," she says in her sweet-as-poison voice, "grandson."

"But," he sputters. "We're *related*. That's incest."

"You said so yourself. So many generations. Five hundred years. You'll be just fine. I think Ariel would agree. Oh, hey." For a moment, Ruby's face tightens with alarm. "With this mandatory childlessness thing and the Generation-Skipping Law. You're not sterile, are you?"

"No! I was harvested before the t-port, and I haven't been entered in the lottery yet. Anyway, I've got a deferment. I'm a skipchild myself."

"Deferment, uh-huh," Ruby says. She darts into the kitchen, returns with Starbright's favorite sherry. She thrusts the bottle and two cordial glasses into his hands. "Then go defer your fine ass up those stairs."

"But this is impossible."

"Impossible, huh? I recall a Heinlein story I read years ago. The premise deals with this very sort of thing. I'll go look it up for you, okay?"

"Ruby, this isn't science fantasy."

"Right. Neither are rocket ships or computers or atomic bombs." She laughs. "Or tachyporters."

"But I can't!"

"I know the Grandfather Principle says you can't kill your grandfather. And probable reality theory says maybe you'll kill an innocent little cat in a gas chamber. But think about it. Do any of your damn Tenets say you can't make love to your great-great-great-grandmother?"

He thinks about it. The more he thinks about it, the more Ruby smiles. And as he thinks about it a bit longer, she laughs a bit harder. And soon he's smiling too and shaking his head.

"Dig it," Ruby says. "I call that the Grandmother Principle. Now get upstairs 'cause she's waiting for you."

GOSSIP, INNUENDO & ALL
THE NEWS THAT FITS

At midnight September 4, tourist season officially ended and for most of the people concerned, so did the Summer of Love. . . .

It all goes to prove what every veteran Haightian knew all along. Most of the summer lovers were out for their vacation thrill. They were tourists, plastic hippies, pseudohip, middle- and upper-class straighties who came down to play the game.

Now the game is over and most of the kiddies have returned to school. . . .

But one thing happened that no one can dispute. In one way or another, almost all these people were turned on. And while they may never again see San Francisco, it's a sure bet that somewhere in the world they'll someday be wearing flowers in their hair.

—From "Haightians Thrill to
Spacious Streets," *Berkeley Barb*, Vol.
5, No. 10, Issue 109 (Sept. 15–21,
1967)

Her hair is everywhere.

On her head, her face, her armpits, her forearms. A couple of hairs sprout from the areolas of her nipples. A patch of down grows beneath her belly button, and more hair, thick and dark, on her calves, between her thighs.

He tries to see her beauty. He strives for the abandon of lust. But that hair, all that hair. The smooth nude skin of Venus Rising captivates his memories of desire, captures him and won't let go.

If she sees his distress, she is not dismayed. She giggles, hiding her face beneath the sheet, regaining her composure, then peeking out at him again, bursting into another peal of laughter.

"What?" he demands.

"You have no hair!"

He follows her gaze. He has never felt ashamed of his perfect nude body before. He turns beet-red all over.

"They didn't give you any hair." She points. "There."

He can feel the blood pounding in his face, down his neck, staining his chest. "Well, they could have. It would just be implants, like my scalp and brows and eyelashes."

"Then why didn't they? Why didn't they give you any hair down there?"

He waves his hands in exasperation. "Oh, hell! I wasn't supposed to get naked in front of anyone. Not in a way that mattered. Not like this."

"You mean the LISA techs sent you back five hundred years to the Summer of Love and you weren't supposed to ball?"

"Of course not! That could have been a violation of Tenet . . . Oh, never mind."

He is completely limp. Despite the urgency of his duty that seems inescapable, he wonders if he can do it. He sits on the edge of the bed, turning his back to her.

"I could have balled anyone I wanted to." He surprises himself with his own bitterness. "I could have used a prophylak."

"Well, now's your chance," she says. "Only you can't use a prophylak, right?"

He is not aroused at all. "This is probably going to be the last blow that kills me."

"Oh, please."

"Sure! You're lousy with bacteria, Starbright."

He peers at her. She lies with a shoulder, a breast, a thigh beneath the sheet. The rest of her is golden in the candlelight.

"Lousy with bacteria," she says. "Isn't that sweet. That's beautiful, Chiron. Don't forget the viruses. Wow! I am really turned on."

But she is laughing still, big brown eyes glancing up at him beneath the fringes of her lashes. "So. What you're saying is you haven't been laid in over two months." Peal of laughter.

He nods, disgusted. He feels her fingers tracing up his spine. He shrugs away from the tickle. "I haven't exactly seen you getting it on."

"Yeah, but I got more than you-ooh," she says in a mocking singsong.

She kneels behind him, pressing her breasts against his back. The fur on her belly scratches his waist. She threads her arms round his chest, leans her head against his ear. Swings her long, tawny hair over his shoulder.

She whispers, "Oh, come on. I'm not a virgin, you know."

She is good black soil from an antediluvian delta.

She is a heifer cantering across a vanished grassland.

She is a delicious odor unfouled by smoke.

She is an owl hooting before an old forest is felled.

She is a shell in clear water, a turtle with omens on her back. She is the twin-tailed siren singing to the sailor. She is the mermaid who tempts him to swim beneath the sea.

She is joy, a mouth and a tongue. She is strong and salty.

She is a cat prowling where there are no gas chambers.

She is the peach of three thousand years, a nectarine, two pears, a plum unspoiled by poison.

She is the night pearl in the oyster's cleft.

She is bright as the first star of the evening.

They touch.

They close a loop across space and time.

that night   sometimes   he sees their bodies glow

21

If You're Going

to San Francisco

Ruby searches her secondhand bookshelves in the Mystic Eye. The shop is closed tonight. It's good to have paying customers, but she loves the shop when it's deserted. Grinning Buddhas, seven-knob candles, rows of gleaming herb jars. Gryphons crouch in perfumed semidarkness.

Seated on the footstool, she becomes so absorbed in poring through her stock that nearly an hour flies by. She finds a copy of *Rosemary's Baby*. This little thriller about scheming Satanists was on the best-seller list all summer. If you ever want to spook ignorant, impressionable minds about practitioners of the ancient ways, this novel is sure to rouse a lynch mob in no time. Witches; right. She picks up another summer best-seller already on the secondhand shelf. *Valley of the Dolls.* White folks on dope, uh-huh. The pill-popping crowd in L.A., the movie starlet scene. She will have to speak to Morgana about buying this kind of trash. But she knows what Morgana will say. Some flower child with a two-month-old baby and no shoes needed fifty cents.

Ah, March '59. *Magazine of Fantasy and Science Fiction.* She whistles, bending back the dog-eared corners, wiping off the dust. "All You Zombies—" by Robert Heinlein. That's it. The story goes like this: A time traveler with a sex-change operation fools his younger self into going to the past, seduces himself, gives birth to himself, steals himself from his own cradle, and recruits himself as a temporal agent. She grins. Let those grumpy LISA techs chew *that* one over when they try to fry Chi for what he's done. And they think *he's* played fast and loose with the Tenets.

She checks the time. Sweet Isis, nearly ten-thirty. She cuts the light, clatters up the back stairs. The living room is empty. Up to the third floor. The sitting room door is closed. She hesitates, then knocks.

"Come in," they both call.

They have set the spare mattress on end, folded the sheets, tidied the blankets, pushed back the coffee tables, and rolled back the rug. Starbright zips her overnight bag, Chiron zips his jacket. Two kids from the burbs, getting ready to go back to school. Starbright is decked out in gypsy finery that will be the envy of her high school pals in Cleveland. The devil box beamed the CBS News Special about the Summer of Love all over America.

"Well?" Ruby stands, tapping her toe like a baby-sitter asking if her charges have brushed their teeth.

Chi whips out the oblong stone and presses it to Starbright's chest.

"The double blip," he says triumphantly. "The scanner shows the double blip."

"Uh-huh, the double blip," Ruby says.

"The Grandmother Principle holds true!" Chi says.

"I'm pregnant," Starbright says.

"Far out." Ruby hands Chi the March '59 issue with Heinlein's story. "Take this. Study it carefully. You may need it."

"Thanks," he says. "But I can't take anything with me. The payload is precisely calibrated to the ME3 Event. I can't take extra mass."

"Then leave something you don't need. Take off the beads. You don't need them anymore, right, am I right?"

He makes a face. "Not supposed to leave evidence of modern technologies, Ruby."

"I'll flush them down the toilet. I promise."

He pulls off his beads. "The purple beads are neurobics. Break them in half and sniff. They pep you up. And these are knockerblockers. They relax you."

"Down the toilet, like I said." But Ruby slips the beads into a drawer. She could use a little pepping up after the Summer of Love.

He takes the magazine, gauges the weight, and frowns. He searches through his pockets, takes out a rectangle of plastic the size of a credit card and even thinner. "You might as well take this, too. A gift for you, Ruby, for your hospitality."

She takes the card, turns it over in her hands. It has a tiny numeric pad, a double row of function signs, and a long clear rectangle across the top. The whole thing is crisp plastic. He takes it from her, holds it up for a second to the lamp in the corner, and hands it back to her.

"What the hell?" Ruby taps at the tiny keyboard with her nail. Numbers appear in the clear rectangle.

"The LISA techs let me take this in case my knuckletop crashed or I needed backup hardware to calculate the probabilities. It's not very smart, sorry."

"Calculate?"

"It's a calculator," he says mildly.

"Like my thirty-pound calculating machine?"

He laughs. "Don't show that to anyone for at least fifteen years."

"What about me?" Starbright chimes in. The kid is suddenly sulky, misgivings burning in her eyes. "Are you ever coming back to see me and our daughter?"

His joy vanishes. "Starbright, I can't. If I were to die in your Now, I'd be trapped in a CTL."

"I thought you loved me."

"I thought you loved *me*. Would you want me to be trapped in a CTL?"

"Didn't I tell you?" Ruby says to Starbright. "These space-age swingers, they are all the same. Warping around galaxies, bumping into girlfriends on exotic planets."

"Lovin' 'em and leavin' 'em," Starbright says, pouting.

Chi glares at Ruby. She shrugs. Maybe he should at least visit, she thinks. But she keeps her mouth shut.

Starbright says in a sweet-as-poison voice, "Then go to your Venus Rising, Chiron. Go to your electric ladyfriend with flowers painted on her head. Leave me and my child. And every year, when this day comes again, I'll think of you."

"You will?" he says gently.

"Yes," she says. "I'll think—*that bastard.*"

She peals with laughter. Ruby starts to cackle, too. Chiron is stony-faced. And Ruby knows it's going to be all right. Got to be.

The Portals of the Past look ghostly at this hour. Antebellum pillars set in a classical portico, white marble luminous beneath the street lights. Not a framework for some stupendous contraption from the distant future. More a doorway into antiquity. Or other worlds?

Ruby isn't sure. The portals are hauntingly beautiful.

The night breeze is refreshed by rain. They all climb out of her BMW, and Chiron strides round Lloyd Lake to the portals. A quarter till midnight. Starbright hurries after him. Ruby lags behind. Something inside her is unwilling to witness his unmasking, his undoing before Starbright's eyes. For, of course, there is nothing inside the Portals of the Past. They look exactly as they always do.

He stands, gazing at the portals. Starbright runs to him and hugs him, clinging passionately.

"No," he whispers. "I've got to go."

But she has knickknacked his jacket pocket. With a cry of triumph, she holds up his maser and dashes off with it.

"Starbright!" he cries. "Damn it, Starbright."

She runs to the portals, drops to a crouch on the steps. Alarmed, Ruby hurries after Chiron. The kid flicks the maser on orange, and with swift, sure movements, she aims the beam at the base of the column.

Ruby sees the shaft of orange light, twirling in the darkness. She and Chi stumble up at the same time. He breathes heavily, as though someone has socked him in the gut.

"Chiron?" Ruby says.

He waves her away.

Starbright jumps up and shows them the graffiti she carved.

"What does it mean?" Ruby says.

"It means *I*," she traces the eye, "*love*," she traces the heart, "*Chiron*," she traces the key. She tucks the maser back in his pocket. "Do you like it?"

He touches her cheek.

He climbs up the stairs and steps through the center of the Portals of the Past. For a split second, Ruby sees a crowd of glowing people, blinking blue and green lights, a sheen of silver. A tall, slim woman stretches her arms to embrace him.

He disappears. It all disappears.

Starbright whispers, "Oh, wow."

Ruby whispers, "You little shit."

The Haight-Ashbury was mobbed with Navajo chiefs, Merlin's magicians, Egyptian pharaohs, guys with four eyes, men from Mars. And time travelers. Strange and wondrous days, with plenty of time travelers. The Summer of Love was psychedelicized and science-fictionalized, and I did not believe you, Ruby thinks. Not in my heart of hearts, not in the back of my mind, not even after all your gadgets and light shows and the most frightful hallucinations I ever saw in my life. I did not totally believe you, Chiron Cat's Eye in Draco.

Do now.

Grandmother Says: T'ai (Peace)

The Image: Heaven and earth unite. Small things fade, and great
   things develop. Peace and blessings upon all living things.
The Oracle: To unite in deep harmony brings a time of universal
   flowering and prosperity.
   When the strong lift up the weak and the powerful smile upon
the meek, when that which is above sinks down and that which is
below rises up, the universe rejoices in peace. The infinite is revealed
in the points of the compass. Time is revealed in the cycle of the
seasons.

   —Hexagram 11, *The I Ching* or Book of Changes

Dear Editor:
What I missed [in your account] was input from the parents who lived
through that time, barely able to comprehend the social changes that
were disrupting their safe middle-class lives, trying to stay in control
and let go at the same time, fighting the terror of not knowing what
was going on.
   Some of us made it; we remained friends with our kids and
adopted some of the better changes for our own. Some of us didn't; we
lost our kids to rags, beads and squalor. Some of them left and never
came back. Some left and came back burned out and weird. Some
parents lost each other as well as their kids. Whom do you blame for
failures and disappointments too painful to bear?
   When the Summer of Love was over, we had new ways of feeling,
dressing, speaking, eating, praying, dancing, marrying (or not),
childbearing, child raising, growing old, even dying. All the old rules
were irrelevant, the new ones uncertain.

It was the Summer of Love for some, the Summer of Discontent for others.

Sincerely,
M. S. M.

—From "Letters," *Image Magazine* (*San Francisco Examiner*, Aug. 23, 1987)

Ruby drives Starbright to the San Francisco Airport. They sit in silence thick and heavy as the fog. The kid cries a little. Ruby tunes the radio to KMPX-FM. "If You're Going to San Francisco" comes on. She turns it off.

They park, unload Susan's overnight bag from the back seat. They drift into the airport. Bright fluorescent lights, garish carpets, ugly plastic walls. A pair of Krishna devotees with shaved-bald heads and orange robes are panhandling the tourists. The squares are staring. Airline folks and citizens from Kansas City with cold, uncomprehending, hateful eyes.

Ruby knows how to handle this scene, but Starbright is cringing, losing her nerve. The kid hasn't been in society this polite in a while. And now she's going to see her parents for the first time in months? This will not do.

"Stop," Ruby commands her. They duck out of the stream of pedestrian traffic. She takes out the vial of sandalwood essence oil she always carries, dabs two dots under Starbright's ears, and two dots under her own. The kid starts to giggle. That's better. In the bottom of her purse, Ruby finds the beaded suede headband Luther gave her in front of the San Francisco Gun Exchange. Very pretty. She ties it over Starbright's forehead, threads it through her hair, fluffs out her frizzy curls.

"You're beautiful, Starbright," Ruby tells her.

And it's true.

"I love you, Ruby," the kid says.

"Then you be strong for me."

They stroll through the airport, two wild-haired, perfumed women. Their exotic skirts rustle. Their bare feet are slipped into sandals. They wear cotton and silk, bracelets that clink, beads swaying over their breasts.

They get to the gate. The plane her parents came on is already there.

He's a handsome man, the kid's father, tall with a bit of belly that goes with his prosperity. The eyes, nose, mouth, and eyebrows he gave to his daughter. His mouth trembles despite his effort to quell it, and that instantly wins Ruby over.

He strides to his daughter and seizes her. "Sweetie pie!" And he cries right there in the middle of the airport, swiping tears off his face. He seizes her again, hugging her.

"Hi, Daddy," Starbright says.

The mother hovers by her husband and daughter. A plucked and dyed dame with deep frown lines, the flabby, stooped shoulders of an old woman, though she can't be more than forty. She joins the reunion, pecks the cheek of her daughter. But she can't restrain her cold look of appraisal even now—look at her *clothes,* look at her *hair,* her *face.* This woman, Ruby thinks, will have to learn a thing or two from her daughter.

"I want to be a doctor, Daddy," Starbright says.

"Well! That's fine," he says, nonplussed.

"I don't want to be a nurse. I don't want to be a dentist. I want to study bacteriology and be a doctor."

The parents exchange an uncertain look. Ruby sees instantly that the daughter as the troublesome child was the glue keeping their fractured marriage intact. And her defection revealed the deep rifts between them. Will the daughter's return restore the reality they knew before? Not likely.

"Also, I'm pregnant," Starbright says. "I want to have the baby. I want to keep her. You can't change my mind, so don't try, okay?"

"Who . . . ?" her father says.

"The father is gone. I'll never see him again. So I don't want to talk about that, either."

They are speechless, these square parents from Cleveland. This is not what they expected of their runaway to the Haight-Ashbury. And everything they expected, and then some.

The father checks out his daughter's costume, then sees Ruby. His eyes flick up and down. The corner of his mouth twitches. Yeah. Yeah, Ruby is beautiful.

Catching his glance, Ruby raises her left hand, extends two fingers, and says, "The Summer of Love did not compel America's children. America's children compelled the Summer of Love."

Ruby kisses Starbright lightly on the forehead, then turns and walks away. In her heart she knows she will never see the kid again.

She will close the Mystic Eye, leave the Haight-Ashbury behind. Get out of town, somewhere like Santa Cruz or Bodega Bay where the air is fresh. Where it's easier to believe in a New Explanation. She has started over before. She can damn well start over again.

And she has business to attend to besides her own. A woman should never be made a criminal for making a choice. The future survives because she, and the women of the world, take care of themselves. Take control of their own destiny.

Dawn glows in the east. The future is hard for the world. But we have a future. We survive.

She feels it as she pulls onto 101 northbound, the forward-moving future plunging beside her like a fellow traveler. Yet the arrow of time is an illusion, Ruby knows that now. Day and night do not move forward, they spin, like the Earth. The hours meted out by the clock are tools for human survival, boundaries and categories, not reality. Dates and years measure the pace of a person's life, mark initiations and graduations, but they are not the woman or the man. In truth, there is but One Day, always new, always coming forth into Being.